BOOK I:

FLIGHT OF THE SOLAR DUCKS

by

CHARLES MORGAN

To Elena

First Published 1988 by Blackie and Son Ltd
This Publication 2009 Lulu Publications

ISBN 978-0-557-07503-4

CONTENTS

CHAPTER ONE: THE GUNGE HOLE

Aracuria is such a stupid name, thought Aracuria. It was so unlike all his friends' names. They were called Michael or Bill or Klut - but, come to think of it, Klut was a pretty stupid name too.

Aracuria was sitting in the kitchen. His dad had just come in from work and was laying a clean bin liner on the table for them to have some tea. Aracuria looked up at the ceiling. A greasy spider's web hung from one side to the other, and the moldy contents of an exploded pressure cooker stuck to the corroded steelwork.

On the far wall there was a poster of a girl walking across a beach. The poster was stained red from the rusty steel behind it. Like the living room and the bedrooms, the kitchen was really a discarded chemical bin. The entire house was a series of giant chemical bins strung together with short lengths of waste tube. Here, they didn't call their homes houses, they called them holes.

Aracuria looked at the poster. The girl was clean, the beach was spotless, and the sea was a deep blue. The surf didn't have any foam on it and, remarkably, no bin liners floated around in the air.

'I bet she doesn't live in a hole,' said Aracuria. But then, she was from the North. That was the peculiar thing about the planet Aracuria lived on; the North and the South were so different that it was difficult to believe they *were* on the same planet.

Dad started preparing the tea. He turned on the methane stove, stood back, struck a match and threw it at the single ring. A bright blue flame shot up high in the air, setting fire to some of the spiders' webs.

Dad reached into the inky blackness of one of the numerous bin liners piled up in the corner and pulled out a couple of tins. He opened them up and poured their contents into a blackened saucepan which he gingerly placed on the ring. The blue flame from the stove completely covered it and immediately began to boil the contents.

The methane stove consisted of a long, thin tube, held upright by a tripod, on the top of which was the methane ring and a little tap to turn the gas on and off. The other end of the tube went out through a hole in the side of the chemical bin, where it picked up all the methane being produced by the thousands of millions of billions of tons of rotting rubbish that surrounded the hole.

At one time the chemical bins that made up their hole lay on the surface of the rubbish. But then, as more rubbish was dumped, the bins became covered and then completely buried. At the moment they were about two hundred meters beneath the surface. A long piece of waste pipe came out of the side of the living room and rose up through the rubbish until it reached the surface. Every day, more and more rubbish was being added, so when Dad came home from work he had to join on another bit of waste pipe so that Aracuria could get out to school.

The stuff in the saucepan bubbled up over the edge and caught light. Dad reached into another bin liner and pulled out a packet of flavor. He poured the yellow powder it contained into the bubbling saucepan, waited a few seconds, then pulled the saucepan off the ring and poured the yellow contents into a bowl.

Aracuria took a long, cold look at the Yellow Stuff as he waited for the bubbling to settle down. Everyone ate the Yellow Stuff in the South. It had its own special name: 'Wholesome Health Food with "Nutr'a'nut" Supplement and Added Vitamin X, Y, and Q'. But everyone called it the Yellow Stuff. Aracuria took a mouthful: bananas. 'Now eat it all up,' said Dad.

'But it's horrible.'

'You should be grateful, young man. In my day we never had the Yellow Stuff, we used to have to ... ' Dad continued talking, but it was the same old thing about how lucky Aracuria was to live in a chemical bin, how lucky it was that they had the Yellow Stuff, and how lucky it was that he had a school to go to. But Aracuria had heard it so many times before that he knew it off by heart.

He looked across at the girl on the beach. 'I bet *she* doesn't eat the' Yellow Stuff.' But then, things were different in the North.

A helmet appeared through the waste tube that connected the living room with the kitchen. It was followed by a body completely covered in a green plastic suit. Mum pulled off her helmet.

'Hello, Aracuria. You ready for school?' Aracuria nodded. Mum seated herself beside the table and turned to Dad.

'Where's my Yellow Stuff? I've been out at work all day cleaning slurry pits and you haven't even got tea on the table.' Mum worked all day in the slurry pits while Dad only worked half the day in a Chemical Decontamination Unit.

'The very least I expect is a little bit of Yellow Stuff when I come in from a hard day's work.'

'Yes, yes.' Dad tried to make up some Yellow Stuff quickly but he was so flustered that he dropped the saucepan on the floor and spilt the powder all over his rubber boots. Mum stood up.

'You're useless. Do I have to do everything around here? The least you could do is make me some recycled tea.'

Dad rushed off to find some second-hand tea bags that had been dumped in the rubbish. Aracuria looked across at the poster. 'I bet she doesn't have recycled tea.' Mum sat down.

'Are you ready for school yet?' Aracuria got up.

'Yes.' He didn't like going to school.

He crawled through the waste tube into the living room. He picked up his empty satchel and made for the exit tube. Five minutes later he was standing out on the surface with the exit tube poking up into the air. Beside it, stuck into the rubbish, was a little sign:

THE GUNGE HOLE

Dad had named it a long time ago. Aracuria looked around. As far as the eye could see there was rubbish; discarded tin cans, fridges, aerosols, clothes, cardboard boxes, old TVs, broken stereos, rolls of waste tube, and here and there chemical bins. Some were being used as holes but most were just empty. The air was filled with flying bin liners carried on the wind.

Aracuria knew things hadn't always been like this, but it was very difficult to find out the truth about the past. Dad always said that when he was a kid things were worse, but Mum said that they were better.

In the South all the land was covered in rubbish, but in the North there was no rubbish at all. In the South everyone worked at recycling the rubbish, but in the North people worked in offices or in fields, or just spent their time walking across the beaches. In the South everyone ate the Yellow Stuff, while in the North they had egg and chips, or pie and chips, or beef burgers and cream cakes. In the South people lived in chemical bins, but in the North they lived in houses made of stone or wood. And no one knew why.

High in the air Aracuria could see one of the giant Refuse Transport Planes of the Air Transport Refuse Disposal Company. They flew over day and night, every five minutes. The back of the plane opened up and a mass of rubbish fell out in a long line. Some of the heavy rubbish fell straight to the ground, but the lighter stuff floated down much more slowly. The really odd thing was that all the rubbish was made by the North and dumped on the South. The South didn't dump rubbish on the North.

Aracuria sighed, slung his empty satchel over his shoulder, and walked off across the rubbish to meet his friend Bill.

CHAPTER TWO: VALLEY OF FIRE

Walking across the rubbish was always difficult. Aracuria dodged around a few broken fridges, then ran and jumped down into the small valley below, where Bill lived. Bill was Aracuria's friend, but they didn't get on that well. All the same, every evening just before it got dark, Aracuria would wait at the entrance to Bill's hole so that they could set off for school together.

That was another thing that Aracuria didn't understand. When his mum and dad had gone to school, they'd gone in the *morning.* Now, every kid in the South went to school just before it got dark and stayed in school throughout the night, coming home in the morning.

He had once heard an explanation for this. In school you weren't supposed to ask questions, but one day one of the girls had asked why all the kids in the South went to school at night. The teacher said that it was because at one time all the kids in the South used to stay up so late at night watching the horror movies on TV that they kept falling asleep in school during the day. Someone had suggested that the kids be taught at night to stop them falling asleep in the day, and that was why every kid in the South went to school just before dark. Aracuria arrived at Bill's hole and sat down, waiting for Bill to appear. Eventually he heard him scrambling up the tube, then a satchel came flying through the air followed by Bill. He was in a foul temper.

'You're late!'

'How can I be late?' said Aracuria. 'I've been waiting for you for ten minutes.'

'You're late, you're always late.' Bill's voice sounded like ground-glass-on-gravel.

'Well, shall we go?'

It was getting dark - they would have to hurry. They strode off together, down past a discarded uranium canister that was gently glowing in the dusk and on into a little gully. There was another hole here, where their friend Klut lived. Bill walked up to the hole and screamed down it:

'IS KLUT READY FOR SCHOOL?' Bill's voice whistled down the hole and they felt a small tremor beneath their feet.

Klut and his family weren't really human. They were the descendants of Civil Servants who had once worked on one of the Star Colonies many, many years ago. Then, the South had been very powerful and important, but no one talked about that time any more.

A few seconds later, Klut emerged from the hole. He was neatly dressed with a newly-washed face and clean white shoes. Klut's head was completely, tabletop flat just above his eyes. It was a good place to keep things, so while Bill and Aracuria held their satchels or slung them across their shoulders, Klut laid his neatly across his head.

Klut was extraordinarily bright, like all his family. He could speak all seventy-two Earth languages, three hundred and ninety-five star languages and was learning a new one every three weeks, while the rest of his family could speak a total of three-thousand and fifty- five languages, which was nearly all the languages anyone knew about. Klut was the youngest in his family. He was nearly seven hundred years old, but since he wasn't really human, earth years didn't count. In his family, seven hundred years was nothing.

They retraced their steps back up the gully, past the glowing uranium canister and then turned left, climbed over a hill of fridges, and went down into a smoking valley. In this neighborhood someone had once allowed a methane stove to blow back and set light to the rubbish outside the chemical bins. As a result, the whole place was on fire underground. The valley had been evacuated years before, but the entrances to the old holes could still be seen.

Klut, Bill and Aracuria started to run: the ground was hot. There were flames coming out of the earth, and here and there pockets of methane exploded sending up swirling red and green flames that danced briefly in the air. They called these Will 0' Wisps. Sometimes they looked like ghosts and other times like people. Everyone was scared of them. Bill was just about to jump off the top of a large waste canister when a multi-colored flame shot up in front of him. It had white eyes like the sockets of a skull, and a green tongue that danced like a snake. All around the skull, there seemed to be a cloak of fire. Bill lost his footing, slipped on the canister and fell under the flames as they rose up in the sky. The skull looked down at Bill and smiled. Then it disappeared. Bill was hysterical.

'Did you see that, did you see THAT?'

Aracuria ran across to him and picked him up. 'Don't worry,' he said, 'it's only a Will O' Wisp.'

‘That's a ghost, that's a GHOST!' Bill started running across the rubbish. Klut looked completely unimpressed.

'What's he scared of? It's only gas igniting.' Aracuria wasn't so sure. There was something about the Valley of Fire that he didn't like.

'Well, if it's just gas, how come it looks like a ghost?' Klut looked out across the valley at the other Will O' Wisps that were rising up and burning away.

'It's all in your mind, Aracuria. You and Bill can see it, but I can't. All I see is burning gas.' Klut was bright, but he lacked imagination.

'We'd better get after Bill before he hurts himself,' said Aracuria.

Bill was running around in circles, screaming at the top of his voice. Aracuria grabbed him by the arm. 'Stop shouting, Bill. We'll be late for school.'

Bill began to calm down, but he looked really scared.

'One, one of them, one of them spoke to me!' he stammered.

'You're lying,' said Aracuria. Bill shook his head furiously. Klut came up to

their side.
'What's the matter?' Aracuria looked from Klut to Bill and back again.
'One of the Will O' Wisps spoke to him,' he said.
'Impossible,' said Klut.
'He did, he did!' said Bill. Aracuria took him by the arm.
'Let's get out of here.'

They started walking towards the end of the Valley of Fire. Klut began reciting a poem to himself in one of the languages he knew. Aracuria gripped Bill's arm as hard as he could to stop him running off.

The Will O' Wisps were growing in number. Klut didn't seem to notice it as he recited his poem, and Bill had his eyes closed, but Aracuria could see that there were more of them, and they were coming together, ahead of them.

The flames were all colors; reds and yellows, greens and oranges, purples and blues. They were coming out of the ground and rising up like phantoms, then disappearing. But more would come, one after the other: hundreds of them.
'I can't go ON!' Aracuria stopped still. Bill opened his eyes and screamed.

Klut forgot his poem and his jaw dropped: they faced an army of fiery skulls, with green tongues that danced like snakes. Suddenly there was a brilliant burst of fire ahead. A monstrous flame rose up in the sky on top of which sat a huge skull.
'Close your eyes and *run!'* shouted Aracuria. They ran through the flaming skulls, through all the other Will O' Wisps and out the other side. They kept on running until Bill ran straight into a fridge and almost knocked himself out. Aracuria and Klut went flying into the rubbish. Aracuria turned to see Klut's white face.
'We, we made it,' said Klut.
'But how are we going to get home again after school? And where's Bill?' he added. They found him lying flat on his back, his eyes closed tight, muttering, 'Are we through the valley yet?' over and over again.
'Bill, open your eyes: we're safe,' said Aracuria.
'What happened?'
'I don't know, it's never happened before. But it scared me,' admitted Aracuria.
'And me,' said Bill. There was silence. Bill and Aracuria looked across at Klut: his face had returned to normal.
'What are you two looking at?'
'We're waiting for you to admit you were scared,' said Aracuria. Klut looked offended. 'How could I possibly be scared of some methane gas?'
Aracuria couldn't believe what he was hearing. 'You're lying, Klut, I saw how white your face went.'
'Impossible. I come from a long line of hyper intelligent civil servants. I am

seven hundred of your Earth years old. How could I possibly be scared by some methane gas?' he said haughtily.

Suddenly the boys realized that it was pitch dark. Night fell in the South very quickly. In the distance they could see the Will O' Wisps burning and dotted about were glowing uranium canisters, but everything else was black.

'What are we going to *do?'* groaned Bill.

'There's no way we can get to school now, it's just too dark,' said Klut smugly.

'We could try getting back home, but we'd have to go through the Valley of Fire again .. .' Before Aracuria could say another word Bill was shaking his head. 'No, no way!'

Klut took his satchel off his head, placed it on the ground and sat down.

'Then we'll just have to sit here until morning.'

'You're right,' Aracuria agreed.

'What's that?' said Bill.

'What's what?' asked Aracuria.

'That bright glow.' Bill pointed into the distance but Aracuria couldn't see anything.

'Nothing.'

'Look,' said Bill, 'there it is again. That bright glow.' Then Aracuria saw it too.

'It's probably a uranium canister,' said Klut, who hadn't bothered to look.

'No, it isn't,' said Aracuria. Far in the distance a shaft of blue light was rising up from the earth, high into the sky, and reflecting off the white clouds like a furnace. Then the shaft of light burst into a brilliant shower of red and purple sparks that spread out like a rain of fire. Aracuria turned to Klut.

'Shall we go and find out what it is?' Klut hesitated, then agreed.

'Where are you going?' said Bill.

'To see where the light's coming from, of course. Anything would be better than sitting around here till morning.'

'Well *I'm* staying here!' shouted Bill.

'OK,' shrugged Aracuria, and started to catch up to Klut who was already marching off ahead.

'What? You're going to leave me here?' cried Bill. 'All on my own?'

'Yeah, you should be safe. Just watch out for the giant worms and earwigs. You should survive until morning as long as they don't get you.'

The next second Bill was at Aracuria's side. The lights ahead got brighter and brighter.

CHAPTER THREE: KING MORCANT

They walked for ages, over fridges and rubble, rubbish and dead cats. Now they stood before a series of hills that rose straight out of the rubbish. At least, they looked like hills. They were really the tops of high mountains, but the rubbish had come to cover the South so deeply that everything else had been completely buried.

The shaft of blue light was coming from the top of the first mountain. Aracuria and Bill followed Klut to its foot. Cut into the rock was a series of steps that led up around the side of the mountain in a spiral. Suddenly, there was an explosion and a shower of sparks and flames rose up high into the sky, falling back down around them. Klut started to walk up the steps with Aracuria following on behind.

'I'm not going up there,' grumbled Bill. 'Anything could happen to us.' Aracuria reached down and grabbed his arm.

'We've got to, Bill, we can't let Klut go on his own.' Bill hesitated a moment and then followed.

The steps were covered in rubbish that had been dropped by transport planes, but the sides of the mountain were too steep for rubbish to cling to. Klut slowed down as he fought his way past the cardboard boxes and bin liners. Eventually Aracuria overtook him.

They worked their way around the mountain in a spiral until Aracuria reached a huge steel gate. He sat down and waited for the others to catch him up. Bill was the first to arrive, followed by Klut. They were all too exhausted to say anything. Across the gate, written in large neon red letters was the message:

DANGER: RADIOACTIVE HAZARD

Klut studied the words for a moment, then pushed the gate open: there was a rusted crunching sound and the gate broke off its hinges and fell clattering to the floor.

'It must be hundreds of years old,' said Aracuria.

Beyond the gate, the steps led up through a cutting in the rock. It was very dark, with only the glow from the blue beam high above their heads to light the way. Finally they came out on to the top of the mountain. It was as flat as a table-top. In front of them was a giant building. The blue beam shone from its top. Suddenly, it went out, plunging everything into darkness.

'What's happened?'

'Don't move: remember we're on a mountain.'

'Help!'

There was silence. Then a door in the side of the building opened, throwing out a brilliant glow. Something came walking towards them. Bill ran back down the steps. Aracuria and Klut just stood and stared as the thing got closer and closer until it was just in front of them.

It was a robot of some kind, and it towered above them. It had two massive legs made of bright shiny steel and above, a plate steel body, with each plate overlaying the next like a suit of armor. Two enormous arms hung at its sides, each with a giant claw that acted like a hand. There were hinges on each of the elbows that were bigger than Aracuria's head. On top of it all was its head, a bright silver dome of steel with a thick sheet of burned glass for a face.

There was a whirring sound and the glass plate that acted as a face slid down. The steel plates that lay across the chest began to slide back over each other until the whole of the robot's chest was opened up. Then someone jumped out: it was an old man with a gray beard and head of white, singed hair.

'What are you doing on *my* mountain?' said the old man. 'Don't you know you could have been killed?' He looked straight at Aracuria, then at Bill peering over the steps and then at Klut.

'Is there something wrong with your head, boy?' Klut pulled his satchel off and said indignantly,

'There is nothing wrong with my head, sir. All my family have heads like this.'

'Huh!' The old man coughed. 'You're an alien. Which of you is human?'

Aracuria held up his hand. The old man walked towards him and pulled out a broken set of spectacles from his waistcoat pocket.

'Say, boy, how do you come to be on my mountain?'

'We were on our way to school and the Will O' Wisps in the Valley of Fire scared us and then before we knew it, it was dark and ... we didn't know what to do,' said Aracuria nervously.

'I don't believe a word of it! Why would kids like you be going to school at night? I suspect you're spies.'

Aracuria tried to explain.

'But it's true! All the kids in the South go to school at night. Honest.'

The old man looked disbelieving, but then he stopped, thought of something and said, 'It could be true, I've been stuck up on this mountain so long I really wouldn't know. With the exception of this *alien,'* he looked disapprovingly at Klut, 'I reckon you deserve a cup of tea.' The old man smiled as Bill came up from the steps and stood behind Aracuria. 'All the. same, if I hadn't closed the reactor down, you would all be dead, just as dead as our once lovely planet.'

The old man turned and headed back to the building.

Klut, who'd been examining the robot, was just about to climb up into it when it turned around and followed the old man. Aracuria, Bill and Klut trailed along behind.

'Who is he?' asked Bill.
Aracuria shook his head. 'I don't know.'

They watched as Klut ran up behind the robot to get a closer look. The old man walked into the building, followed by the robot. As Aracuria walked through the door, he noticed how vast it was; ten or fifteen meters high, as many wide and about four meters thick. It was made of solid lead. The building inside was bigger still; it was square with an open roof, and in the center of the building, set into the floor, was a massive lead dome with a great hinge at one end.

The old man stopped. Klut went around to the side of the robot and peered up at some writing on its left knee.
'What does R.O.G.E.R. stand for?' he asked. He turned towards the old man for an answer, but before he could say anything the robot itself turned around to face him.
'NONE ... OF ... YOUR ... BUSINESS ... FLAT ... HEAD,' it said.
'Shut up, Roger, and close the door: I'll do the insults,' said the old man.
'It stands for Roboticized Organizer and General Engineering Robot,' he said. 'I'm very lucky really, there's no way I could have carried on working here without him. He fell from the back of an Air Transport Refuse Plane: they use them to offload heavy items like uranium canisters. I suppose he just forgot to let go.'
Aracuria drew closer. 'What sort of work do you do?' he asked. The old man ignored him.
'Roger, go and make some tea, there's a dear.' The robot finished closing the door, and trundled off to the far side of the building where the wall seemed to open up, allowing him to pass into a room beyond.
'What?' said the old man.
'I said what sort of .. .' Aracuria was cut short in mid-sentence.
'I clean, repair, and recycle failed pressure vessels for Nuclear Fusion Reactors,' said the old man. He reached into the top of his waistcoat pocket and pulled out a piece of paper. 'Here's my card. If ever one of your reactors has to be closed down, fusion or fission, I can repair it. We do reduced rates for bulk orders.' Aracuria looked at the card:

KING MORCANT & Co. LTD INC.
SOUTHERN REACTOR REPAIR AGENCY
NO I
MORCANT CASTLE
MORCANTLAND

'You're a *king?'* he gasped.
The old man smiled. 'Not really applicable these days, what with things being the way they are, but we used to be kings, so if we still had a land to

be a king in, I suppose I'd be him.'
Klut wandered over and took the card from Aracuria's hand.
'If you're a king, Morcant, then where is Morcant Castle?' Klut looked smug.
The old man smiled. 'Ah, a little accident, in the early days, before we really knew what we were doing, I suppose. My father, King Morcant CXLVIII, was alive in those days. We'd just lost the war against the North and our Off World enterprises had been confiscated by the Northern Corporations. They'd started dumping all their rubbish on us when Dad thought he'd go into the Nuclear Repair business. Everyone was doing it in those days, and we were down on our luck, so we set ourselves up in business. Everyone said it was dead easy . . .' He reached up and scratched the top of his head. 'All lies, of course, but how were we to know? A nuclear reactor around the corner had just been closed down; we told them we could repair it. They flew the pressure vessel up to the castle and left it with us. Dad thought it was just a matter of opening up the pressure vessel and cleaning around the inside with a brush and some wire wool. I was up repairing one of the Solar Ducks at the time. I suppose he must have undone one of the bolts on the inspection hatch ... Dad, the pressure vessel and the castle just disappeared in an enormous nuclear explosion. Pity really, because it was a lovely castle,' said the old man wistfully.

The wall at the back of the building opened up again, allowing Roger through with a tray full of mugs of tea.

Aracuria looked back at the old man. 'The Solar Ducks?' he enquired.
'Yes,' said the old man, without a word of explanation. Roger trundled up and started handing around the tea. Klut took his and then started asking questions.
'So how did you start again after the explosion?'
'Oh, it was simple,' said the old man. 'I applied to one of the Northern Corporations for some money to set up my own business. At first I wanted to carry on repairing Solar Ducks but they weren't interested in that. So then I told them about the Nuclear Reactor Repair business that Dad had started and they became really enthusiastic. They gave me a grant to build the Dome,' he tapped the lead lid that he was sitting on, 'and off I went! Been paying my way ever since!' The old man coughed and started slurping his tea.

Aracuria took a sip of his tea and noticed how nice it tasted. He had so many questions he wanted to ask Morcant, but all he could think of was the Solar Ducks. He was on the point of asking about them when Klut said, 'And what is the Dome for?' Morcant yawned.
'Using Roger, I pick up any pressure vessels the Corporation drop off on their transport, pop them into the Fusion Pit beneath the dome and then open up the side of the pressure vessel with a massive can opener.'
'Is that what caused the blue beam we saw going up to the sky?' asked Klut.

'Yes, that's right.'
'And the sparks, why did that happen?' asked Aracuria.
'Well, once I've opened it up, Roger and I climb inside and clean it all out with a brush and wire wool: Dad had the right idea all right, he just lacked the Dome to help him do it.' Morcant smiled. 'And now I'm getting tired. I don't usually stay up this late, I just had to get this last pressure vessel repaired for the pickup tomorrow.' He stood up.
Aracuria wanted to ask about the Solar Ducks, but something else came into his mind. 'King Morcant, what was the South like before the North started dumping all their rubbish on us?'

Morcant stopped still, then he looked down at Aracuria and spoke softly: 'Oh, it was beautiful, so beautiful you couldn't even begin to imagine it. There were lakes, rivers, waterfalls, and streams, forests and birds in the forests and fish in the sea, and tigers and leopards and lambs. Each year was divided into four seasons, and sometimes you'd have rain and other times snow and sometimes just sunshine. And people used to go to the beach and lie on the sand in the sun and eat ice-cream by the sea.' A tear appeared in the corner of Morcant's eye. 'And then everything started dying; first the trees, then the birds and before long even the people who lay on the beaches. Then came the war and after that no one really cared about anything.'
'Were we rich in those days?' Klut asked, Morcant laughed and thumped his fist into his chest.
'Rich, rich? You don't know the meaning of the word! Everyone was rich then; even the poor were rich. We had everything we wanted! We made money from the land and from the sea, but most of our money came from Off World. We had whole fleets of star ships taking goods from one part of the Universe to the other, that's where we made our money.'
'And the North; what was the North like?' asked Aracuria.
'Poor,' said Morcant. 'They spent all their money on weapons and they didn't have any money left over. That was why the war started: they decided to take what was ours.'

Without saying another word, Morcant turned and walked across to the far wall, which opened up for him. Aracuria, Klut and Bill followed Morcant out into the night air. Behind the building was a series of steps that rose up the side of another mountain. On top of that stood a second building. Once they were half-way up the steps, Morcant stopped and turned around. He looked out across the land. As far as the eye could see there was rubbish, but Aracuria could tell from Morcant's eyes that he was looking at it the way it used to be. Then he turned around and carried on up the side of the hill.

Once they reached the top, Morcant headed for a series of portacabins and caravans that were bunched together. He threw open one of the doors to the portacabin and went in. Aracuria and the others followed. Inside was a long table with a candle at each end. At the far end of the table

sat a girl wearing a glass bubble over her head. She was trying to eat some food with a fork while at the same time keeping the bubble on her head. Morcant addressed her.
'Rhiannon, this is Aracuria, Bill, and an alien called Klut who is too bright for his own good. I'm going to bed. Wake me up when the transports arrive in the morning.' With that, Morcant turned on his heel and walked out of the portacabin.

Rhiannon pulled a face at Morcant's back, then turned to the guests.
'What are you punks doing in my granddad's portacabin, anyway?' she said nastily.
Aracuria stepped forward. 'We saw the blue beam ... '
'So?' said Rhiannon.
'And we were late for school ... ' said Klut.
'So?'
'And it was dark ... ' said Aracuria.
'So?'
'And the Will O' Wisp had scared us ... ' said Bill.
Rhiannon looked around at the three of them.
'You're not spies, are you?' she said, quietly and meanly. The three of them shook their heads. 'Just as well, or we'd have to recycle you,' she said.

Rhiannon went back to eating her food. Aracuria pulled out a chair and sat down at the table. He was hungry. Rhiannon didn't seem to notice, or care.
'What are you eating?' asked Klut.
'What does it look like, Alien?' said Rhiannon. It didn't look like anything they had ever seen before.
'I don't know,' said Aracuria.
Rhiannon looked at him sideways with disbelief. 'You've never seen egg, bacon, chicken and chips before?'
Aracuria shook his head. 'Only on posters from the North.' Rhiannon sat back in her chair. 'So what do you eat?' she asked.
The three of them answered at the same time. 'The Yellow Stuff.'
She almost choked on a chip. 'That means you can't smell, doesn't it?' she said. Aracuria looked confused. 'That means you can't smell how horrible you stink,' she said.
'What do you mean?' asked Klut, rather alarmed.
'Well, you can't be that bright if you didn't know that the Yellow Stuff is only handed out free so that no one in the South knows how horrible this place smells. Why do you think I wear this bubble over my head, Alien? For fun? It filters out the stench of living above a thousand million billion trillion tons of garbage, that's what it does.'
Aracuria couldn't believe his ears. 'But King Morcant doesn't wear a bubble,' he said.
'That's because he had his nasal passage surgically removed by Roger in a

fifteen hour operation. And while we're about it, if you're going to call my granddad King, you might as well call me Princess Rhiannon, because that's what I am, and if I'm a princess then you're a bunch of plebs.'
Bill stepped forward. 'Could we have something to eat? We're very hungry.'
Rhiannon went back to her meal and answered without looking at him. 'Yeah, take what you want, the transport's coming tomorrow with re-supply; the fridge-oven is over there.' She pointed at the fridge in the corner that nobody had noticed.

Aracuria, Bill and Klut ran towards it, threw the door open and began pulling out the contents. There were chips and beans and eggs and beef burgers and dozens of different kinds of colored fizzy pop. And the really weird thing was that this fridge-oven not only stopped the food from going off, it kept the pop cool and the food warm, all just ready to eat and drink.

Aracuria, Bill and Klut sat down on the floor and began to eat as they had never eaten before. They were so busy that when Rhiannon got up after finishing her meal and said to them,
'You'll regret it,' they didn't even hear.

CHAPTER FOUR: THE SOLAR DUCKS

Aracuria was the first to wake. He opened his eyes and saw the light streaming in through the portacabin window. Suddenly, the most awful stench filled his nostrils. Aracuria jumped up. Klut and Bill were still asleep on the floor beside the fridge. They must have all fallen asleep after stuffing themselves full of food. But the stench!

Aracuria felt sick. His head swam with the smell of decaying food, rotting clothes and dirty skin. He ran to the door and threw it open. The smell of putrid fish hit him full in the face. It was even worse with the door open; he closed it. What was he going to do? He pinched his nostrils together and started breathing through his mouth. It helped a bit, but even so he could still smell it.

All the noise had woken Klut. He rubbed his eyes, looked at Aracuria, then began to cough. 'What's that *smell!* What is it?' he yelled. He ran for the door and threw it open. The same smell of putrid fish hit him in the face. He slammed the door shut again.

'Aracuria, what's happened!' he groaned.

'I don't know,' said Aracuria, who still had his fingers over his nose.

All the shouting had woken Bill. He stood up, walked towards the fridge to get some more food, then fell flat on his face without saying a word; the stench had made him collapse.

Aracuria turned to Klut. 'Put your fingers over your nose, it helps.' Klut did as he was told. The stench became less strong. Finally, Klut felt calm enough to go and sit at Aracuria's side.

Rhiannon came into the room wearing her bubble. She took one look at Klut and Aracuria sitting at the table with their fingers over their noses, saw Bill flat out on the floor, and burst out laughing.

'Ha, ha, I told you you'd regret it,' she said.

'Regret what?' asked Klut.

Rhiannon ignored him, wandered over to the fridge, pulled out a bowl of muesli and sat down to have her breakfast.

'Eating real food,' she said.

'What?' said Aracuria, not understanding.

'The second you start eating real food, it destroys the substance in the Yellow Stuff that stops you from smelling. With all those millions and billions and trillions of tons of rubbish covering the South, you'd expect it to smell awful, wouldn't you?' she said.

'So what are we going to do?' asked Klut. Rhiannon shrugged her shoulders.

'Go back to eating the Yellow Stuff. In about three months' time you'll lose your sense of smell again.'

'Three months?' groaned Klut and Aracuria together.

'Yeah, three months, give or take a month,' she said confidently. An idea came into Aracuria's head.
'Couldn't we each borrow a bubble?' he asked hopefully.
'Sorry, this is the only one I've got. All the others have been broken. They break easily, you see.'
Aracuria suddenly felt terribly miserable. He couldn't go back to eating the Yellow Stuff, not after having tasted real food for the first time. But he could hardly go on holding his nose for the rest of his life.

Suddenly his thoughts were interrupted by a deep, dull sound. The portacabin started to shake, and the ground began to vibrate. Rhiannon jumped up. 'Blast and pus, that's the Transports arriving and I haven't got Granddad up.' She threw down her bowl of muesli and ran out. Aracuria followed her.

The door to the portacabin led into a courtyard, beyond which was a line of steps that climbed up yet another mountain. Aracuria watched as Rhiannon came running out of a nearby caravan and started bounding up the steps, while trying to pull on a purple jacket. Aracuria made for the steps, but before he could reach them, Morcant came running past and climbed up in front of him. He was carrying a suit of armor over his arms and was trying to put on a silver breast plate and some steel gloves.

Aracuria walked slowly up the steps, making sure that he didn't let go of his nose. The ground was vibrating heavily and in the air there was a dull, crackling sound like an electricity fuse about to blow. When he reached the top, he saw that Morcant and Rhiannon were standing next to each other. Morcant had the top half of a suit of armor on his head and body, while Rhiannon had buttoned up the purple uniform. Away to his left, Aracuria saw a neat row of nuclear pressure vessels, which Roger had just finished positioning.

The crackling got louder and the whole top of the mountain was shaking. The Transport came into view. It was a massive airplane with huge extended wings and a fat body. It came slowly towards them until it was right overhead, then hovered over the pressure vessel. Aracuria tilted his head back to get a clear view of the Transport. Its underside was all blackened with smoke and there were burn marks along the wings. Above the burn marks were streaks of rust and written across the side of the body were the words:

AIR FLEET ONE NUCLEAR
CONTAMINATION TRANSPORT
THE TRANS-UNIVERSE CORPORATION

The underside of the Transport opened up and then, one by one, the clean, shiny pressure vessels drifted up into the air to disappear into the holds. Once the last one had been sucked up, the doors closed. Then another door opened and out came a dozen burned and battered pressure vessels. They fell straight down and smashed and bounced on the ground. Some began to hiss steam, while others rumbled as if they were about to explode.

Aracuria ducked in fear, but when nothing happened he stood up again. He looked across at Rhiannon and Morcant and saw that they had their hands up to their heads in a salute. Morcant said something, but it was impossible to hear because of all the crackling in the air. Another door opened in the side of the Transport and a large white package tumbled out, falling halfway down before a parachute opened and allowed it to drift gently to the ground. Morcant and Rhiannon remained still while Roger walked over and picked up the first pressure vessel and carried it towards the dome. Before he had even reached the steps, all the doors on the Transport had closed up and the giant airplane began to move slowly away. When it was finally out of view, the crackling in the air and the vibrating of the mountain stopped.

Rhiannon ran forward and began to tear open the white package. Morcant seated himself on the ground. Aracuria went over to him.

'Good morning, King Morcant,' he said. Morcant looked exhausted; he pulled out a hanky from beneath his breastplate and wiped the sweat off his forehead.

'What's the matter with you, boy? Why are you holding your nose?'

'I ate real food yesterday. We all did,' he said.

Morcant nodded knowingly. 'I'm so sorry for you. I should have guessed.' Morcant turned away to look at Rhiannon, who was pulling out bars of chocolate from the white package.

'What are we going to do?' asked Aracuria. 'We were going to go home today, but now we can't, not knowing how awful this planet smells.'

Morcant shook his head and pulled the burned white hair on his chin. 'I don't know, Aracuria, I don't know. The only reason the North gives everyone in the South the Yellow Stuff is so that no one can smell how awful everything is. If they did, then no one would stand for it any longer; everything would have to change,' he said wistfully.

Aracuria sat down at his side, and said excitedly. 'But that's it! That's the way to do it. If everyone could smell how terrible it was, they'd all come out of their holes and demand that something be done!'

Morcant turned to look at him; his face was old and wise and sad. 'There isn't enough real food in all the South to feed everyone. Up here we've only got enough to feed ourselves.'

Klut appeared. He had his fingers over his nose and looked very unhappy. Just then something caught Morcant's eye. The old man stood up, shaded his eyes and pointed into the distance.

'Ah, it's the Solar Ducks,' he said. 'I forgot they were due to arrive today.'

Away in the distance was the fourth mountain. It was the highest of them all and high in the air Aracuria could see three birds winging their way

through the sky, coming in to land on the highest of the peaks. Without another word, Morcant started climbing up the fourth mountain to meet the ducks. Klut turned to Aracuria.
'Shall we go and see them land?' Aracuria nodded.
'Maybe it'll smell less up there,' he said hopefully.

They walked across the open space; past Rhiannon who was busily munching her way through bar after bar of chocolate; past Roger, who was carrying the second pressure vessel down to the dome; past the hissing and rumbling pressure vessels themselves and then up the steps to the fourth mountain.

At the top they found Morcant sitting on a rusted pipe waiting for the ducks, his helmet beside him. The top of the fourth mountain was a mess, with broken pipes dripping water, rusted buildings and maintenance sheds with collapsed roofs. Aracuria gazed around him in surprise.
'What's this place?' he asked.
'Oh, this is the maintenance depot for the Solar Ducks,' Morcant replied.
Aracuria didn't understand. 'What are the Solar Ducks?' he asked. 'What are they for?'
Morcant tutted disapprovingly. 'Don't they teach you anything in school these days?'
Aracuria shook his head. 'No,' he answered, truthfully.
'Well,' said Morcant, 'years and years ago in the time of the great Emperor Thesaurus, when the South was extraordinarily rich, it was decided that it might be a good idea to invest some of our vast wealth on another planet, just in case anything ever went wrong. So, the Emperor Thesaurus gathered together all the kings of the South, among them one of my ancestors, King Morcant the Unsteady, and they decided that they should look for some form of currency that would always be acceptable throughout the universe, regardless of place or time, and then find a really safe place to store it.
'What happened then?' asked Klut.
'Well, it took hundreds of years, but finally, in the time of my great grandfather, King Morcant the Slow Witted, they eventually discovered that the most valuable thing in the whole Universe was a particular kind of cheese, produced by the Lesser Spotted Silurian Cow, known as Silurian Dripping Cheese. And the reason this unlikely substance was so valuable was because there had only ever been one Lesser Spotted Silurian Cow and it had died 30 million years before, leaving just eleven thousand tons of Silurian Dripping Cheese behind it. What's more, it tasted really good. So King Morcant the Slow-Witted and the other kings sent out a whole fleet of space treasure ships and bought the Cheese from the planet of the Silurians, whose ancestors had owned the original cow ... '
'If the Cheese tasted so good,' Klut interrupted, his fingers still clutching his nose, 'why didn't it all get eaten by the Silurians?'
'Because the Silurians regarded the Lesser Spotted Silurian Cow as sacred, as

was the Cheese,' snapped Morcant cuttingly. 'Well,' he continued, 'once the treasure ships had been exchanged for the Cheese, we had to find a place to store it. That wasn't too difficult, as we already knew of a planet of Demi-Demons who had moved into the banking business a long time before. We asked them if they would look after the Cheese for us until the time came when we needed it and they said they would. The only problem was that they had to be paid for keeping it and we had just spent all our money on the treasure ships. Of course, at the time, we all thought that it wouldn't be that long before we were extraordinarily rich again, so we agreed to pay them a certain amount each year until the time came for us to sell the Cheese.

'Now, we had made our money by trading with other planets and civilizations and we owned a vast fleet of space cargo ships that carried our goods from one planet to another. But, in order to pay the Demi-Demons each year, we decided to build a small fleet of solar ships that would use the energy of the sun to travel from our planet to theirs.'

'And that's where the Solar Ducks came from!' exclaimed Aracuria.

'Exactly,' said Morcant. He stood up and held out his hands in a wide sweep. 'And this was where they were built by King Morcant the Slow-Witted, and this is where they came back once a year to be maintained. Everything was automatic; the computers on the ducks had been programmed to fly first to the Southern National Reserve Bank and pick up the year's treasure, then they were programmed to fly here and be serviced and then they would fly off to the planet of the Demi-Demons with their treasure, using the power of the sun.'

Morcant sat down again with a sad look on his face. 'That was over two hundred years ago.'

'What happened then?' asked Aracuria.

'Shortly after they started flying, the North attacked us and stole all the money out of the Southern National Reserve Bank. For a while after that, up until I was a boy in fact, we continued maintaining the Solar Ducks as they flew in, hoping that things might get better, but they never did.'

'And the Cheese, what happened to the Cheese?' asked Aracuria.

Morcant turned to look at him.

'Oh it's still with the Demi-Demons, all eleven thousand tons of it. They won't let anyone have it. I heard that the North tried to get it back, but the Demi-Demons destroyed every warship that was sent out to take it. The Demi-Demons of Draco can be appallingly evil if anyone breaks a pact with them.'

The Solar Ducks were coming in to land. Far off in the sky a giant bird winged its way in to the mountain top. Aracuria and Klut watched in amazement. Its huge webbed feet landed in the open space between the buildings and then slowly it folded its giant rusted wings.

Then a second one arrived. It was making a terrible squeaking sound as it flapped its wings, one of which was obviously loose. It came up behind

the other and brought its webbed feet crashing to the ground. Its bill hit the Duck in front, shunting it along like a train. Then, with a terrible creaking sound, it folded up its damaged wings. Finally the third bird came in to land. Its wings sounded even worse than the second Duck and even before it landed Aracuria could see that it had lost one of its legs.
'How's it going to land?' asked Aracuria.
Morcant shrugged his shoulders. 'With difficulty,' he said wryly.

Eventually, swaying from side to side, the third bird came above the mountain top. It settled one webbed foot on the floor, folded up its creaking wings and, with a loud crash, fell over on its side.

Aracuria walked over to it. It was covered in streaks of red rust, there were black burn marks around its huge bill and along the edge of its wings, and it had two large eyes, each the size of Aracuria himself. The eyes were bright blue, and as Aracuria watched, two battered steel eyelids slid down to cover them.
'What's happened to it?'
Morcant drew along side. 'They've been flying for over a hundred years and no one has looked after them for sixty years or more. Each re-entry takes a little bit more out of them. I think this is the last time Glenys will make it.'
Klut looked up at him. 'Glenys?'
'Yes, Glenys; and those are Margaret and Deborah,' he pointed at the other two, 'and last year there were also Susan and Jennifer and Genevieve and the year before that there were Elena and Zoe. But one by one they either break down in space or fall apart on re-entry and burn up in the atmosphere. At one time there were two hundred of them. These are the last three. '

Morcant sat down on the ground beside Glenys and took off his helmet.
'What's this?' Aracuria asked, pointing at a large, silver bag strapped to the back of the Duck.
'Oh, that's the Solar Rucksack; that's what gives the ducks the power to fly.'
Aracuria was about to touch the rucksack when Rhiannon appeared, her face and neck and the inside of the bubble smeared with chocolate. She approached Aracuria and was just about to say something when there was a scream.

Bill came running up the steps and across the open place.
'The smell, the smell, I can't stand it!' he shouted. 'Aracuria! Help me!' Then suddenly Bill's foot hit Morcant's helmet and he was airborne. He flew through the air and Rhiannon just had time to scream, 'NO!' before Bill came crashing down on the bubble, which exploded into a million pieces of glass. Bill fell straight to the ground.

For a few seconds Rhiannon just stood there in shocked disbelief, then the smell hit her. 'HE'S BROKEN MY BUBBLE! HE'S BROKEN MY BUBBLE!' She immediately set about trying to strangle Bill who lay stunned on the floor. 'I'M GOING TO KILL HIM!'

Aracuria, Klut and Morcant had to work together to drag her off before she caused him any serious harm. Rhiannon was furious.
'What am I going to *do?* This planet stinks! And there won't be another transport for three months!'
'Pinch your nose with your fingers, Rhiannon,' gasped Aracuria. 'It'll stop the smell.'

Everyone was unhappy now. Klut sat down beside Morcant, who stared dreamily at the closed eyes of the Duck; Rhiannon walked round and round in circles, occasionally shouting abuse at Bill. What were they going to do? thought Aracuria. Spending the next three months like this was too appalling to contemplate. Everything had gone wrong; everything in the South had gone wrong for *years.* If only everyone could smell how dreadful it all was, they'd soon get something done about the rubbish, and the schools, and having to work in slurry pits and live in chemical bins and all the rest of it. If everyone could smell ...

Aracuria ran back to Morcant. 'How much Cheese do the Demi-Demons of Draco have?' he asked excitedly.
Morcant looked confused. 'Ah, eleven thousand tons.'
'And it's real food, isn't it?'
'Yes,' said Morcant.
'And it belongs to us, doesn't it; we paid for it with the treasure ships?'
'Yes,' said Morcant again, his face a picture of bewilderment.
'Then why don't we fly there in the Solar Ducks, get the Cheese, bring it back here and feed it to the people of the South?' cried Aracuria. 'Once everyone's tasted real food and smelt how awful everything is, they won't let the North dump the rubbish here any more.'

Morcant thought it over for a few seconds, frowning, and then said, 'Impossible.'
'Why?'
Morcant explained. 'The Demi-Demons of Draco are the most evil things in the whole Universe. The entire Northern War Fleet was destroyed trying to get the Cheese from them, so what chance have you got?'
Aracuria smiled. 'But that doesn't mean it's impossible, just unlikely,' he said, resolutely. He turned to Klut. 'What do you think of the plan?'
Klut smiled wryly. 'Sounds insane to me, Aracuria. But do we have any choice? Even if we could put up with the smell for three months, the second we got back to school ... ' Klut drew a finger along his neck. 'Kids who miss school disappear,' he said ominously. Bill nodded in agreement.
Aracuria looked at Rhiannon. 'And what about you'!'
She shrugged her shoulders. *'Anything* to get off this planet,' she said.
Aracuria turned to Morcant. 'When do the Ducks take off?' he asked.
'Just before midnight.'
'Then just before midnight we leave,' said Aracuria.

CHAPTER FIVE: THE VOYAGE OUT

They had all day to get prepared. Aracuria and Rhiannon spent most of the time loading up Glenys with real food, while Klut and Bill looked for weapons to take with them. Morcant hunted around for a book on the Demi-Demons of Draco.

Towards evening, just as darkness fell, it started to rain. Rhiannon and Aracuria had finished loading up Glenys. Klut and Bill had got together a collection of antique laser weapons that had been stored away in one of the buildings. No one had seen Morcant since early morning and Rhiannon was beginning to get worried. She didn't want to leave without saying goodbye to her granddad. They waited on the fourth mountain peak, sheltering from the rain under one of the Ducks. They waited all evening and still Morcant hadn't appeared. Then, just before midnight he came running up the steps shouting out loud:

'I found it, I found it.' In his right hand he clutched a book. 'I found it!' He ran up to Klut. 'Did you load those laser weapons?' he asked, half out of breath.

Klut nodded.

'Then get rid of them,' said Morcant.

Aracuria turned to Morcant in astonishment.

'Why do you want us to get rid of the lasers? We're going to need them, aren't we'!'

Morcant was out of breath, it was coming up to midnight and he didn't have time to explain. 'This book,' he said, waving the book in front of Aracuria's face, 'this book has all the answers. It's a detailed account of the Demi-Demons of Draco and their leader, Lucifer. It was written by the Emperor Thesaurus himself, seven hundred years ago. Believe me, if they find so much as a penknife on you, they'll blow you out of the sky before you've had time to ask a question, let alone steal the Cheese.'

Aracuria reached across and took the book out of Morcant's hand. He read the cover: *The Demi-Demons of Draco: The Guardians of the Tree of Life,* and turned to Morcant. 'What's the Tree of Life?' he asked.

Morcant looked scared. 'I found the book this morning and I've been reading it all day. To reach the Cheese, you'll have to trick your way past the eight sub princes of Draco and then past their leader, Lucifer. Just go for the Cheese, nothing else. When I told you the Demi-Demons of Draco had gone into the banking business, I didn't know that they had been looking after something else for far longer.'

Aracuria didn't understand, but he could see fear in Morcant's eyes. 'What's the Tree of Life?' he asked again.

Morcant was just about to answer when there was an enormous creaking sound. Rhiannon screamed out. 'The DUCKS! The Ducks are moving!'

They all looked in horror as the first Duck walked to the edge of the mountain. It opened its wings and jumped off into the night. It disappeared out of sight, then a few seconds later reappeared, flapping its wings, rising higher and higher in the air. Then there was another loud creak as the second Duck began to move off.

'Quickly!' shouted Morcant. 'Climb up before she flies off.'

Rhiannon and Aracuria started scrambling up one of the legs while Klut and Bill grabbed for the other. The four of them managed to get to Margaret's knees, but then, just as they reached the edge, the Duck opened her wings and the jolt they received as the wings started to flap made them all fall off. For a moment they just lay there, then there was a giant creak.

'OH NO!' screamed Rhiannon. 'It's Glenys!' They turned around to see the last Solar Duck trying to get to her one foot and make her way to the edge, Morcant shouted out at the top of his voice.

'ROGER: EMERGENCY!'

At once Roger appeared at the top of the steps, brandishing a Zulkon Gamma Gun. Morcant shouted again. 'Put that down, you great lump of tin and help them!' Before Roger could move, Glenys was up on her foot and had started to hop towards the edge. Roger ran to the edge as fast as he could, overtaking the hopping Glenys, reached down and picked up Rhiannon, Aracuria, Bill and Klut. But it was too late, Glenys had reached the edge and was just about to unfold her battered wings.

'Roger: stop Glenys!' screamed Morcant. Without thinking, Roger turned around and gave Glenys a firm push. Glenys fell flat on her face. 'Roger: put them on Glenys!' shouted Morcant. Roger neatly dropped the four of them on to Glenys' back as she struggled to stand back up.

Morcant picked up a helmet, and threw it at Klut. 'Put it on your head, Alien, then the demons won't know that you're brighter than the others; it might come in handy.' He reached down again to pick up the book by Thesaurus. At that moment, Glenys stood up, stretched out her wings and fell off the edge. Morcant grabbed the book and threw it down off the edge after them. Aracuria reached up and caught the book just as the duck plummeted down into the void below.

They clung on to the Solar Rucksack for dear life waiting for the duck to start flapping her wings; but nothing happened. They were shooting downwards through the air at a hundred miles an hour, past the sheer rock face, and still the wings wouldn't work.

'What's the matter?' yelled Aracuria. 'Why won't the wings work?'

'The Solar Rucksack; we're sitting on the Solar Rucksack!' said Klut.

Aracuria looked at him in disbelief. 'But it's night!' he shouted. A look of terror crept across Klut's face, Then Aracuria looked up at the sky; high above was a brilliant moon. The rubbish was fast approaching; there wasn't

time to explain.
'GET OFF THE RUCKSACK!' Before anyone could ask why, he pushed Rhiannon and Bill on to one wing and then jumped with Klut on to the other.

As the moonlight hit the rucksack, the wings started to beat, slowly at first, then faster and faster. Gradually they began to pull out of the dive, but they were still dropping. Slowly the rubbish came up to meet them. Glenys' foot banged against the rubbish, which was lit lip by the glow of uranium canisters and the flames of Will O' Wisps. Just as they were about to start rising again, her foot caught on a fridge. There was a terrible ripping sound as her leg was torn off. She blinked a few times, then continued flying upwards, straining to catch up with the others.

Aracuria lay across the wing looking down on the world below, with the book by Thesaurus tucked into his jumper for safe-keeping. Klut was beside him. He had just pulled on the helmet that Morcant had given him and even though he didn't say so, he quite liked it.

On the other wing Rhiannon and Bill were staring down at the ground. They were rising higher with every beat of Glenys' wings, and it looked magical. Everywhere there were glowing objects, reds and yellows, blues and greens, while the flames of the Will O' Wisps seemed to be dancing in the rubbish.

Gradually the air became thinner; the smell of rotting rubbish began to go away and the air cleared. Ahead of them, down below, a great silver expanse appeared. It was wide and so immensely long that it seemed to go off either side of the world.
'That's the Equatorial Sea,' said Klut. 'It goes right the way around the world and it divides the North from the South.'

The sea was silver from the light of the moon. Slowly Glenys began to pull them over until they could see the other side. There were long strings of yellow lights running in straight lines and great clusters of red and yellow lights bunched together. Aracuria had never seen anything like it before.
'What are the strings of lights?' he asked.
'Those are road lights,' said Klut.
'And the clusters?'
'They're cities, Aracuria,' answered Klut. 'That's where the Northerners live.'

Down below there was the sound of music, and people shouting and laughing. The North seemed so different from the South, so different from anything Aracuria had ever known.

Slowly even the North fell out of view. The whole world was getting smaller and more rounded. Glenys rose higher and higher until they left the world behind and were finally in space. Aracuria sat up and looked back at Earth; it looked so small and so alone. It was just a blue ball getting smaller with every second.
Something was coming into view ahead.
'It's Margaret and Deborah,' said Aracuria, as the outline of the other Solar

Ducks appeared. Glenys began to catch them up.
'Do you remember what Morcant said?' asked Aracuria. Klut nodded silently.
'What did my granddad say?' shouted Rhiannon across the rucksack.
'That if we have so much as a penknife on board, they'll blow us out of space,' Aracuria continued. 'And that means we have to empty out the laser weapons from the other Ducks.' He turned to Rhiannon. 'Is there any way we can get Glenys to fly above one of the other Ducks?'
Rhiannon grinned. 'Yeah. Just ask her; she's not as dumb as she looks.' Glenys started beating harder with her wings and slowly began to pull above the Duck in front of her.
'I don't believe it!' said Aracuria. 'She did it without me asking.' Rhiannon shrugged her shoulders. 'I said she wasn't dumb.'

Glenys and Margaret were now flying close together. Aracuria turned to Klut. 'So who's going to jump down on to Margaret, climb in through her bill and clean out all the lasers?'
Klut shook his head. 'Not me,' he said.
'Well, is anyone else going to do it?' There was silence. 'Very well then, I'll have to do it,' said Aracuria. He climbed off the wing and on to Glenys' neck.

All around were stars. He climbed up the neck and over the head until he was sitting on the edge of Glenys' bill. Ten meters beneath him was Margaret and beneath her was a bottomless void. He went to jump.
'Take care!' shouted Rhiannon. He pushed off with his feet, expecting to come down on Margaret's back; instead he floated up into the air. Klut walked across and grabbed Aracuria's leg, but didn't take his feet off Glenys.
'Don't you realize we're in space and that everything is weightless? The Solar Ducks must have some kind of gravity, so, as long as you don't take your feet off them, you don't float away.'
Aracuria looked down at Klut. 'So how do I get on to the other Duck?' he asked.
'Simple!' replied Klut. 'I just walk around Glenys.'

With that, he began to walk down off Glenys' wing, on to her underside, whilst still holding Aracuria's ankle. Aracuria simply reached out and grabbed Margaret's Solar Rucksack. Klut let go of his feet so that he could climb on to Margaret's back, and then he walked up her neck, over her head and climbed into her bill. Once inside, a light came on automatically. Ahead of Aracuria was a huge oval room that seemed much bigger than he'd expected. There were Zulkon Laser Guns lying on the floor, together with Franchini Proton Weapons and IPM Plutonium Carbines. One by one, Aracuria threw them out of Margaret's bill, and they drifted slowly off into the blackness of space.

When he had finished, he climbed on to Margaret's back, reached up and took hold of Klut's hands so that he could pull him back on board Glenys. No sooner was he there than Rhiannon began to complain that she was hungry.

'I'm going to get some food from the hold,' she said. 'I won't be long.' She set off up Glenys' neck and disappeared over the top of the Duck's head. About twenty minutes later she returned carrying a whole armful of food. While Klut, Rhiannon and Bill tucked in hungrily, Aracuria pulled out the book that Morcant had given him. It was very old, bound in thick leather with brass hinges on the edge. He opened it up and started to read:

'I, Emperor Thesaurus, leader of the South, mighty ruler of the western ring of the Solar System, Chief of the Trans-Universe Trade Federation .. .' And so it went on, page after page of all the titles and business corporations that Thesaurus had. Then the writing changed, ' ... warn you and all those who come after me; never ever go near, visit or have dealings with the Demi-Demons of Draco. They are not only the most evil thing in the Universe but have among them a terrible secret, of which I will now tell you ... ' Aracuria closed the book and looked up at the others.

'We're in big trouble,' he said.

CHAPTER SIX: DRACO

It was impossible to tell how long they'd been traveling. There was no night or day and around them the stars didn't seem to move at all. Aracuria had put away the book because it scared him too much. But he knew he would have to read it all before they arrived.

It seemed to be only a short while after he had put down the book that something strange happened. Everyone except Aracuria was asleep. Rhiannon lay flat out on the wing, while Klut lay asleep underneath. Bill had climbed inside Glenys where the food was and Aracuria was lying on Glenys' neck with his head propped up against the Solar Rucksack, looking out at the other Ducks. Suddenly the leading Duck was bathed in a brilliant orange glow. Aracuria shouted out.

'Klut! Come here!' Klut's flat head popped up from beneath Glenys.

'What's happening?' he asked sleepily.

Aracuria pointed at Deborah as the glow seemed to completely cover her. The next moment there was a streak of brilliant blue light which shot out like a comet from the orange glow and burned its way across the Universe, disappearing between the stars.

'Deborah; she's gone!' exclaimed Aracuria. Deborah, and the glow too, had indeed vanished. Aracuria's cry woke up Rhiannon and Bill. Rhiannon scrambled up beside him, while Bill poked his head out through the bill.

'What's happened?' asked Rhiannon.

'I, I don't know. Deborah ... just vanished,' said Aracuria. Rhiannon turned to Klut, 'Do you know what happened to her?' He opened his mouth to answer when, up ahead, Margaret began to be covered in another orange glow.

'Oh no, it's happening again!' cried Aracuria in dismay. The glow grew bigger and brighter and bigger and brighter until it completely covered Margaret. As they watched, she seemed to tilt over and then there was another blue streak, which once again burned its way through the stars, disappearing on the other side of the Universe.

'She's vanished too!' gasped Rhiannon. Margaret and the glow had gone.

Bill screamed out, 'I want to go *home!'* but everyone ignored him.

Aracuria looked at Klut. He had his hand on his chin and his hyper-intelligent brain was working overtime. He just had time to say, 'I think I know what's happening ... ' when the glow burst out right in front of them. They gazed in wonder as the glow grew into a giant sheet of orange, extending from the edge of Glenys' bill high above them and far below. The farther they traveled the bigger it grew, until eventually it began to come down around them, covering the Duck.

Klut cried out, 'It's a rubber sheet! We're at the edge of the Universe.' Then suddenly Glenys tipped over, the orange glow turned into a brilliant blue and

the next second all the stars turned into great long streaks of white light, until it looked as if they were surrounded by white spaghetti.
'What's happening?' Rhiannon clutched Aracuria in terror. Klut wasn't scared, he just stood on Glenys' head and kept on repeating to himself. 'This is amazing.'
Aracuria shouted to him, 'Klut, do you know what's going on?' Klut turned around. 'On the planet where my family used to live, there was a story that the wall of the Universe was made of rubber. And now I know it's true. The Ducks just hit the edge of the Universe and bounced off.'
Aracuria was mystified. 'Then where are we going now?'
Klut smiled. 'To Draco, at the speed of light. That's why all the stars have gone stringy.'

Gradually the blue glow began to fade and the long streaks of light shortened to become stars once again. Up ahead a giant circle of silver stars appeared. Aracuria and Rhiannon jumped up and ran to stand beside Klut.
'What's that?' asked Rhiannon, pointing at the circle of stars.
'That's the head of the Dragon. Draco means the Dragon.' Aracuria let the words sink in, and then he cried out in horror.
'You mean we're already there?'
Klut nodded.
'Then we're really in trouble,' said Aracuria.
'Why?'
'Because the first real line by Thesaurus tells anyone who reads his book never to go to Draco and that's all I've had time to read,' he said, pulling the book out from under his jumper.
'Let me,' said Klut, taking the book out of Aracuria's hands. Up ahead the circle of stars was getting bigger and bigger as Klut thumbed through the book, reading each page super-fast. When he had finished, he gave the book back to Aracuria.
'Oh boy,' he said. 'We are in *trouble!'*

Slowly they passed through the center of the circle of stars and came out on the other side. Up ahead was a giant red planet. Glenys was heading straight towards it. Aracuria looked down at Klut.
'What did the book say?'
'The Demi-Demons of Draco are *real* demons. The only way we can get past them to get to the Cheese is by answering the questions of each of the Demons who hold the keys to the Pit.' Klut rolled over and looked up at Aracuria. 'Getting in is the easy bit; getting out is the problem. These demons don't just collect Cheese, they collect everything ... including souls.' Klut looked across at the glowing red planet. 'If we're ever going to get off there again, we need a lot of luck.'
Aracuria had a question to ask, 'What's the Tree of Life?'
Klut looked horrified. 'Don't ask!'

The planet was like a ball of fire. Slowly Glenys came down into the atmosphere and headed for a mountain. The whole planet was covered in a sea of molten, burning metal that bubbled and spat great fountains high into the sky. Glenys flew in over the sea and, just before she reached the mountain, Klut grabbed the book from Aracuria and threw it into the molten sea where it burst into flames. A long slit opened in the side of the mountain and a white glow appeared. Glenys flew through the opening into a vast hall of white light. She stopped flapping her wings, touched down on her belly, slid along the floor and with a terrible screeching sound turned over, catapulting Rhiannon, Klut, Bill and Aracuria off her back.

Aracuria stood up. To his left were the other two ducks. Both were covered in black burn marks from having bounced off the edge of the Universe.

They were in a vast hall of glass. Klut picked himself off the ground and straightened his helmet.

'Well at least they let us in. I tell you, Aracuria, your idea in coming here was really stupid. If Morcant had let me read that book before we took off, I would never have come.'

Rhiannon looked around at the sheer glass walls. 'And yet the place looks deserted.'

Klut grimaced. 'The demons are just watching us, listening. The first thing they're going to do is find out whether we've come here to deposit something. Things are going to get really difficult when they find out we want to take something away.'

Aracuria looked down and saw Bill curled up in a tight ball on the ground. His head was tucked between his knees.

'Bill, you can get up now.'

Bill lifted his head and looked around at the hall. 'Where, where are we?'

'Draco.'

Suddenly there was a terrible smell, like the stench of rotting maggots and festering wounds.

'Ugh! What's that?' yelled Rhiannon, placing her hand over her mouth.

'That'll be one of the demons coming to see us,' said Klut.

Out of one of the glass walls came a huge dragon with outstretched wings and a long winding tail. Its mouth was closed, but on its back rode a creature with three heads. The first head was a ram's, the second head a bull's and the third a man's. The creature carried a spear in his left hand, which he pointed at Bill. Bill's eyes were wide open in terror. The dragon strutted towards them and then stopped. Everyone was terrified, except Klut, who had read the book and knew what was going to happen. Klut pulled off his helmet.

'Oh, Asmodee, I do this as a mark of respect,' he said, bowing slightly. Aracuria and Rhiannon looked at Klut in disbelief.

'WELCOME!' roared the creature on the dragon. 'WELCOME TO DRACO! DO YOU WISH TO MAKE A DEPOSIT?'
Klut straightened up. 'Ah, no. You see, we have come from the planet Earth to collect the eleven thousand tons of Silurian Dripping Cheese that was deposited with you by the ancestors of Aracuria, Rhiannon and Bill,' said Klut. The creature's jaw fell. 'But how do we know that it belongs to you? The Cheese was deposited a long, long time ago. You don't think we'd allow anyone to come and take it, do you?'

Rhiannon lifted her head. 'It was only two hundred years ago,' she said. The beast looked down at her and a smile came across his face, then the smile broadened and he started to laugh. 'HA, HA, HAA!' he screamed, as his voice echoed around the glass hall. 'Two hundred years ago! More like a hundred million!' At that moment the walls of the hall lit up with stars, in the center of which appeared a fantastic explosion of light.
'That was a super-nova that ninety-three million years ago wiped out your planet and everything for a billion light years around. Do you still want the Cheese?' he said. Before anyone else had time to answer Klut shouted out, 'Yes!' Rhiannon looked at him. 'Is the demon lying?' Klut shook his head.
Suddenly Rhiannon burst into tears. 'Then what's the *point* in getting the cheese? We haven't even got a world to go back to!' The demon looked straight at her. 'Are you thinking of your grandfather, child?'
She nodded. 'And what became of him?' She nodded again.

Suddenly the stars disappeared, to be replaced by the top of the fourth mountain of Morcant's castle. Her granddad was there, waiting by the edge, with Roger at his side. He was looking out through a set of binoculars at the sky, waiting for Rhiannon to return. Then he grew older, much older, with long gray hair, and before long he was sitting in a wheelchair being pushed around by Roger. Finally he disappeared from the scene, although Roger still waited, standing on the edge, year after year, waiting for the Ducks to return, though they never did. Finally, even Roger died, though by then even the mountain had been worn down by the rain. Rhiannon couldn't stop the tears.
'What happened to him?' she said.
'Your grandfather waited twenty-five years for you to return and you never did. Roger waited twenty thousand until his uranium core expired.'
Rhiannon sat herself on the ground.
'Why did you bring us here, Aracuria? Why?'
Aracuria was too stunned to say anything. Klut lifted up his head. 'But we still want the Cheese.' he said.
Aracuria couldn't see the point; if there was no planet left to save, what was the point of having the Cheese?
'I failed,' he said. 'Let them keep the Cheese; it's worthless now.' He sat down beside Rhiannon, but Klut was still insistent.
'We want the Cheese,' he shouted.

'Even though you have no use for it?' asked the demon.
'YES!' shouted Klut.
'Then you will have to pass all the tests to show it belongs to you. If you fail one, just one, you lose ... your souls. Do you understand this?' The demon smiled.
'YES!' shouted Klut.

Then suddenly, the demon vanished. Klut looked down at the other three; Rhiannon, who was crying for her grandfather; Aracuria, who felt awful for having brought them there; and Bill who didn't understand a thing.
'Don't worry,' said Klut.
'Don't *worry!'* screamed Rhiannon. 'Don't *worry,* he says. I've lost my grandfather, Aracuria and Bill have lost their families, we've all lost the Earth, we haven't got the cheese, we're stuck on a planet on the other side of the Universe, inhabited by demons who are about to take our souls away and you say don't worry! I am terrified!'
'Don't you understand?' said Klut. 'When we bounced off the edge of the Universe, we were accelerated up to the speed of light. Anything that travels *that* fast travels through time. We've gone forward in time a hundred million years, but when we go back we'll travel back in time by a hundred million years as well. As far as your granddad is concerned, we'll only have been away a second. What we saw up there in the glass is what will happen if we don't get back; that's what will happen if we *don't* get the Cheese.' Klut sat down on the floor exhausted.
'You mean it'll all be all right in the end if we get the Cheese?' asked Aracuria.
Klut nodded. 'If,' he said ominously.
'It, it'll, it'll be all right in the end?' asked Bill, white-faced.
'Yes,' said Klut.
'The demon said something about tests,' said Rhiannon. 'What kind of tests are those?'
'All kinds. That was the first one and, thanks to me,' he said, puffing out his chest, and popping his helmet back on his head, 'and no thanks to you, we passed with flying colors. The first test was to see whether we wanted the Cheese for its own sake rather than to sell it or use it in some other way.'
'And we passed!' said Rhiannon excitedly.
'Yes, but each of the seven other sub-princes of Draco will set us tests. If we pass them all, they'll allow us in to see Lucifer, who guards all the treasure - not just the Silurian Dripping Cheese, but all the treasure in the Universe that the demons have managed to gather in from the very beginning until now.'
'Is the Tree of Life part of it as well?' asked Aracuria innocently. Klut gasped in horror.
'I told you never to mention it!' After a moment he calmed down. 'You realize, Aracuria, that before we leave here - if we leave here - you'll be permitted to see it, and *only* you. And none of us will be allowed to help you

get away.'
Aracuria smiled.
'That's easy: I'll just walk away,' he said.
'It won't be that easy, Aracuria; according to Thesaurus, a thousand million people have come here from the beginning of time, looking for the Tree of Life, and *none* of them ever got away. Remember what Asmodee said; these demons collect souls as well as Cheese.' Aracuria stopped smiling.

CHAPTER SEVEN: MS BAD BREATH

Aracuria and the others sat around on the floor waiting for something to happen. Klut had told everyone to be quiet, as the demons could hear every word and he had already had to give away a lot of secrets. Glenys was leaking oil from where her last leg had been ripped off. The other two birds stood silently by.

A girl appeared. She seemed to walk straight out of the glass wall. She was young, beautiful and wearing a long silver dress. She held out her hand.

'Would you step this way, please? The game show is about to begin.' Her voice was soft and gentle.

'Game show?' said Rhiannon in disbelief.

'Game show!' said Bill excitedly as he jumped up from the ground. 'I've always wanted to go on a game show.' The girl turned around and headed back towards the glass wall, only now there was a large white door in it. The door opened and she stepped through to the other side with Bill close behind.

Aracuria turned to Klut. 'Is this a trick?'

Klut shrugged. 'Of course, but we have to beat them at their own game, there's no other way.'

He followed Bill through the door.

'I don't like it,' said Rhiannon. 'I don't like *her.'* All the same, she followed Klut through the door, as did Aracuria.

They found themselves in a large TV studio. They had come in at the back of an entire audience of people.

'There are other people here from Earth,' said Aracuria.

Klut shook his head. 'The demons have conjured up an image, that's all; none of them are real.'

Aracuria couldn't believe it, but he didn't have time to look closely. Another girl appeared and tagged little labels on to their clothes. Each of the labels had their names written on.

'Bill; come on down!' shouted the girl at the front. Immediately the audience began to clap, shout and whistle their applause. A big smile broke out on Bill's face.

'This is brilliant,' he said happily. 'I *always* wanted this.' He ran down the steps towards the front, heading straight for the girl. She smiled, put her arm around his shoulders and turned him to face the audience.

She picked a piece of paper off her desk and shouted. 'Klut; come on down!' Klut ran down the steps to more applause. The girl made him stand beside Bill.

'Aracuria; come on down!' she screamed again, with the audience going even wilder. Aracuria turned to Rhiannon and grinned, then he too ran down to the

front to stand beside Klut.
'Rhiannon; come on down!' roared the girl for the last time. Rhiannon made her way to the front and came to stand beside Aracuria.

At last the audience quietened down. The girl turned to the four of them and said. 'This is Bill, Klut, Aracuria and Rhiannon and you're from Earth.' The audience began shouting and screaming again. 'And in case you didn't know, that was a puny little planet that was blown up by a super nova 93 million years ago. So, whatever you win here tonight, you won't be taking *anything* back.'
'I don't like her,' Rhiannon whispered in Aracuria's ear. The girl continued.
'My name is Astarot, I'm your hostess for this evening.' She smiled. Klut looked down at her dress; on the left hand side she wore a white brooch shaped like the moon.
'Oh no!' he whispered to Aracuria. 'She's a demon. We *are* in trouble!'
Astarot raised a finger to her lips.
'No talking among yourselves. That could be counted as cheating.' She turned to the audience. 'And what do we do with cheats?' She raised her hands in the air and the audience screamed in response:
'WE CUT THEIR HEADS OFF!'
The smile on Bill's face vanished. 'Wh-what? I thought this was a game.'
Astarot beamed. 'And so it is, and we're all going to have some fun tonight!' The audience shouted wildly. 'OK,' she said. 'These are the rules; you each have to answer one question. If any one of you gets the answer wrong, you all die. If you all get the answers right, you win tonight's star prize!' She swung around and behind the desk a broad silver curtain opened, revealing eleven thousand tons of Silurian Dripping Cheese, stacked up in a great pile. At the sight of the cheese the audience gave a loud 'Ahh!' Astarot continued. 'And just in case you didn't know, this cheese is the most valuable form of money in the whole Universe, so if you win tonight's star prize you'll be really lucky, won't you?' She turned towards them, and then breathed out. Bill almost fell over and the others rocked back on their heels. She had the most horrible bad breath that any of them had ever smelt.

'OK then, Klut; the first question for you. If you had the choice between eating a Carmel Consolidated Baal Beef burger from the star system of Yummyville, or a Draco Fried Dodo with Rats' Entrails and Bat Brain Puree Sauce, which would you choose?' The smile on her face turned nasty.
'That isn't a proper question,' said Klut.
'I'll have to hurry you, you flat-headed alien squirt.' She smiled again. Klut knew most things. He knew, for example that a Carmel Consolidated Baal Beef burger from the star system of Yummyville was without question the best tasting thing in the whole Universe, but if he said so the demons would be offended.
'The Draco Fried Dodo with Rats' Entrails and Bat Brain Puree Sauce, of

course,' replied Klut, feeling sick at the thought of it. Astarot's smile glittered nastily. 'Then this is just your day, because not only did you get the question right,' the audience screamed with joy, 'but we've got your favorite dish right here!'

From behind her back she produced a bowl of Draco Fried Dodo with Rats' Entrails and Bat Brain Puree Sauce. A spoon stuck out of the side.
'Eat it all up!' she screamed. Klut took one look and fainted. Astarot put the bowl down on the table. 'So far, so good,' she said. 'Now, Bill, the second question; if you had the choice between going home to be with your mum and your dad, to sit in front of the TV and then fall asleep with your head on your mother's lap, or being eaten alive by the dreaded Twelve-Eyed Child-Gobbling Beastie of the Draco Schools Inspectorate, which would you choose?' Bill wasn't very bright, but he knew he would rather be at home with his mum than with the Twelve-Eyed Child-Gobbling Beastie. He didn't understand that if he said he wanted to go home rather than be eaten by the monster, then it meant he didn't really want the Cheese that badly. However, Bill often had the habit of saying the opposite to what he meant, and this was one of those occasions.
'The Twelve-Eyed Child-Gobbling Beastie of the Draco Schools Inspectorate, please,' he said quietly, thinking that he had said the opposite. Astarot looked really upset, then she said. 'Well here he is!'

The curtains opened again and a two-legged, twelve-eyed, eight-armed, blood-red monster appeared. It had a huge wide mouth with giant razor-sharp teeth. Its body was covered in slimy scales and each of its feet and arms had seven black claws.
'RUN!' shouted Rhiannon. Bill tried to move but was rooted to the spot in terror. The monster loomed over him; it reached down for Bill - but at that moment Aracuria rushed forward, grabbed the bowl of Draco Fried Dodo with Rats' Entrails and Bat Brain Puree Sauce and threw it into the monster's mouth. It stopped, started to chew the bowl and its contents, and walked away, obviously satisfied with its meal.

Astarot looked really angry. Rhiannon ran across and planted a kiss on Aracuria's cheek. 'You're a genius, Aracuria, a genius. You saved Bill's life.' Bill was too stunned to say anything. Klut raised his head.
'What's, what's happened?' he asked, picking himself up. Astarot looked straight at him.
'Nothing - yet! But it soon will!' She lifted her hands and the audience began to scream uncontrollably. She turned to Aracuria. 'OK then, bright boy, let's see if you can answer this question. According to the ancient mythologies, the Universe is made out of one of two things. For several million years the inhabitants of Draco have known which of these two stories is correct. Now, all you have to do is tell me which of the stories is the right one. First: that the Universe is an egg laid by the Greater Zachlumia Warbling Snail of

Draco on the head of Tzachus the Awesome Mega Parrot, brother of Vukan Sky-God.' The audience roared uncontrollably; Astarot continued. 'Second: that the Universe is in fact made of rubber. ' Aracuria looked anxiously at Klut, who said nothing. He knew the real answer, because they'd found it out on the way to Draco, but from the roar of the crowd it seemed that wasn't the answer they wanted.
'The first one,' said Aracuria nervously. Astarot smiled.
'You mean that the Universe is an egg laid by the Greater Zachlumia Warbling Snail of Draco on the head of Tzachus the Awesome Mega Parrot, brother of Vukan Sky-God?' Aracuria nodded.
'You're sure you don't want to change your mind?' She was still smiling; what was he going to do? He closed his eyes.
'No,' he said. There was silence. When he opened his eyes again he saw that Astarot looked furious. 'You got the right answer, lucky boy. Let's *hope* your luck holds out.'

Finally she turned to Rhiannon. They had answered three questions correctly, just one more to go. Astarot produced another card.
'OK then, the last and final question to find out if you get the Cheese, or if you lose a lot more than you bargained for. How old is Aracuria?' There was total silence.
'What?' said Rhiannon.
'How old is Aracuria,' Astarot repeated.
'That isn't fair!' shouted Aracuria. 'I don't even know how old I am, no one knows. My dad can't count.'
Astarot smiled menacingly; she turned to Rhiannon. 'Answer!'
'I don't know,' said Rhiannon, desperately. 'No one does.'
'Answer!' screamed Astarot again.
'This isn't fair! How can you ask a question that no one knows the answer to. It's impossible,' shouted Klut angrily.
'Answer!' screamed Astarot, and she added quietly, 'And if you get it wrong or fail to answer, you lose your souls, all of you.' She looked around at the others.
'But how can I answer it? Even if I guess it right, you won't know if it is... '
An idea occurred to Rhiannon. At the same time Klut's face lit up.
'Of course!' he said. 'Whatever you say *has* to be right, because she has no way of knowing if you're wrong!' The evil smile disappeared from Astarot's face.
'You mean, it's a trick question?' said Rhiannon. Klut nodded.
'A thousand and one!' shouted Rhiannon. Astarot and the audience went quiet.
'Yes,' said Astarot, and then she smiled again. 'You are, of course, right.' Then she reached out and touched Aracuria. Suddenly he started to age; first he was twenty, then thirty, then middle-aged, then an old man with long

white hair and wrinkled skin.
'No!' screamed Rhiannon. But Aracuria kept on aging, older and older, year after year, until he could no longer stand. He collapsed to the floor, a thousand and one years of age. Rhiannon went to his side.
'I didn't mean it, honestly! Oh, please come back young again,' she cried. But Aracuria just lay there. Astarot started to laugh, as did the audience.
'Stop it!' screamed Rhiannon. 'You're all monsters, you're all evil.' She felt angry with them, but when she looked back down at Aracuria, old and wrinkled when he had just been so young, she started to cry. Her tears fell from her cheeks and landed on his face.
Astarot turned to her. 'I can give you one thing. Either Aracuria young again, or the Cheese,' she said. Rhiannon was just about to say, 'Aracuria,' when Klut shouted, 'It's a trick!'
Astarot swung around and touched his lips, sealing them so that he couldn't talk. Rhiannon thought it through; if she asked for Aracuria young again they would all die, but if she asked for the Cheese ...
'The Cheese,' she said quietly, turning her head away in shame. Astarot looked awful.
'As you wish,' she said. Suddenly Klut could speak again.
'Look!' he cried, pointing at Aracuria. Rhiannon looked; he was young again.
'What happened?' said Aracuria. 'I seemed to fall asleep.' Rhiannon helped him up. 'It doesn't matter,' she said.
Astarot turned to him. 'Her tears saved you, young man.' Then she turned around and vanished into thin air.
'Where did she go?' said Bill.
Rhiannon ran forward. 'I don't know and I don't care. Let's get the Cheese and go.'

They all ran towards the Cheese, but just in front of it a hole opened up in the ground. Rhiannon, who was in front, fell into it. Aracuria, Bill and Klut followed.

The hole was like a tunnel of light. They fell over and over, crashing into each other and bouncing off the walls. It seemed to be bottomless and there was no way that they could ever stop.

CHAPTER EIGHT: DR MAGOT AND THE FLY

Aracuria was dizzy. They'd been falling for ages. Suddenly he felt his face being flattened, then Klut landed on his head and the next moment the four of them were bouncing back up in the air, then down again, then back up. They had landed on a trampoline.

'This is really weird,' said Klut. Rhiannon bounced off the trampoline.

'Weird isn't the word. Where are we?' she said. Aracuria looked around. They were in a tunnel carved in rock. He jumped down off the trampoline. The tunnel went both ways, straight and long, so long in fact that they couldn't see either end.

'Which way do we take?' asked Bill.

Klut shook his head. 'It doesn't matter. Whichever way we go, we'll meet up with one of the demons again.'

Aracuria pointed to his left. 'Well, let's go this way.' The others followed on behind.

They had walked for perhaps twenty minutes between the rough, solid rock walls when suddenly a man appeared ahead. He was sitting at a desk. Aracuria approached. The man was looking at some notes. Then he glanced at Aracuria.

'Please take a seat,' he said. A seat appeared on Aracuria's side of the table. 'My name is Doctor Magot. If you want to get past me you have to pass your medical, is that clear? Before I can allow you past me, at least one of you has to pass the medical. The medical in this case is to see if at least one of you is normal. If no one is normal, then I'm afraid none of you can get past. Is that *clear?'* he said again. They all nodded. Aracuria sat down.

'Right then,' said the doctor, pulling out some notes from a drawer beneath his desk. 'Your name is Aracuria?' Aracuria nodded. 'How old are you?' Aracuria shook his head.

'I, I don't know.'

'You don't know?' said the doctor. 'And how long have you been suffering from this terrible illness of not knowing how old you are?' Aracuria looked uncertain, then Klut prodded him in the back.

'Since ... I was seven.'

'Since you were seven,' said the doctor, smiling. 'And how long ago was that?'

Aracuria looked confused. 'What, what do you mean?'

'I mean, how long is it since you last knew how old you were?' said the doctor curtly.

'If I don't know how old I am, how can I know how long ago it was that I knew how old I was?' asked Aracuria. The doctor looked away.

'Well, I'm afraid not to know how old you are, and to have suffered from this ailment since you were seven, and now not to be able to know exactly when it was that you were seven and so not to know in turn when it was that the ailment started in relation to your current age, means that I cannot in any sense of the word give you treatment. You are therefore untreatable and untreatable people who do not know how old they are are not normal. NEXT, PLEASE!' said the doctor, ripping up some notes and throwing them on the floor.

'What?' said Aracuria, who remained seated. The doctor stared across at him through his wide, black rimmed glasses.

'You failed the medical, you imbecile,' he shouted.

Aracuria jumped up. 'I only asked.'

Rhiannon took the seat. The doctor pulled out some more notes, looked through them and then glanced at Rhiannon.

'Your name is Rhiannon, is it not?' Rhiannon nodded.

'And you like chocolate?'

'Yes,' said Rhiannon.

'And how long have you liked chocolate?'

'Since I was very small, a baby I think.'

'Since you were a baby,' repeated the doctor. 'And yet you are not fat.'

'No. I'm not. I do a lot of jogging, with Roger, back home in Morcant Castle. We run up and down the four peaks every morning. It keeps me fit and exercises his Uranium Core.'

The doctor looked horrified. 'You *exercise,* in order to stop yourself getting *fat?'*

'Yes,' said Rhiannon.

The doctor took off his glasses. 'Don't you know that being fat is the body's way of telling you that you're healthy, and that to eat chocolate and be thin is therefore a gross abnormality. But to compound this ailment with exercise is absolutely unheard of. Do you not know that no less an authority than Professor Zosimus, the chairman of the Draco Committee on Flatulence and Toad-Eating for the Terminally Fit has conclusively proved that exercise is the cause of *all* illnesses.'

'You're mad,' said Rhiannon.

'And you, my dear,' said the doctor, ripping up another set of notes, 'have failed your medical, as no one who is normal would ever contemplate exercise to stay thin. Next, please!' Rhiannon stood up.

'This is all rigged,' she said to Klut as he sat down opposite the doctor.

The doctor read a new set of notes for a while and then looked up.

'Ah, you're called Klut, are you not?' Klut nodded.

'Could you take your helmet off, please?' Klut did as he was told.

The doctor took one look at Klut's flat head and said. 'No one with the top of their head missing can possibly be healthy.' He scribbled something on a piece of paper and handed it to Klut.

'This prescription is for Head Growth Hormone. Take one tablet four times a day and then come and see me again in four weeks' time. Until then you are clearly not normal. Next, please!'

Klut remained seated. 'But all the people on my planet have flat heads. That's why we're so intelligent.'

The doctor looked up. 'What is normal on your planet is irrelevant. What is normal on Draco is all that matters. Next, please.' Klut stood up clutching his prescription, allowing Bill to sit down.

Klut turned to Aracuria. 'If Bill fails his medical, that's it, we lose everything,' he whispered. Aracuria and Rhiannon looked horrified.

'Your name is Bill,' said the doctor. Bill nodded. 'How old are you?'

'I don't know,' said Bill quietly.

'And how long have you not known how old you were?'

'Since I was three.'

'And how long ago was that?'

'Ten years ago,' said Bill without thinking.

'So you don't know how old you are and the last time you knew how old you were was when you were three and when you were three was ten years ago. Correct?' Bill nodded. 'Good. Do you eat chocolate?'

'No,' said Bill truthfully.

'And yet you're fat; do you do any exercise?'

'No,' said Bill.

'And do you have a flat head at all?' Bill reached up and felt the top of his head.

'No,' he said.

'Good, very good. Well you don't eat chocolate, but you are fat so it doesn't matter; you don't exercise; you've got no flat head; you don't know how old you are and you know how long you haven't known. You're obviously fit and so you're clearly normal and so you've passed this medical with flying colors. Your friends could obviously take a leaf out of your book.'

The doctor stood up. Bill was smiling from ear to ear.

'I passed! I passed!' he shouted with joy.

Rhiannon looked at the doctor. 'Can we go through now?' she asked.

'Of course,' said the doctor. 'All you've got to do is get past me.' Rhiannon stepped forward when, suddenly, the buttons bounced off the doctor's jacket and it ripped open.

'What's happening?' gasped Rhiannon. Suddenly the doctor began to grow in size; his skin started to become wet, white and slimy.

'UGH!' screamed Klut. 'It's Magot! The third of the eight sub-princes.' Before their eyes the doctor turned into a massive maggot that filled up the whole of the tunnel, crushing the table and chairs. Then he started to slither towards them.

'Run!' shouted Aracuria.

They all turned and ran back down the tunnel the way they had come, with the maggot slithering after them. They soon reached the trampoline and bounced over it to the other side, but the maggot was getting closer; the tunnel was just the right size for it.
'I knew there was something funny about the name of that doctor,' Klut puffed as he ran. 'I thought I'd heard it before.' Gradually, as they ran down the tunnel, it began to get warmer. Aracuria was the first to notice it since he still had a jumper on.
'It's getting hotter,' he shouted breathlessly, as he pulled off his jumper and threw it to the ground. No one answered; they were too busy running. A red glow appeared at the end of the tunnel. As they got closer, the glow became brighter and more intense.
'What's that?' gasped Bill, clutching his sides as he ran.
'Looks like something burning,' said Klut. The heat intensified until finally they were sweating. The whole tunnel was red, but the end was just up ahead. They could run no longer; it was too hot. They walked through the glow and came out of the tunnel into a vast open cavern.
'WOW!' said Rhiannon.
'I don't believe it!' said Aracuria.

In front of them, a bridge made out of solid stone stretched from one side of the cavern to the other, with the tunnel continuing on the other side. Beneath the bridge the cavern dropped sheer through hundreds of meters to a red bubbling river of fire. Above them it rose into the giddy heights before stopping at a vaulted roof. Rhiannon stepped out on to the bridge with Aracuria right behind her. They looked to their left and saw a brilliant red waterfall of fire coming from the roof and falling thousands of meters to land in the river below. The fire fall was bubbling and screeching, and flames shot out in every direction. The cavern itself was glowing bright red from the flames.
'I've never seen anything like it!' Aracuria exclaimed in wonder.

Klut came up to join him.
'Do you remember how the surface of Draco was covered in a sea of burning fire?' he asked. 'Well this must be where it leaks down to the core of the planet.' At that moment, Bill screamed.
'It's the MAGGOT!' Instinctively, they ran across the bridge, but just then they heard a buzzing sound. Aracuria was just about to run into the tunnel when Klut grabbed him.
'Stop!' he shouted. They listened as the sound grew louder; it was coming from deep inside the tunnel. Suddenly he groaned. The maggot had appeared at the entrance to the other tunnel.
'What is it?' shrieked Rhiannon. 'Why can't we go down this tunnel away from Magot?' Before Klut had time to answer, a giant fly came buzzing along the tunnel; its wings spanned the width of the tunnel and its two vast

eyes stared intensely at Rhiannon.
'That's why,' said Aracuria, as the buzzing became too loud to bear.
'Oh no!' said Klut. 'It's Beelzebub, Lord of the Flies.'

Aracuria turned to Rhiannon. 'What do we do now?' he asked desperately.
Rhiannon shook her head. 'I don't know.'

Klut was thinking furiously. He noticed that at each of the tunnel entrances were two stone statues of warriors with their heads bowed. In their hands they held stone swords. 'That's it!' he screamed. 'There are four statues with four swords and there are four of us; we're meant to defend ourselves with them!' He shouted with joy, but it was short-lived.
'It's too late,' said Rhiannon, pointing at the maggot. Magot had already slithered past the first two statues and it was impossible for anyone to pass it on the bridge.
'But what about the other two?' cried Klut. Without waiting for an answer, he ran to the other tunnel entrance. Beelzebub was coming close, but he hadn't reached the statues. Klut got to one of the statues first and tried to pull off the sword. It was a huge double handed, double-edged sword, but it was stuck in the hands of the warrior. 'It won't budge!' he shouted. He stepped aside. Bill tried to pull the sword from the statue's hands, but again it wouldn't move. They tried together, but still nothing happened. The fly was almost on top of them. Klut thought quickly. If they didn't get the swords out, they were all going to die. He and Bill hadn't been able to get the sword; so they weren't meant to fight.
'Aracuria!' screamed Klut straight away. Aracuria ran and grabbed hold of the sword's hilt; the warrior's hands opened up, allowing the sword to come free.
'Rhiannon!' shouted Klut. But Rhiannon was already running to the other statue and grabbing the hilt. Once again the warrior's fingers sprung open, allowing the sword to come free.
'This is great!' yelled Aracuria as he settled the sword into his hands. It was still made of stone, but it was as light as a feather. Rhiannon swung the sword around her head. 'Now we've got you!' she roared.
Aracuria ran out across the bridge to meet the maggot.
'All get into the middle!' ordered Klut. He and Bill positioned themselves between Aracuria and Rhiannon. The maggot slithered towards them. It was white and huge and left a trail of slime behind it.
Aracuria lifted up his sword and shouted. 'You weren't much of a doctor anyway!' Then he swung the sword around his head and brought it crashing down on the maggot's side. The sword cut through its flesh like a razor, slicing from one side to the other. Gallons of white pus and slime spilled out over the bridge and flowed into the river of fire. Aracuria was just about to hit it again when the maggot collapsed and slipped over the edge of the bridge on its own slime. They watched it fall through the air until it hit the

river of fire. Immediately there was a huge explosion as the maggot blew apart, sending great sheets of flame rising high into the air.

Now it was Rhiannon's turn. She braced herself for Beelzebub to come at her, but instead he flew out of the tunnel and went up into the air, high in the cavern.

'Why won't he fight me?' she asked. Then Rhiannon saw that there was more than one fly; there were hundreds. They all came pouring out of the tunnel, one after the other, each one as big as a house. Suddenly the air was filled with the buzz of beating wings.

A thought occurred to Klut. 'Of course; Beelzebub is the *Lord of Flies.* These are all the others.'

'Great!' said Rhiannon mockingly. 'Aracuria gets a dud maggot and I get ten thousand enormous flies. Don't they like girls on Draco?' Klut didn't have an answer.

Once all the flies had come out into the cavern, the first one attacked Rhiannon. It dropped down from near the roof in a straight dive, then, just above the bridge, it leveled off and headed straight for her. She saw its huge eyes get bigger and blacker; its mouth opened, revealing a sticky black mass of hairs and teeth. It was going to swallow her whole. Just before it reached her, she ducked away and brought the sword swinging up through the air into its path. She missed its body, but the tip of the sword sliced through the fly's buzzing wing. The wing was cut clean off and went flapping away into the distance on its own. The fly itself began to corkscrew, spinning uncontrollably, heading down through the cavern until it too, eventually, hit the river of fire and exploded.

'I got it! I got it!' cried Rhiannon, brandishing her sword. The next moment, at a command from Beelzebub, all the flies dived from the roof and headed straight for Rhiannon.

'Aracuria! HELP ME!' she shouted. Aracuria came around to her side. 'What are we going to do now?' she asked.

Aracuria turned to Klut and Bill. 'Lie down on the floor,' he said. Klut and Bill did as they were told, then he turned to Rhiannon. 'We fight,' he said defiantly.

The first flies pulled out of their dive and headed straight towards them. Rhiannon ducked, then took a swipe with her sword at one of them, but she missed and her blade swung wildly in the air. Aracuria just stood still and allowed the fly to come straight towards him. He held up the point of his sword and the creature flew straight on to it. The sword dug deep into its body, but Aracuria couldn't hold it. He was forced backwards towards the edge of the bridge.

'Aracuria!' screamed Rhiannon, as she watched him fall towards the edge. Klut immediately jumped towards him and grabbed his legs. Aracuria fell backwards, his sword relinquishing the fly, allowing it to fall angrily into the

abyss below.
'Just take swipes at them,' said Rhiannon. Aracuria picked himself up, but no sooner was he on his feet again than the other monster flies arrived.
'Watch out!' shouted Rhiannon, as another fly headed towards him. Aracuria positioned the sword behind his back and brought it swinging up from behind his head, straight into the path of the oncoming fly. The sword cut the gigantic insect clean in two. Its buzzing stuttered and stopped, as it fell uncontrollably into the river of fire.
'That's the way!' Rhiannon swung up her sword to hit the next attacking fly.

Eventually all the flies except one had been killed. Beelzebub hovered alone in the air. He buzzed around at the top of the cavern for a little while and then, seeing that there was nothing more to be done, flew off down one of the tunnels and disappeared.
'You've done it!' cried Klut, as he jumped up off the floor.
'Brilliant!' said Bill, clapping Aracuria on the back as Klut shook Rhiannon's hand.
'What do we do now?' asked Aracuria.
'Find the Cheese,' said Klut, 'and then get out of here. It's just as well we've got these swords; they might come in handy again.' Aracuria and Rhiannon slung the swords over their shoulders.
'Which way now, then?' asked Rhiannon.
Klut took a look at both tunnel entrances. 'I don't think it makes much difference. Let's go the way Beelzebub went,' he said.

They made their way across the bridge and towards the statues, heading off down the tunnel. Suddenly the swords on their shoulders began to get unbearably heavy.
'What's happening?' gasped Rhiannon.
Aracuria shook his head. 'I don't ... know.' The swords were too heavy to handle. They staggered on a few paces past the statues, but finally they both had to drop them and neither could pick them up again. 'Why have they become so heavy?' said Aracuria.
Klut stroked his chin and was just about to answer when there was a terrible grinding sound.
'What's that?' shouted Bill in alarm. Rhiannon was the first to reply.
'The statues; they're moving!' Everyone stared as the two statues slowly came to life and got down from their pedestals. They turned to face the four children, then started to walk down the tunnel. They bent and picked up the stone swords. Then they returned to their pedestals and took up their positions once again, heads bowed. Everyone was astonished. Aracuria ran back to take another look at them. On the bottom of each pedestal was a name. Aracuria read the names to himself and then turned to Klut.
'What do the names Gog and Magog mean?'
Klut looked horrified. 'It means we're getting close to Lucifer; this is where it starts getting difficult!'

CHAPTER NINE: THE FOUR GUARDIANS

Aracuria, Rhiannon, Klut and Bill entered the tunnel. It was dark and long, in stark contrast to the giant red cavern they'd just left. Without the swords they felt a little scared. The tunnel wound its way through the earth for miles. After all the fighting, Aracuria and Rhiannon were tired, but they walked as fast as they could in order to reach the Cheese as soon as possible. They had outwitted or fought their way past four of the chief demons; they had another four to face.

The tunnel began to get bigger, the roof rose and the walls widened. A wind began to blow. The farther they walked, the stronger the wind blew until eventually the tunnel, which had become a vast cavern, was filled with a storm.

'What's happening now?' shouted Rhiannon.

Klut pulled his helmet tight on his head. 'I don't know,' he said. 'I think we must be getting close to Lucifer.' Aracuria turned to him.

'What should we do, Klut? Stay here and wait for the wind to go down?'

Klut shook his head. 'That's what they want us to do, they want us to give up. We've got to keep going until we can't go any further.'

They battled on until the storm became a hurricane. The roar of the wind was deafening. Rhiannon tried to speak to Aracuria, but he couldn't hear her. She lifted her arms to put her hands around her mouth, but as she did so, she took off.

'Rhiannon!' Aracuria shrieked. He watched as the wind tossed her high in the air.

The next moment, Aracuria, Klut and Bill had been picked up as well. The wind spun them around and around. They went right up to the roof, hundreds of meters above the ground. Then, suddenly, the wind stopped.

They plummeted down like stones. Just before they reached the ground the hurricane returned. It caught hold of them like an invisible hand and spun them forward, head over heels, just meters above the ground. Then they were picked back up in the air and dropped again. This happened over and over again. Each time, the wind became more violent, until they didn't know where they were or what was happening. Then the wind stopped completely and the four of them landed in a heap on the ground.

'Oooh, what happened?' groaned Bill, as he picked himself up.

Aracuria staggered to his feet, trying to brush the hair out of his eyes. He took one look and cried out, 'Oh my ... Klut!'

'What is it?'

Aracuria pointed. 'What are *those?'*

They were in a vast place with a roof of rock miles above their

heads. The walls were too far away even to see. In front of them stood four statues, each a mile high. They stood with their backs around the edge of an immense circle, in the center of which was a pit that went right down to the center of the planet. Out of the pit leapt flames and lightning flashes.
'Let's, let's escape while we can,' stuttered Bill in terror.
Aracuria turned to Klut. 'What are those four statues?' he asked.
'I'm not sure. I think they're ... ' But he never finished the sentence. Instead, he walked off towards the statues on his own. No one followed.
Aracuria looked at Rhiannon. 'What should we do?'
'Well, we can't turn back now, can we? We're in it up to our necks, and we can't leave Klut to face those things on his own. We've got to go on.' Aracuria nodded, and the two of them followed Klut. Bill reluctantly tagged along behind.

Klut headed for one of the biggest statues. It stood about half a mile away. When he reached it, he stopped and read the name that was written on the base of its pedestal. He waited for the others to arrive, then turned to them and said. 'It's Oriens, he's one of .. ' But before Klut could finish speaking there was a deafening clap of thunder.
'Who calls my name?' bellowed the statue. Klut looked up at Oriens. He was tall and white-faced. In his right hand he had a sword and in his left, a smoking cauldron.
'Who spoke my name? Answer! or I will burn thee with fire!'
'I did!' said Klut.
The head of the statue peered down at him. 'I am the Guardian of the East,' it said. 'What is it that you want of me?'
'We've come for the eleven thousand tons of Silurian Dripping Cheese, please,' said Klut.
'I know nothing of this Silurian Dripping Cheese. I am Oriens, the First Guardian of the Pit. What do you want of me? Answer, or I will burn you with fire!' The statue tipped the cauldron slightly, allowing a river of burning oil to fall down through the air and hit the ground a few hundred meters away. They watched aghast as it burned like a furnace.
'Klut,' said Rhiannon urgently, 'you've got to give him the right answer or it's the end of us.'
Klut shook his head, baffled. 'I don't know what I'm supposed to ask him. I thought asking for the Cheese was the right question.'
'Answer me!' roared the statue.
'Think!' said Aracuria. 'What did the book say?'
Klut stroked his chin. 'The book said that there would be Four Guardians of the Pit. It didn't say anything about how to get past them, though.'
An idea came into Aracuria's head. 'That's it!' he said. 'That's what we want: to get past him!'
Klut thought for a second and then looked up at the statue. 'We want to get past you, Oriens,' he said. For a moment there was silence, then the statue

spoke again.
'To get past me, you must answer a riddle of the Guardian of the East. If you fail to answer, accursed be you and all your kind and kindred. If you fail, I will burn you with fire. Your tongues will molder in your mouths and your eyes will rot in their sockets. Will you turn away?'
Bill reached out and tapped Klut on the shoulder. 'Let's, let's go home. I rather like my tongue.'
Rhiannon stepped forward. 'We will not turn back!' she shouted defiantly. The statue looked down at her and smiled.
'Very well then. What has never been, and never will be, and yet is?'
Rhiannon was horrified. She turned to Klut. 'Well,' she said, 'answer him.' Klut said nothing. Aracuria looked up at the statue.
'How many answers will you accept?' he shouted.
'Only your first,' said the statue mockingly.

Klut sat down in despair.
'We're finished!' he said. 'I'm no good at riddles. We've only got this far because I'm a genius and get all the difficult questions right and Bill is stupid and gets all the obvious questions wrong, which turn out to be right, and Aracuria and Rhiannon are brave and so could fight the Maggot and the Flies. Now we're finished; no one knows how to answer riddles.' Klut let his head drop into his hands.
Rhiannon looked across at Aracuria. 'There has to be some way we can work it out. What was the riddle again?'
Aracuria repeated it, 'What has never been, and never will be, and yet is?'
Rhiannon thought it through. 'It has never been, means that it never existed in the past, right?' she said. 'And if it will never be, then whatever it is will never exist in the future, right?'
'Right,' said Aracuria.
'So what is it that doesn't exist either yesterday or tomorrow but still exists?' Her eyes lit up at the same time as Aracuria's. They turned to Oriens and shouted out together. 'TODAY!'

The mocking smile vanished off Oriens' face.
'You have answered the riddle of the Guardian of the East. You must now answer the riddles of the other three Guardians to gain entrance to the Pit. You need no longer fear fire.'
Oriens fell silent. Klut raised his head. 'What happened?' he asked.
Rhiannon looked down at him. 'We answered the riddle!' she said. 'Now we've only got to answer another three and then we've only got Lucifer to deal with.'
'Only!' cried Klut bitterly. He jumped up and headed off towards the next statue.
Rhiannon turned to Aracuria. 'I thought he'd be pleased.' Aracuria watched Klut walk away. 'I think he feels unwanted because he isn't any good at

answering riddles,' he said.

'And what about me?' said Bill. 'I never get anything right.' Rhiannon placed her arm around his shoulders. 'And it's just as well you don't, otherwise we wouldn't even have got this far. '

The three of them set off behind Klut in the direction of the next statue, while the flames and lightning from the pit grew ever more fierce and violent. It took twenty minutes to reach the second statue.

'This is it,' said Klut grumpily. 'To all of you who can't read, his name is .. .'

'I *can* read!' bellowed Rhiannon. 'How dare you suggest that I can't read! I was taught to read when I was five years old on my grandfather's knees, you flathead alien!' Klut's face fell. He turned around and sat down against the pedestal. Rhiannon read the word written in stone above Klut's head.

'His name is AMAIMON!' she shouted. There came a terrible roar.

'Who calls my name?' The voice was louder and deeper and more violent than the first statue. They all looked up, even Klut, and saw the statue of a man with a monstrous dragon's head. A blood red mouth lined with razor sharp fangs spurted a shooting flame of burning sulfur. In his right hand he held a sword, and in his left a globe of Earth.

'This is ter ... ter ... terrifying,' stuttered Bill.

'Who spoke my name? Answer! Or I will bury thee with earth!'

'We did!' said Rhiannon. The dragon's head looked down at them. Its bloodshot eyes swiveled around in its eye sockets; there were no eyelids.

'I am the Guardian of the South,' said the statue. 'What do you want of me?'

'Who's going to do the talking?' asked Rhiannon.

'Answer!' bellowed the statue and, as he did so, he gripped the globe tightly in his hand. Suddenly the ground beneath them shook, and hairline fractures appeared, out of which burning sulfur smoked.

'We've come for the eleven thousand tons of Silurian Dripping Cheese,' shouted Aracuria hurriedly.

'I know nothing of this Silurian Dripping Cheese. I am Amaimon, Guardian of the South. I am the Second Guardian of the Pit. What do you want of me?'

'We want to get past you!' shouted Rhiannon. The dragon spoke again.

'First you must answer a riddle. If you fail to answer, accursed you will be and all your kind and kindred. If you fail I will bury you with earth, your tongues will molder in your mouths and your eyes will rot in their sockets. Will you turn away?'

'No!' shouted Aracuria. The dragon blew out a massive flame of burning sulfur and then continued:

'Very well then; what crawls on its belly and yet is faster than a man, what hangs in the air and has the breath of the damned?' Rhiannon turned to Aracuria. 'Any ideas?' she asked.

Before he could answer, Klut shouted. 'You see how difficult it is! It could be anything, anything at all. We've been lucky so far, that's all.'

'Quiet!' shouted Rhiannon. She turned back to Aracuria. 'Well?'

Aracuria wanted to sit on the ground as his legs were tired, but smoke was still rising up out of the cracks and the smell of the sulfur was making it difficult to think.

'I don't know, I don't know. It crawls on its belly and yet travels faster than a man, it hangs in the air and has the breath of the damned. What does that mean? It could be anything, it could even be a dragon!' he cried out, pointing up at the statue as he went to sit beside Klut by the pedestal. Before he got there, Amaimon spoke.

'You have answered the riddle of the Guardian of the South. You must now answer the riddles of the other two Guardians of the Pit. You need no longer fear earth.' Aracuria was astonished.

Rhiannon ran across and slapped him on the back. 'Well done! Well done!' Aracuria still looked confused.

Bill patted him on the back. 'You made it look easy,' he said.

'What?' said Aracuria. 'You mean *dragon* was the right answer?'

'That's what it said,' said Rhiannon. 'And a dragon headed statue should know.'

Klut got to his feet. 'Luck, luck! That's all it is. Our luck's going to run out, you mark my words.' He walked off alone in the direction of the third statue.

Klut stopped in front of the pedestal and looked at the name that was written there. The others soon arrived. Aracuria looked up at the massive figure. In its right hand it held a sword that was a hundred meters long. The point of the sword rested on the pedestal next to his feet, each toe of which was bigger than any of them. In his left hand he held a bowl, but Aracuria couldn't see if it was filled with anything. The statue had the head of a goat.

'This one looks spooky, doesn't it?' said Rhiannon.

Aracuria nodded. He turned to Klut. 'Well, are you going to read out his name?'

Klut said gruffly. 'Why don't you read it?'

Aracuria could see that Klut was still upset because he was no good at riddles.

'Because I don't know what it says,' said Aracuria. They never encountered words like that in school.

'OK,' said Klut, happy that he was needed again. 'This name is Paimon!'

'Who calls my name?' bellowed the statue. 'Answer! Or I will drown thee!'

'We did!' shouted Aracuria.

'I am the Guardian of the West,' said the statue. 'What do you want of me?'

'We want the eleven thousand tons of Silurian Dripping Cheese,' said Aracuria.

'I know nothing of this. I am Paimon of the West. I am the Third Guardian of the Pit. What do you want of me?'

'We want to get past you, Paimon!' screamed Aracuria.

'To get past me, you must answer a riddle. If you fail to answer, accursed be you and all your kind and kindred. If you fail, I will drown you with water and your tongues will molder in your mouths and your eyes will rot in their sockets. Will you turn away?'
'No,' shouted Rhiannon.
'Very well then: what is it that no one wants and yet everyone has, that is mocked in a man and yet good to have?'
Klut put his hands to his head. 'How can we answer this?' he cried. 'This is impossible! Riddles are impossible. They can have lots of answers, but only one can ever be right. This is awful!' He walked away and sat down on his own.

Once again Rhiannon turned to Aracuria. 'What is it that no one wants, and yet everyone has?' she said.
'I don't know. I can't think of anything that we've got but don't want,' he said.
'And it's something that is laughed at in a man, but it's good that everyone has it,' said Rhiannon. Aracuria sat down on the ground.
'It's something that is laughed at in a man; does that mean it isn't laughed at in a woman?'
Rhiannon looked up at Paimon. 'Can we ask you a question?'
'No!' said the statue, his voice booming out through the vast cavern. Rhiannon sat down on the ground beside Aracuria.
'I don't know,' she said: 'I really don't know the answer to this one. It's far harder than the others.'
'How long have we got to answer it?' asked Aracuria.
'All of your lives!' said the goat head, and it began to laugh, horribly.
Bill shuddered. 'I don't know about you, but if there was one thing I could do without, it would be being scared. That goat head really frightens me.'

Aracuria and Rhiannon turned to look at each other and then said simultaneously, 'What is it that no one wants and yet everyone has, what is mocked in a man and yet is good to have!' They looked up at the statue and shouted together. 'Fear!'
The goat head straightened up. 'You have answered the riddle of the Guardian of the West. You must answer the riddle of the last Guardian to gain entrance to the Pit. You need no longer fear water.'

Rhiannon jumped for joy, then swiveled around and kissed Bill on the forehead. 'You're a genius, Bill, a genius!'
Bill looked really pleased; it was the nicest thing anyone had ever said to him. 'Why? What did I do?' he asked.
Rhiannon smiled. 'It's a pity you're too dumb to realize how bright you are,' she said.
'I see you answered another riddle,' said Klut, looking really glum.
'Actually, Bill answered it,' said Rhiannon.
Klut's face became even more dejected. Without a word he walked across to

the next statue. They were all tired and hungry. But all the same, no one, not even Bill, complained. They hurried along as fast as they could.

Klut was the first to reach it. He sat down without even bothering to read the name. Instead he took off his helmet, scratched the top of his flat head and started to sulk.

Rhiannon read out the name. 'This one is called Ariton!' her voice echoed out. Aracuria saw that Ariton was less frightening than all the others. He had a man's head; in his left hand he held a sword, and in his right a set of keys.

'Who calls my name?' said Ariton. The voice was quieter than the others, but still very loud.

'We do!' shouted Rhiannon. The head of the statue looked down at them.

'I am the Guardian of the North,' said the statue. 'What do you want of me?'

'We want the Cheese!' shouted Bill, who up till now had said nothing to the statues.

'I know all there is to know of this Cheese. I am Ariton, Guardian of the North, Keeper of the Keys of the Pit. What do you want of me? Answer or I will deprive thee of air!'

Aracuria shouted out. 'We want to get past you!'

The statue smiled. 'To get past me, you must answer a riddle. If you fail to answer, accursed be you and your kind and kindred. If you fail, I will deprive you of air, your tongues will molder in your mouths and your eyes will rot in their sockets. Will you turn away?'

'No!' shouted Rhiannon.

'Very well then; upon your own heads be it. This is the riddle of the Guardian of the North. What has twelve legs and two heads, nine arms and shares in Trans-Galactic Oil?' Ariton smiled.

Rhiannon and Aracuria were dumbfounded. 'What?' they both said. 'We're finished!' they cried.

Bill sat down beside them. 'Is that it then?' he asked.

Rhiannon nodded. 'I'm afraid so. There's no way that we can answer that one.'

'Ah, well, we almost made it,' said Bill sadly.

They sat there for about half an hour. Finally, Klut, who had been sitting apart from the others, got bored, stood up and walked back to the other three.

'Well, did you answer it?' he asked tetchily.

Aracuria shook his head. 'We can't, it's too difficult.'

Klut looked surprised; he had been too busy scratching his flat head to hear what the statue had said. 'What was the riddle then?'

At this the statue shouted out; 'What has twelve legs and two heads, nine arms and shares in Trans-Galactic Oil.'

Klut couldn't believe it.

'Is that the riddle?' he asked. Aracuria nodded. 'Well, that's dead easy,' said Klut, looking up at Ariton. 'It's a librarian who works in the Beta Star-

College for the Inter-Galactic Mineral Company.'

The smile vanished from the statue's face. 'You have answered the riddle of the Guardian of the North. I hereby give you the Keys to the Pit. The abode of Lucifer. You need no longer fear air. '

Aracuria, Rhiannon and Bill were stunned into silence as they watched the left hand of Ariton open and allow the Keys to fall to the ground.

'Well, shall we go?' said Klut calmly.

'Go, go where?' asked Bill.

Klut smiled. 'Straight into Hell, my dear friends. This is the last and most awesome test. If we pass it, we get the Cheese. If we don't, well, we'll just be like everyone else who has come here...'

Aracuria looked confused. 'What do you mean; everyone?' he said.

'No one, but no one, in the history of the Universe has ever got past Lucifer.'

And with that Klut turned and headed in the direction of the Keys.

Rhiannon turned to Aracuria. 'I wish he'd told us that before!' she said.

CHAPTER TEN: LUCIFER

Aracuria, Rhiannon and Bill followed Klut to the Keys. They were enormous; each one bigger than any of the children. There were three in all, made of blackened steel, and each was tied to the others by a chain of silver.
'What do we do with these?' asked Aracuria.
'I'm not sure,' said Klut. Rhiannon reached across and rubbed one of the Keys; the blackened powder came away, revealing shiny metal underneath.
'Look!' said Rhiannon, 'There's something written on them.' She tried to read what was said, but it wasn't in any language she knew. Klut bent over and took a closer look. He read out the words in the most extraordinary language any of them had ever heard: 'Et in arcadia ego. '
'What?' said Rhiannon.
Klut turned to her and smiled a superior smile. 'It's a very ancient language that was once used over the whole Universe. I learned it from my grandmother,' he said smugly.
'But what does it mean?' Aracuria asked.
'Oh, something like, "This is the key to the Treasure Chamber" said Klut.
Bill looked confused. 'What Treasure Chamber?'
'Presumably the place where the Cheese is kept,' said Klut as he started rubbing the black sooty powder away from the second Key. Once again, more writing came into view. 'Ah!' said Klut, straightening up. '"Terribilis est locus iste."'
'And what does that mean?' asked Aracuria.
Klut smiled, he smiled one of those long, self-satisfied smiles that only someone who knew it all could smile. 'Well, a loose translation would be: "This is the Key to the Pit."'
'That's it, that's the one we want!' said Rhiannon excitedly. 'Let's take it and the one for the Treasure Chamber off the ring and carry them with us.'
Aracuria looked at the third Key. 'What's this one for?'
Klut bent down and rubbed the powder away from the surface. He was still smiling in a smug way. Immediately he read out the words that appeared. 'I tego arcana dei,' he said, and as he spoke, so the smile disappeared off his face.
'What does it say?' asked Aracuria.
Klut's face went white. 'Nothing, I, I couldn't make it out,' he stammered.
'You're lying! You read it all right. What did it say?' Aracuria demanded.
'It would be best if you didn't know, Aracuria. It's only been given to tempt you.'
'I want to know,' said Aracuria resolutely.
Klut shook his head. 'I shan't tell you,' he said. Then there was a terrible grinding sound, 'Tell him or I will!' It was the voice of Ariton. Everyone

looked up to see the statue's face staring down at them. 'Very well,' said Klut, 'if you force me. On the Key is written: "This is the Key to the Tree of Life."'

Rhiannon became scared. 'Quickly! We've got to break the chain and dump that Key. If it's only been given to tempt Aracuria, then it must be bad luck for us.' She immediately set about trying to break the silver chain. Klut and Bill helped her, but Aracuria did nothing. Instead he looked up at the face of Ariton as Ariton began to laugh.

'Why are you laughing?' shouted Aracuria.

'Because those links were forged in Hell. You will never break them!' Ariton straightened his head again. After a short while of trying, Rhiannon and the others gave up.

'It's no good,' she said. 'We'll just have to take them all along.' She turned to Aracuria. 'But promise me this, Aracuria, that you will throw this Key away when we get the Cheese. OK?' Aracuria nodded.

'I promise,' he said.

They each took hold of the silver chain and slowly began to drag the Keys across the ground. The Keys were heavy, but working together they were able to move along at a slow walking pace.

Finally they reached the edge of the Pit. By now they were all exhausted. Klut, Aracuria and Rhiannon sat down on the edge and dangled their feet over the Pit, while Bill stood back next to the Keys. In front of them, great, billowing clouds of sulfurous smoke and steam rose up into the air, while every now and then great sheets of flame burst up from down below and exploded out into the cavern.

'Well, what do we do now?' said Rhiannon. 'There are no steps down through the Pit. It just looks like a bottomless hole. ' Aracuria thought for a moment. 'I think we've got to jump down it.'

'What!' cried Bill, terrified.

'I think Aracuria is right,' said Klut.

'But we'll be killed,' said Rhiannon. 'If the flames don't kill us, then the shock of hitting the earth at the bottom certainly will.'

'And what about all the smoke: how can we possibly breathe in all that?' asked Bill. Everything they said seemed right. Klut didn't have an answer, but Aracuria did.

'Remember what the four statues said: that we need not fear fire, water, earth or loss of air,' he said.

'Yes!' said Rhiannon. 'That means that the flames won't burn us and we'll be able to breathe in the sulfur, and when we hit the ground at the bottom, we won't be hurt; but what about the water?' Everyone thought hard.

'Getting down there is easy, coming back up might be more difficult,' said Klut uncertainly. 'Maybe the power over water is to do with that?'

But there was no way of knowing until they were actually down there. Everyone fell silent. They sat on the edge of the Pit for a long time, doing nothing. Eventually, Aracuria spoke.

'Shall we jump then?' A look of fear crossed each face, but there seemed no other way.
'What shall we do with the Keys?' Rhiannon asked.
'I think we should all hold on to the chain and then jump off the edge with them,' said Aracuria.
'No!' cried Bill, who couldn't believe what he was hearing.
'There's just no other way, Bill,' said Aracuria taking hold of the chain. Rhiannon and Klut did the same.
'I'm not going!' said Bill. 'I'm not going!'
'If you don't come with us, you'll be stuck here for ever and ever and you'll never get back home,' said Rhiannon firmly. Bill hastily stepped forward and grabbed the chain.
'All right, then, but I'm going to close my eyes, and don't tell me when you are going to do it; just jump!'

Aracuria looked at Rhiannon, Rhiannon looked at Klut. 'NOW!' the three of them shouted together, and simultaneously jumped off the edge. Bill plummeted like a stone behind them.
'Keep hold of the chain!' shouted Rhiannon as they whizzed around, tumbling back and forth with the massive Keys dancing in the air. They were passing through the billowing clouds like a rocket, past the sheer rock walls, through the burst of flames, past condensing steam and down, down, all the time ever faster, ever deeper into the pit.
'This is *amazing!'* shouted Aracuria, who was loving every second of it.

The farther they went, the faster they seemed to go. The clouds came at them with frightening speed, and no sooner had they entered one than they were out again and into another. Aracuria noticed that one of the Keys was beginning to glow red.
'Klut! What's happening?' he asked, pointing to the Key.
'It's burning up!' cried Klut. Even as he spoke, the metal went white hot and parts of it began to burn away. As they watched, the Key to the Pit finally disappeared in a cloud of smoke; it had done its job.

A split-second later they hit the ground. They must have been doing a thousand miles an hour, but they bounced high up in the air, then came down again for a second time. Everyone was dazed.
'I guess you must have been right, Aracuria. The earth didn't hurt us. *Much!'* said Rhiannon.
Aracuria, his head spinning, struggled to his feet. 'Oh my ... !' he said.
Rhiannon picked herself up. 'What's the mat…'

She stopped in mid-sentence and her jaw dropped. All around them was a vast sea of fire. They seemed to be standing on an island of flat rock which was only inches above the level of the bubbling lake of molten fire. From the island, a narrow walkway led across the fiery lake to a hole in the rock in the far wall. All this was terrible enough, but ahead of them, not a hundred meters away, was a vast serpent. It had a massive, skull-white head and a long coiled body covered in red and yellow scales. Out of the head came seven horns and along its back were two long, transparent wings. The head was as big as a house with huge, bloodshot eyes and a cavernous mouth filled with white teeth. On the end of the serpent's nose were another three horns.

The serpent was curled up around a solid gold throne that rose up out of the center of the earth. It coiled around a dozen times or more. In the throne sat a man dressed in silver.

'What, what is that?' stammered Bill.

'It depends on what you mean by *that,* my dear Bill,' replied the man. He stepped off his throne and began to walk over the scales of the serpent, climbing down each of its coils as if he were descending a staircase. Aracuria looked at the man's face and saw that his eyes were firmly fixed on the set of keys that lay a few meters away.

'Quickly! Get the Keys!' he shouted. 'He wants them!' He ran forward and snatched up the silver chain with its two remaining Keys. The others quickly joined him. The man in silver stopped just as he stepped off the last coil of the serpent. Aracuria watched him bite his lower lip, hesitate and then step forward.

'I must congratulate you on getting this far,' said the man. 'It isn't often that Leviathan and I get visitors.' He looked at Aracuria and smiled. 'You *must* be Aracuria; I've heard so much about you!' he said, staring deeply into Aracuria's eyes. The man was handsome, with thick, black hair and deep-set eyes, but there was something about him that was utterly evil. He wasn't a man to be trusted. He held out his hand; instinctively Aracuria went to shake it.

'DON'T!' shouted Klut. Aracuria withdrew his hand before the man had time to shake it. 'If you shake his hand, it means you accept his friendship and hospitality; it gives him power over us.'

The man looked straight at Klut and a flash of anger burst through his eyes. 'Well, if you know so much about me, my flat-headed friend, why don't you tell your companions who I am. It is the height of impertinence not to be introduced.'

Klut said nothing. Rhiannon spoke. 'You're, you're Lucifer?' she said hesitatingly. The man half-bowed and smiled.

'At your service, madam.'

Aracuria looked at Rhiannon and saw that she was flattered.

'We've come for the Cheese,' he said quickly. 'Give it to us and then we'll go and never bother you again. '

Lucifer took one look at Aracuria and laughed, a long, low, loud laugh. 'Bother me! *You!* Bother *me!'* Lucifer laughed again, and as he laughed, so the diamond rings on his fingers glistened with red and silver light and the gold chain around his neck glowed. 'I'm not *bothered* by you, I

intend to *keep* you here!' He turned to the serpent, 'Don't we, Leviathan!' The serpent opened its mouth and a cloud of sulfurous breath burst out and the scales on its body began to glisten. Bill shuddered.
'What you want isn't important!' shouted Rhiannon. 'We've come for the Cheese. It belongs to us, we passed all your silly tests and now we want to leave this place and go back in time to our planet, Earth.'

Lucifer swung around; there was hate in his eyes.
'That Cheese was deposited here a hundred million years ago by King Morcant the Slow-Witted on behalf of the Kings of the Southern Earth Federation, thus fulfilling the wish of the Emperor Thesaurus. We have been in the banking business since the beginning of the Universe a thousand million years ago. People and life forms come from all over the Universe to make deposits here. Do you really think that I am going to let a bunch of second-rate half-wits take away the second most-valuable Treasure in the Universe just because they ask for it?' Lucifer turned on his heel and walked back towards his throne.

Klut stepped forward. 'You have just spoken to Rhiannon, granddaughter of the last king of the South, the current King Morcant, direct descendent of King Morcant the Slow-Witted. She has the right to take what was placed here by her ancestor,' he said.

Lucifer froze in his tracks. At that moment the whole of Draco began to shake and shudder and violent flashes of lightning crackled up the entire length of the Pit. Lucifer turned to look at Rhiannon.
'I didn't ... realize ... ' he said slowly. 'Very well then, I suppose you want to return to the Chamber of the Treasure and claim your Cheese. '
Klut nodded, and Aracuria said, 'Yes!'

Lucifer climbed back up the coils of the serpent to the throne, where he seated himself. 'You can only enter the Chamber of the Treasure if there is one among you, just one, who is fit to enter. He, or she, must be pure in heart and spirit, must never have told lies or want gain for him or herself. Only this person can enter the Chamber because of what is held there.'
Klut interrupted impatiently: 'What do you mean, "because of what is held there"? It's only Cheese, there's nothing holy about Silurian Dripping Cheese!'
Lucifer's eyes flashed. 'I agree, although the inhabitants of Siluria might disagree, if they hadn't all been killed in a terrible war twenty million years ago. No, it isn't the Cheese that's holy.'
'Then what is?' said Rhiannon, suspecting a trick.
'The Tree of Life,' said Aracuria quietly.

Lucifer smiled, as Rhiannon and Klut looked at Aracuria in horror. *'Exactly!'* exclaimed Lucifer. 'How very bright of you to think of that.'
Klut faced Lucifer defiantly. 'But why do you have the Tree? It's no good to you. You already have eternal life. '

'Of a sort ... ' said Lucifer, looking suddenly gloomy. 'But it has other uses... '
Klut was mystified, but Aracuria understood. 'You mean ... ' He fell silent without uttering another word.
'Exactly! Again he gets it. Brilliant! Right at the birth of the Universe, we stole the Tree of Life from the Garden of Eden and placed it in our Treasure Chamber. Because for ever after only those who are pure in heart can come anywhere near it, it has kept away absolutely everyone who has ever come here, even if they owned what was deposited in the Treasure Chamber in the first place.'
'That makes you a thief!' shouted Klut indignantly.
'Of course, flathead. I am Lucifer, after all!' He let out another burst of terrible laughter. Suddenly, he became serious. 'Well, since you are so eager to get to the Cheese, I shan't keep you a moment longer. First you have to answer my questions and then, if one of you passes, you will all be allowed to make your way to the Treasure Chamber. I must warn you though, that if anyone tries to go in without proving themselves here, you will all be burnt to ashes. Do you understand?' Everyone nodded. 'I will give you no help whatsoever in either task, because of course I want you to fail, but what I will say is, that while you have lost your immunity to air, fire and earth in falling down through the Pit, you may continue not to fear water. One other thing; you were right to protect the Keys from me, as without them you would never, ever have stood a chance of making it out of my abode. Tell me when you are ready, and I will begin the questioning.'

Lucifer stopped. Rhiannon, Aracuria, Klut and Bill looked at each other. 'What have we got to lose?' said Rhiannon.
'Our souls!' replied Klut mournfully.

CHAPTER ELEVEN: THE FINAL TEST

Aracuria stepped forward. The molten sea of fire was bubbling more ferociously. Sulfurous fumes and bursts of steam rose up out of the sea and filled the pit above their heads. The golden throne was glistening brilliantly and the serpent's scales glowed. It wasn't going to be easy to say, but it had to be done.

'We're ready,' he said.

Lucifer smiled. 'Very well then; let the test begin.' Lucifer seated himself more comfortably in his throne. 'I, of course, will know when you are lying, but just in case you think I am cheating...' He clapped his hands together and immediately the ground in front of Aracuria erupted and shattered into fragments. A black stone burst into view. It was old and worn with a crack along its top.

'What's that?' said Rhiannon, who came forward to examine it more closely.

'That,' said Lucifer, 'is the Stone Of Destiny. It was taken from your planet long before you were born. It was once used to crown the rightful kings of the Earth.'

Rhiannon's eyes lit up. 'I've heard of it; I thought it was a myth,' she said.

'And if you have heard of the Stone Of Destiny, then you know that it cannot abide lies,' he said.

'Yes,' said Rhiannon.

'And that anyone who places his hand upon the stone and tells a lie will make the stone crack open even more.' said Lucifer.

'Yes,' said Rhiannon, who knelt down and touched the top of the stone, feeling its smooth, black surface. 'And there is something else ... '

Lucifer cut her short. 'That needn't concern us!' he shouted. 'We've wasted enough time as it is; who will go first?'

'I will,' said Aracuria.

Lucifer smiled. 'No, no, I want you to wait till last.' He raised his hand and pointed at Rhiannon. 'Let the little princess go first, since she already has her hand on the stone.'

Rhiannon felt scared, but she didn't know why. 'OK,' she said. 'I'm ready.'

Lucifer looked straight at her; the smile slid from his face and his features became harder, more cruel. 'Have you ever told a lie?' he shouted.

Rhiannon looked confused. 'What kind of a question is that? Everyone tells lies; you know the stone hates lies ... '

'Then tell the *truth!'* screamed Lucifer.

'Yes,' said Rhiannon angrily. The stone made no noise whatsoever.

'Are you missing someone?' said Lucifer.

'Yes.'

'Is it your grandfather?'

'Yes.'
'Do you love him?' said Lucifer. She began to think of her grandfather.
'Of course,' she said.
'And is there anyone else you love?' Rhiannon fell silent. 'Answer!' shouted Lucifer.
'Yes,' she said quietly. Lucifer looked across at Aracuria.
'Have you ever stolen?' he said quickly.
'No.'

Her eyes shot up at Lucifer; she had answered too quickly, it was a trick; he had made her think about one thing, one line of questions, and then asked a completely different one. The Stone Of Destiny began to creak, and then there was a loud crack and she felt the stone shudder beneath her fingers as another fracture appeared in the rock.

Lucifer closed his eyes. 'I can see you,' he said. 'A young child, five or six years of age. You have come to the kitchen of your castle when no one is there. A servant has cooked cakes for your grandfather. You steal one and then later when your servant asks where the cake has gone, you lie.' Lucifer opened his eyes. 'Difficult to believe, isn't it, that it was a hundred million years ago when that happened?'
'You tricked me!' Rhiannon shouted. She jumped up and began to cry. Turning away, she walked to the edge of the burning lake to look out at the flames.

Lucifer merely smiled. He raised his bejeweled hand and pointed his finger at Klut. 'Flathead; your turn!' Klut walked forward, knelt on the ground and placed his right hand on the stone. 'Have you ever told a lie?' said Lucifer. Klut didn't want to say yes but it was impossible for someone not to tell a lie at some time in their life.
'Yes,' he said.
'Is there anything that you do not know?' said Lucifer. Klut liked to think that he knew everything, but at the same time he knew that no one could know everything that there was to know.
'Yes,' said Klut.
'Are you jealous of anyone?' said Lucifer.
Klut hadn't been expecting that one. He looked down at the stone. 'Yes,' he said quietly.

Once again Lucifer looked at Aracuria. Then he smiled. 'Have you ever felt fear?' Lucifer spoke quickly.
'No,' said Klut without thinking. Then he looked up into Lucifer's eyes; Lucifer was smiling. 'You tricked me! Just like Rhiannon!' It wasn't fair; he was jealous of Aracuria because Aracuria was brave and although Klut was super-intelligent he got scared easily, although he had never told anyone and he didn't like to admit it, even to himself.

The Stone Of Destiny gave a loud crack and Klut felt the stone shudder beneath his fingers as a second new fracture appeared in the rock. Lucifer closed his eyes. 'I see you in the Valley of Fire. The Will O' Wisp has just appeared in front of you. You are scared, but when you are asked if you are scared, you lie.' Lucifer opened his eyes. 'And there are many other occasions like this.'

Klut felt awful. He stood up and walked away with his head bowed. Lucifer raised his hand a third time and pointed his finger at Bill. 'Now it is your turn,' he said. Bill stepped forward, knelt down on the floor and placed his hand on the Stone of Destiny. 'Have you ever told a lie?' said Lucifer. Bill started to think; he wasn't sure, he was certain he had, but he couldn't remember the particular occasion. So, if he said he had, like Rhiannon and Klut had, and he really couldn't remember, then would it be counted as lying? By now he was so confused he didn't know what to say.

'I, I don't know,' he said finally. Lucifer smiled and then waited for the stone to crack: nothing happened. The smile vanished from Lucifer's face.

'You really are a fool, boy, aren't you?' said Lucifer cruelly.

'Yes,' said Bill sadly.

'And so is your father?' said Lucifer.

'Yes,' said Bill bowing his head.

'Have you ever felt fear, boy?'

'Yes,' said Bill.

'Have you no pride, boy?' said Lucifer.

Rhiannon swung around. 'Stop it! You monster! You're being deliberately cruel!' she shouted angrily.

'Answer!' screamed Lucifer.

'No,' said Bill who was on the verge of tears.

'Do you admire anyone?' said Lucifer.

'Yes,' said Bill. Once again, Lucifer looked at Aracuria.

'Are you glad you came to Draco?' Lucifer smiled.

'No.'

Lucifer had expected him to say this, as had everyone else, but what happened next took everyone by surprise, except Lucifer. The Stone Of Destiny gave a loud crack, shuddered beneath Bill's fingers and a third new fracture appeared in the rock.

Rhiannon stepped forward. 'I don't believe it! You lied, Bill?' she said.

Bill nodded. 'Yes, I didn't mean to, it just came out like that, it always does.' He walked away to stand beside Klut. Bill had been complaining all the time since they'd left the Earth; complaining that they were in danger, complaining that he was hungry, that he was tired. But really, deep inside he was glad they had come, because it was an adventure, and because it was the only way to save the South from being buried in rubbish.

Lucifer smiled. 'You haven't done very well, have you? None of you is worthy to enter the Treasure Chamber - except maybe Aracuria.'

Lucifer pointed straight at him. 'Take your place!'

Aracuria knelt down in front of the stone and placed his right hand on it. This was their last chance and everyone knew it, especially Aracuria.

'Have you ever told a lie?' shouted Lucifer, confident of the answer. Aracuria tried to remember: everyone told lies, but had he ever told one? He must have, but if he said he had and he hadn't, then he'd be lying anyway.

'No.'

Lucifer smiled and waited for the stone to crack, but nothing happened.

'You've never told a lie?' asked Rhiannon in disbelief.

'I've never had a need to,' said Aracuria.

'Have you ever stolen anything?'

Aracuria shook his head. 'No.'

'Have you ever been jealous?' said Lucifer.

'Yes,' said Aracuria.

'And who were you jealous of?' asked Lucifer.

'A girl on a poster. She was walking across a beach and the beach didn't have any rubbish on it,' said Aracuria.

'And is that the only person you have ever felt jealous of?'

'Yes,' said Aracuria. Lucifer waited for the stone to crack, but still nothing happened.

'Have you ever felt fear?' asked Lucifer, angrily.

'Yes, twice; in the Valley of Fire and when I saw the serpent Leviathan for the first time.'

'Just twice?' asked Lucifer.

'Yes.'

'In your *whole* life?' he asked in disbelief.

'Yes,' said Aracuria quietly. Lucifer waited patiently for the stone to crack, but still nothing happened. He continued the attack.

'Are you glad you came to Draco?'

'Yes,' said Aracuria.

'Why?' said Lucifer.

There were many reasons that Aracuria could think of, but there was one reason that was above all others, and he had only just realized what it was. And it had nothing to do with the Cheese.

'So I can return the Tree of Life to the Garden of Eden,' said Aracuria quietly. Everyone was shocked, above all Lucifer.

'And, and do you think you will succeed?' asked Lucifer, who was obviously upset. Aracuria wasn't sure of the answer.

'No, no not this time. But I think I may come back here one day and I will succeed in the end, though I don't know why.' Everyone fell silent. Lucifer waited for the stone to crack; nothing happened.

'ENOUGH!' screamed Lucifer as he jumped out of his throne. A terrible flash of lightning burst out through the length of the smoky pit and a

monstrous clap of thunder had everyone covering their ears. Aracuria watched as the Leviathan began to uncoil from the throne and slip its head beneath the bubbling molten mass of flames.
'You have the Keys to the Treasure Chamber. If you can find your way there then take the Cheese and *go!'* cried Lucifer in fury.

Klut and Bill jumped for joy and began to whoop with laughter. Rhiannon remained silent. She walked up to Aracuria, who was still kneeling on the ground, bent down and then whispered in his ear.
'Sit on the Stone of Destiny, Aracuria.' Even though the words had been spoken as silently as she could say them, Lucifer's eyes flashed.
'What did you say?' he screamed. Rhiannon said nothing. Aracuria turned to look at her.
'Just do as I say,' she said. Aracuria seated himself on the stone. Suddenly, an awesome scream burst through the cavern and echoed up the pit. Lucifer looked horrified.
'What does it mean?' asked Aracuria.
Before Rhiannon could answer, Lucifer shouted out. 'It means we will meet again, Aracuria!' he sneered arrogantly.

Rhiannon helped Aracuria to his feet. 'What does your father do?' she asked. Aracuria was more confused than ever.
'He cleans out chemical bins,' he said. Rhiannon smiled.
'The Stone of Destiny only screams out under the rightful king of the South. Somehow, you must be descended from...'

Suddenly there was an enormous explosion in the sea of fire, throwing flames high into the air. While they had been talking, Leviathan had slipped beneath the sea and was about to stir up a storm that would drown them all in fire.
'Quickly!' shouted Klut. 'We've got to escape!' He ran past the throne and headed for the walkway, just as a wave of fire swamped part of it. Bill and Rhiannon started to run, but Aracuria was rooted to the spot.
'Who am I descended from?' he shouted.
'It won't matter if we're burnt up!' cried Rhiannon, as Leviathan caused another wave to crash over the rock.
'Until we meet again, Aracuria,' called Lucifer, as he seated himself back on his throne and began to laugh.

Klut ran across the walkway. There was a small pool of fire that blocked the way but he was able to jump over it. 'Come on!' he screamed, as the storm began to get wilder. Bill ran across the walkway and jumped over the pool of smoking fire to land at Klut's side. 'Come on!' they shouted to Rhiannon. She ran as fast as her legs could take her and then jumped over the pool. She turned around, expecting Aracuria to be behind her; but he was still standing by the Stone, staring at Lucifer.
'Come on, Aracuria!' she screamed.
'We can't get away without you!' shouted Klut.

'You still have the Keys!' cried Bill, horrified.

Aracuria woke out of a daydream; the Keys, everything depended on the Keys. He pulled the silver chain over his shoulders and began to run towards the walkway. There were millions of things running through his mind; everything was confusing. Just as he reached the walkway, Leviathan burst through the sea of fire, sending a shower of flames high into the air and causing a tidal wave of flames that came straight towards him. Aracuria ran as fast as his legs could carry him, but the Keys were heavy and they were slowing him down. All the same, he made it to the walkway, then stopped at the pool of fire that burned on it.

'I can't jump it!' he shouted. 'The Keys are too heavy!' The tidal wave of flame was coming closer. In the distance, Aracuria could hear Lucifer's cruel laugh.

'Throw them!' shouted Rhiannon. Aracuria took the Keys off his shoulder, grabbed the chain and swung the Keys twice around his head before letting go. Klut just managed to catch them, and then he and Bill ran across the walkway to where it entered the rock. *'Jump!'* screamed Rhiannon. Aracuria turned back to take a run at it; the tidal wave of fire had completely covered the throne and was set to break over him. He turned and ran, leapt over the pool of fire and then, hand-in-hand, Aracuria and Rhiannon ran to the hole in the rock where Klut and Bill were waiting for them, holding open a large steel door. They threw themselves through it just as the wave of fire was about to smother them. Klut and Bill slammed the door shut and barred it. The wave of flame hit it and it glowed a dull red. Rhiannon and Aracuria picked themselves off the ground.

'Where are we now?'

Aracuria looked up. Above them soared a tube through solid rock. It was so long he couldn't even see the end.

'Looks like we're in another Pit,' said Aracuria. They weren't out of Draco yet.

CHAPTER TWELVE: THE TREE OF LIFE

The steel door was getting hotter. It had changed from a dull red color to bright red. Aracuria continued looking up the endless shaft.
'I don't understand it,' said Rhiannon. 'This is the only way out, but it doesn't lead anywhere.' Klut and Bill stared at the glowing door.
'This steel is turning white!' cried Klut. 'It's going to melt unless we find some way of cooling it.'
Cooling it? Aracuria remembered something. 'What did Lucifer say? That we still need have no fear of water?' he said.

Klut's eyes lit up. Aracuria had a look around. Under their feet was a steel floor. In the center of it was a key-shaped hole. Aracuria went across to it and knelt down; there was some writing on the steel.
'What does this say, Klut?'
Klut walked across and started to read. 'I tego arcana dei.'
'What does that mean?' said Aracuria. Klut became excited.
'It's the keyhole to the Treasure Chamber,' he said in disbelief.
'But, I thought the Treasure Chamber was near the surface, not all the way down here,' said Rhiannon. At that moment, part of the glowing steel door fell away.
'The door's *melting!'* screamed Bill.
'Quickly! Fit the key in!' shouted Klut. Aracuria picked up the two remaining keys and fitted the right one into the keyhole. It slid in slowly, as if something was gently pulling it down. Once it was fully in, it began to turn around on its own.
'It's hydraulic,' said Klut, obviously impressed.

The key turned slowly around as more bits of molten steel began to drip from the white-hot door. Finally, the key turned right the way around, then it too started to glow; first a dull red, then bright red; then it went white and started to melt.
'What's happening?' said Rhiannon. Finally there was nothing left of the Key. Aracuria picked up the silver chain with the last remaining Key and threw it over his shoulder. Just then there was a deep hissing sound.
'The *door!* It's *going!'* shouted Bill. Everyone turned to look, but instead, the floor started to tilt. The hissing grew louder and then suddenly the shaft began to fill with water.
'What's happening?' screamed Aracuria, as the water rushed around his legs.
'It's the floor!' said Klut. 'It's really a door to a reservoir!' As the floor opened up, more and more water began to gush into the shaft. Aracuria was scared. Rhiannon looked at him just before the water covered their heads. 'What's the matter?' she asked, pleased that they now knew what was happening.
'I'm scared of water!' shouted Aracuria. Rhiannon was about to laugh when

there was a burst of water like the force of a thousand dams breaking. Aracuria, Rhiannon, Klut and Bill were propelled up the shaft like bullets from a gun.
'This is amazing!' shouted Bill.
'We're floating like corks!' laughed Klut. 'We have no need to fear water!'

The force of the water grew stronger and stronger. The sheer rock face of the shaft seemed to blur as they shot past, getting ever higher, ever further from the center of the planet. And, in spite of the force of the water and their weight, they never once got their hair wet.
'Wow!' screamed Rhiannon as they went even faster.

A spot of light appeared above them. It started to grow larger and larger. They must have been traveling at several hundred miles an hour.
'We're going to hit the surface!' shouted Klut.

Suddenly, they found themselves inside a vast gold hall on top of a fountain of water. They were flying through the air, slowing down all the time. The fountain fell back and then they stopped and began to fall back too. They fell a hundred meters or more, straight back into the shaft of water. Aracuria was the first to drag himself out, and the others followed. The water had stopped just at the lip of the shaft so as not to flood the hall. Aracuria lay on his back with his feet just clear of the water and waited to get his breath back.

'I never knew you were scared of water,' said Rhiannon as she looked down at him.
'Neither did I until now,' said Aracuria. Klut stood up. He cleared the water out of his eyes and then looked around.
'I don't believe it!' he said. Bill took one look and couldn't say anything. Aracuria stood up and opened his eyes wide.
'We, we've come up in the middle of the Treasure Chamber...' he managed to say before his jaw dropped.

The hall was immense; it ran for miles in every direction. The walls were covered in pure gold, stripped from a thousand planets and a thousand civilizations. The roof was made of solid silver and glowed like the moon. Across the floor there were billions of tons of gold and jewels; diamonds lay discarded in heaps sixty meters high, and gold bars had been used to tile the whole floor. There were massive thrones, sitting side by side, and hundreds of gold horses with silver chariots and other strange animals from other worlds that had been carved out of onyx and opal. There were statues of emperors a hundred meters high made of platinum and silver, surrounded by thousands of warriors with swords and laser guns carved in gold. It was all so dazzling, so brilliant, that Aracuria had to close his eyes to stop himself going blind.
'It's like being inside a diamond,' said Klut, as he rubbed his eyes for a second time.

In the center of the hall, rising up on a solid gold pedestal, was a

column of glass which rose up almost to the roof.
'What's that?' said Aracuria. Without waiting for an answer, he started to walk towards the column, past the piles of diamonds which littered the floor, through the legs of the horses and beneath the wheels of giant chariots. The others followed instinctively. To their right was a single green diamond, forty meters high. Klut stopped in front of it.
'Do you know what this is?' he gasped. 'This is the green gemstone of Thlagtha. It was one of a pair that made up the eyes of the Idol of Thlagtha.' He walked right up to it and stared inside the stone; at its very center he saw a ring. 'And it's *true!'* he cried.
'What's true?' asked Rhiannon.
'In the Legends of Thlagtha,' said Klut, 'it is said that at the beginning of the world there were two rings cast which could give all power to the holder. The gods placed the two rings into these green gemstones so that no man could ever have them or the power they contain. The gemstones were dropped on Thlagtha where the people placed them as the eyes of their idol. I thought it was all myth.'
'So how did it get here?' said Rhiannon. Klut shrugged.
'How did any of this stuff get here? It was deposited with the demons for safe keeping and never returned.' He looked around for the other stone, but it was nowhere to be seen.

Aracuria had walked off on his own. He left behind all the statues and the chariots and passed some white stuff before stopping at the foot of a gold pedestal. The pedestal itself was over thirty meters high, too high to climb. Along the base something was written, but Aracuria couldn't make it out. The words were large and deeply cut into the gold:

NOVUS HIEROSOLYMITANUS SAPIENTIA ET INCUBUS

Instead he just stood there, looking up at the huge column of white glass that rose up out of the pedestal to the roof of the hall.
'You found it! You found it!' shouted Rhiannon. 'You found the Cheese!' Aracuria turned around and saw, for the first time, that only a few meters away, stacked up in a giant pile, were hundreds of cheeses; Silurian Dripping Cheese.
'We found it! We found it!' cried Klut and Bill, who immediately began to dance up and down. But Aracuria didn't care. He turned back to look at the column of glass. The glass was all frosted and it was impossible to see clearly what was inside, but it was enormous. Rhiannon saw him looking and came over to his side. She looked at the column of glass and then at the writing on the gold pedestal.
'Klut! Come here and read this; it's that ancient language again,' she said. He joined her and read the writing. He was so happy, there was a smile right across his face. But as he read the words, the smile melted away, to be

replaced with a look of horror.
'You, you don't want to know,' he said nervously.
'What do you mean, I don't want to know? I asked you to read it, didn't I?'
Klut looked at Aracuria and then back to Rhiannon. 'Read it!' she said.
Klut read it quietly to himself.
'And what does it mean Klut? Have you gone dumb or something?' she shouted.
'It says, THIS IS THE TREE OF LIFE.'

Rhiannon gasped in horror. She looked at Aracuria, whose eyes were fixed on the column. 'Klut! Bill! Go get the Solar Ducks, Margaret and Deborah. Fly them in here. I want to get out as soon as possible.'

Klut and Bill ran off through the hall, past the statues and the chariots, the thrones and the diamonds. They headed back the way they had come, past the shaft of water, until they came to a massive silver arch. This led straight out into the Hall of Glass where they had first arrived. The Solar Ducks were there; Margaret and Deborah standing upright, Glenys lying forlornly on her side. Bill and Klut ran down the Hall of Glass and climbed up on to the backs of each of the ducks.
'How do we make them work?' asked Bill.
Klut didn't really know, but all the same he shouted a command.
'Fly into the Treasure Chamber!' The ducks immediately began to run and flap their wings. A second later they were airborne and heading for the arch.

Back in the Treasure Chamber, Rhiannon had seated herself on the Dripping Cheese while Aracuria just stared silently at the column of glass, inside which was frozen the Tree of Life. The Solar Ducks appeared, flying gingerly between the statues and over the thrones. Rhiannon jumped up as Klut brought the first one in to land.
'Eat up the Cheese,' she cried. Margaret settled herself on her legs, lowered her head, opened her huge, blackened bill and began to gobble up the Cheese. When she was full, Deborah came alongside and started to eat what remained. Before very long, all eleven thousand tons of Silurian Dripping Cheese had vanished. Rhiannon started to climb up on top of one of the Solar Ducks. She turned and saw that Aracuria was still looking at the Tree of Life. The Key hung around his shoulders.
'It's time to go, Aracuria. The South is waiting for us.' Aracuria looked over his shoulder; she could tell by the look in his eyes that he didn't want to leave.
'Do you remember what you promised me, that once we got the Cheese you would throw the Key away. You weren't lying, were you?' At that word a deep groan filled the hall. It came from the Tree of Life.

Aracuria looked up at the column of glass and then back to Rhiannon. 'You're right,' he said. 'Though how I can ever come back here and unlock the Tree of Life from the glass without the Key, I don't know.'

Aracuria climbed up on to the back of the Solar Duck and then took

the chain off his shoulder. Maybe he never would return, maybe Lucifer and the Demi Demons would always have the Tree.
'Throw it away,' said Rhiannon. Klut and Bill nodded in agreement. Aracuria swung the chain once around his head and then released it. The Key flew through the air like an arrow, much faster than he had thrown it.
'Look!' cried Bill. 'It's heading straight for the glass!'

The Key buried itself in the side of the column. Suddenly there was an enormous explosion, as the glass column fractured into a thousand pieces and then shattered apart like an iceberg breaking. A brilliant blue light began to fill the hall as the full glory of the Tree of Life came into view.
'Don't anyone look at it except Aracuria!' shouted Klut as he hid his eyes.
'Fly away!' shouted Rhiannon. The Ducks began to flap their wings as the Treasure Chamber started to glow.

Aracuria turned to look at the tree as the last of the glass fell away. 'It's *awesome!'* he gasped.
Rhiannon, Klut and Bill turned their heads away and closed their eyes, but the blue glow was so bright it filled the Treasure Chamber and shone through their eyelids. The Ducks flapped their way over the statues and thrones and on through the silver arch, out into the Hall of Glass. But still the glow could be seen. Ahead of them a wall of glass opened up, revealing the red hot surface of Draco and, beyond it, the night sky filled with stars. They flew through the Hall of Glass, past Glenys, who was furiously flapping her wings, but unable to take off without her legs.

As they passed by, Rhiannon shouted down. 'Don't worry, Glenys; we'll be back for you one day!' They flew through the exit and out over the surface of the planet, then up into the sky. And still the glow could be seen. It burst out like a shaft of light high into space and seemed to be growing brighter by the second. The Ducks flew through the ring of stars and then on out into the depths of space. And all the time Aracuria looked back at Draco while the others hid their eyes. The glow had come to cover the whole planet and from it, four shafts of light had appeared forming the shape of a cross and were extending on out into space. The farther they traveled, the brighter the glow became, until it seemed as if a new sun had appeared in the night sky.

Aracuria seated himself on the back of Margaret's wing, with his head resting against the Solar Rucksack. From here he could clearly see the new star that was taking its place in the night sky. None of them had eaten since they had landed on Draco, so Rhiannon went into the hold of the Duck and brought out one of the Cheeses. She laid it down on Margaret's head and peeled off the outer skin. The Dripping Cheese was white and pure. She cut out a slice and placed it in her mouth.
'Mmm! This is delicious,' she said. At that, Klut took a mouthful of the Cheese and the expression on his face said it all.
'What about me?' complained Bill, who still sitting on the other Duck.

Rhiannon cut out a large segment of Cheese and threw it across to him.
'And if you want any more, climb inside Deborah; you've got five and a half thousand tons of it. But don't eat it all!' she shouted. Bill's face lit up as he bit into the Cheese.
'This is great!' he said.

Everyone was happy, everyone was eating - except Aracuria. He just sat on the back of Margaret's wing and watched the star getting farther and farther away. Rhiannon came to the back of the wing to see him. She was carrying a large portion of Cheese.
'Here, eat this,' she said. Aracuria shook his head.
'No, thanks, I don't feel hungry.' Rhiannon was going to argue with him, but as she looked into his eyes she could tell that it would be no good. She put it down beside him.
'Maybe you'll feel like it later,' she said.
'Maybe,' said Aracuria quietly.

They were all tired. It had been so exhausting fighting the demons and answering all their trick questions. Now that they'd eaten, everyone felt tired. Rhiannon stretched out next to Aracuria and quickly fell asleep, while Klut lay down on the other wing and soon did the same. Bill kept on eating right through the piece of Cheese that Rhiannon had given him and then climbed inside Deborah to get some more. He eventually fell asleep among the Cheeses. Aracuria stayed awake for a while longer. He watched the star grow in the sky and thought over all that had happened and wondered how long it would be before he saw the Tree of Life again.

CHAPTER THIRTEEN: HOME AT LAST

Aracuria was woken up by a loud thump. He jumped up; all around them was an orange glow, the orange glow of the edge of the Universe. Rhiannon just had time to say, 'What was that?' when suddenly all the stars began to streak in the sky. The streaks turned into long lines of white light, into which the Ducks were propelled like cannon shot.

'I think we're going back in time,' said Aracuria.

Klut stood up on the other wing and peered over the Solar Rucksack. 'I hope so!' he said.

Rhiannon jumped up. 'What do you mean; hope so?' You're the one who told us we'd go back in time!' she cried angrily.

'We will, we will travel through time, but in which direction and by how much, no one can know.'

'You told us we'd come back the next second after we had left. And now you're telling us you don't know!'

Klut nodded. Aracuria had to reach out and restrain Rhiannon from climbing over the Solar Rucksack and hitting Klut.

'Whatever happens,' said Aracuria, 'it isn't in our hands.'

The great streaks of white light began to shorten. Then they turned back into pin pricks of light. Ahead of them was a planet. Aracuria looked back to see where Bill was, but there was nothing to be seen. Then the second Duck appeared out of thin air, as if by magic.

'It's Bill!' shouted Klut, who was also looking behind. The second Duck came close up behind and Aracuria could just make out Bill's head poking from Deborah's bill. He was eating.

Aracuria turned back to look at the planet. It was growing bigger and closer all the time. The Ducks dived down and entered straight into the atmosphere. There was a brief shower of sparks and then they leveled off high above the land. The ground was covered in darkness, so it was impossible to make out where they were, but ahead of them were the four peaks of a large mountain, one rising above the other. Rhiannon held her breath; was it Morcant Castle? she thought to herself. The Ducks were heading straight for it. Then suddenly Aracuria noticed something coming towards them.

'What's that?' he shouted. Everyone turned to look.

Approaching them were three large birds, each flapping their wings. Two of the birds had long legs, but the third had no legs at all.

'It's the Solar Ducks!' exclaimed Rhiannon in disbelief. On the back of the Duck with no legs there were four children.

'And that's us!' said Klut. 'We really have come back in time just seconds after we left, a hundred million years ago!' Aracuria, Rhiannon and Klut looked at the three Ducks and their riders as they passed by; it was like watching a movie of the past. Bill didn't notice as he was too busy eating.

The two Ducks headed straight for the fourth peak of the castle. Margaret was the first to touch down. She ran along the runway for a few yards and then stopped. Deborah soon joined her. Ahead of them was a large silver robot; to its left stood an old man in a breastplate.

'Granddad!' shouted Rhiannon as she slid down off the Duck and ran into his arms.

'What, what's happening?' he said. 'Rhiannon! What are you doing back? Have you lost your nerve or something? The blood of Morcant the Unsteady and of the Emperor Thesaurus runs through your veins! I didn't bring you up to be a coward!' he roared defiantly. Rhiannon was so happy to be back she burst into tears. 'And now you're crying like a woman! I know you *are* a woman, but that's no excuse. I don't know what's got into you!' said Morcant crossly.

Aracuria was about to speak when Morcant interrupted. 'And you, boy, why is your face all red?' Aracuria looked into Morcant's shiny breastplate and was surprised at what he saw. Then he looked at Rhiannon's face and Klut's and Bill's. Morcant looked at each of them as well.

'Your faces! They're glowing!' cried Morcant in amazement. Aracuria looked up into the sky until he found a star brighter than any other shining high in space.

'It's a long story, King Morcant, but do you see that new star up there?' Aracuria pointed up into the sky.

'Well, I never; it's a new star, you're right, this is wonderful! There hasn't been a new star for thousands of years!' exclaimed Morcant.

'We've just returned from it,' said Aracuria quietly. 'The star is Draco.'

'What?'

'With the eleven thousand tons of Silurian Dripping Cheese,' said Bill, proudly.

'How?' said Morcant.

'We traveled through time,' said Klut.

'A hundred million years,' said Rhiannon, 'and it's good to be back.' She planted a kiss on her grandfather's wrinkled cheek.

'But, but your faces; you must have been irradiated!' said Morcant in alarm.

Aracuria turned to him. 'It isn't radiation,' he said. 'We saw the Tree of Life.'

Morcant's jaw dropped. 'Rog… Roger: fetch me a drink!'

All that night they sat on the fourth peak telling King Morcant what had happened. It was morning before they finally came down and went into one of the portacabins, where they spent the whole day planning what they were going to do next. Rhiannon took charge of the operation, while Morcant acted as counselor. The next day, Rhiannon, Klut and Bill set off with a charter drawn up by Morcant, who had now styled himself 'King Morcant the Very Fortunate', summoning all the people of the South to come to Morcant Castle at once. Along with them went Roger, who carried all eleven thousand tons of Silurian Dripping Cheese piled up in his hands.

The four of them went out into the rubbish wastes of the South. First of all they went to Klut, Bill and Aracuria's parents and told them where they had been and what had happened. Then they began the important task of distributing all the Cheese to the people in the holes; the people going to work; the people in the slurry pits and those who were on their way to school. Once they had tasted the absolutely delicious Cheese, they couldn't eat the Yellow Stuff again. And once they started to smell how awful the South was, they became very angry. The final proof was the appearance of the new star in the sky, at the sight of which they immediately made their way to Morcant Castle as they had been told.

The one person they wanted to see was Aracuria, without whom they would never have been able to taste the Cheese, and they gathered at the castle gates and over the rubbish piles around the castle for as far as the eye could see. Aracuria seated himself on the fourth peak and told them that things had to change and that the North had to be told to stop dropping all their rubbish on the South.

Everyone agreed, and it wasn't long before Rhiannon had put Aracuria's words into action. She went out into the slurry pits and the holes where the people worked and lived and told them that they all ought to go to the North and tell the Northerners to their faces how awful things were in the South. Soon, thousands of people were following her across the Equatorial Sea in boats made of discarded fridges and chemical bins. They went into the cities and towns of the North and started talking to everyone they met. The people in the North were so shocked at the state of the people from the South, and so fearful that they might turn nasty, that they immediately stopped dumping their rubbish on them.

Stopping the dumping of the rubbish was only the beginning of the things that they had to do, but everyone felt that with Aracuria in charge, there was nothing that they couldn't accomplish. Aracuria was glad that he had achieved what he set out to do, but in all truth his mind was on other things. He sat and walked alone on top of the fourth peak, where his family, the people, and dignitaries from the North came to visit him. Yet, all the while, all he thought about was returning to Draco, and rescuing the Tree of Life.

BOOK II:

ARACURIA AND THE IDOL OF THLAGTHA

by

CHARLES MORGAN

CONTENTS

CHAPTER ONE: SOMETHING IS WRONG

Aracuria sat on the fourth peak. He was bored. He sat in a red leather chair that the people of the North had given him. He had his feet up on a fur-covered foot-rest in the shape of a big dice that someone from the South had given him. In front of him was the biggest TV set that anyone had, anywhere on the planet. This was given to him by one of the Northern Corporations. On his left was an antique table loaded with cream cakes, chocolates and sticky sweets. To his right was another antique table stacked with different kinds coke and pop.

Aracuria was bored, but there was something else: he was beginning to feel cold. On the TV was a revolting game show with people throwing buckets of mud over each others' heads. The remote control to the TV was built into the arm of the chair: he turned it off. Aracuria climbed out of his chair: immediately two servants came running up out of nowhere and placed a pair of gold colored slippers on his feet.

"I'm bored." said Aracuria. The servants looked upset.

"Shall we get you your motorbike?" said the one.

"Or your airplane?" said the other.

"Perhaps you'd like to watch a film?"

"Or play a computer game?" Aracuria stared down at them and then shook his head slowly, walking away.

He had everything. He was the most loved person on the whole planet. In the six months since he, Klut, Bill and Rhiannon had returned from Draco with the Silurian Dripping Cheese, having outwitted Lucifer and his Demi-Demons, everybody, rich and poor, had given him anything he wanted. He had airplanes, he had motorbikes, he had speedboats waiting on the Equator sea, more food than he could eat, more DVDs than he could watch. The fourth peak of Morcant Mountain had been turned into his personal home. All the rusting old sheds had been knocked down and in their place a garden had been built with fountains and lawns covered in little gnomes with personal stereo headphones on their heads. At the far end between a row of recently planted trees sat the two remaining Solar Ducks on which they had flown to Draco, Deborah and Margaret. No longer covered in rust and burn marks, they had been serviced, painted and oiled, and when they weren't asleep they would strut around the garden or go for the odd fly around the planet. But there was something wrong: the trees had begun to shed some of their leaves and some of the flowers in the garden had begun to die. Aracuria noticed this, but didn't know what to make of it.

He walked to the edge of the fourth peak and looked over the edge: all the rubbish that the North had been dumping on the South for years had been cleared from around Morcant Castle, so that no one who actually lived on the castle had to smell anything horrible anymore. But there was still rubbish over the rest of the South, as far as the eye could see. It would take years to get rid of it all. At first they hadn't known what to do with it and some people actually suggested that they should dump it all back on the North for a few hundred years since it was their rubbish. But then Aracuria came up with the suggestion that the air fleets of the Northern Corporations should start picking up all the rubbish, take it into space and drop it into the Sun, where it would all be burned up to nothing. And that's what they were doing, all the time, day and night.

Aracuria had achieved so much, everyone said so, but he was still bored and he didn't feel right: something had gone wrong.

"I've got to see Bill." he said to himself. He turned towards the stone steps that now had a hand rail made of pure gold on one side, and walked down to the third peak.

This was where Bill lived. Bill had the second biggest TV set on the whole planet and he spent all his time watching really scary horror films on it. Aracuria approached the TV set, from which loud screams were coming: Bill was nowhere to be seen. In front of the TV set was another leather chair, only this one was yellow, and empty. Aracuria looked around the third peak: it had also been cleaned up, but instead of being turned into a garden it was an amusement park with big dippers and dodgem cars, pinball machines and juke box machines scattered everywhere.

"Bill: where are you?" shouted Aracuria. A little, frightened face topped with a bobble hat popped up from behind the yellow chair.

"Here, here I am," said Bill shakily. He looked at Aracuria, then saw the head of a monster appear on the TV and quickly ducked behind the chair again. Aracuria switched the set off. Bill immediately jumped up.

"What did you do that for?" he said indignantly. "I was watching it."

"Something's wrong," said Aracuria.

Bill became alarmed.

"What ? What's the matter? We've got everything up here; what on earth can be wrong?"

Aracuria shook his head slowly. "I started feeling bored and then it occurred to me: something is wrong." Bill began to look really frightened. "I think we ought see Klut."

They left the third peak and walked down the stone steps to the second peak where Klut lived. The second peak had also been cleaned up, only instead of being turned into a garden or an amusement park, it had become a gigantic library filled with copies of all the books in the whole Universe.

"Klut, where are you?" shouted Aracuria, as he and Bill walked between row upon row of book shelves. "KLUT! Where have you got to?" Klut was nowhere to be seen. Suddenly there came a voice from high above.

"What do you two want: can't you see I'm busy?"

Aracuria looked up and saw that high above him, sitting on top of a great pile of books, was Klut, with a scarf around his neck and an open book in each hand. He was reading both at the same time.
"Something is wrong," said Aracuria.
A frown appeared on Klut's face. "What do you mean, something is wrong? How can anything be wrong? We got the cheese didn't we? We're cleaning up the South by firing the rubbish at the Sun as I suggested..." Bill cut him short.
"You didn't suggest it: Aracuria did!" he said.

Klut looked down at them haughtily. "If you had a brain to remember correctly Bill, you would remember it was I who suggested we fire all the rubbish at the Sun and so get rid of it completely and for ever."

Bill became indignant. He was just about to shout at Klut when Aracuria stopped him.
"It doesn't matter who thought it up. The fact is I started to feel bored on the fourth peak and then I realized that something was wrong."

Klut closed his books and said, "Well if there is something wrong, then I suppose I had better solve it."
"I think we ought to go and see Rhiannon," said Aracuria. Klut jumped down off the pile of books and together they walked down the stone steps that led to the bottom peak.

The bottom peak, like the other peaks, had been cleaned up, only instead of having a garden, or an amusement park, or a library on it, Morcant Castle was being rebuilt the way it used to look before the nuclear explosion that blew it away many years before. The work on this was still taking place and there were gangs of workmen around, building towers, walls and drawbridges: but one part of it had already been finished and that was the Great Hall. Aracuria, Klut and Bill walked under a tangle of scaffolding and through a huge wooden door into the Great Hall. In front of them was an enormously long table with Rhiannon sitting at one end and King Morcant sitting at the other. Half way along the Hall was an enormous fireplace set into the wall, in front of which sat ROGER, with his steel feet gently warming in the flames.

In front of Rhiannon on the table was a pile of half-chewed chocolate bars. In her right hand she held a dagger with diamonds encrusted in the handle. She was using the dagger to eat the chocolate. She looked up from her task as they came in.
"Hi Aracuria. What do you and the plebs want?"
"I was on the fourth peak and feeling bored when I suddenly realized: something is wrong."

Rhiannon became alarmed. ROGER twitched his massive shiny steel head and reached down for the gamma gun that he always kept at his side.
"Wrong, what's WRONG?" she shouted. "I've got everything I've ever wanted. I've got all the chocolate I can eat and more, I've got all the decent

clothes I never had when we were poor, I no longer have to wear that blasted bubble on my head to keep the awful smell of the rubbish out of my nose and I've got a castle to live in at last, instead of that POXY portacabin. What on earth can be wrong?"
"I don't know," said Aracuria, "but something is."

He walked to the far end of the table where King Morcant was sitting, asleep in a gold throne. He had his feet up on the table and on his head was a crown. He was snoring gently.
"What do you mean YOU DON'T KNOW WHAT IS WRONG?" bellowed Rhiannon, upset at not getting an answer. Aracuria still didn't answer but the shout woke up Morcant, whose heavy crown fell off his head into his lap.
"What! What's happening?" he growled. Immediately two servants ran up, picked up the crown and placed it back on his head before he knew he had dropped it. He looked up and saw Aracuria.
"Why, my boy! What a pleasant surprise," he beamed. Then he shivered and pulled his coat closer. "ROGER: put another log on the fire would you, it's getting cold in here." Morcant straightened himself up and then said, "And what can I do for you, Aracuria?"
"I was sitting on the fourth peak feeling bored when suddenly it occurred to me: something is wrong." said Aracuria. Morcant looked lost.
"What do you mean, wrong? Everything is excellent. I no longer have to clean out nuclear pressure vessels for a living, I've got my castle back, I spend all my time asleep and people call me king: how on earth could anything be wrong?"

Aracuria didn't know what to say. Suddenly he found himself surrounded by them all. Rhiannon, Klut, Bill and Morcant were all staring at him.
"Yes, what IS it that's supposed to be wrong?" said Rhiannon.
"Come on, answer." said Klut and Bill, annoyed at having been forced to leave their peaks. But Aracuria didn't have an answer. Morcant gave another shiver and shouted across to ROGER.
"Put ANOTHER log on the fire: it's getting colder in here."
"THAT'S IT!" cried Aracuria. "The leaves are falling off the trees, the flowers are dying: it's getting colder!"

There was a stunned silence. Klut looked down at the scarf he wore around his neck, Bill looked up at the hat on his head, Morcant realized he had his warmest coat on and ROGER put his feet back in the fire. Morcant was the first to speak.
"But it's coming up to summer," he said. "It should be getting warmer."
"Exactly," said Aracuria, but before he could go on, Rhiannon had swiveled round and gone back to her chair.
"Is that all it is? I never feel the cold, winter or summer: chocolate keeps you warm all the year around." She let out a long laugh and then ignored

everyone. Aracuria turned to Klut, the one person who might know why it was getting colder.
"Do you know what's happening?" asked Aracuria.

Klut looked troubled. "I, I think I might," he said, walking towards the door. Everyone except Rhiannon followed him outside. Once he was out in the open, Klut looked up at the sky.
"ROGER! Come here!" he shouted. " I want you to take two readings, one now and another one a second later. I want you to measure the temperature of the sun." Aracuria, Bill and King Morcant were confused. ROGER, being a Roboticized Organizer and General Engineering Robot, could do anything, especially something simple like measuring the temperature of the sun: he raised his hand up to the sky and then put it down again.
"One...million...one...hundred ..thousand.. and.. .fifty. ..eight...degrees. . centigrade...cooling. ..to...one. ..million...one...hundred. . thousand. ..and...fifty...seven.. degrees.. .one ...second...later." said Roger.

Klut looked horrified. "You mean the sun is COOLING DOWN?" Roger nodded.
"But that means..." Roger finished Klut's sentence.
"Life...will...be...extinguished...on...earth...in...three...years..eight...months...and...seven...days."
"WHAT!" gulped Bill. Klut put his head in his hands.
"How can this be?" asked Morcant. "The sun has always shone."
Klut shook his head. "It's all Aracuria's fault," he said. "It was his decision to fire all our rubbish at the sun: well now it's putting it out."
Aracuria's jaw fell. Bill became angry.
"You said a few minutes ago that it was your decision to do it."
"No I didn't," said Klut, "Everyone knows it was Aracuria's." Bill went to hit Klut but Aracuria stopped him.
"It doesn't matter who took the decision, the fact is it's happened." he said. He turned to Roger. "If we stop dumping any more rubbish on the sun, will it get warm again?"
Roger slowly shook his head. "The. ..process...cannot. ..be... reversed," he said solemnly.
Aracuria suddenly felt very sad and not at all bored. "That means our sun is going to die," he said.
"And we along with it," said Klut, grimly.

CHAPTER TWO: SOMETHING HAS TO BE DONE

Aracuria walked to the edge of the peak and sat down. He dangled his legs over the edge and put his head in his hands.
"It was all for nothing! Going all that way to Draco to get the cheese, and beating Lucifer: it was all for nothing!" Klut, Bill, King Morcant and Roger gathered around him miserably. No one said anything. At that moment Rhiannon came out of the Great Hall with a large bar of green chocolate in her hands.
"Hey! Taste this chocolate: it's amazing! It tastes just like..." She was just about to say what it tasted like when she saw how glum everyone was looking. "What's the matter with you lot?" she asked. Roger was the first to speak.
"Life...will...be...extinguished...on...earth...in...three...years..eight...months...and...seven...days." he said.
Rhiannon looked at him dumbfounded. "Has someone poured ketchup in your circuits, Roger? You sound strange."
Morcant explained, "He sounds strange because he's unhappy and the reason he's unhappy is because he's telling the truth."
"WHAT/" shouted Rhiannon, dropping the bar of chocolate. "How can that be?"

Morcant told her what had happened. Before he had finished Rhiannon had reached across and started hitting Klut across the head.
"What are you doing that for?" he squeaked.
"Because you were the dumb dingo who told us to fire all that rubbish at the sun!" she said.
"No I wasn't!" he shouted, moving his head around, trying to dodge the blows, "It was Aracuria."
Rhiannon took no notice."But it's been you who's been SAYING it was your idea for the last six months and boring us to death as a consequence."
Klut dodged another blow and ran to hide behind Roger.

Rhiannon came and sat down beside Aracuria.
"What are we going to do?" she asked.
"I don't know." said Aracuria, his head still in his hands.
"Well SOMETHING has to be done," she cried.

Aracuria raised his head and looked up at the sky: in the distance he could see the bright light from the new star in Draco that had been created when he threw the key at the Tree of Life. It was still shining and would shine forever.
"All the stars are just far away suns," said Aracuria. "Klut told me that the other week."
"Then it must be wrong," said Rhiannon sarcastically.

"I think we've only got one choice," said Aracuria. "We'll just have to find another planet to live on before our sun goes out."
"That sounds like a brilliant idea!" said King Morcant.
"Excellent!" cried Bill. "He's done it again! All we've got to do is find another planet."
Bill and Morcant felt happy again, but Klut and Roger looked glum.
"Impossible," said Klut.
"What?" said Morcant in dismay. "Why is it impossible?"
Klut stepped from behind Roger. "All the good planets in the Universe are already inhabited by people, or other life forms, or renegade robots, so if we were to leave Mother Earth, we would have to end up on some slag heap of a planet where life would be simply awful. And even if we did have a good planet to go to, it would take us hundreds of years to get everyone off Earth. Isn't that right Roger?" Roger nodded sagely.
"So you see, in the three years that we have left we could only get a few hundred thousand people off in time and that would leave about 5 billion people to die horribly."

Aracuria, when he heard that put his head back in his hands: it wasn't such a good idea after all.
"In fact," continued Klut, who once he had started talking had no intention of stopping, "It would probably be easier to get a new sun to keep us warm than it would be to get a new planet to live on."
Aracuria clapped his hands and jumped up in the air. "That's IT!"
"What's it?" said Rhiannon.
"That's the answer to our problem!" he cried. Everyone was still mystified, except Klut.
"Aracuria, I know you are not a very bright person, unlike myself, but even a total idiot could see that it would be impossible to bring a new sun into being to replace our old one. Suns were created when the Universe was created and I'm afraid no one has yet learned to tow one around like a torch."

Aracuria was still smiling. "But don't you see: that's EXACTLY what I'm saying!" Everyone looked at him as if he had gone mad. Even Roger thought so.
"You're obviously not feeling well," said Rhiannon consolingly. "Why don't you go and have a lie down: it's simply impossible to tow a sun through space and everyone, even a total idiot like Bill, knows that." Bill nodded in acknowledgement, but Aracuria ignored them both.
"Klut, didn't you tell me the other week that stars are just suns that are very far away?" Klut nodded. "Well, look up into the sky in the direction of Draco: there's one star that we COULD tow away!"
Klut, Rhiannon, Bill, King Morcant and Roger all looked up into the sky. "You mean: THE TREE OF LIFE?"
Aracuria nodded."Remember how it made our faces go red when we left Draco: it must be warm enough to keep Earth from freezing over."

Klut's jaw dropped: he turned to Roger. "Is, is what Aracuria saying, true? If we towed the Tree of Life here, would it stop the earth from freezing over?"

Roger blinked a little as he worked out in his head how much light the Tree of Life was giving out at such a great distance and how much heat it would give out if it was set up next to the earth. "Tow...it...to...Earth." he said. Everyone jumped for joy: except Klut.

"You've done it! Aracuria, you've done it!" cried Rhiannon, but the smile disappeared off Aracuria's face as he noticed that Klut wasn't happy.

"What's the matter Klut?" he asked.

"There are two outstanding problems," said Klut, "Firstly, how do we tow the Tree of Life 108 million light years from Draco to Earth in just the three years we've got to do it in. Remember that a light year is the distance that light travels in one whole year and light travels at 186000 miles a SECOND."

Rhiannon interrupted, "Easy: we just bounce it off the edge of the Universe and travel though time and space, like we did with the Solar Ducks," she said confidently.

Klut looked at her disdainfully.

"The Solar Ducks are made of steel and steel is a metal and all metals are cold. The edge of the Universe is made of rubber: if we tried to bounce the Tree of Life off the edge of the Universe it would burn a hole straight through and the whole Universe would blow up like a balloon bursting!" Rhiannon looked shocked and terrified. "If you have any more bright ideas - keep them to YOURSELF." Klut was obviously angry at Rhiannon for hitting him.

Aracuria intervened. "But surely there must be machines that can travel through space faster then the speed of light?"

Klut nodded. "Oh yes, the North has hundreds of them, but no one has one big enough to carry the Tree of Life in its hold. Remember, the Tree of Life is HUGE."

"But someone, somewhere, must have a space ship big enough to carry one," said Morcant.

Klut nodded, "Yes, you're right. In the whole Universe there is just one space cargo carrier that is big enough to take the Tree of Life."

"Great," said Aracuria. "Where is it?"

"Draco," said Klut, "I remember reading that the Demi-Demons built it especially to carry the Tree of Life from the Garden of Eden in the first place: it's called the Morrigan Deep Space Cargo Transport. And that, Aracuria, brings me to the second problem that we are facing, and that is the fact that the Demi-Demons are not going to let us take the Tree of Life away from them, any more than they'll let us take their cargo ship." Aracuria was unabashed. "But it could be done, couldn't it?" he said.

"It's not...impossible," agreed Klut, "Just so very, very unlikely that only a bunch of idiots would ever try to do it."

"Do we have any choice?" said Rhiannon.
Klut stared for a moment an then turned to Roger, "Well, do we?" said Klut.
Roger shook his head, "No." he said solemnly.
A smile burst out on Aracuria's face, "Great. Now that's settled all we've got to work out is how to do it."
Klut sank his head into his hands."Here we go again," he said.

Aracuria turned to King Morcant, "Would it be all right if we borrowed the Solar Ducks again? It's just that if we try to go to Draco in one of the Northern spaceships, then word will soon get out why we've gone there and when people learn that the sun is going out, they'll all start to panic, and that's the last thing we want while we're away."
Morcant nodded enthusiastically, "Of course you can borrow them! I'd come myself if I were a little younger. As it is, you'd best take one for yourself and let Roger ride on the other: he might come in handy."
Aracuria was just about to thank him when Klut butted in, "I can't believe what I'm hearing! Have you gone crazy, Aracuria? What do you intend to do, just fly to Draco again and steal the Tree of Life from under Lucifer's nose?"
"Something like that," said Aracuria.

Klut shook his head in disbelief. "Last time we were lucky; very, very lucky. This time they'll be waiting for us. Lucifer is one of the most powerful creatures in the Universe and YOU, Aracuria, will have to do battle with him. Are you prepared for that?" Aracuria nodded.
"Oh you are, are you?" said Klut sarcastically. "Well then, how are you going to get into his presence, which is where the fight will take place?"
Aracuria looked a little lost. "I'll, I'll just go the way we went before." he said uncertainly,
"Oh, I see, so you'll just go the way we went before. If you weren't stronger than me I'd club you for being so dumb. All the questions will have been changed. Can you answer them all again, on your OWN? Because none of us will be allowed down there to fight him, you can be sure of that."
Aracuria shook his head.
"So you see, you won't even be able to get to see him in the first place. And even if you could, how do you think you could defeat Lucifer, Leviathan and all the hosts of Hell that they can summon up to help them?"
Aracuria looked really unhappy.
"I couldn't, could I?" he said quietly.
"Even if we were there to help you, you couldn't and if we tried flying there with any weapons, they'd blow us out of space before we could land," said Klut.
"So it IS impossible." said Rhiannon, who was looking as miserable as Aracuria.
Klut shook his head. "No it isn't, there might just be a way." Aracuria and Rhiannon looked up as Klut continued, "Lucifer is very powerful, but he isn't all-powerful. I remember reading in one of my story books as a child

that the Universe was brought into being by two rings called the Rings of Ra. When the rings were brought together, everything was created. Now those rings couldn't be destroyed, but anyone who possesses just one of them would become one of the most powerful creatures in the whole Universe and anyone who possessed both of them would become ALL-powerful. To stop that from ever happening, the great gods sealed the rings into giant green gemstones and then dropped them on the desert planet of Thlagtha. When the inhabitants of Thlagtha saw the giant green stones drop from the sky, they immediately set about building a massive idol into which they could fit the gemstones as eyes. It took them thousands of years to build it, but eventually it was completed."

"And what happened then?" asked Bill.

"The statue was so big it could be seen from space and the green gemstones used to reflect the light of the stars so that people could see them glowing for light years around. That's when disaster struck, because space pirates came and stole one of the green gemstones. I know this because that was the stone that I found in the Treasure Chamber on Draco."

"I remember seeing it!" said Rhiannon excitedly, "and it had a ring inside it."

"Exactly!" said Klut. "The space pirates must have deposited it with the Demi-Demons for safe keeping and never been allowed to get at it again. But somehow Lucifer doesn't know that it's there, otherwise he would have broken it open, placed the ring on his finger and increased his own power immeasurably. All the same, that ring is in his possession and so no one else can use it."

"What happened to the other ring?" asked Aracuria.

"No one knows. The last time anyone saw it was when it fell out of the eye of the Idol of Thlagtha when the space pirates toppled it over to get the other ring." said Klut. "But if we could find it, and put it on your finger Aracuria, then you might stand a chance of beating Lucifer."

"Excellent!" cried Morcant. "I knew there would be a way to do it. Once Aracuria has that ring I'm sure he'll give Lucifer a run for his money."

Everyone was pleased with the solution. Klut, however, didn't look so happy.

"But first, we have to find that ring," he said solemnly, "because without it we don't stand a snowball in Hell's chance of winning: if you see what I mean." They did.

CHAPTER THREE: OFF WE GO AGAIN

Just as Klut had finished speaking two heralds ran up to Aracuria, pulled out two bronze horns from under their oversize jumpers and let out a piercing honk that nearly split everyone's ear drums.
"What do you WANT?" screamed Rhiannon, annoyed at the noise.
"We've come to announce the arrival of Hubert Mega-Dollar Star System the Third and his wife Belinda Mega-Buck Star System, joint President and Presidentess of the Northern Botulism Corporation."
Rhiannon looked particularly unimpressed, "What do they want, small-fry?"
"They wish to pay their respects to our beloved leader, Aracuria."
Aracuria looked horrified. "I can't see them: if they find out what's happening to the sun and how we've got to leave the planet and go to Thlagtha, then they'll spread panic everywhere."

Rhiannon turned to the heralds. "Can Belinda and Hubert keep a secret?" she asked.
"You must be joking!" said one of the heralds.
"Biggest gossips on the planet," said the other.
"Right then, that does it," said Rhiannon, "Tell them that Aracuria, beloved or not, is not at home."

But it was already too late, because up the steps to the first peak came two enormously fat people, one of whom was wearing an evening suit with a bow tie and the other a bright fluorescent yellow evening dress with an emerald tiara.
"Aracuria!" bellowed Hubert, "Good to see you again, my young man: I've brought you another TV set as a little present, and then we can discuss whether you would like to meet our little daughter, Angelica Mega-Buck."
"She's very fond of you, Aracuria," added Belinda, "VERY!" Aracuria turned away in horror. "Oh no," he gulped.
Rhiannon had had enough. "Right that does it: ROGER!" she shouted out loud, "Show our guests the gate." Roger jumped forward, picked up Belinda and Hubert by the necks and frog marched them back down the steps, with a whole load of workmen, carrying an absolutely massive TV set, scurrying down in front of them.

Klut turned to Aracuria. "The longer we stay here the more likely it is that idiots like that are going to find out what's happening: if we are going to go to Thlagtha to get that ring, then we are going to have to go right away."
Aracuria nodded. "You're right."

Just then Roger reappeared on the steps. King Morcant called to him. "Go and tell the Solar Ducks to get ready for take off. They are to fly to the

planet of Thlagtha in the shortest possible time: arrange all the details yourself." Roger went off up to the fourth peak to do as he was told.
"Is there anything we'll need to take, like weapons or something'?" asked Rhiannon.
Klut shook his head, "Thlagtha is a peaceful planet: there's no need even for a pocket laser, and anyway, if Roger is coming along he can look after us if need be."

Now that they knew they were going to go off into space again, Rhiannon walked up to her grandfather. She was about to tell him not to worry while they were away and how she was certain that if there was any chance of getting the ring then they were the ones to get it, but she never did, because as she opened her mouth to speak to him she noticed that something was happening on the fourth peak.
"The DUCKS! The Ducks are moving towards the edge!"

Aracuria, Klut, Bill and Morcant looked in horror as Deborah began to saunter towards the edge of the cliff. At that moment Roger returned to the first peak. "I... have... sent... the... ducks... on... their... way... to... Thlagtha." he said.
Morcant went red with rage. "But Aracuria and the others aren't on them YET!"
In spite of his immense size, Roger suddenly looked extraordinarily dumb.
"Can't we call them back?" asked Bill.
"No." said Morcant, "Once they receive an instruction they obey before listening to any others. That means..."
Aracuria butted in, "...that means they'll fly straight to Thlagtha but..."
Rhiannon butted in, "...no one has told them to come back...ROGER, you idiot: DO SOMETHING!"

Without waiting for another word Roger dashed up the steps towards the fourth peak, with Rhiannon, Klut, Bill, Aracuria and King Morcant running as fast as they could behind.

Deborah was getting close to the edge. She was taking her time, inspecting her shiny golden wings and blinking her massive black eyes before take off. Roger dashed up the steps, past Klut's library, past Bill's amusement park, then on to the fourth peak. Deborah was right on the edge, she stretched out her wings, raised her beak to the wind and was about to launch herself when Roger crashed into her side, sending her tumbling across Aracuria's garden, scattering gnomes everywhere, until she landed, appropriately, in the duck pond.

Rhiannon, Klut, Bill and Aracuria finally arrived, totally exhausted, on the fourth peak: King Morcant was nowhere to be seen. Klut was exhausted. He walked towards the edge, where Roger was lying flat on his steel face, turned his head and was about to say something to Aracuria when his foot caught on a gnome that was lying on the floor. The next second he

was flying through the air. He did a complete somersault, hit the edge of the fourth peak, and then slipped over.
"AARRAGH!" he screamed, as he realized what was happening. Aracuria rushed forward, dived for the edge and just managed to grab Klut's foot before he disappeared completely. But Aracuria couldn't stop himself: he too started to go over the edge. First went his head, then his arms and then his body.
"AARRAGH!" he screamed as his legs went over. Rhiannon, seeing what was happening, made a dive for Aracuria's legs and managed to catch him at the knees, but with the weight of Klut and Aracuria to hold there was nothing to stop her going over as well. First went her head, then her arm, then her body, "AARRAGH!" she screamed as her legs went over. Bill dived for Rhiannon's legs just as she disappeared over the edge. Somehow he managed to catch her left foot, but there was now no way that he could hold the combined weight of Aracuria, Klut and Rhiannon, and so he started slipping over the edge.
"AARRAGH!" he screamed as he began to plunge off the cliff.

At that moment King Morcant appeared on the fourth peak, wiping the sweat off his brow and panting: he looked around, but all he could see was Deborah climbing out of the duck pond and shaking herself dry, Margaret making her way across the garden towards the edge and Roger lying sprawled on the ground. He was about to ask, "Where has everyone gone'?" when he saw Bill's feet disappearing over the edge of the cliff. "ROGER - DO-SOMETHING!!"

Immediately Roger jumped up, saw what was happening, dived for the edge of the cliff and just managed to grab Bill's right foot as it disappeared out of view. For a moment he just lay there, as Aracuria, Klut, Bill and Rhiannon dangled over the thousand foot drop.
"Don't look down!" shouted Morcant, who was only trying to be helpful. Immediately, Rhiannon, Klut, Bill and Aracuria, looked down at the ground a thousand feet below.
"AARRAGH!" they all screamed.

Deborah had now recovered her dignity and was walking once again to the edge, and Margaret was doing exactly the same, crushing gnomes underfoot in the process. Something had to be done fast.
"ROGER!" shouted King Morcant, "Put Aracuria, Klut, Bill and Rhiannon on Deborah." But Deborah was now once again about to take off. Roger ran along the edge of the cliff to where Deborah was already stretching out her wings, with Aracuria, Rhiannon, Bill and Klut dangling and swinging in mid air. When he reached her, Roger put his foot out in front of Deborah just as she launched herself into the air. The second she hit the foot, she stopped dead with a loud clunk. Roger then pulled up Aracuria, Bill, Klut and Rhiannon and dropped them on to Deborah's back. When they were all on, he moved his foot away, allowing Deborah to drop like a stone off the edge.

"Have a good journey!" shouted King Morcant, as the four of them plummeted out of sight down the cliff face. Just then Margaret reached the edge and without more ado launched herself off the edge of the cliff. Morcant turned to Roger.
"Quickly Roger: jump." Without pausing for thought, Roger ran along the edge of the cliff and dived off with his arms outstretched. He caught hold of Margaret's neck just as she began to flap her wings. She gave an enormous squawk as the massive weight of Roger swung beneath her. Immediately her wings folded up and together they plunged down through the air.

Meanwhile Aracuria and the others were desperately trying to get off Deborah's Solar Rucksack so that the sun could hit it and make her wings start flapping. As they dived ever faster down the sheer cliff wall and with the ground looming up below them, one by one they managed to clamber on to the wings. Slowly, the giant wings started to flap and they began to come out of the dive. Just then Margaret and Roger came shooting past like a bullet.
"What was that?" said Bill. They all looked down as Margaret tried as hard as she could to flap her wings. But with the weight of Roger around her neck it was almost impossible.
"They're going to hit the ground!" shouted Aracuria,
"They're going to be smashed to pieces!" cried Klut.
Any moment now they were going to hit the ground. Rhiannon shouted down, "ROGER-DO-SOMETHING!"

Roger saw what was about to happen. He at once began running in mid air with his giant steel legs as fast as he could. The next second they hit the ground, but instead of being smashed to pieces, all that happened was that they suddenly shot forward at a terrific speed.
"Wow!" exclaimed Rhiannon, as Roger and Margaret roared across the ground like a racing car. Now at last Margaret's wings began to work properly and with Roger running as fast as he could they began to lift gently into the air. The only trouble was that up ahead was a massive mound of rubbish that was yet to be cleared away. Margaret tried as hard as she could to lift them into the sky and so fly over it, but it was too late, they were going to hit. Just then Roger stopped running with his feet and instead began kicking, left, right and center. The next moment, Margaret and Roger hit the rubbish, but instead of crashing into it, Roger's huge feet began bashing the rubbish away. From where Aracuria and the others were, high above, it looked as if a small explosion had taken place, as thousands of black rubbish sacks burst open, spilling their contents in a cloud of filth. Fridges went flying here and there like rockets and even discarded uranium vessels were flung high in the air.

"Wow!" said Aracuria, as out from the cloud of filth came an exceedingly grimy Margaret, with Roger still clinging to her neck, a black

rubbish sack over his head and his body covered in rotten tomatoes, bits of dead cat and moldy ketchup.
"You made it!" cried Rhiannon, as Margaret gradually gained height and came up beside them. However, Roger, unable to see with the black bin liner over his head, was still kicking furiously.
"You can stop that now," shouted Klut. Roger stopped kicking, "And take that stupid bag off your head," yelled Rhiannon.

Roger opened his laser eyes and instead of removing the bag with his hands, which would have been impossible, burned it away into nothing. Then, with a neat somersault, he swung himself around until he landed on Margaret's back.

It was time to relax. Aracuria and Rhiannon lay down on one wing while Klut and Bill lay down on the other. They all looked down at the world below as they passed over the Equator Sea, just as they had six months before. Gradually, they rose higher and higher into the sky until the whole world began to fall away. And then it was just a ball of blue and white, floating alone in space. The Solar Ducks kept on flapping. They seemed to be going a different way this time, because up ahead they could see the Moon. The Moon was smaller than the earth; it was all white and pockmarked where meteorites had landed thousands of years before. Deborah and Margaret winged their way towards it. Slowly the Moon grew larger and larger until it started to pass beneath them, just a few thousand miles below.

An idea entered Rhiannon's head.
"Hey! Why didn't we dump all that rubbish on the moon instead of firing it at the sun: no one lives there after all."
Klut shrugged his shoulders. "Don't ask me, ask Aracuria. He's the bright one who said let's fire it at the sun. He's the one's got us into this mess."

Rhiannon was just about to lean across Deborah's neck and clout Klut across his flat head when Aracuria reached out and stopped her. "It doesn't matter now, does it?" he said. "If we don't get the Ring of Ra then we're done for."
Rhiannon nodded, "Yeah, guess you're right. All the same, it was a pretty dumb idea to fire all that rubbish at the sun." Aracuria hung his head in shame: it was indeed the dumbest idea he had ever had. Even if Klut had boasted about it being his idea, it was really Aracuria's .He just had to get that ring and sort everything out.

The rise and fall of Deborah's beating wings sent them all off to sleep, one by one. Roger leant back against Margaret's Solar Rucksack, crossed his feet and then put them up on the back of her head. It had been quite an eventful day for him, so he closed down his thermo-nuclear reactor core and, like the others, went to sleep. Soon they would be on Thlagtha.

CHAPTER FOUR: GREEN GOO AND SLIME

Aracuria was woken with a thump. He looked up and saw that Margaret was bathed in a brilliant orange glow. He shouted out.
"Wake up everybody! Here we go again!"
Roger had already woken and was now standing on Margaret's head, unsure of what was happening, as the glow seemed to completely cover her. The next moment, there was a streak of brilliant blue light which shot out like a comet from the orange glow and burned its way across the Universe, disappearing between the stars. Margaret, Roger and the glow had vanished.

Rhiannon and the others woke up.
"What's happening?" Rhiannon asked dreamily.
"We've hit the edge of the Universe. Roger and Margaret have just bounced off it and disappeared," said Aracuria.
"Oh, is that all?" said Rhiannon, as she curled back up on the wing. "I thought something important had happened." She went back to sleep. Klut and Bill stayed awake though; they sat up on the edge of the other wing and watched as Deborah came up to hit the edge of the Universe, which was really just a giant sheet of rubber. The next second, a brilliant glow burst out right in front of them. They gazed in wonder as the glow grew into a giant sheet of orange, extending from the edge of Deborah's bill high above them and far below. The farther they traveled the bigger it grew, until eventually it began to come down around them, covering the duck.

Klut cried out. "It's the rubber sheet! We're at the edge of the Universe." Then suddenly Deborah tipped over, the orange glow turned into a brilliant blue and the next moment all the stars turned into great long streaks of white light, until it looked as if they were surrounded by white spaghetti.

They were now traveling faster than the speed of light, just as they had when they went to Draco, but what was different this time was that slowly Deborah began to spin around and around and around.
"What's happening?" cried Aracuria.
"I don't know," said Klut. The spinning started getting faster and faster and faster.
"What's happening?" said Rhiannon, as the spinning woke her up again. "Why do I feel sick?" She lifted up her head and saw that the whole Universe seemed to be spinning around and around, getting faster and faster every second.
"Aarragh!" she screamed.
Klut grabbed the Solar Rucksack."Quickly! Hold on to this, everyone, before we get thrown off and disappear forever into space." At the thought of that

everyone dived for the Solar Rucksack and clung on to it for dear life, as the spinning got worse and worse.

"Deborah!" shouted Klut. "Fold up your wings or they'll be ripped off by the force." When she heard that Deborah blinked and hurriedly folded up her wings, but the moment she did so the spinning became uncontrollable. The Universe turned into a white blur around them.

"Now I know what my jeans feel like in the washing machine," groaned Aracuria, but no one answered. They all felt too sick to speak. Instead they closed their eyes and waited for it to stop.

After a few moments, Aracuria became aware of a wind in his hair. He opened his eyes and saw that everything was light and that sometimes above him and sometimes below him there was a sky.

"What's happening now?" he asked.

Klut opened his too. "Deborah!" he shouted, "You can open up your wings now: it looks like we're in Thlagtha."

Deborah opened her eyes at once, then unfolded her wings. The spinning began to slow down and gradually the sky stopped appearing first above them, then below them and eventually stopped above their heads.

"We're on Thlagtha!" cried Rhiannon, overjoyed that the spinning had stopped. Aracuria and others looked down: below them was what looked like an emerald lake that stretched out for miles, and in the center of the lake was what looked like a big black spot.

"Hey !This place is beautiful!" shouted Rhiannon. High up in the sky was a brilliant sun that was making the emerald lake glow a beautiful shiny green.

"Where shall we land?" asked Aracuria.

Klut looked across from horizon to horizon, but he couldn't see what he was looking for.

"I thought we should come down where Roger and Margaret landed, but I can't seem to see them anywhere."

Rhiannon became alarmed. "What do you mean, you can't see them? Where's my Roger gone? He was my nanny when I was a baby: where is he?" Rhiannon leaned out precariously over Deborah's head, but Roger was nowhere to be seen.

"Maybe he's landed by that big black spot," said Klut. "Perhaps it's some kind of town. If we land there we ought to find him." Rhiannon looked relieved. "Yes, you're probably right," she said. "It would just be awful if we lost Roger: there's just no way we could defend ourselves or fix anything if he wasn't around." Everyone nodded: without Roger things would be just terrible.

Deborah headed out towards the big black spot and then gradually came down to land. The strange thing was though, that the closer to the spot they came and the lower over the lake they flew, the more the big black spot didn't look like a town. In fact, it didn't look like anything that they had ever seen before, because it just didn't look like anything. Deborah came in low

over the gleaming emerald sea with the spot coming up right ahead of them: she was going to land right in the middle of it. Aracuria was about to say to Klut, "I'm glad we don't have to land in this green sea as I'm scared of water, whatever color it is..." but he never did because at that moment a look of absolute horror covered Klut's face.
"That isn't a town!" he screamed, "It's a HOLE!"
"WHAT?" shouted everyone in terror.
"Quickly Deborah: land in the water and start flapping backwards!"

Deborah did as she was told. She dived into the emerald sea, opening out her webbed feet to make as big a splash as possible. But when her feet hit the green sea, there was no splash at all. Instead there was a mighty GLUG, as if someone had just punched a fist into a bowlful of jelly. And worse still, they didn't stop moving. Instead, Deborah's webbed feet began to skid over the surface of what was clearly not a sea at all, straight in the direction of black spot.

"What's happening?" cried Aracuria, as great lumps of green slime began to fly past his head.
Klut looked horrified, "I don't know, I don't know," he said. Up ahead, the black spot that was really a hole began to get closer and closer.
Rhiannon was now getting scared as well. "Aracuria, do something!" But Aracuria didn't know what to do. Suddenly Deborah, who was furiously trying to beat her wings backwards at the same time as trying to skate over the sticky slime of the green sea, began to lose her balance.
"Oh no!" shouted Bill, as Deborah began to spin around, and around, and around.
"Hold on to the Solar Rucksack!" cried Klut, "Or we'll all get thrown off." But it was too late: Deborah had lost control. The slime had covered her webbed feet and as she spun around and around, so it began splattering over her wings and her head and her tail. Finally, with the massive hole only meters away, it became too much for her and she toppled over, catapulting the four of them high into the air.

"AARRAGH!" everyone screamed. The next moment, they all came crashing down into the green slime. Deborah gave an uncharacteristic 'squawk' as she too splattered into the slime, burying her head and wings.

There was total silence, except for the deep, but gentle whistling of the wind. Aracuria stood up. He had been thrown the furthest from Deborah and his head and body were covered in green goo. But the goo was only about three feet deep, so it was possible to look out over it. He looked around and saw Rhiannon, Klut and Bill slowly emerging from the slime. Then Deborah lifted up her head from beneath the slime and blinked. Aracuria started laughing.
"What are you laughing at?" yelled Rhiannon furiously, as she pulled thick lumps of green slime from her hair.
"You all look so funny!" said Aracuria.

This really annoyed Rhiannon, who struggled forward to hit Aracuria across the head. At that moment Klut asked, "What's that whistling sound?" just as Aracuria stepped backwards to avoid Rhiannon's fist. But instead of putting his foot down through more green slime, there was nothing but pure, sweet, empty air.

"AARRAGH!" he screamed, as he started to fall backwards. Rhiannon, instead of hitting Aracuria reached out and grabbed him by the hair just as he fell backwards into what was the biggest hole that any of them had ever seen, ever.

"Oh my!" cried Rhiannon, looking down into the depths of what was clearly a bottomless pit. "AARRAGH!" screamed Aracuria as the pain shot through his head from where Rhiannon was holding him. Then he screamed again as his head turned and he saw the enormous hole into which he was going to fall if Rhiannon let go. Klut and Bill ran forward, grabbed Aracuria and pulled him back from the edge.

Exhausted, frightened and covered in slime as they were, they all lay down on the rim of the hole and looked down. The hole was absolutely gigantic: it must have been two miles across and went down sheer into the depths. Beside the sound of the wind whistling up the shaft, they all listened as Aracuria's scream echoed down, seemingly forever.

A terrible thought occurred to Rhiannon: she turned to Klut. "You don't think Roger and Margaret could be down there, do you..?."

Klut looked really frightened. "No, no, I don't think so. If they had, we'd still be hearing their cries: I would have thought a sound coming out of a hole this big would echo for years." Rhiannon was relieved: she could still hear Aracuria's scream echoing around, so it was just impossible for Roger and Margaret to have fallen into the hole.

"Oh, I'm glad you said that Klut. It's just that without Roger, we'd be doomed on this planet, I'm certain we would." Everyone nodded: without Roger they'd all be in a right state.

Just then Aracuria, who was rubbing his aching hair furiously, looked up. High in the sky he saw something that looked like a missile.

"What's that?" he shouted, pointing up into the sky. Rhiannon, Klut and Bill all looked up into the air, where something large was coming straight towards them at an incredible speed.

"I don't know, but it could be..." Before Klut could go on, the object came close enough for them all to see that it was Margaret, traveling at a frightening speed, spinning around and around, with Roger clinging desperately to her neck.

Rhiannon turned frantically to Klut. "Why doesn't Margaret open out her wings?" she demanded.

The answer soon became apparent as Margaret came closer, "Because they've been RIPPED OFF!" cried Aracuria.

The next second, Margaret crashed into the slime like a missile. There was a fantastic explosion of green goo that burst out like a tidal wave, showering everyone and everything. Deborah hid her head as everyone else dived for cover. The trouble was that the shock of the explosion sent Roger flying high into the air. He turned over once, twice, three times and then fell straight into the center of the massive hole.

"...AA...RR...AA...GGH...!" he screamed, in a metallic sort of way.

"Oh no!" wailed Rhiannon. But worse was to come. After crashing into the slime, Margaret hadn't slowed down enough. She continued sliding along beneath the surface of the goo, and came out only at the edge of the hole: she slipped over the edge and, without any wings to stop her, plummeted down into the depths alongside ROGER,

"SQUAWK!" she screamed, but there was nothing that anyone could do.

Aracuria, Rhiannon, Klut, Bill and Deborah watched in horror as Roger and Margaret crashed down the hundreds of miles of hole, sending up a shower of dust as they banged off first one wall then the next, until finally they could be seen no more. When eventually everything went quiet, Rhiannon, with tears in her eyes, turned to Aracuria.

"Roger and Margaret are gone. What are we going to do now? There is no way they could have survived that." Aracuria's face was blank with horror.

"I, I don't know." he said. Thlagtha was going to be worse than Draco, and that was saying something.

CHAPTER FIVE: THE NOSE AND A BIG TOE

Everyone felt awful.

"What are we going to do now?" asked Bill glumly but no one answered.

Rhiannon turned to Klut. "How come Roger and Margaret came out of Hyper-Space after us when they went in first? I just don't understand?"

Klut sighed. "Margaret must have slowed down drastically when her wings were torn off. If only she had folded them up when she began to spin."

Bill looked down into the dusty hole. "What are we going to do now?" he asked again.

Aracuria looked down into the hole and then out over the great expanse of green slime that stretched in front of them.

"Well, there's no use staying here. We've got to make our way through this green stuff until we can find someone to talk to. Maybe then we can find out where the Ring of Ra might be."

Klut suddenly became very upset. "But we don't KNOW that the Ring of Ra is even on this planet: it disappeared 700 million years ago - it could be anywhere in the Universe."

Aracuria nodded. "I know, but have you got any better ideas?" Klut remained silent and no one else said anything. "Well then, let's get going."

They had just started moving off through the green goo when Deborah, whom everyone had forgotten, gave a kind of metallic duck-like whimper. Aracuria looked back and saw her, still standing by the edge of the hole where her sister duck Margaret had plunged just a few minutes before.

"I'm sorry Deborah," said Aracuria, "But there's nothing we can do about it. You had better stay here until we come back with help." Deborah blinked her shiny eyes and settled down on the edge of the hole for the long wait.

Walking through the thick green slime was really difficult. Every time one of them put a foot down, it squelched in the green goo until it hit the hard rock beneath; then, when they tried to lift up the foot, the goo stuck to it like glue. After about half an hour they were all exhausted, but they had only traveled a couple of hundred meters from the edge of the hole.

"How much further have we got to go?" asked Bill, who beside being extraordinarily stupid most of the time was also a little short sighted.

"About another hundred miles," snapped Klut, still annoyed that he had ever decided to come on this dumb trip to Thlagtha.

"We're not going to be able to walk on like this for ever," panted Rhiannon. "When are we going to stop?"

Aracuria looked up at the sky: high overhead the sun was burning fiercely. "When it gets dark," he said. "We'll have to stop then."

Klut unstuck one of his feet and added, "If we don't drop dead first."

They continued walking through the slime, on and on, and the more they walked, the more covered in the goo they became. All the time they were hoping that it would get dark so that they could have a rest, but the strange thing was that even though it felt as if they had been walking absolutely ages, they couldn't have been, as the sun was still in the sky, burning in the same place that it had been when they started off. Finally, after what must have been another hour of walking, (although because no one had a watch they couldn't tell), they came in sight of a set of steps, set into a bank that rose up out of the goo. Rhiannon was the first to see them and she set off as fast as she could to get to them.

"Look what I've found!" she cried, as she finally made it to the marble steps and began running up them. Aracuria and Klut followed. The steps were wide and clean, while the bank on either side of the steps seemed to run right around the green slime.

"It looks like an enormous lake!" exclaimed Aracuria. "But who would want to build a lake of slime?"

Not even Klut could answer that one. By the time they reached the top of the steps, Rhiannon was already trying to clean her clothes and hair of slime. Aracuria started doing the same, but Klut stepped forward and looked out over the planet at something. "Do you see what I see?" he said.

Rhiannon looked up, then she saw it too. "You mean that..."

Klut nodded. Aracuria looked up, he pulled a big lump of green slime out of his hair and then he saw what the others were looking at. "It's a nose!" Away in the distance, standing alone on the horizon was the outline of a massive nose.

"I don't believe it!" said Klut.

"What don't you believe?" asked Bill, who had only now managed to climb up the steps, but no one answered him as they all knew he was short sighted and that he wouldn't believe them unless he could see it himself.

"Let's take a closer look," said Klut. "This strange phenomenon demands further investigation.

Once again they set off, only this time the walking was easy as they didn't have to trample through all that goo. Very soon the outline of the nose began to loom over them. When they got really close, Rhiannon noticed that she could see something else, half hidden by the massive nose.

"Is that a big toe, or am I seeing things?"

Klut ran forward to get a better look. "It's a big toe!" he shouted back, "It really is a big toe and an enormous nose."

They all came to a halt in front of the huge nose that now towered hundreds of meters above their heads. Klut walked into one of the nostrils with Aracuria while Rhiannon and Bill stayed out in the open.

"IT'S A NOSE!" screamed Bill, who had only just realized what was looming above him. Rhiannon ignored him. Meanwhile Aracuria ran up to Klut.

"How do you think this got here?"
Klut didn't answer, he was too busy looking up at gigantic arch of the nostril and the thousands of hairs that stuck out from each side, "I don't know," he said finally, "but I wouldn't like to be around when it had a cold."

At that moment Bill's scream of 'It's a nose!' burst into the nostril. It echoed up into the heights and then far into the back, and wherever it went the hairs began tingle. The next moment, all the tingling set up a huge pressure wave of air that mingled with the sound of 'It's a nose!' and then exploded from the back of the nostril, heading straight for the entrance at a fantastic speed. Aracuria and Klut found themselves out in the open, crashing along the ground with, 'IT'S A NOSE' bellowing along behind them.

They picked themselves off the ground and began to dust themselves off.
"That was a stupid thing to do." said Klut crossly to Bill. "If that nose had had a cold, we could have been drowned."
Rhiannon reached out and hit Bill across the head. "Idiot," she said condescendingly. Klut was just about to do the same when out of the sky came a small piece of stone that hit him straight in the middle of his flat head and sent him crashing to the ground. All at once there were more stones landing all around them.
"What do you think you're doing? Hooligans! Leave my nose alone!" The voice was distant and weak, like the voice of an old man, and it came from high above.
"It's God!" gasped Bill. Before he could fall to his knees, Rhiannon hit him over the head once again.
"Idiot," she said once more. "Don't you know God's a woman? Don't you know anything about mythology?"
Bill, not knowing what 'mythology' meant, said nothing.

"Who is it?" shouted Aracuria, straining to see where the voice was coming from while yet more stones landed on the ground.
"I'll give you beef burgers, young lad!" came the reply. "I'm a vegetarian and that's the way things are going to stay.

Aracuria turned to Rhiannon with a puzzled look. "Did I mention anything about beef burgers?" Before Rhiannon had time to reply, a hammer came flying down through the sky and landed straight on Aracuria's foot.
"Aarragh!" he screamed, hopping around holding his damaged toes. The next second, a chisel came flying down and hit Bill on the toe.
"AARRAGH!" he screamed. He tried to do what Aracuria was doing but instead of hopping when he lifted up his sore foot, he fell over, crashed into Rhiannon and sent them both clattering to the floor.

With Klut, Rhiannon and Bill lying on the floor, only Aracuria saw what happened next: a giant yellow bucket appeared from the top of the nose and descended on a long rope until it touched the ground. Inside it was an old man with a black beret and a wrinkled face.

“I’ll give you beef burgers, young lad! A vegetarian I am and a vegetarian I’ll stay!” Aracuria stared at him, speechless in amazement. Klut stood up, rubbing his head: he was really angry. He walked over to the yellow bucket and was about to shout at the old man when he noticed, as he peered over the rim of the bucket, that not only was the old man wearing no clothes, but the bucket was filled with water.

Klut spun around. “We’ve got a loony here: he’s taking a bath!” The old man retorted at once: “And what’s wrong with cleanliness, young man? At least I wash myself regularly, unlike you city types.”

At this point Aracuria thought he’d better explain who they were.

“We’re not from any city, sir. We’re not even from this planet; we’re just visitors here, just passing through. Who are you?”

The old man looked at him and noticed the green slime in his hair. “Guess you’re right: not even waiters are dumb enough to go swimming in the pond now that there’s no water in it. My name is Gayomart, and if you don’t mind I’ll just get my hammer and chisel and get on with my work.” The old man went to get out of the bucket just as Rhiannon picked herself up. Aracuria hurried forward and picked up the hammer and chisel before the old man had time to climb out.

“You’d better not, Mr. Gayomart,” he said apologetically. “There’s a princess present.” The old man nodded gruffly, took the hammer and chisel and reached over to turn a switch on the side of the bucket that would take him back to the top of the nose.

“Before you go, said Rhiannon urgently, “Is there anyway we could get our robot and a damaged solar duck out of that big hole in the center of the green slime? You see, they fell down it when we crash-landed on your planet.”

The old man began to laugh. “You must be joking: that’s the shaft of the Most Holy Fountain of Theom. It goes straight to the center of the planet. Nothing that goes down there ever comes out.”

Rhiannon turned away wretchedly. “Well that does it! Without Roger there’s no way we’re going to get the Ring of Ra.”

But at those words the old man’s eyes lit up. “Have you come looking for the Ring of Ra?” he asked excitedly.

“Yes,” said Aracuria, “Do you know where it is?”

The old man shook his head.

“Do you know where it might be?” asked Klut. The old man shook his head again.

“Then do you know what happened to it?” asked Rhiannon.

“Oh yes,” said the old man, “Oh yes, I know what happened to both of them, but what business is that of yours?”

Aracuria, Rhiannon, Klut and Bill gathered around the bucket, but not too closely, then Aracuria explained.

"The sun on our planet is going out and what we thought we'd do is steal the Tree of Life from the Demi-Demons of Draco and take it back to our planet Earth to keep it warm. But to do that we need at least one of the Rings of Ra in order to overpower Lucifer."

The old man scratched his chin. "You're all crazy. You know that, don't you?" The four of them nodded. "But now you come to mention it, you say your planet is Earth: that rings a bell with me. I've heard of it before. If I remember rightly, it used to be a very special place, though for the life of me I can't remember what it was, something to do with the Tree of Life I think...." The old man had started to ramble: Aracuria cut him short.

"Unless we find that ring, Earth is going to freeze over. Can you tell us what you know about what happened to the Ring of Ra?"

The old man smiled. "How old are you kids?" he asked, "Rhiannon and Bill are almost teenagers and Klut is several hundred years old," said Aracuria. "No one knows how old I am."

"And how old do you think I am?" asked the old man.

"About seventy," suggested Rhiannon.

The old man burst out laughing, "I'm 700 million years old if I'm a day!"

"What?" gasped everyone, including Klut. The old man continued. "It was 6900992 years ago this week, if I'm not mistaken, that the Zombie Pirates from the Dead Zone Solar System turned up here. I had just celebrated my eighth birthday when they arrived and devastated our lovely planet of Thlagtha." He paused. "Do want to hear what happened next?" Everyone nodded "Well you'd better listen well, because the only way you're going to save your planet Earth is by finding out what happened to the second Ring of Ra." That was just what they wanted to hear.

CHAPTER SIX: HEAD BANGER

The old man leaned across the edge of the yellow bucket.
"In the beginning, there were the two Rings of Ra that brought this Universe into being. The Rings of Ra were therefore immensely powerful and the Great Gods didn't know what to do with them. Finally, after billions of years of discussion, they cast them inside two green quartz glass globes, which they dropped on an unnamed desert planet where no one lived, except for a few convicts who had been left there to die. Now one of those convicts was the great one-eyed magician Mug Ruith, who had been arrested for stealing the Great Gold Chalice of the god-King Cormac mac Airt. Mug Ruith had been dropped there with his daughter Thlagtha, and together they lived in abject poverty along with the other convicts in one of the many caves that littered the planet. Now when the giant green gemstones dropped down from the sky, Mug Ruith, once he realized what they contained, immediately tried to break them open, but of course without success. But his pious daughter Thlagtha, instead of being greedy for power, lit a fire on the ground and offered prayers to Theom, the Great Mother of all the Universes, thanking her for the gift, not of the gemstones, but of hope."

Klut butted in. "You mean there's more than on Universe?"
"Thousands," said the old man. He continued with his story. "Straight away, Thlagtha's prayers were answered and where the fire was lit the ground opened up and a giant shaft appeared which went straight to the center of the earth where the Sweet Waters lie. A huge fountain at once erupted and the waters that flowed up to the surface made the desert grow. From that day to this, that unnamed desert planet has been called Thlagtha in the memory of what she did. And when she died, everyone stopped speaking the ancient language they had always spoken, since without her, they said, no one was worthy to utter its sounds."

Rhiannon interrupted, "Was that the hole which Roger and Margaret fell down?"
"If Roger and Margaret are the names of your robot and duck, then the very one," said the old man.
"But where has the fountain gone?" asked Aracuria. "All we found was green slime."
"I'm coming to that, my boy, and indeed the green slime is all that is left of the dried up lake which once watered our planet," said the old man. "Once the desert bloomed, everyone became healthy with all the vegetables that started growing and for some reason everyone who ate the vegetables and nothing but the vegetables lived for a very long time. Then people started making things, and selling things and within a few hundred years of the death of Mug Ruith and his daughter, the people of Thlagtha were so rich they

could afford to raise up a statue in the honor of the one who had lit the fire. Well, it took them thousands of years to build, but in the end they had the biggest statue in the whole Universe: I should know, I was one of the last master craftsmen employed to finish her off, her nose being the very last bit. Once the statue was completed, for her eyes they used the green gemstones containing the Rings of Ra, which, as it turned out, was the dumbest thing they could possibly have done..."

"It attracted the space pirates didn't it?" said Klut who already knew part of the story.

"Yes it did," said the old man. "They came, saw the gemstones, and thinking they were just that and nothing more, pulled one of them out of Thlagtha's head. The trouble was, they had to use so much force to get it out that the statue toppled over and smashed into pieces."

"And did that devastate the planet?" asked Rhiannon.

"Oh no," said the old man. "It just woke everyone up. No, what devastated the planet was Head Banger."

Aracuria and Rhiannon looked at each other in bewilderment.

"Head Banger?"

"Head Banger," repeated the old man. "It's a computer game. You see, the Zombie Space Pirates from the Dead Zone Solar System might not have recognized that the Rings of Ra were inside the gemstones, but in other respects they were fiendishly clever. Thlagtha in those days was incredibly rich and like most incredibly rich planets everything was controlled by computers. The computers paid people, they sold things to people, they built things for people, they did everything for the people. Then along comes Head Banger, the most infuriating computer game that had ever been devised. We should have realized that there was something wrong with it because it was made by the 'Brain Damaged Virus Software Company'.

"Well, one of our children picked up this computer game that the Space Pirates had dropped out of their spaceships before they left; he took it home and put it into his computer. The game was simple, all you had to do was zap a bug called Computer Virus. The problem was that no matter how hard he tried he could never win the game. So, he made some copies and gave them to his friends, but they couldn't beat it either, so they made some copies and gave them to their friends, and so on. Then their parents got hold of it and started playing it at work during lunch breaks, but still the virus couldn't be beaten. So they made some copies and gave them to other parents, and so on. And so gradually Head Banger spread across the whole planet into every computer system of every firm, business, company and home." The old man stopped.

Klut leaned forward."But how did that devastate the planet?"

"Simple," said the old man, "Head Banger contained two programs. One was the game that everyone played and couldn't win and the other was a hidden program called 'Dead Zone Strikes Again' .One evening every computer on the whole planet suddenly flashed the following message on the screen: YOU ARE A BUNCH OF WALLIES; DEAD ZONE ZOMBIE STRIKES AGAIN; ERASE ALL FILES.

"And that is exactly what it did! All the files to pay people money, order them goods, build them cars and TVs: everything was erased in a millisecond. A whole civilization was made bankrupt overnight. Every other planet placed us in technological quarantine, so as not to catch the virus, so we could no longer buy new computers from outside."

Rhiannon interrupted impatiently, "But you could still grow vegetables. You could have started from scratch again."

"Yes we could have, if it wasn't for what an outraged group of accountants did. After having seen all their money disappear in a few seconds, in a fit of temper they picked up the other green gemstone that had been lying around on the ground since the statue fell over, and threw it down the Most Holy Fountain of Theom. That was a really dumb thing to do, as a few hours later the fountain stopped flowing: that was nearly 700 million years ago and it has never flowed from that day to this. A few little springs popped up here and there in its place, but there was never enough water to grow vegetables, only to stop people dying of thirst, although they soon started dying of old age."

Rhiannon was horrified. "That's awful," she said.

"If it wasn't for the fact that I've got a little spring up behind Thlagtha's big toe all to myself, around which I grow my melons, I doubt if I would have lived as long as I have," added the old man.

"What did you do after that?" asked Klut.

"Oh, some of the people went to try to find the gemstone. This planet is filled with caves and lots of people went down into them. Of course we never found out if they found the gemstone because none of them ever returned and their descendants still live underground today: we call them the Ghouls, as living underground for seven hundred million years has made them mutate into hideous shapes."

"And what about the rest of the inhabitants?" asked Rhiannon.

"The rest of us stayed above ground. Everyone else went into the beef burger business, but having helped build the statue I decided to break up what remained of it and sell off bits to lost or crash-landed space travelers. They've taken away most of it, either as building blocks for houses or used the interesting pieces as garden ornaments: if anyone present wishes to buy a nose or a big toe, I'm sure we could come to some sort of arrangement. I can offer credit." The old man looked hopeful, but the same thought had occurred to the four of them at the same time.

"The beef burger business?" they said in unison.

"Yes, it seemed a good idea at the time, so good in fact that everyone went into it. After all, they couldn't grow vegetables anymore and people have to eat. Now of course the trouble is that everyone else sells beef burgers, but there's no one with any money to buy any beef burgers, as everyone is trying to sell beef burgers. A right pig's armpit, if you'll excuse the expression."

"If everyone is so poor," said Klut suspiciously, "then how come they managed to get meat for beef burgers in the first place?"

"Oh," said the old man apologetically, "as I said, people who don't eat vegetables. ..die..."

Rhiannon gasped in horror. "But that's cannibalism!" she cried.

"Don't shout at me young lady," said the old man, "I'm a Vegan."

Aracuria felt sick. "You must be REALLY poor if you have to eat each other," he said.

"Oh, I'm not poor, I'm actually staggeringly rich. Over 700 million years I've managed to amass a vast fortune of Hyper-Space Dollars from selling off bits of the statue - some parts went for extraordinarily high prices - but being a Vegan I refuse on principle to eat any meat, and since that's all those stupid waiters are willing to sell me, I'm afraid there's no way I can spend my money."

Bill looked up at the old man: he was fascinated at the idea of cannibalism. "And, and do they still eat dead people, even now?" he asked rather timidly.

The old man shook his head. "Oh, no. That was only a long time ago. People live so long on Thlagtha anyway, even without the vegetables, that there would never be enough bodies around to be turned into beef burgers, and anyway, once people found out where their dead relatives were going they started hiding them away. No, for the last few hundred million years all the beef burgers of Thlagtha have been made out of regurgitated sick."

"OH NO!" screamed Rhiannon, clasping her hands to her mouth, almost sick at the thought.

"Oh yes," said the old man splashing the water in his yellow bucket, "and because regurgitated and reprocessed sick soon loses its meaty flavor, they add worms and maggots taken from the ground to it." Aracuria and Bill turned away in horror. "Now perhaps you can see why I'm a Vegan," he said. Klut nodded vigorously.

While Aracuria, Rhiannon and Bill were doubled up at the thought of it all, Klut bent towards the old man, "Gayomart, sir," he said, "you said that the people who went underground had mutated into ghouls: do you know whether they ever found the green gemstone that the accountants threw down the Most Holy Well of Theom?"

The old man rubbed his chin. "If they ever did find it, they never told anyone. This planet is riddled with caves, so maybe one of them leads to the bottom of the shaft, but one thing's for sure, no one on the surface knows where it is."

Aracuria at last straightened up. "So if we went to see these people underground, they might be able to tell us where it is?" he asked.

The old man smiled wryly. "They might know where it is, but another thing that's for sure is that those ghouls are no longer people. Some of them are hideous, some of them are monstrous and all of them are very weird, with weird long names and weird ideas on everything. For example, I happen to know that they believe they are all descended from a thing they call the Great Chicken, and that when they die they go to an unpronounceable place where the Great Chicken lives and then they are re-born as little chicks and they live with her there forever. Now if that isn't weird and strange I don't know what is."

Rhiannon, who had now stopped feeling sick, nodded.

"So, if we wanted to see these ghouls, how do we get to where they live?" asked Aracuria.

"Oh, that's easy," said the old man. "You just go along past Thlagtha's remaining big toe and you'll see the Mountain of the Dead in the distance. There's an entrance in the side of the mountain called the Demon's Mouth that leads down to where the ghouls live. But first you'll have to get past the waiters and their beef burger bars: the moment they see four newcomers to the planet, they'll be around you like flies."

Aracuria turned to the others. "Well, it looks as if that is the way we are going to have to go: are we all agreed?"

Rhiannon, Klut and Bill nodded.

Aracuria turned back to the old man. "Thank you for telling us what happened to the Ring of Ra, Mr. Gayomart," he said.

"You won't be thanking me when you see what the ghouls look like," said the old man, as he flicked the switch on his yellow bucket and began to soar upwards. Aracuria glanced up at him as he rose away.

"It's not as if we have a choice," he said sadly. "We have to do this to get the Ring, so that we can take the Tree of Life to Earth."

They left the old man and walked off in the direction of Thlagtha's big toe. They shouted out their goodbyes, but the old man was wrapped in thought as he rose up past Thlagtha's massive nostril, "The Tree of Life," he kept on saying over and over to himself, "The Tree of Life: why does that ring a bell when I think of the Earth? What used to be so special about the Earth that I should remember it? After all, it's so far away..." Gayomart switched off his bucket and shouted down to the others as they disappeared in the distance, "Hold on: this is very important. You must wait until I think this one out." But none of them heard him, which was just as well, as it was going to take him all day to find the answer.

CHAPTER SEVEN: VATS OF SICK

Aracuria tapped Rhiannon on the shoulder.
"Did you hear something just then?" he asked. Rhiannon shook her head. Then her eyes caught something, "Look at those carrots!" They were passing behind Thlagtha's massive toe, where Gayomart had laid out a small vegetable garden. There were carrots, and melons, and turnips, and other sorts of fruit that none of them had ever seen before. At the center of the garden was a small spring which rose out of the ground and watered everything around. Rhiannon and Aracuria wanted to take a closer look at the garden, but Klut was impatient to get moving. They walked out from behind Thlagtha's toe and headed up a small rise. Over the top, they saw a wide plain stretched out in front of them. In the distance was what looked like a small town and beyond that, standing on its own in almost pitch darkness, was a huge mountain.

"Is that the Mountain of the Dead?" asked Bill.
"It must be," said Aracuria.
Klut took a good long look at the mountain and then glanced up at the sky where the sun was still burning, "I wish Roger was with us," he sighed. "There's something not quite right about this planet, but without him there's no way I can be certain."
"What's wrong?" asked Rhiannon. But Klut didn't answer. Instead he mumbled something to himself, then walked off in the direction of the town with the others following.

It took about an hour to get to the town, although 'town' was probably the wrong word to use. There was one street running in the direction of the Mountain of the Dead, and on either side of it, instead of proper houses or shops, there were just pretend walls made of wood, with pretend windows cut into the walls. Behind the pretend windows sat pretend people cut out of cardboard at pretend tables. All the cardboard people had happy painted faces and they were all biting into pictures of beef burgers.
"This is really weird!" said Aracuria.
Rhiannon shook her head in disbelief. "This is beginning to phase me: I mean, why is everything so unreal?" No one answered. Instead Bill went up to one of the windows and stared at a cardboard family busily chewing picture beef burgers and French fries. Behind the cardboard family stood a waiter. He had on a little red apron with the words 'MONSIGNOR GUTROT BEEFBURGER PARLOUR' written across it. Bill stared closely at the waiter.
"Hey! Look at this one," he called. "They've even painted sweat on to his face!"

Aracuria and the others huddled together and looked through the pretend window, past the pretend family, at the sweating waiter who looked too real to be made out of cardboard.
"He really is life-like," said Rhiannon.
"No he isn't," said Klut. "That waiter is too ugly to be life-like: when was the last time you saw someone that ugly?"

At that very moment the waiter's moustache twitched, his eyes rolled and then his mouth opened.
"A REAL CUSTOMER!" he screamed.
"AARRAGH!" yelled Bill, jumping back from the window in fright and hitting Klut on the chin with the back of his head. Klut screamed with pain, threw his own head back and hit Rhiannon on the nose. Tears flooded into Rhiannon's eyes. She swung out wildly with her fist and hit Aracuria across the side of the face. He immediately fell to the ground in a heap. Rhiannon, Klut and Bill then fell over him in the confusion and all four ended up sprawled across the floor with aching heads or noses.
"A customer! A customer!" shrieked the far-from-cardboard waiter, jumping up and down with joy. "I haven't had a customer here for seven years, not since the last spaceship crash- landed." All the noise he was making seemed to wake up the whole pretend town. From behind pretend counters behind every pretend shop front came similarly dressed waiters. They all looked out of their pretend windows, saw a pile of people in the streets and at once began to shout, "A customer! A customer! We're all going to have a customer!" Aracuria staggered to his feet and saw what was happening. "We've got to get out of here! This place is crazy!"

Rhiannon, Klut and Bill dragged themselves up, just as the first waiter came running out of his pretend shop clutching a menu. "Would you like one of Monsignor Gutrot's Beef burger Specials?" he shouted at no one in particular.
Rhiannon, rubbing her nose and in a foul temper bellowed out, "CANNIBAL!" but the waiter didn't even seem to hear, he just held out his menu card and Bill, who was a bit hungry, began to read it. At that, all of the waiters came running out into the street clutching menu cards.
"We've got to get out of here!" cried Klut in horror, as a hundred waiters descended on them from all directions.
"This way!" called Aracuria, and at once Rhiannon, Klut and Aracuria all ran off in different directions, while Bill didn't do anything at all. Instead he held the menu close up to his face, reading what was available to eat, while the waiter gleefully led him through a pretend door.

Rhiannon, glancing back, saw what was happening.
"BILL!" she cried. But Bill couldn't hear anything through the stampede of waiters' feet as they ran to grab some customers.
"Aracuria! Klut!" ordered Rhiannon, "Follow me!" Aracuria and Klut, who were now running around in circles as the waiters bore down on them, turned

to face Rhiannon. Once she was sure they were going to follow her, she dashed forward, jumped up high in the air and brought both her feet crashing down on the back of the waiter who was leading Bill away. The waiter went flying forward and smashed into the pretend wall of his pretend shop. Rhiannon grasped Bill's arm and knocked the menu out of his hands.
"Bill, you IDIOT! Didn't anyone ever tell you not to walk off with STRANGE WAITERS?"

Before Bill had time to answer Rhiannon ran with him straight in the direction of the pretend window.
"JUMP!" she bellowed. Bill instinctively obeyed. The next moment Rhiannon and Bill went crashing through the window, scattering the cardboard family and their painted beef burgers all over the place. The next moment Aracuria and Klut came bounding through as well; they both landed on the wooden table, which shattered under their weight. Meanwhile Monsignor Gutrot was trying to get up, but all the other waiters, seeing that he had failed to make a sale, were now convinced that they were going to get a customer. They charged towards the pretend door like a stampede of cattle and crushed the poor Monsignor underfoot.
"RUN!" shouted Rhiannon, leaping over the shop counter. Bill also tried to jump over, but only succeeded in landing on top. Aracuria and Klut picked themselves up off the floor, just as the first waiters began to pour through the door. They both dived for the counter, but failed to clear it. With the weight of the three of them now on it, the whole counter collapsed, sending Klut, Bill and Aracuria flying out through the back of the pretend shop. At that moment the rest of the hundred-odd waiters tried to get through the door in one go. They all became terribly jammed in the doorway, and then, with the weight of all of them pushing, the whole side of the shop began to topple over.
"RUN!" shouted Rhiannon, as the whole pretend building came crashing down around them.

Aracuria, Rhiannon, Klut and Bill found themselves out in the open while a huge pall of dust rose up from the ground where Monsignor Gutrot's shop had just been.
"We've got to hide somewhere!" said Rhiannon. They all looked around desperately. Suddenly, Bill spotted something, standing on its own at the back of the pretend houses. "Let's hide in that water tank!" Without pausing to think what they were doing, Bill, Rhiannon and Klut ran towards a very large, round, steel water tank, out of which a light whiff of steam was rising. However, Aracuria, who hated water, remained where he was. "Where am I going to hide?" he called, but no one answered. Instead Rhiannon, Klut and Bill ran headlong for the water tank and dived in. But instead of the massive splash that everyone had expected, there was a kind of a deep GLUG. Aracuria dashed up to the water tank and peered over to see what had happened: the water tank wasn't a water tank at all. It was, in fact, a heated

vat of steaming sick, filled with wriggling worms and maggots, from which the waiters made their beef burgers. Three heads popped up above the surface.
"UGH!" the three heads screamed, but it was impossible to tell which one of them was Rhiannon, Klut or Bill, as covered in sick they all looked the same.

At that moment, the hundred waiters came running out of the cloud of dust where the shop used to be. One of them caught sight of Aracuria and began shouting, "There they are!"
Aracuria turned back to the others. "Stop messing about in there and RUN!"
Rhiannon, Klut and Bill dragged themselves out of the vat, while Aracuria ran off in the direction of something that had caught his eye.
"Wait for us!" spluttered Klut, as the warm sick dripped off him. Rhiannon ran around blindly trying to hit Bill, who was now more scared of her than he was of the waiters. Aracuria, however, had seen something which looked like a beach buggy parked behind one of the rows of the pretend shops. It had huge wheels, four seats and a bull-bar up front. Over the top of the buggy was stretched what appeared to be a gold mirror. He jumped up on one of the seats; in front of him was a wheel and on the floor was a simple on/off switch. "Where's the engine?" he muttered, pressing down on the switch with his right foot. The next second, the beach buggy's wheels spun around in a cloud of dust as Aracuria and the buggy went crashing through the back of another shop, smashing the counter, table and a cardboard family of four to pieces in the process.
"AARRAGH!" screamed Aracuria, as he emerged through another shop window and landed back in the street. "It's a Solar Buggy!" he exclaimed, opening his eyes as the pretend shop collapsed behind him.

There was no time to lose. The hundred waiters were bearing down on the others, who were now so covered in sick that they were unable to escape. Aracuria aimed the wheels straight at another shop, pressed down with his foot and headed straight for the window: he went crashing through, shattering everything around him until he burst out on the other side. He then spun the buggy around, drove between the waiters and the others and then skidded to a halt.
"Jump in!" Klut and Bill leapt into the buggy without a word, while Rhiannon wiped the sick from her eyes and exclaimed, "Where did you get this from?"

At that moment the first waiters grabbed hold of the other side of the buggy.
"There's no time to explain!" said Aracuria, hitting the switch with his foot and wrenching the steering wheel around. They seemed to spin out of control as the fat tires threw up a dust storm. Rhiannon quickly jumped into one of the seats as Aracuria aimed the buggy straight at the remaining row of shops.
"What are you doing? she yelled. "Have you gone crazy?" But Aracuria didn't answer, as there was a waiter hanging on his side, thrusting a menu

into his face. A moment later, the buggy crashed into yet another pretend shop. Rhiannon, Klut and Bill closed their eyes while Aracuria spun the steering wheel around from one side to another trying to shake off the waiters.

Suddenly the menu disappeared from in front of his face and he could at last see that they were out into the street and heading for the row of shops on the other side. He spun the wheel again, but it was too late: the buggy scraped along the side of the pretend shops and the whole row keeled over and collapsed. Aracuria was no longer in control of the buggy. It went charging back across the street, straight through another of the shops and came out on the other side into the midst of the waiters.

"Oh no!" Aracuria spun the wheel frantically, but the buggy careered on, crashing into the side of the vat of sick, which promptly split open, spilling its contents everywhere. The huge wheels of the buggy began to spin uncontrollably, sending out a shower of sick in the process. Some of the waiters began falling about as they slipped on the sick, while others were drenched in the spray from the buggy's wheels.

"AARRAGH!" they all screamed, as finally Aracuria took control of the buggy and aimed it out of the town.

Rhiannon at last opened her eyes and saw they were now out in the open, racing along at an amazing speed. She turned around in her seat and looked back at the pretend town: both rows of shops and houses had now collapsed and in their place there was just a billowing cloud of dust, "Looks like we wrecked it," she said. "Now all I need is a bath." She settled back into her seat for a moment, then sat bolt upright again. "What's that?" she exclaimed: in front of them was a towering black mountain covered in shadow, at the center of which was a huge opening, shaped like a demon's mouth.

"That's the Mountain of the Dead," said Aracuria solemnly. He had been silently staring at it since they had left the town. By the look of that demon's entrance, their troubles had only just begun.

CHAPTER EIGHT: INTO THE PLANET

Aracuria kept his foot down on the switch as the Solar Buggy raced towards the entrance to the Mountain of the Dead, which was still a few miles off. Suddenly everything went dark. The wheels of the buggy began to slow down and then everything ground to halt. "What's happening?" asked Rhiannon in alarm.

Aracuria jumped out of his seat. "The sun, the sun: it's gone!"

Klut also jumped out of the buggy. "I knew it, I knew it!" he repeated over and over to himself.

Aracuria turned to him."What did you know?"

Klut was jumping up and down in excitement."This planet, this planet doesn't revolve like other planets," he said. "That's why the sun never appeared to move in the sky: because it never did."

Rhiannon sprang up out of her seat. "So that means we re now on the dark side of the planet," she said.

"And that's why the solar buggy stopped," said Aracuria.

"Yes, exactly," said Klut.

Bill also climbed out of his seat.

"I don't understand," he said, but everyone ignored him.

Leaving the now useless buggy, Aracuria and Rhiannon led the way to the mountain. Everything was dark and eerie, but up ahead they noticed that on the side of the mountain there were two flickering lights. No one said anything until they finally reached the foot of the mountain and then everyone froze in terror: in front of them, carved out of the rock of the mountain, rose the monstrous face of a demon. He had horns coming out of the top of his head; out of the side of his head came long, pointed, dog-like ears; his face was covered in hair; his nose was squat and wide and on either side of it were two huge eyes in which flames were burning.

"Wha, wha, what's that?" said Bill, as if he didn't already know.

"That...is the entrance to the Land of the Dead," said Klut.

They walked closer to the demon's head. His mouth was open wide, and around both edges of it, above and below, there were rows of jagged teeth.

"I don't like this," said Rhiannon. "He just looks so evil."

Aracuria nodded. "I wish there was another way in, but this is the only one."

Bill started chattering. "Yes, maybe there is another way in. Perhaps we should look for that first, perhaps..." but everyone ignored him as usual.

Aracuria walked right up to the demon's mouth. Inside the mouth there was what looked like a long tongue but otherwise everything was dark and quiet. Then he noticed that there was something carved into the demon's face just above the mouth:

“HIC JACET SPULTUS CAUSA NON MORTIS POPULUS THLAOTHANUS HOC MONUMENTUM POSUIT.”
“What does that say Klut, I can’t make it out.”
Klut came to Aracuria’s side. “Roughly translated it means, ‘Here lie buried the living dead: the people of Thlagtha erected this monument.” A feeling of horror overcame every one of them.
“The living dead!” said Rhiannon.
Bill began to shake. “I, I am not going in there,” he stuttered.
Aracuria walked right up to the demon’s mouth. “We have to: there’s no other way.” He took hold of two of the stone teeth and pulled himself into the mouth: no one else moved. “Come on!” he shouted, “We’ve GOT to go in this way.”
“But it’s so dark,” shivered Rhiannon. “How are we going to see if it’s pitch black in there.”

Rhiannon had a point. Aracuria stepped on to the demon’s tongue and peered into the darkness. Once his eyes had become accustomed to the lack of light, he began to see flickering shadows.
“There’s some kind of light in here: it’s only really dark at the entrance.” For a moment no one else moved, then Rhiannon grabbed one of the stone teeth and climbed inside. “You’d better know what you’re doing Aracuria,” she said, stepping on to the demon’s stone tongue. Aracuria thought it best not to reply; he really didn’t have a clue what he was doing.

Klut climbed through after them, but Bill just stood alone outside, repeating over and over again, “I’m not going, I’m not going.” Finally Rhiannon’s patience ran out.
“If you don’t climb in here, I’m going to hit you so hard...” Bill immediately clambered through the demon’s mouth, as he was more scared of Rhiannon than he was of any demon.
“You see,” said Aracuria, once they were all inside and standing on the stone tongue, “that face is only there to scare people away: there’s really nothing to be frightened of.” And with that he stepped forward to the far edge of the demon’s tongue. “Follow me,” he said, confident that there was nothing to be worried about. Now that they were all inside the demon’s mouth, all the others began to feel the same.
“Yes, there’s nothing to be worried about,” said Klut in a superior sort of way, as he stepped forward to join Aracuria on the far edge of the tongue.
“Nothing to worry about at all,” agreed Rhiannon, as she followed Klut.

But as she did so I there was suddenly a terrible creak and the next moment the edge of the tongue where Aracuria was standing began to fall, while the edge of the tongue where Bill was standing began to rise high in the air.
“AARRAGH!” screamed Bill as he shot up through the air. Klut just had time to shout out, “The tongue is a see-saw, when Bill’s head hit the roof of the demon’s mouth and he came sliding down the tongue and crashed into

the others, throwing all of them off on to the ground. Just then the darkness was filled with an enormous grinding sound, like the sound of two enormous stones being rubbed against each other. Aracuria jumped up from the ground in time to see the stone mouth of the demon begin to close.

"The mouth is closing!" he cried, running back up the stone tongue, which quickly crashed back down into its original position. But it was too late. He dived for the demon's mouth, but the giant fang-like teeth had already closed down one upon the other, so that now they resembled the bars of a cage through which only air could pass. Rhiannon came to his side. "NOTHING TO WORRY ABOUT!" she screamed.

Aracuria stood up."OK, so I was wrong," he said quietly.

"WRONG!" shouted Rhiannon furiously.

Aracuria shrugged his shoulders, "Well, you can't win them all." And he proceeded to walk away down the demon's throat.

"Where are you going?" yelled Rhiannon.

Aracuria answered without turning around. "This tunnel must somehow lead down to the bottom of the Most Holy Fountain of Theom. That's where the Ring of Ra is and that's where what remains of Roger and Margaret are. That's where we've got to go and there's just no other way of getting there except down this passage." Rhiannon looked at Klut, who nodded in the semi-darkness.

"He's right." he said.

Together they started to follow Aracuria. Bill glanced wistfully through the now closed teeth of the demon and then, realizing he had been left alone, hurried to catch up with the others as they walked into the underworld Land of the Living Dead.

CHAPTER NINE: THE EARTH SHAKER

Aracuria led the way down the passage. It was almost completely dark, but up ahead there was some kind of light that was casting shadows across the stone roof. After a few hundred meters, it became clear that there were flames coming from either side of the passageway, casting flickering shadows everywhere. The flames were coming from the mouths of little stone demon heads that had been carved out of the walls and ran along the length of the passageway at regular intervals. Rhiannon took a look at one of them and shuddered.

"This is really creepy," she said. Everyone felt the same way, except Klut.

"Do you know what I think?" he said, "I think that this whole place is empty. I think that whoever came down here 700 million years ago eventually died out and that the people on the surface have just made up frightening stories about this place to stop their children coming down here." Aracuria, Rhiannon and Bill suddenly started to feel better.

"What a sensible idea," said Rhiannon.

"Excellent," said Aracuria.

"You mean, there's really no one down here?" asked Bill, rather timidly.

Klut looked very superior. "No one at all: of that I'm absolutely sure. The flames in the demon's eyes and coming out of these gargoyles are just natural gas seeping out of the ground; the closing of the demon's mouth was just a mechanical trick. We are the only ones down here: you can count on that, Bill." He folded his arms and smiled a satisfied sort of smile, but the smile was soon wiped right of his face,

"YOU WANNA BET?" A harsh, gruff voice echoed out down the passageway. Everyone ran to hide behind Aracuria.

"Who, who is it?" quivered Rhiannon.

Aracuria suddenly became aware of someone standing only a few feet away, hidden beneath one of the gargoyles. The next moment a man dressed like a Red Indian stepped out of the shadows.

"I am Hahgwehdaetgah: who are you?" Rhiannon stepped out from behind Aracuria. "Hahawhat?" she said.

"HAHGWEHDAETGAH!" boomed the Indian.

"THERE'S NO NEED TO SHOUT!" Rhiannon yelled back, but her voice didn't sound even half as loud, The Red Indian folded his arms.

"I shan't repeat this again: who are you, why have you come here? I am HAHGWEHDAETGAH! The first Guardian of the land of the Living Dead. Answer, or you will die at my hands."

Aracuria stepped forward.

"We are looking for the Ring of Ra, held inside the gemstone of the Idol of Thlagtha. Does this passageway lead to the bottom of the Most Holy Fountain of Theom..?"

He was cut short by the scream of a horrific battle cry. From each side of the Red Indian's neck, the head of a reptile and the head of a lion burst out, while fangs appeared in the central, human head. "AARRAGH!" screamed Rhiannon as Hahgwehdaetgah charged at Aracuria. The reptile's head was dripping in saliva, while the lion's head had blood on its razor sharp teeth. Aracuria took one look at the three-headed monster and collapsed to the ground.

Hahgwehdaetgah, however, was now traveling at full speed: his feet caught on the now slumped body of Aracuria and he took off. Rhiannon turned to run, but only succeeded in hitting Klut, who immediately fell back and hit Bill. Just then Hahgwehdaetgah hit the three of them and they all crashed to the ground in a pile. For a moment there was total confusion then Bill opened his eyes to see that he was staring into the bloodshot eyes of the reptile, Klut found that he had his arms around the lion's neck, while Rhiannon discovered that she had somehow got her finger in the ear of the Red Indian head, a fact which he didn't seem to appreciate.

Simultaneously, all three heads tried to eat Rhiannon, Klut and Bill.
"Aracuria: DO SOMETHING!" shrieked Rhiannon.

Aracuria quickly jumped up. His eyes darted around the passageway to see if there was something that he could hit Hahgwehdaetgah with. Then he caught sight of a club propped up against the wall. He snatched it up, rushed back to where Rhiannon, Klut and Bill were trapped on the ground, swung the club once around his head and then brought it crashing down against one of the heads. Under the force of the blow, the head of the reptile came right off and in its place a thick, green fluid oozed out all over Bill.
"UGH!" screamed Bill.
Aracuria swung the club once again and this time brought it down on the lion's head. The lion's head broke off from Hahgwehdaetgah and in its place yet more of the thick green stuff began to pump over Klut.
"Ugh!" said Aracuria, as he realized what he had done. Klut, Bill and Rhiannon quickly scrambled out from under Hahgwehdaetgah, who as far as anyone could tell was now dead.
Rhiannon was very angry. "'No one here', he said!" she fumed. "No one here: then what exactly is this three headed monster that has just tried to eat us, you flat-headed alien squirt?"

Klut, however, didn't answer, as he was too busy trying to clear the green, glue-like stuff from his clothes.
"It's, it's a monster," said Bill in horrored disbelief. Aracuria was just about to say that it was when he noticed that Hahgwehdaetgah was starting to move.
"He isn't dead!" he gulped. "RUN!"

Without another word the four of them ran as fast as they could down the passageway, just as Hahgwehdaetgah dragged himself to his feet.

"I AM HAHGWEHDAETGAH: THE EARTH SHAKER!" His voice echoed out down the passageway. Suddenly the ground began to shake, the roof began to crack and the next moment the whole rock ceiling of the passageway above Hahgwehdaetgah collapsed, burying him completely. The ceiling down the whole length of the passageway now started to crack open and slowly it all began to crumble and crash to the ground behind Aracuria and the others. All four of them ran as fast as they could, but the collapsing passageway was catching them up.

"We're going to be buried!" wailed Bill, as the dust from the roof engulfed them all.

Suddenly they all found themselves flying through the air and the next moment they were crashing down a flight of steps, until they hit an earth floor. Then everything went very quiet and in the silence all they could hear was the sound of bird-song. Aracuria picked himself up and looked around him. He saw that they were in a large amphitheatre carved out of the rock.

Above them, at the top of the amphitheatre, was the passageway, only now it was blocked with fallen rocks, while on the left of the amphitheatre was another, open, archway on which sat a blue humming bird, of which none of them took any notice.

"Where are we?" panted Rhiannon as she dragged herself to her feet.

"It looks like an amphitheatre," said Aracuria.

"A what?" said Bill.

"Don't you know anything?" grumbled Klut. Bill shook his head quietly. "An amphitheatre is a place where gladiators used to fight each other in ancient times: a barbaric practice if ever there was one..." Klut was about to say more but he was suddenly cut short by a loud voice that echoed out through the amphitheatre.

"SAYS WHO?"

Everyone fell silent: on the far left of the amphitheatre, just where the blue hummingbird had been singing, had appeared a gladiator dressed up in what looked like a half finished suit of armor. On his head he had a wide brimmed steel helmet; over his right arm and chest he wore steel plates that were shaped to fit his body; in his left hand he held a net and in his right he had an enormous double bladed sword.

"Who, who are you?" asked Klut quietly,

"I am Huitzilopochtli, the Second Guardian of the land of the Living Dead. My mission and my task is war. I slaughter who I will and I eat who I slaughter. Now answer me: who are YOU, flat-head, and what are you doing here?"

Klut suddenly looked very frightened. Rhiannon, seeing that he was frightened stepped forward and decided to speak for him.

"Look here Mr. Huit-whats-your-name, we are looking for the Ring of Ra, held inside the gemstone of the Idol of Thlagtha. Do you happen to know if this archway leads to the bottom of the Most Holy Fountain of Theom...?"

But as it turned out, that was the worst thing that she could have said. Suddenly Huitzilopochtli let out a fearsome roar: his eyes flashed red and his skin blistered with horrible sores which began weep a thick yellow stuff. The next second he charged at Klut, threw his net over his head and dragged him to the floor.

Huitzilopochtli raised his great sword above his head and brought it crashing down on to the ground in order to cut Klut in half.

"Aracuria: DO SOMETHING!" screamed Rhiannon. But Aracuria and Bill were frozen to the spot in horror. Without waiting any longer, Rhiannon charged forward, raised her feet in the air and brought them crashing down on Huitzilopochtli's side. She bounced off and landed flat on the ground, but the blow also knocked Huitzilopochtli momentarily off balance and his huge sword sliced harmlessly through the air. However, he would soon be on his feet again and they needed weapons to fight him with.

"Aracuria: do something!" shouted Rhiannon in desperation. Aracuria looked around the amphitheatre, but saw nothing of any use. He ran off in the direction of the archway and there, hidden in the passageway, he found a shield, a spear and two swords.

"I've got some weapons!" he cried. But Huitzilopochtli was now back up and about to strike Klut again. Aracuria picked up the shield and rolled it along the ground to where Klut was lying. Huitzilopochtli raised his sword once again and brought it crashing down, just as the shield rolled in front of Klut. Klut quickly forced his hands through the net, grasped the shield and, just in time, managed to lift it up as the sword came down to cut off his head. There was a massive CLUNK as the sword hit the shield and Klut shuddered under the impact. Aracuria picked up the spear.

"Rhiannon: catch!"

Rhiannon jumped up from the ground where she had been lying, just as the spear came whizzing through the air and landed in her hand. Aracuria picked up the two remaining swords and threw one to Bill, who tried to grab it but missed. Meanwhile, Huitzilopochtli had gone into a frenzy and was now repeatedly trying to hit Klut, who was now holding the shield above him for dear life.

"Quickly!" shouted Aracuria, "We've got to kill him before he kills Klut." Rhiannon ran forward and prodded the spear into Huitzilopochtli's side. Huitzilopochtli growled in pain, turned, slashed out with his sword and cut Rhiannon's spear in two.

It was now up to Aracuria and Bill. Aracuria ran forward with his sword, swung it once around his head and brought it crashing down on Huitzilopochtli's back. Huitzilopochtli roared in agony, spun around with his sword and tried to cut Aracuria in two. Aracuria raised his sword and managed to block the blow, but all the same he was knocked off his feet. Just then Bill, who had only just managed to pick up his heavy sword, began to whirl it around his head like Aracuria had done, only once he had started spinning he found that he couldn't stop. Like a top, he spun across the ground with the sword outstretched. He came right alongside Huitzilopochtli, and without a clue what he was doing, cut off Huitzilopochtli's left leg. Everyone was astonished, Huitzilopochtli most of all. He looked down as his left leg fell away and, not being able to stand on one leg, he keeled over and crashed to the ground.

"Quickly !Let's get out of here!" shouted Aracuria. Rhiannon rushed forward and helped the dazed Klut out of the net and together they dashed after Aracuria though the archway and down the passageway that lay beyond. For a moment Bill just stood there and stared at Huitzilopoehtli as he lay sprawled, helpless, across the floor.

"I cut off his leg! I cut off his leg!" he shouted triumphantly, though a little unsure as to how he had done it. Then realizing that he was all alone, he threw the sword away and chased after the others.

CHAPTER TEN: THE GOD OF DEATH

Aracuria finally stopped running. Rhiannon and Klut came to halt beside him. They waited, panting, for Bill to catch them up. Aracuria looked around the passageway, with its rows of flaming gargoyle heads and tried to decide what to do next.
“"This place is worse than I thought,” he said. “At least on Draco all we had to do was answer questions, but here we’ve got to fight our way through past everyone.”

Klut was still very shaken up, but he felt he had to say something. “The reason for that is obvious,” he said.
“What do you mean by that’?” asked Rhiannon.
Klut tried to calm himself and then continued. “Both Huitzilopochtli and Hahgwehdaetgah went crazy when we said that we wanted to get to the Most Holy Fountain of Theom. Well, do you remember what Gayomart said, how the people who lived down here, when they died, would go to a place with an unpronounceable name where there lived a Great Chicken? Now what if the Most Holy Fountain of Theom and this place with the unpronounceable name are one and the same...?” Everyone understood, except Bill.
“So you mean, they think we’re going to harm this Great Chicken?” said Aracuria.
“Or steal her eggs,” said Klut, “which they believe contain the souls of their dead ancestors.”
“So,” said Aracuria, “as long as we don’t mention what were down here for, we should be able to get past the Ghouls without having to fight them?”
“Exactly,” said Klut. Everyone began to feel much better, except Bill who hadn’t really understood what Klut had been talking about.
“Come on then,” said Aracuria, “let’s find out what lies at the end of this tunnel.” Without another word the four of them set off down the long, sloping stone passageway.

After about half an hour of walking, the passageway suddenly opened up into an enormous graveyard. There was a circular stone wall with an old gate beyond which lay hundreds of lopsided gravestones and in the distance there were the ruins of an old church with a rickety steeple.
“This looks really creepy,” shivered Rhiannon, pushing open the rusty gate.
“Remember,” said Klut, “Whatever happens, never say anything about the Most Holy Fountain of Theom: got it?”
Everyone nodded, including Bill, who repeated quietly to himself, “Never say anything about the Most Holy Fountain of Theom.”

They entered the graveyard cautiously. There was a single stone path that led straight past the ruined church. As they were walking along this, Klut began looking at the names on the gravestones: they were all very long and utterly unpronounceable. Everything was eerily quiet, so quiet in fact that no one dared speak. Finally, they came to the open doorway of the church. Aracuria glanced in and saw that there saw someone inside it, standing by what remained of the altar. He was dressed from head to foot in a black cape, only the cape was all tattered and torn. Aracuria and the others were just about to walk on when the figure suddenly spun around.

"WHO IS IT?" he bellowed.

Klut timidly stepped forward and said, "Klut, and some friends."

The man in the tattered black cape stepped forward. He was middle-aged, with white, unhealthy looking skin and hair. "My name is MICTLANTECUHTLI! Third and last Guardian of the land of the Living Dead. What are you doing in my churchyard?"

"We're just passing through," said Rhiannon hopefully.

"To WHERE?" said the man.

"Oh, nowhere," said Aracuria. A suspicious look came across Mictlantecuhtli face, and then he suddenly smiled viciously.

"If you're going nowhere, then you've come to the right place." He began to laugh and as he laughed so a row of black and yellow teeth came into view.

"Looks like they have a sense of humor down here," said Rhiannon.

"And no dentists," added Aracuria.

"WHAT DID YOU SAY'?" shouted Mictlantecuhtli, his smile disappearing. Suddenly Bill spoke out as if he were reading a script, "Never say anything about the Most Holy Fountain of Theom."

Klut, Aracuria and Rhiannon stared at him in horror. Then Mictlantecuhtli ripped the cape from off his back, his eyes shriveled up in his head, his skin peeled away from his face and his bones began to protrude from his flesh.

"I AM MICTLANTECUHTLI: GOD OF DEATH!"

"AARRAGH!" they all screamed, as Mictlantecuhtli, who was now little more than a skeleton, ran at them at a frightening speed. Aracuria, Klut and Rhiannon jumped out of the way, but Bill just stood where he was, unsure what to do. The next moment Mictlantecuhtli

bore down on him. Bill finally turned and tried to run, but before he could move off the spot Mictlantecuhtli had reached down and with his long, bony fingers he grasped Bill's jumper and gently picked him up.

"I'm going to skin you alive," said Mictlantecuhtli, "and then I'm going to stew what remains of you." His skull-like head peered down at Bill as Bill wailed in terror.

"Aracuria: DO SOMETHING!" shouted Rhiannon. Without a second thought Aracuria jumped forward and punched Mictlantecuhtli in the side of the head. But his fist hit solid bone and all he could do was yell in agony as his knuckles bruised heavily. While he nursed his hand, Mictlantecuhtli, who hadn't even noticed Aracuria's punch, turned around and began to walk back into the church with Bill dangling from his fingers. Something had to be

done quickly. Rhiannon noticed that there was a rope hanging just beside her. She looked up and saw that at the top of the steeple was a large bell to which the rope connected.
"If you want something done, you have to do it yourself," she muttered. She took hold of the rope and pulled on it with all her might: nothing happened.
"Klut: HELP ME!" Klut grabbed the rope and pulled as well: nothing happened. Then Mictlantecuhtli turned to look at them.
"And after I've eaten him, I'm going to eat both of you as well," he said.
"You wanna bet?" shouted Aracuria angrily, as he rushed forward and swung on the rope alongside Rhiannon and Klut. Suddenly, high above, came an enormous CREAK. Mictlantecuhtli just had time to look up to see the massive bronze bell come crashing out of the belfry, before it hit him square on the head. Under the force of the blow, Mictlantecuhtli exploded into a mass of bones that shattered and splintered everywhere.

When the dust had cleared Mictlantecuhtli was nowhere to be seen, while Bill was standing alone next to the bell with his eyes tightly closed.
"Come on, let's got out of here!" shouted Aracuria. They raced through the rest of the graveyard, jumped over the far wall and then shuddered to a halt: in front of them was a vast marble staircase, lit by thousands of gargoyle heads. The staircase seemed to go down into the center of the earth. In fact it was so long that none of them could see where it ended. "What are we going to do now?" asked Rhiannon. "It'll take us years to walk down all those steps." Aracuria had an idea. He ran back to the graveyard and jumped back over the wall. "Give me a hand to dig up one of these gravestones." he shouted.
"What?"
"Just do as I say!" The others bounded over the wall and began to dig at the foot of one of the gravestones, trying as hard as they could to pull it out of the ground. Finally, the gravestone came loose and they were able to pull it free.
"What do we do with it now?" asked Rhiannon, but before Aracuria had time to answer, something terrible happened: the hand of a skeleton burst through the ground beneath their feet and clutched the bottom of the gravestone.
"Quickly! We've got to carry it to the stairwell." Aracuria kicked the skeleton's hand off the gravestone and the four tried as hard as they could to carry the heavy stone towards the wall.

As they staggered away, so more bony hands and skulls began to appear from other graves in the cemetery. By the time they had reached the wall, the graveyard was full of skeletons dressed in rotten rags, all of whom were making their way towards them. Rhiannon glanced behind and shuddered.
"I hope you know what you're doing!" she called to Aracuria. Hurriedly they slid the gravestone over the wall and stumbled towards the stairway. The skeletons were now clambering and falling over the wall. As they reached the

stairs Aracuria shouted, "Put the gravestone down on the ground and then jump on it. Once the three of you are on, I'll push the stone down the stairs and jump on myself. Then we can all slide down to the bottom." Rhiannon, Klut and Bill looked at him in horror.
"You must be kidding!" they shouted. Just then the first skeleton grabbed Aracuria. Aracuria turned around and kicked him away, "Have you got a better idea?" They hadn't .

The three of them jumped onto the gravestone, Aracuria pushed it over the edge and jumped on board. At that moment all of the skeletons finally reached the stairway and as Aracuria and the others whizzed away into the distance, the skeletons began tumbling and crashing down the stairs, until all that was left of them was a mass of broken bones.

The gravestone was now sliding down the steps at a frightening speed. Rhiannon, Klut and Bill hung on grimly, while Aracuria knelt behind them. The flaming gargoyle heads were flashing past so fast they were beginning to blur into two continuous strips of light. The stairway seemed endless as it plummeted down to the center of the earth, but the longer it seemed the faster they seemed to go, until in they end they all had to close their eyes as everything became a blur.

The next moment there was an enormous crash as the gravestone hit something and shattered into a thousand pieces. Aracuria found himself catapulted into the air, while Rhiannon and the others went rolling away to one side. There was utter confusion. When he opened his eyes, Aracuria found that he was hanging over the branches of a tree.
"Where am I?" he groaned. Rhiannon, Klut and Bill were all crumpled together up against something which looked like a giant cabbage. One by one they picked themselves up, while Aracuria scrambled down out of the tree and looked around. They appeared to be in a kind of garden or ornamental park, filled with strange trees and odd looking plants. Rhiannon came to Aracuria's side. "Do you think this is IT?" she said, without mentioning the name that had got them into so much trouble.
Aracuria shook his head. "I don't know."

In front of them was a pathway that led through a ruined stone arch and on into another tunnel that was covered in darkness, while in front of the stone arch, set right in the middle of the path, was a round stone pillar sticking up out of the ground. Klut walked up beside them.
"I think that's the way we've got to go," he said, pointing at the arch.

They waited for Bill to join them and then made their way towards the arch. Suddenly, before they had even reached the stone pillar, three men appeared out of nowhere and blocked the archway. One was all black, the other was all white and the third was half black and half white, with the join running straight down the center of his face. Rhiannon took one look at them, turned to Aracuria and said, "Our troubles aren't over yet." She had never spoken a truer word.

CHAPTER ELEVEN: BEYOND THE ARCHWAY

The all-black man stepped forward,
"My name is Mangarkunjerkunja: What do you want here?" he said
"We want to pass through that archway," said Rhiannon defiantly. Then the all white man stepped forward.
"My name is Tamapoulialamafoa," he said, "Why do you want to pass?"
"Do we have to give you a reason?" said Aracuria.
Then the half white and half black man spoke.
"My name is Andriambahomanana. You have done well to get so far. We are the Questioners. Beyond this archway lie the two Doorkeepers of the Most Holy Unpronounceable Place, where the spirits of our dead ancestors sleep. The Doorkeepers will do all they can to stop you entering the Unpronounceable place, but first you must pass by us. The Doorkeepers are so awesome they will destroy anyone they meet, but if you satisfy us we will give you the information you will need to pass them." The black and white man stopped. "Do you understand all this?" Aracuria nodded silently. "Good, but first you must satisfy us." he said.

Andriambahomanana walked forward until he was standing in front of the pillar. Then he opened out his hands and passed them through the air in front of him. Suddenly, a series of lights, like little stars, appeared on the top of the pillar. The lights were red and blue and gold and they seemed to flash on and off and move around in mid air. Inside the lights something began to appear. Gradually it took shape. Andriambahomanana stepped back and as he did so the lights disappeared and in their place was the most exquisite golden chalice that any of them had ever seen. It had a round, conical shaped stand, above which was a wide brimmed bowl with two handles on either side. All this was in bright, yellow gold, but set around the base of the stand and around the side of the bowl were rubies and emeralds, each with its own intricate pattern-work of gold setting.

"Wow!" said Rhiannon, as the chalice began to glow of its own accord.
"This is the chalice that Mug Ruith the Magician stole from the god-king Cormac Mac Airt. In a fit of temper Cormac Mac Airt consigned both the Mug Ruith and the chalice to this desert planet and when our forefathers came underground to look for the gemstone of Thlagtha they brought this with them. This chalice has special properties that will test whether you are fit to pass us by." Andriambahomanana fell silent for a moment; he looked into the eyes of each of them, looked down at the chalice and then stared at Rhiannon. "Are you scared of what is to come?" he asked. No one knew what to say: Andriambahomanana hadn't said anything about how they were going to be tested, and if they gave the wrong answer presumably they wouldn't be allowed through, so no one said anything.

"We can wait, forever, if need be," said Andriambahomanana. The fact that Andriambahomanana was staring at her all the time and the thought of waiting there forever really annoyed Rhiannon, "No, of course we're not scared." she said.

Suddenly there was a loud noise as a crack appeared in the side of the chalice. Andriambahomanana continued talking as if nothing had happened but his gaze had shifted to Aracuria,

"Did you desecrate the graveyard of our ancestors before coming down the great stairs?" he asked quietly,

"Of course not," said Aracuria, "We just made our escape by the only way we could..."

Before Aracuria could finish speaking there was a loud noise, like the sound of metal splitting as yet another crack appeared in the chalice. Aracuria looked at it in horror, but before he could say anything Andriambahomanana started speaking again, only this time he was staring at Klut. "Have you ever been made to look foolish by being shown to be wrong in something you said?" he asked.

Klut folded his arms haughtily. "I don't know about these others, but I never have." he said proudly. Suddenly a loud ripping sound began to fill the air and then, in front of their very eyes, the golden chalice fell apart into a hundred pieces. Gold decoration, emeralds and rubies crashed on to the top of the stone pillar until there was nothing left but a rubble of jewelry.

Andriambahomanana stepped back.

"You are unfit to pass us by," he said, "When three lies are spoken over the chalice of Cormac Mac Airt, the chalice breaks into pieces."

Rhiannon, Aracuria and Klut looked at each other in horror: that was the test, and they didn't know anything about it. They had all lied, and they knew it. Rhiannon had been scared of what the two monster Doorkeepers might be like; in ripping up a gravestone Aracuria had desecrated the churchyard and Klut had been wrong about there not being anyone underground, although he didn't like to admit it.

"What are we going to do now?" asked Bill. None of them had an answer. For a moment there was silence and then Andriambahomanana stepped forward.

"Restore the chalice to its former shape and then answer a few more questions and we will let you pass." Immediately Rhiannon and Aracuria ran forward and tried to put the chalice together. They tried fitting the emeralds and rubies back into their gold settings, but they kept falling out again; they tried putting the gold pieces of the base back together, but none of them seemed to fit; they tried putting the handles back on what remained of the bowl, but they just didn't seem to join up.

Finally, Rhiannon gave up in exasperation. "This is pointless," she said. "We'll never do it."

Aracuria tried a little while longer, but then he too gave up.

"You're right: not even a master craftsman like Gayomart could put it together: it's impossible." He turned away in disgust. Then Bill stepped forward. He looked at the broken chalice and remembered how wonderful it had looked when it was all whole and then he said,
"It was stupid to tell lies in front of something as beautiful as this: I'm sorry we ever broke it." Andriambahomanana smiled to himself. The next moment the lights appeared on top of the stone pillar: they completely covered the ruins of the chalice. Bill watched in amazement as they floated and hovered in the air. Then, as suddenly as they had come, they vanished and in their place was the golden chalice, fully restored once again.
"How did you do that?" shouted Rhiannon in disbelief, but Bill remained speechless, as he didn't know either.
Then Andriambahomanana spoke. "Tell three lies over the chalice of Cormac Mac Airt and you will destroy it: tell three truths and you will make it whole again, and it is true that trying to put it together by hand was pointless, and that not even Gayomart could rebuild it, and that the young man was sorry you had broken it." Andriambahomanana fell silent, but neither he nor the other two men moved out of the way of the arch.

"You said we had to answer other questions to get past," said Aracuria. "What are they?" Andriambahomanana turned his gaze upon him.
"On the way down here you passed the Three Guardians of the Underworld: Mictlantecuhtli, Huitzilopochtli and Hahgwehdaetgah. Our first question is: tell us the meaning of one of their names."

Everyone turned to Klut, who was the only one who might possibly know. Klut looked glum. "Why are you looking at me? I don't know what those names mean,' he said, "I can hardly pronounce them, let alone tell you what they mean: in all the books I've ever read I have never, ever heard of them before, or of any of the other weird names that everyone seems to have down here." Everyone now felt equally unhappy. Rhiannon turned to Andriambahomanana.
"How can we work them out if we have never heard of them before?" she said, but Andriambahomanana said nothing.
"They knew that already," said Klut sorely, "and if they knew that already then they know that we couldn't answer the questions at all."
"But that is not true," said Andriambahomanana. Then an idea came in Aracuria's head. "If what Andri-whats-his-name says is true..."
"It is, the chalice would crack otherwise," said Andriambahomanana.
"...Then the meaning of at least one of the Guardians' names must have been given to us when we were with them." Andriambahomanana smiled to himself. Rhiannon saw the smile and then said, "Well, when we saw Hahg-whats-his-name, he sprouted three heads: does his name mean 'Man-with-three-heads'?" she asked.

Andriambahomanana gave her a kindly glance, "No it doesn't, but you're on the right track."
That cheered everyone up. "When we met the second guy, the God of War..."
"Huitzilopochtli," said Andriambahomanana.
"Yeah, him," said Aracuria, "when we first met him he had a suit of armor on. Is he called something like: 'One-who-wears-a-suit-of-armor.'?"
Andriambahomanana almost burst out laughing. "No." he said.

Then Bill said something which seemed unimportant.
"Before he appeared there was a blue humming-bird on the left," he said, but everyone ignored him, except Andriambahomanana.
"You are right." he said. Everyone looked in astonishment at Bill, who was himself astonished. "Huitzilopochtli in our language translates directly into yours as 'Blue-humming- bird-on-the-left."' Everyone was silenced. Rhiannon was so impressed she reached across and kissed Bill on the cheek. "You're a genius," she said, which made Bill blush terribly.

Andriambahomanana stepped forward and picked up the chalice.
"If we let you pass, will you harm the eggs of the Great Mother Chicken that contain the unhatched souls of our dead ancestors?" he asked.
"No," said everyone: the chalice didn't crack.
"If we allow you to pass, will you damage or desecrate our most Holy of Places," asked Andriambahomanana.
"No," said everyone again, and again the chalice didn't crack.
"If we let you pass and you make it to the Most Holy of Places, do you know how to get out again without returning the way you have come?"

Everyone looked horrified. "No," they all said. Once again the chalice didn't crack, though everyone present knew it wouldn't.
"Very well then," said Andriambahomanana, "you may pass and meet the Doorkeepers of the Most Holy Place. To help you pass the First Doorkeeper, 'The-great-one-who-opens-to-the-sky', I will just say this: all life comes from the open sea. And to help you pass the Second Doorkeeper, 'Lord-of-the-house-of-dawn', I will just say this: the tongue of the Unpronounceable place is the ancient and holy language of Mug Ruith and his daughter that we are all forbidden from uttering, except the Second Doorkeeper." Once he had finished speaking, Andriambahomanana, the Chalice, the all black man and the all white man disappeared into thin air as if they had never been there.

"What do we do now?" said Bill. Aracuria stepped forward.
"We go see the two Doorkeepers and hope our luck holds out," he said.

They walked around the stone pillar, under the stone archway, through a passageway and then stopped: it had suddenly became very hot. In front of them was a waterfall which fell like a curtain over the end of the passageway. The water was as clear as glass and beyond it Aracuria could see a huge chamber that seemed to be full of flames: it looked the most uninviting place he had ever seen. They were going to need their good luck more than ever.

CHAPTER TWELVE: THE SEA DEMON

Aracuria walked towards the waterfall and stopped: inside the flaming room he could hear screams. He glanced across at Rhiannon, who looked really scared, then he took a deep breath and walked through the waterfall. When he came out on the other side he was confronted not by a room at all, but an immense sea which curved around, to left and right, in a ring shape. On either side of the sea rock walls rose straight up out of the water and then shot up miles into the air where they came together as a vaulted rock ceiling. Aracuria looked down at the water and saw that it was bubbling and boiling, with great jets of steam breaking to the surface, and as each jet broke through into the air, it gave a scream that sounded just like a human voice. The waters themselves seemed to be on fire: deep inside them Aracuria could see flames and fires burning fiercely, and every now and then huge bubbles would reach the surface and a brief flash of flames would burst out.

In front of him was a steel suspension bridge that ran from the waterfall right across the sea to the far side, where there was another waterfall in the opposite wall. He walked on to the bridge and stared down at the sea. Beneath the water there was a dull red glow that lit up everything, as if the molten core of the earth lay beneath the sea, just a few miles down.

"Are you okay?" called Rhiannon from the other side of the waterfall.

"Yeah," he shouted. Rhiannon summoned up her courage and stepped through the waterfall.

"WOW!" she exclaimed as she saw the sea. Hearing her cry, Klut and Bill stepped through it together: both of them were speechless.

"What is this place?" wondered Rhiannon. Klut peered down at the dull red glow coming up from beneath the sea.

"We must be close to the very center of the planet," he said. "These must be primeval waters that somehow got trapped down here long ago. The molten core of heavy metals at the center of the planet must heat them up like this, and I suppose when the fountain of Theom was flowing it was the pressure generated by all this heat that threw it up to the surface."

Rhiannon turned to Aracuria. "But this place is empty and that half black and white man said that the second Doorkeeper lived here. How could he? Nothing could live in these waters."

Aracuria shook his head. "Maybe he meant that we had to go over the bridge first."

"Whatever he meant," said Bill, "let's get out of here: this place is scary."

Everyone agreed. One by one they set off along the suspension bridge with the screaming jets of steam and flaming bubbles bursting around them. As they walked in silence, so the bridge began to sway gently, but it was made of such heavy beams of steel that this didn't worry any of them.

They had just passed the halfway mark on the bridge when Rhiannon stopped.

"Did you hear something then? It sounded like..." Rhiannon never finished her sentence, because just then the whole flaming sea parted and a gigantic monster burst above the waters.

"AARRAGH!" everyone screamed as the huge beast continued growing out of the sea until it towered high above them. The monster was unlike anything they had ever seen, it was huge and red and covered in shiny scales. It had seven heads and ten horns and on each of the heads part of a name was written into the flesh. The first head was the head of man with big bulging eyes and a long, pointed tongue that flapped about its face; the second head was the head of a lion with massive teeth; the third head was the head of a bear with what looked like three red ribs in its mouth, as if it had just eaten something; the fourth head was the head of a leopard with a black, silky face and evil eyes; the fifth head seemed to be all bone with just sockets where the eyes should be and with teeth made of iron; the sixth had the head of a ram with wide, curved horns and the seventh head was the head of a dog with sharp, pointy ears.

Aracuria stared at the Beast with his eyes wide open and his jaw touching his chest.

"How do we get past THAT?" No one answered, but the first head began to laugh.

"My name is PAHUANUIAPITAAITERAI!" His voice exploded around the vast walls of the sea and made everyone clasp their ears. "I am the First Doorkeeper to the Most Holy Unpronounceable Place." Nobody knew what to say for a moment, but everybody was filled with terror.

"Run for it!" screamed Aracuria at last, as this was the only thing he could think of doing.

In blind terror they raced across the bridge as fast as their legs could carry them, and all the time they ran, all they could hear was the booming sound as the first head laughed uncontrollably. Aracuria glanced over his shoulder as he ran and noticed that the monster hadn't moved an inch. The second waterfall was only a few hundred feet away and he was certain they could make it.

"We're in with a chance!" he gasped.

Just then, up ahead of them, a huge, shiny tendril looking for all the world like the limb of an octopus, burst through the surface of the sea beside the suspension bridge. It shot high into the air, a thousand meters or more, like some fleshy skyscraper. Aracuria gazed up at it, but he couldn't believe it had anything to do with the monster that was now so far away. Suddenly, the skyscraper of flesh toppled over. At a lightning speed it came down and hit the top of the suspension bridge, while the rest of it crashed into the water for a thousand meters or more. A moment later, the tendril burst through the waters on the other side, flew up into the air, came down again across the bridge and back into the water on the other side.

"It's wrapping itself around the bridge!" cried Klut. Everyone shuddered to a halt, as the winding coil went spinning faster and faster around the bridge like an almighty Catherine Wheel. The coils of the tendril began to race towards them, as the chains that supported the bridge were crushed flat.

"RUN!" shouted Rhiannon as the coils came spinning towards them and the water exploded around. Aracuria and the others turned and fled in the direction of the monster. The bridge itself now began to shake wildly, and before they had finished running, they were all thrown off their feet on to the floor of the bridge and knocked against the supporting chains which hung on either side.

Aracuria clung with all his strength to one of the chains as the bridge lashed about, completely out of control, threatening to throw them into the boiling water. When the movement of the bridge had slowed a bit, he looked over the side and saw that the tendril, which was now completely out of the water, was nothing other than a limb of the Monster. The beast gradually came closer as it pulled itself along by the tendril. Finally it stopped once again beside them. All the heads were gnashing their teeth, except the first, human one, which was about to speak.

"You really are silly, aren't you?" it said. "I am Pahuanuiapitaaiterai, the sea Demon of the deep and nothing can get past me unless I will it."

Aracuria waited until the bridge stopped swaying and then he dragged himself up and looked at the first head; he watched for a while as the long, forked tongue of the monster slicked back the human head's hair, and then he said, "How do we get past you?"

The first head smiled. "Simple: answer one question and I will let you through."

Rhiannon stood up. "What is it?" she demanded.

The human head swiveled right round on its socket and came back to face them again.

"Which is the greater: salt water or sweet water?"

Aracuria and Rhiannon looked at each other, then at Klut, who was getting to his feet. Aracuria and Rhiannon both spoke at the same time.

"What on earth is sweet water?"

"It's not on Earth at all actually," replied Klut. "In fact it isn't supposed to be anywhere, it's just a name that people used to give to what they thought were imaginary waters that lay beneath the salt seas of the Earth and other planets. I suppose at one time they thought that if there were whole seas of salt water on the surface of the planet, then there must be whole seas of sweet water beneath the surface. Sweet water would accordingly taste a bit like cream soda."

Rhiannon loved cream soda.

“Well then sweet water must be better than salt water,” she said to Klut.
“Is that your answer?” asked the monster.
“NO!” said Klut quickly, rounding on Rhiannon, “Just because you like cream soda doesn’t mean that sweet water is greater than salt water: do you remember what Andriambahomanana said? He said that ‘all life comes from the open sea’ .The open sea is salt water.”
Rhiannon stared at him, puzzled. “So is salt water the answer?”
Klut shook his head. “I don’t know, and I don’t know because it isn’t as simple as that.” He looked down at the some of the puddles of water that had splashed on to the bridge. He knelt down, dipped his finger into one of them and then put it into his mouth.
“Don’t do that,” said Rhiannon, “it must taste horrible: salt water always does.”
“But it doesn’t,” said Klut. “That’s the whole problem.”

A look of amazement came over Rhiannon’s face. She knelt down and tasted one of the puddles at her feet.
“IT IS CREAM SODA!” she cried.
“It’s a whole sea of cream soda!” retorted Klut, “or, as it’s always been known, sweet water. So which is the greater, the salt water that gives life to all living things, or the sweet water that gave life to THIS THING?” He pointed to the Monster. Rhiannon straightened up.
“Now I understand why it isn’t so simple,” she said.

All this time Aracuria had been listening quietly: he knew the answer because a quiet voice inside of him had just said what it was.
“It’s salt water,” he said. “The answer is salt water.”
Rhiannon, Klut and Bill looked at him in horror, thinking that he had just guessed the answer. Then the human head of the Monster nodded.
“You are right, young man.” Everyone jumped for joy. Rhiannon ran across and kissed Aracuria.
“What a brilliant guess!” she cried, “What a brilliant guess.”
“It wasn’t a guess,” said Aracuria, “someone told me the answer,” but with all the jumping and shouting no one heard him.

As quickly as the coils of the tendril had wound around the bridge, so now they unwound. When the way was clear and the bridge had stopped swaying, Aracuria and the others walked across it to the far edge, while the sea demon Pahuanuiapitaaiterai slipped beneath the waters. Up ahead was the second waterfall and beyond it lay the second Doorkeeper and the last and most difficult test that they would have to face before they came to the Most Holy Place with the Unpronounceable name.

CHAPTER THIRTEEN: THE LAST QUESTION

Aracuria left the suspension bridge and walked up to the waterfall: it seemed to be glowing. He stopped for a moment, and then walked through the waterfall. When he came out on the other side he found himself blinded by a brilliant light. He half-closed his eyes and looked down to the ground, but the ground was glowing white; he looked up above and stared at the sky, but the sky was burning with light; he turned around and around, but all he could see was this intense whiteness that was already beginning to give him a headache.

"Rhiannon!" he shouted. The next moment Rhiannon and the others stepped through the waterfall and found themselves in the same predicament.

"What is this place?" asked Rhiannon. "I can't see a thing."

"Close your eyes," said Aracuria. "Everyone, close your eyes or we'll all go blind."

For a few moments they stumbled about in the light, but the light was so intense and it seemed to be coming from everywhere, so that there was nothing they could do, nowhere they could walk. In fact, if it continued like this they would have turn back.

"Will someone put out this light!" shouted Aracuria in desperation, his headache becoming intolerable. As soon as he spoke, the light vanished. He opened his eyes and saw that they were standing in a dark place, but high up in the air he could see a brilliant golden glow that seemed to be half hidden. Aracuria still couldn't see very well: he stood still and waited for his eyes to clear. When they did he had the shock of this life: high above him there was a woman clothed in the circle of the Sun. Beneath her was the horned crescent of the Moon on which her bare feet rested and on her head she wore twelve stars as a crown.

Aracuria was astonished; although he couldn't see her face, he could tell that she was beautiful. He was just about to step forward to see who she was when a loud voice bellowed out behind him, "What are you DOING HERE?" He swung round and saw that there was a man standing in the sun, without any moon or stars, and for that reason he didn't look half as amazing as the woman.

"Who are you?" asked Aracuria.

"I am TLAUIXCALPANTECUHTLI!" exploded the man, "The Lord of the House of Dawn. What are you doing HERE?" Rhiannon walked up to Aracuria's side.

"We want to go through to the Unpronounceable Place," she said. "Do you know where it is?"

"Yes, I do," said the man, "but first you will to tell me your names, your first names and family names."

Klut turned to Aracuria. "This may be easier than we thought," he said. He looked up at the man in the sun. "My name is Klut, and my family, or surname is Ibalwattle."
"What?" burst out Aracuria and Rhiannon, falling about laughing.
Bill stared at Klut. "I didn't know that was your surname," he said.
"So what's new?" said Klut sarcastically.

The man in the sun bellowed out, "You others, what are your names?"
"My name is Bill," shouted Bill.
"What is your family name?" said the man in the sun.
"I, I don't know," said Bill apologetically, "I don't think we've got one."
"Very well," said the man in the sun, "Let me hear from the rest of you."
"My name is Aracuria," said Aracuria, "but I don't know what my surname is either: if I've got one then my parents have never told me."
"Very well," said the man in the sun, "let me hear the last name."
"My name is Rhiannon," said Rhiannon, "and my family name is Morcant."

The man in the sun went strangely quiet, and then he said, "Are you from Earth'?"
"Why yes," said Rhiannon. "How did you know?"

But the man in the sun didn't say, in fact for a little while he didn't say anything at all, almost as if he were thinking about something. Then he suddenly bellowed, "There are two tests that you must pass to go the Unpronounceable Place. First, tell me what your names mean. Aracuria and Bill looked at each other in astonishment and said, "What they mean?" But Rhiannon and Klut didn't seem to mind.
"Oh, as I said, "said Klut, "this is going to be easy." He puffed out his chest and proclaimed, "Klut is an ancient word meaning 'Wisdom' and Ibalwattle is a not quite so ancient word which means 'Higher Executive Officer Grade One."'
"How boring," said Rhiannon. "They sounded so interesting before you explained them."
"And what does your name mean?" said the man in the sun to Rhiannon.
"Well, Rhiannon is a very ancient word in the ancient language of the people of Morcantland in which I am a Princess and it means 'Great Queen', while Morcant means 'Sea-Born."'
The second she said that, the light from the woman who was standing behind them flamed out in a brilliant glow that briefly filled the room before dying away again. "What was that for?" asked Rhiannon.
"You will find out, one day," said the man in the sun. "But now I want to hear what the other names mean."
There was an awkward silence. Then Aracuria shouted out, "I don't know what Aracuria means, and I'm sure Bill doesn't know what his name means either." Bill nodded vigorously.

"Oh, you two don't know anything," shouted Klut, "Bill is a shortening of William and William means Resolute Helmet."'

Bill's eyes lit up, "You, you mean Bill actually means something?" he said.

"It means what I just said it means and no more," said Klut curtly, "and Aracuria is a name derived from the Earth province of Arauco." Aracuria turned to Klut, "Why didn't you tell me that before?"

"Because you never asked me," snapped Klut.

The man in the sun stepped forward.

"You have answered the first question, but now you must answer the second." He stopped and turned, and as he turned so the sun which he was standing in also turned and lit up a far wall on the right that none of them had seen before. Set into the wall was a door made of solid marble and above the door, carved in marble was a long name. "That is the Door to the Most Holy Place of the Unpronounceable Name. All I want you to do is to look at the name, one by one and then to tell me what it is and what it means."

Klut stepped forward. "Can I ask a question?" he asked.

"Of course," said the man in the sun.

"Most of the names I've encountered down here are unlike anything I have ever seen before," said Klut, "and I have read millions of books from different worlds and civilizations. If this Unpronounceable Name is like those others, then none of us will stand a chance at saying what it means."

"You have no need to fear on this account," said the man in the sun, "the Unpronounceable Name is an Earth word."

"Then this should be easy," Klut said smugly, as he walked off to look at the name.

For about ten minutes Klut stood in front of the marble door looking up at the name. Then he hung his head and walked slowly back to the others.

"I thought you said it would be easy," said Rhiannon, but all Klut could say was, "I've never seen anything like that before: it's the longest word in the UNIVERSE'."

Aracuria then stepped forward. "Well, if it's an Earth word then maybe I'll know what it means." He too walked up to the door, took one look at the word and then came straight back to the others. "It's IMPOSSIBLE!" he cried, "It's the biggest word I've ever seen."

Then Bill stepped forward. "Let me have a look." he said quietly. As Bill walked across to the marble door, every eye was on him: even though Bill was incredibly dull he had a knack of getting things done.

For about twenty minutes Bill stood in front of the door looking up at the word, then he came back to the others.

"Did you find out what it means?" asked Rhiannon anxiously.

Bill shook his head. "No, but it's a very nice door."

At that Rhiannon swung out and clubbed him across the head. "Well, it's your turn," said Aracuria to Rhiannon.

"What chance do I have?" she said, "I'm never any good at this sort of thing."
"But you might as well try," said Aracuria. Rhiannon shrugged and walked up to the door.
She stood in front of it for about ten seconds reading the word and then began to jump up and down.
"I KNOW IT, I KNOW IT!" she shouted joyously. The others ran up to her side at once.
"Tell me what it is, child," said the man in the sun, as Aracuria and Klut picked Rhiannon up on their shoulders so she could see it better.
"It's called: Rhiannon drew a deep breath and then shouted out the name, "LLANFAIRPWLLGWYNGYLLGOGERYCHWYRNDROBWLLLLAND YSILIOGOGOGOCH."

Total silence descended on everyone, then at last Aracuria spoke.
"How did you say that?" he asked in awe.
"It's easy," said Rhiannon, "it's the ancient language of Morcantland, the same language as my name." Aracuria and Klut put her back down on the ground.
"But that means," said Klut, who had suddenly become very serious, "that Mug Ruith and his daughter Thlagtha must have come from Earth."

Everyone was astonished, but before they had had time to take this in the man in the sun bellowed out, "You have told me what the Unpronounceable Name is, now you must tell me what it means." Rhiannon turned to face him, took a deep breath and then said, "It means: 'Church of St Mary in a hollow of white hazel near to a rapid whirlpool and to St Tysilio's church near to a red cave."' Aracuria, Klut and Bill stared at Rhiannon in admiration.
"You have answered all my questions," said the man in the sun, "You may now pass into the Most Holy place."

As he spoke those words so the massive marble door began to open. Beyond it, in the Most Holy place, they could hear the gurgling sounds of rushing water, the gentle noise of birdsong - and the harsh sound of someone sawing wood. Once the door was fully open the others rushed in ahead. Aracuria, however, waited a moment. He turned to take one last look at the beautiful woman who stood silently on the moon, clothed in the sun and with a crown of stars on her head. 'Who is she?' he wondered to himself, before following the others through the marble door, which closed behind him, forever.

CHAPTER FOURTEEN: THE GREAT CHICKEN

Aracuria walked through a marble passageway and came out into the most beautiful place he had ever seen. Green grass covered the ground, there were trees scattered everywhere of all shapes and colors, there were fruiting plants and flowers. Rhiannon and the others ran on ahead while Aracuria gently picked his way past the flowers. Up ahead was a stream which flowed down over moss covered rocks and then fed into a small pond which at its center disappeared into a whirlpool. Aracuria jumped over the steam. On the other side the ground sloped away into a grassy hollow that was filled with the budding shoots of white hazel trees. Green and yellow birds were singing in the branches. He could also hear the occasional sound of sawing wood, but he assumed that it must be some strange bird noise. He walked past the trees, noticing that a little way off was the stone shell of a chapel: only the wooden roof which had once covered it had been completely taken off. Aracuria was just about to take a closer look when he head Rhiannon's voice calling him.
"Aracuria! Come and see THIS!"

Aracuria ran in the direction of her voice. He jumped over a few flowerbeds, ducked under a couple of branches, ran down a gentle slope and then stopped dead.
"I, I don't believe it!" he said. Dumbfounded, he staggered down to where Rhiannon, Klut and Bill were standing side by side. High above them was the bottom of the shaft down which Roger and Margaret had fallen. The shaft was huge and wide, and rays of blue light cascaded down from high above, bathing everything in their glow. But that was as nothing compared with what sat directly beneath the shaft: in front of them rose the biggest chicken they had ever seen. It was a hundred meters high and as many wide. It sat, brooding, on the ground with its huge wings folded up and its eyes closed.
"It's a chicken!" said Bill.

For a while everyone just stood there, staring up at the massive fowl, then one by one they walked around it just to see if it was as big as they thought it was. And it was. When they came back together Aracuria said, "Well, as amazing as this chicken is, we've got to look for the gemstone of Thlagtha. It has to be around here somewhere, so we all ought to spread out and look for it." Everyone nodded in agreement. They all split up to look for the gemstone that contained the Ring of Ra. Aracuria was going to go in the direction of the dismantled chapel, but Rhiannon had gone that way, so he set off towards a small wood instead.

He had only been searching among the trees for a short while when he heard Rhiannon. "Aracuria! Everyone! Look who I've found!"

"Rhiannon where are you?" he shouted, as he dashed out of the trees, up a rise to the chapel.

"Over here!" Her voice came from beyond the chapel, near to where the walls of the chamber began to rise up. Aracuria ran past the building, jumped over some fallen logs and then stopped dead in amazement: in front of him was a dull red cave carved out of the rock, but in its entrance stood Rhiannon and beside her was the unmistakable silver shape of Roger. Roger was holding a large saw and file, while next to him sat Margaret with a brand new pair of wooden wings.
"ROGER!" cried Aracuria, running as fast as he could to the cave entrance.
"Isn't this AMAZING!" said Rhiannon joyously. "My little Roger survived the fall. He really is the best nanny a princess could ever want. And we all thought you were done for!" In spite of his massive bulk Roger began to look a little embarrassed. The next moment Klut and Bill came running up.
"It's ROGER!" they both shouted in happy disbelief. Klut walked around Margaret, to see what kind of a job Roger had done in making the new wings.
"This is an EXCELLENT piece of work, Roger," he said. "You really know how to carve wood. Did you chop down any of the trees to do it?" Roger shook his steel head.
"No ..I.. dismantled. ..the. . church.. .... .hope...no...one...minds?"
"Of course not!" said Rhiannon, hugging Roger's leg.
"But how did you two survive the fall?" asked Aracuria, "We didn't think anyone would last plummeting down that shaft."

Roger folded his arms. "We...landed...on...the...chicken .She...broke...our...fall."
"I bet that upset her," said Bill.
"It...did," said Roger. "She...hit...me...with...her...beak." At the thought of that everyone began to laugh.

They all stood around talking for a while and then Aracuria said, "We've still got to find this gemstone; after all, that's what we came here for. So shall we all look, Roger and Margaret included?" Everyone nodded, including Roger and Margaret, who immediately hopped off to try her new wooden wings.
"Right then," said Aracuria, "let's all split up and not give up looking until we've found it." They all set off to look once again for the gemstone of Thlagtha. Aracuria made straight for the ruined chapel, but instead of finding a gemstone all he found were hundreds of green, football-size eggs, some of which seemed to be about to hatch out, as they were beginning to move around. This gave him an idea, but first he went off to look elsewhere.

An hour passed, then another hour and still they hadn't found anything. Roger roamed around the garden looking with his infra-red eyes, Margaret hovered and flew through the air looking down on the ground while Aracuria and the others searched beneath the trees. When the third hour had passed and they still hadn't found anything, Aracuria called a meeting.

"We've been searching here for ages," he said, "and we haven't found a thing. That can only mean one thing."
"What's that?" asked Rhiannon.
"That the gemstone of Thlagtha must be under the giant chicken." Everyone turned to look at the massive, sleeping fowl.
"But how on earth could we shift her?" exclaimed Rhiannon.
"It's impossible," said Klut.
Aracuria shook his head. "No it isn't impossible, it's just very difficult," he said. "First of all, let's see if Roger can move her, and if not then I might have an idea."

Without further ado Roger tried to move the giant chicken. He ran straight at her at a ferocious speed, but instead of shifting the chicken he just buried himself in her feathers before bouncing off. Then he tried to push her out of the way, but all he succeeded in doing was digging a hole in the ground with his feet. Before he finally buried himself Aracuria told him to stop. However, Roger had managed to wake the chicken, although without making her angry. Now she just sat silently, staring out over the ground as sleep slowly began to overcome her again. When Aracuria saw this he called over to Roger.
"Roger, go up to the chapel and bring out the eggs. I want you to lay them down in the light, just in front of the chicken so that she can see them." Roger immediately ran off to do his task while everyone else stared at Aracuria, unsure what was happening.

When Roger had finished, Aracuria sat down on the ground.
"What are you going to do now?" asked Rhiannon.
"Nothing," said Aracuria, "Except wait." No one understood, but trusting Aracuria they all sat down and waited. Aracuria stared at the eggs, he watched as the warm sunlight came down the shaft and hit the eggs, he watched as the eggs began to move more and more and then he watched as the first chicks began to hatch out.
"How nice," said Bill as they began to run around, clucking to themselves, "But what has this got to do with getting the Ring of Ra?"

Everyone else was thinking the same thing. Then Aracuria said to Roger, "Climb up on to the chicken's head and hit her across the beak." For a moment Roger looked unsure. "You're not scared of her, are you?" said Aracuria. Steeling himself, Roger scaled up the sleeping chicken, climbed on to the bridge of her nose and thwacked her one across the beak.

"CLUCK!" came the monstrous reply as the chicken opened her eyes, shook her head and flung Roger a hundred meters away. Then her eyes caught sight of the chicks that were running around in front of her. She immediately jumped up, clucked happily to herself and walked off to look after her brood. And as she rose off the ground and walked away so the glowing green gemstone of Thlagtha came into view.
"WOW!" said Rhiannon.

"It's the GEMSTONE!" shouted Klut.
"It's the gemstone!" repeated Bill. The three of them rushed off to see it while Aracuria walked slowly and silently behind them.

The green gemstone was just like the one that Klut had seen in the Treasure Chamber on Draco, only here it was embedded deeply into the ground.
"This must have been here for 700 million years!" exclaimed Klut, "and that dumb chicken must have been sitting on it all this time thinking it was one of her eggs."
"She was waiting for it to hatch," said Aracuria, "when all the time her real eggs were sitting in that chapel. When Roger took the roof off the sunlight started to warm them up, which is what gave me the idea of how to get her to move." He knelt down and looked into the gemstone. At its heart was a single, glowing ring, while deep beneath the gemstone there appeared to be gurgling water.
"So now we've found gemstone of Thlagtha," said Rhiannon, "how do we get the gemstone out of the ground, the Ring of Ra out of the gemstone and the six of us out of the bottom of this pit?" Aracuria said nothing.
"Especially since Margaret with her wooden wings can't even fly one of us up the shaft, let alone all of us," said Klut.

Aracuria shook his head. "I, I don't know." he said. Their problems weren't over yet.

CHAPTER FIFTEEN: THE COSMIC SEA

Aracuria looked down at the gemstone: there was no way that any of them could budge it. "ROGER!" he called, "I want you to remove this gemstone from the ground." Straightaway Roger knelt down, placed his arms around the stone and began to pull it upwards. By squeezing as hard as he could he ensured that his steel arms didn't slip, but no matter how hard he pulled, the gemstone didn't move. Instead his steel feet began to sink into the ground. "You can stop now, Roger," said Aracuria. Roger straightened up.
"What are we going to do now?" asked Bill.

Aracuria thought for a moment, then turned back to Roger. "Do you know how to play rugby?" he asked.
"I...know...all...games," said Roger.
"Good," said Aracuria, "then I want you to take a long run at the gemstone and kick it out of the ground as if it was a rugby ball."
Roger looked confused, "But...a...rugby...ball...is...not...round."
"Just do as he says," said Rhiannon impatiently.

Roger walked away into the distance. He walked past the chicken playing with her chicks, he walked past the trees and the chapel, then he crossed the stream and continued walking until he was standing by the closed marble door.
"I think we ought to get out of here," said Klut.
Just then Roger shouted, "...READY..."

Aracuria and the others dived for cover while Roger began his long run up. He set off from the marble door, jumped the stream, whizzed past the chapel, blasted the leaves off the trees, blew the feathers off the chicks and then shot like a bullet straight for the gemstone. He lifted himself off the ground, stabbed his steel foot beneath the gemstone and kicked with all his might. Suddenly there was a great GULP as the gemstone dislodged from the ground and shot against the wall, but before anyone could shout 'Hurrah' an enormous fountain of water erupted from the ground where the gemstone had been. It caught hold of Roger and everyone watched in amazement as he was hurled high up the shaft until he disappeared out of view.
"It's the FOUNTAIN!" shouted Rhiannon, "The gemstone was blocking the Holy Fountain of Theom!" At that moment, the gemstone that Roger had dislodged from the fountain's mouth hit the far wall with such a terrifying force that it shattered into a thousand pieces. There was a great flash of lightning that burst out through the chamber, followed almost at once by a monstrous clap of thunder.
"WHAT WAS THAT?" screamed Bill, who was really frightened of thunder.
"It's the RING OF RA!" cried Aracuria, running around the Fountain and heading for the far wall. Klut and Bill were about to follow him, but

Rhiannon stopped them, as it was Aracuria who had brought them here and the Ring really belonged to him.

Aracuria slowed as he got to the wall. There were large and small chunks of green glass lying everywhere. He searched among the trees and looked through the grass, but the ring was nowhere to be seen. Then he looked up and saw that part of the wall was glowing. He reached up and from a cleft in the rock pulled down the Ring of Ra. It was exquisite: the most beautiful thing he had ever seen. The ring itself was made of a kind of gold, although it was different from anything he had ever seen before, while on top of the ring was a little blue diamond that glowed hauntingly. He slipped the ring over the second finger of his right hand: it fitted perfectly. Then he walked back to the others.

"I've got it!" he said. Everyone gathered around to look at the Ring and they were all amazed by what they saw.

"Can I try it on?" asked Bill. Aracuria nodded and tried to get the ring off his finger: but it wouldn't budge.

"It looks like you're stuck with it," laughed Rhiannon. Aracuria tried a little longer, but gave up when he realized that it just wouldn't come off.

"What can you do with it?" asked Bill.

Aracuria's face went blank, "Well, I'm not sure," he said.

"It's supposed to confer all power on to the wearer," said Klut. "Do you feel all-powerful, Aracuria?"

Aracuria shook his head."I don't know how to make it work!" he said in alarm.

Rhiannon intervened. "You've got to wish something..." Before she could even finish her sentence a brilliant blue bolt of lightning shot out of the diamond of the ring and burst up the length of the shaft.

"AARRAGH!" screamed everyone, including Aracuria, as the thunder clap hit their ears.

"It works! It works!" shouted Aracuria, "I wished just then for lightning and it works!"

Rhiannon looked anxious.

"You promise to be careful with that thing," she said, "or someone might get injured."

"Let's hope it's Lucifer," said Klut, and suddenly they all realized what they had to do next.

For a moment they were silent. All they did was stare at the ring and then at the roaring fountain, and then back again.

"We've done it." said Bill, and indeed they had.

"And we also know how to get up the surface now," said Rhiannon, to the others' surprise. She shouted across to Margaret. "Margaret: fly up the shaft and pick up Roger!" Then she turned to the others and said, "Just follow me." The next moment she stepped straight into the fountain and immediately shot up the shaft like a bullet.

"It's GREAT..." came her voice, until she was too far away to be heard.
"I suppose it beats an elevator," said Klut as he stepped into the jet of the fountain and rocketed to the surface.
"See you up there," said Bill quietly as he stepped into the water and disappeared.

Aracuria was now all alone. He stared into the fountain but no matter how hard he tried, he just couldn't step into it.
"I've got this all powerful ring and yet I'm still scared of water!" he cried. "How on earth can I defeat Lucifer and get the Tree of Life off him when I'm still scared of water? It's impossible!" He slumped to the floor in despair. Then, suddenly, the waters of the Fountain began to glow a brilliant blue.
"Nothing is impossible."
"Who said that?" said Aracuria jumping up. He spun around but there was no one to be seen. "Come out, or I'll blast you with this RING!" he shouted, holding the Ring like a weapon.
"And yet I was the one who put the power in the Rings of Ra."

Aracuria froze still and then turned slowly around. The voice was soft and gentle, it was the voice of a woman, and it was coming from the center of the fountain. He stared in amazement into the flowing waters and at its heart he saw once again the image of the woman clothed in the sun, standing on the Moon, with a crown of stars on her head. "Who are YOU?" he asked in disbelief.
"I have many names: Tiamat and Theom; Ananta and Manna. Which do you wish to call me by?"
"I, I..." Aracuria stuttered, not actually saying anything.
"Don't be afraid," said the voice, "for I will be with you. There is no need to fear Lucifer, for Lucifer holds no power over you or me. Go and do whatever you have to do. The Tree of Life has remained with him for far too long: now it is time to return it to its rightful home." Aracuria almost felt like crying.
"But I'm scared of water," he said miserably, at which the woman clothed in the sun laughed. "Can you really be scared of me when I am the Waters of Life? Upon my Cosmic Sea sleeps the Lord who day and night dreams the Dream that is your Universe."
"Is everything just a dream?" asked Aracuria.
"Just a dream," said the voice, "and when you wake up, as all living things must, then everything will be perfect."

Aracuria no longer felt scared. He stepped into the fountain and suddenly found himself bathed in blue light as he rose like a bullet through the shaft to the surface of the planet.

CHAPTER SIXTEEN: TO DRACO

A few moments later Aracuria found himself sitting on top of a giant fountain of water high above the surface of Thlagtha. Rhiannon and the others were bobbing around beside him, "What took you so long?" shouted Rhiannon. The waters of the Fountain were now beginning to fill the dried out sea and all the green goo was slowly dissolving. Just then Margaret emerged from the shaft, flew into the fountain and picked up Roger, who climbed straight on to her back.

"Go straight to Draco!" ordered Rhiannon. "We haven't time to go back to Earth, we've taken long enough on this planet as it is." As Margaret winged away across the sky so Deborah, who had been cleaning all the green goo off herself in the waters of the fountain, finally took flight. She soared up on an air current, flew into the fountain and picked up the others, who at once set about making themselves comfortable on her wings. When they were all aboard, Deborah swung out of the fountain and then swooped low across the sea before rising up in the air.

"Just follow Margaret to Draco," said Rhiannon to Deborah. As the Solar Duck beat her wings ever faster to catch up with her sister duck, whom she had thought lost, so Klut noticed that all the waiters and their families were leaving the pretend town and coming to the edge of the sea, which was now rapidly filling with water. Most of them stood in amazement as they watched the waters rise high in the air and cascade down, while others jumped for joy and a few more had the good sense to dive in the waters and wash off the sick that had dried into their clothes.

"I think the beef burger business just closed down on Thlagtha for good!" said Klut, "And not before time," declared Rhiannon.

As the Solar Duck began to rise in the air so they caught sight of Gayomart, who was still sitting, thoughtfully, in his yellow bucket halfway up Thlagtha's nose. As Deborah swooped by, Gayomart noticed for the first time that the Fountain of Theom was flowing again after 700 million years. For absolutely ages, ever since Aracuria and the others had left him, he had been trying to remember what it was that was so special about the Earth and the Tree of Life and now he suddenly caught sight of the blue waters of the Fountain. His eyes lit up as he remembered what it was. He flicked the switch on his yellow bucket and shouted up to Aracuria and the others.

"You are in great danger! The Tree of Life used to grow on Eden, but after Lucifer stole it away they changed the name of Eden to EARTH! Lucifer will do all he can to stop you returning it to its home."

But the old man's voice was weak and as Aracuria and the others passed by they didn't hear a word of what he had said. Instead they waved their farewells and journeyed on their way to Draco, where Lucifer and his demons were waiting for them.

BOOK III:

ARACURIA AND THE TREE OF LIFE

by

CHARLES MORGAN

CONTENTS

CHAPTER ONE: DEEP SPACE

The Solar Ducks, Deborah and Margaret, began to rise high in the sky. Rhiannon, Klut and Bill lay back on Deborah's wing and stared down at the huge stone nose of Thlagtha, all that remained, with the exception of a big toe, of the giant statue of Thlagtha that once stood on the planet of the same name. In the distance a bright blue fountain of water, the Most Holy Fountain of Theom, was flowing up from the core of the planet of Thlagtha and filling the desert with water.

"Oh, I feel so tired." said Rhiannon.

"So do I." added Klut.

"And me." yawned Bill. They were all tired, except Aracuria, who sat alone against Deborah's solar rucksack, thinking quietly. They had good reason to be tired, as they had just been through the most extraordinary adventure. They had flown all the way from the planet Earth to Thlagtha on the backs of the Solar Ducks in order to get the Ring of Ra, one of the most powerful things in the whole Universe, only to find that the ring was at the bottom of an enormous shaft which went right down to the center of the planet. It had taken them absolutely ages to get down there through a mass of tunnels, having to fight their way past devils, demons, monsters, questioners and other people, all of whom had the most unbelievably unpronounceable names. In the end though, they had got the ring and now it glowed hauntingly on Aracuria's finger.

"I'm going to go to sleep," said Rhiannon, but there was no reply: Klut and Bill were already sleeping.

Down below, the planet grew smaller and smaller as the ducks rose up into space. Aracuria looked back at the other Solar Duck, Margaret, on whose back sat ROGER, Rhiannon's Roboticized Organizer and General Engineering Robot, who was also at one time her nanny. Roger had made the journey from Earth with them, but although everyone had thought that he would be extremely useful, on account of his enormous strength and intelligence, in fact he had been almost completely useless. This was because the moment they had landed, he and Margaret had fallen down the great shaft that led to the center of the planet, and they hadn't seen or heard anything of them again until most of their problems were over. He had, however, managed to get the Ring of Ra out of the huge green gemstone into which it had been set by the Great Gods so that no one should ever wear it, so it was worthwhile him coming along after all.

The Solar Ducks were now out in space, with the planet of Thlagtha looking like a huge football, floating motionless in a sea of stars. Far away in space, Aracuria could see one star which was brighter than all the others. It was millions of light years away, but all the same it was the brightest star of all. That was Draco. Actually the light wasn't coming from the star at all; it was in fact coming from the Tree of Life, which was held in a Treasure Chamber on Draco by the Demi-Demons of Draco. That was how it all started, and it seemed as if it had happened a long, long time ago. But as Aracuria had learned before, the Universe was such a strange place that time really didn't exist at all. All the same, they were now flying to Draco. They were going to try to steal the Tree of Life from the Demi-Demons and their evil leader Lucifer, and then they were going to take it back to Earth and put the Tree of Life in space next to the Earth's natural sun, which was going out and threatening to turn planet Earth into a giant snowball.

And why was the Earth's natural sun going out? Aracuria didn't like to think about that, not just because it all became so mind bogglingly complex that he didn't have the energy to remember how it had all started one night when he, Bill and Klut were late for school, but because all their problems had to do with rubbish, and that was all that need be said.

Anyway, Aracuria didn't have time to think about the past: he was too busy thinking about the future and how they were going to get the Tree of Life off Lucifer. Perhaps it was impossible. But then again nothing was impossible in this Universe: it was that sort of place. At the very least, though, it was going to be extremely difficult, and if they failed Aracuria knew what would happen to them all: Roger would be melted down and he and his friends would be killed, if not worse.

All this thinking was making Aracuria sleepy. He rested his head against the Solar Rucksack, looked down at his glowing ring, said to himself, 'I hope this isn't radioactive', and began to fall asleep to the gentle beat of Deborah's wings. When they awoke, he thought to himself, they would be in Draco. But as was sometimes the case, on this point Aracuria was completely and utterly wrong.

Aracuria thought he was dreaming. In the dream there was this crazy hairdresser with three heads, who was blow-drying his hair with a vacuum cleaner. The problem was that his hair was all stuck up on end and he didn't like it that way as he looked ridiculous. With his eyes still closed, Aracuria raised his hand and touched his hair: it was all standing up on end.

"WHAT THE...!" He jumped up, opened his eyes, shook his head and shouted out, "What's happened to my..." But he never finished the sentence, because he caught sight of something that had made his eyes open wide and his body freeze. The Solar Ducks were still flying side by side, but beside them, floating in space, was the most enormous, most stupendous spaceship that Aracuria had ever seen in his entire life. It went for miles to his left, it went for miles to his right, it towered high above him and it sank deep below: it was vast.

"Rhiannon! Klut! Bill! You'd better wake up!" Nothing happened. "WAKE UP!" yelled Aracuria, without taking his eyes of the spaceship for a moment: still there was nothing. Then he turned around and saw that the others were

already awake. They were standing on the wing, staring in awestruck silence at the spaceship. However, frightened as he was, Aracuria noticed that all the others' hair was pointing up in the air too.
"Your hair!" said Aracuria, "It's like mine: what's happening here?" Klut answered without taking his eyes off the spaceship. "Static electricity," he said. "It's being induced by this...THING."

Aracuria gave a sigh of relief. "Thank goodness," he said, "I thought it was that hairdresser who did it." The others turned to look at him in horror.
"Did you dream of a hairdresser?" asked Rhiannon.
"With three heads?" added Klut.
"And a vacuum cleaner?" gulped Bill.
Aracuria was stunned. "Yes, that's it exactly!" he said. Klut scratched his chin.
"This is very strange. Each of us dreamt the same dream. Rhiannon, Bill and I were just talking about it before you woke up."
Aracuria pointed to the spaceship. "When did THIS appear?" he asked.
"We don't know," said Klut. "It was here when we woke up."

They were in deep space now and the planet of Thlagtha was nowhere to be seen, so there was no way of telling how long they had been asleep. The giant spaceship was gently passing them by. All along its sides there were glowing lights, reds and yellows, greens and purples. Some looked like warning lights, others looked like windows. The whole spaceship was covered in burn marks and rust and for some reason, in spite of its size, it didn't half look old. Gradually as it gently moved past them a series of huge letters became visible along one side. Each letter was vast, painted in white paint a hundred meters high and as many wide. Because the spaceship was moving from left to right, the words that the letters were spelling out appeared in front of them backwards, so when Rhiannon asked, "What does it say?" only Klut could work it out, as he was particularly good at that sort of thing.

"Spell out the letters as they appear," said Klut. Rhiannon and the others did as he asked.
"T.R.O.P.S.N.A.R.T.O.G.R.A.C.E.C.A.P.S.P.E.E.D.N.A.G.I.R.R.O.M." The trouble was, none of them had bothered to tell Klut where one word ended and another began, so it took a while for him to work it out. When he had, however, everyone could tell, as his face suddenly bleached white. Then he looked down at his feet and said grimly, "Oh no!"
"What is it?" asked Rhiannon, "What do the letters spell?"
Klut turned to look at her. "They spell: MORRIGAN DEEP SPACE CARGO TRANSPORT."
"What?" said Aracuria, "Isn't that the thing that Lucifer and the Demi-Demons used to carry the Tree of Life from Eden to Draco?"
Klut nodded.
"And that means..." said Rhiannon,

“That means that before we even get to Draco, Lucifer and his demons have come to get us.”

Just then there was an enormous creaking sound like the opening of an ancient door. Everyone looked at the spaceship. It had now moved in front of them and they could all now see that the whole thing was shaped like a letter ‘Y’. The forked end of the ‘Y’ seemed to be moving to the right. They watched in silence as the giant spaceship positioned itself so that the Solar Ducks were now flying into the center of the fork.

“What’s happening?” asked Bill in alarm.

“They are trying to capture us,” answered Klut glumly.

The two sides of the forked spaceship were now passing them by on each side. Aracuria shouted to the ducks, “Deborah! Margaret! Quickly: turn around and fly away!” Immediately the two ducks turned on their wings and began flying back they way they had come: but it was too late. The giant spaceship was now traveling backwards faster than the ducks could fly forward and with every beat of their wings the two sides of the forked spaceship came closer and closer.

“What are we going to do?” cried Rhiannon, “There’s no way we can out-run THAT!” She shuddered as the massive spaceship began to loom all around them.

“There’s nothing we can do,” said Aracuria. “Deborah and Margaret: you can stop flying.”

The Solar Ducks stopped beating their wings and glided gently to a halt. They were now at the end of the fork where both sides of the spaceship joined together and although the ducks had stopped moving the spaceship hadn’t. It looked for a moment as if the Morrigan Deep Space Cargo Transport was about to run them down, but just before the side of the spaceship hit them, two giant, rust red doors opened up. The doors were huge and as they opened so the Solar Ducks gently passed through them into the pitch blackness of what seemed to be Deep Space, with no stars or suns or lights of any kind. Once they were inside, the doors began to close, and as they closed so Aracuria and the others took their last look at the stars, because it seemed as if they wouldn’t be seeing them again for a long time to come.

“Oh no!” groaned Klut, as the doors slammed shut with a deafening clang, and everyone else felt exactly the same way.

CHAPTER TWO: THE LITTLE PEOPLE

The four of them stood silently in the pitch blackness. It was eerie and frightening not to be able to see or hear anything.
"Where are we?" whispered Rhiannon.

Before anyone could answer her, a huge gantry of brilliant lights came on, high above their heads. The next moment another gantry lit up, only this one was a few meters in front of the first. Then another came on that was further in front of that one again; and so on it went, gantry after gantry of lights, each one farther and farther away. Aracuria and the others stood in amazement as the size of the place they were in became apparent. Finally the last set of lights came on and they could all see the huge room that stretched out in front of them.

"This cargo bay is VAST!" said Klut in astonishment, which was unusual because Klut wasn't normally impressed by anything.
"What shall we do now?" asked Rhiannon. Aracuria scratched his head: it was then that he noticed that his hair was no longer upright.
"My hair! It's back to normal!" Everyone else reached up and felt the top of their head.
"So's mine!" said Rhiannon.
"And mine!" said Bill.
Klut, however, didn't say anything as the top of his head was completely flat and he didn't care at all whether his hair was upright or not.

Feeling glad that his hair was normal again, Aracuria peered down the long corridor. "I think someone wants us to go down there."
"Well that's a good reason for not going down there," said Rhiannon. Aracuria shrugged his shoulders. "I don't think we have much choice: either we go to the end of the cargo bay or we sit here, possibly forever. And we've got a planet to save and only three years to do it in."
"Less," said Klut unhelpfully.
"OK then, let's get walking," said Rhiannon, as she started to climb off the back of the duck.
Aracuria stopped her. "Why walk when you can fly..." And with that he called to Deborah and Margaret; "Fly to the end of the cargo bay."

Straightaway the Solar Ducks began to beat their wings. They ran forwards a few paces, lifted their legs and gently took to the air. A few seconds later they were swooping low and fast over the cargo bay floor, heading for the place where the last lights were burning.

A few moments later they touched down. In front of them, blocking off the end of the cargo bay, was a steel wall in the side of which was a small door. Aracuria jumped down from Deborah and made for the wall.

"It looks as if this is where we'll have to leave the ducks behind: this door is too small for them to pass through." The others joined him. Rhiannon took a look at the door. "I don't know about the ducks, but it looks as if Roger will have a job getting through there," she said. "Roger! What do you think?"

Roger climbed down off Margaret's back and walked over to the door: he was about three meters too high for it and about two meters too wide. "I...am...too...big..." he said in a metallic sort of voice.

"No you're not," said Rhiannon teasingly. "Just try going through it."

Roger reached down, opened the door with his hand, went to go through it and instead burst through the wall, leaving a clear robot outline in the buckled steel.

"You see," said Rhiannon with satisfaction, "it just needed a little widening." Roger, now on the other side of the wall, was just about to turn around and say 'sorry', when suddenly a net came tumbling down from above and completely covered him. Then hundreds of squeaky little voices broke out in harmony, "We got it! WE GOT IT!"

Aracuria and the others stared in amazement through the gashed doorway as hundreds of little coiled ropes began to spin down through the air to land on the floor. The next moment, they were even more amazed to see hundreds of tiny little dwarfs descending the ropes. Each one either carried a curved sword or else had a knife between his teeth. Some of them wore little hats and others had patches over their eyes.

"I don't believe this," gasped Rhiannon. "Am I the only one who is seeing hundreds of dwarf PIRATES coming down those ropes?"

"KILL it! KILL the monster!" came the voices as the dwarfs swarmed around Roger's feet, while others began landing on his head.

"KILL the MONSTER!" squeaked the voices as the dwarf pirates began stabbing and hacking at Roger's steel legs with their little knives, to no effect of course.

Roger peered down at them and then looked helplessly to Rhiannon.

"What...shall...I...do?" he asked.

""I, I don't know!" stammered Rhiannon, too dumbfounded to think properly. Suddenly all the dwarf pirates froze. They stopped attacking Roger and turned towards Rhiannon. "There's TWO of them!" squeaked one of the pirates.

"THREE of them!" screamed a second as they caught sight of Bill.

"FOUR of them!" shrieked another as they saw Klut.

"FIVE of them!" screamed yet another as they laid eyes on Aracuria.

"FIVE of them! Let's kill the five MONSTERS!" And with that all the dwarf pirates came charging at Aracuria and the others, leaving Roger all alone.

"What do you mean 'monsters'?" said Rhiannon indignantly. "We're not..." But she got no further with her sentence because one of the pirates came running up, raised his sword and tried to hit her with it.

"KILL the MONSTER!"

The next moment the sword came whizzing through the air. Rhiannon ducked to one side, but all the same the blade of the sword cut through her coat, narrowly missing her skin. For a second she just stared at the gaping hole. "You've ripped my clothes!" she said in disbelief. "You've ripped my COAT!" she said again, only louder this time. "YOU'VE RIPPED MY 700 INTER-SPACE DOLLAR JACKET!" Without a second's delay Rhiannon, who like most princesses had a foul temper when she was angry, kicked out with her right foot, caught the dwarf full in the stomach and sent him flying high in the air, until he crashed on the ground in a heap a couple of meters away. "Take that, you little SQUIRT!"

All the other dwarfs froze still. They stared at Rhiannon, who lashed out with her fist. "CLEAR OFF! All of you! Before I get my hands on you! Rip my jacket INDEED!"

At that all of the dwarf pirates burst into tears. Some of them threw away their weapons and all of them ran away. In the new found silence, Rhiannon suddenly felt rather sorry for them. Then she remembered how they had just ripped her jacket and she was glad they were gone.

"Well," said Aracuria, "You certainly showed them what for."

"That was really weird," said Bill. "I wonder who they were."

Klut scratched his chin. "I don't like this," he said.

"What do you mean?" said Aracuria. "They all ran away in tears when Rhiannon shouted at them: they were no trouble at all." Klut shook his head.

"This spaceship is the Morrigan Deep Space Cargo Transport, built to carry the Tree of Life to Draco from Eden. When I first saw it I thought the Demi-Demons had sent it to intercept us before we reached Draco, but if that is the case, how on earth did those dwarf pirates get on board?" Everyone was mystified.

"What does it mean?" asked Rhiannon.

Klut shrugged. "That's the problem: I don't know."

Aracuria pointed in the direction the dwarfs had run.

"Let's follow them then, and find out where they've gone."

"That's a good idea," said Rhiannon. "At least we've nothing to be frightened of anymore." Aracuria wasn't so sure.

Rhiannon ordered the Solar Ducks to wait in the cargo bay until they returned, then the four of them stepped through the ripped steel wall, while Roger tore up the net that the pirates had thrown over him. Aracuria led the way through what looked like another empty cargo bay, only this one was much, much smaller. The dwarf pirates had disappeared down a dark, unlit corridor at the far end of the room. The corridor itself was quite large; large enough for Roger to walk upright, so Aracuria asked him to light the way for them. Without further ado, Roger's glass eyes began to glow and then a piercing beam of light, like a car's headlamp, burst out from each eye, lighting up the way. Aracuria and the others made their way down the corridor with Roger shuffling along behind.

After about five minutes' walking they came to large door that blocked off the way. On the door was some writing. Aracuria leaned forward and read what it said.
"Air Tube Inter-Ship Transport." He turned to Klut. "What does that mean?" Klut peered at the words. "I'm not sure," he said, with a puzzled look.

Rhiannon stepped forward. "Look!" she cried. High up on the right of the door was a red and yellow button with the word PRESS written across it. "Maybe this will tell us what it means," she said, stretching up and pressing the button.

At once there was a deep gushing sound of rushing air and then the whole door began to revolve open. The next moment the four of them were staring into a round room, which looked like the inside of a large tin can. Aracuria and the others stepped inside followed by Roger. "What do we do now?" asked Bill. But before anyone had time to answer the whole round room began to turn and as the room turned so the door closed. Everyone felt rather scared at that, but no one moved. It was then that Rhiannon noticed that right in the center of the round room, in the middle of the floor, was another red and yellow button.
"Hey, there's another of these buttons: shall I press it?"
However, she didn't wait for an answer. Instead she reached down and pressed the button, just as Klut said, "I don't think you should because..." Klut never finished his sentence, as the instant Rhiannon pressed the button there was another sound of rushing air and then the whole floor opened up.
"AARRAAGH!" they all screamed as they all plunged down what looked like a bottomless shaft which glowed eerily in red light.
"What's happening?" yelled Rhiannon, as they fell down hundreds of meters of empty air.
"It's a TRAP!" cried Bill. But he was wrong. After they had fallen a few hundred meters there was the sound of rushing air again, only this time the sound was really loud. The next moment a gale force wind hit them from below. Gradually they all began to slow down, except Roger, who continued to fall down the shaft. The wind got stronger and stronger, so strong in fact that Roger eventually stopped falling while the others began to rise up the shaft. Then the wind got stronger still and finally Roger also started to rise slowly up the shaft, while the others began to shoot along.
"What's happening?" shouted Aracuria to Klut, but Klut seemed lost in thought.

At great speed they rose up the shaft until they were back up where they had started falling from. Just before they reached the round room the ceiling opened up allowing them to pass through into yet another shaft that seemed to rise above them forever. Aracuria stared up into the red shaft as he and the others hurtled into it at a frightening speed.

“What’s happening?” he shouted again to Klut. Klut tried to face him but instead he began to spin around and around in the air. All the same he tried to answer.
“This is an elevator, it’s a lift, designed to get people from one side of the ship to another,” he called. “This must be a really old spaceship, because on all the other big ships they use magnetic fields to move things around.”
Aracuria stared back at the endless shaft.
“But where are we going?” he asked. Klut shook his head: no one knew, which was just as well, as it was straight into deep trouble.

CHAPTER THREE: THE DEAD ZONE

They were now flying through the shaft at a fantastic speed. Rhiannon had just come out of a spin when she noticed that up ahead the shaft seemed to be completely blocked.
"We're going to DIE!" she wailed, as they all hurtled at what appeared to be a solid steel wall. But just as they were about to hit it, the wind suddenly blew them away to one side and they started flying down another shaft, which didn't seem to be straight at all. Instead they now found themselves in a twisting tube that hurled them from one side to the other.
"It's OK!" shouted Klut, "This is a transport tube: we're in no danger." While Klut closed his eyes and enjoyed the ride, the others watched in terror as the tube twisted first this way then that, while they all spun around in mid air.

It was while Rhiannon was spinning around that she thought that she could hear voices. First of all they were distant and faint so she ignored them, but when they started getting louder and more distinct she started getting worried.
"Aracuria: can you hear someone laughing or am I going crazy?" she asked.
"I can hear laughter," he said. The laughter was getting louder. It was shrill and high-pitched, more like kids screaming than a normal laugh. Everyone was wondering what it was when suddenly, up ahead, through the twists and turns in the tube, Rhiannon caught sight of a pair of short legs. Then another pair appeared, and another.
"What the...?" Then some bodies came into view, then some heads and finally Rhiannon noticed that some of the heads had eye-patches.
"It's those blasted dwarf PIRATES!" she bellowed.

Hearing her voice, the pirates stopped laughing and giggling. They turned in mid air, saw who was coming up rapidly behind them and shouted out as one, "The MONSTERS! The MONSTERS are COMING!" Some of the pirates stopped spinning around. Instead they straightened themselves and as they did so they seemed to rocket back towards Aracuria and the others. They were all waving their swords around their heads and screaming, "The MONSTERS! KILL the MONSTERS!" Half a dozen pirates came shooting past Aracuria, slashing out left and right with their swords. Aracuria, Klut and Bill just managed to avoid being cut, but Rhiannon, although she tried to dodge the blows, was unlucky, as two of the cuts hit her jacket, one on each of her arms. Immediately the stitching came away and both sleeves of the jacket floated off down the tube.

For a moment Rhiannon was speechless as she watched the remains of her jacket drift away, then she started shouting and screaming and nothing could stop her.

"I'M GOING TO KILL YOU!" she bellowed. The half dozen or so pirates were now between her and Roger, so Rhiannon did as they had done; she straightened herself and shot back down the tube to get them.
"Help us!" squeaked the dwarf pirates, as Rhiannon approached them at great speed. But it was too late. She was soon among them and she was in a really foul temper. She grabbed the first two she reached by their necks and began battering them together until they let go of their weapons and began to cry. Then she did a somersault and kicked another two in the teeth, which made them burst into tears. Then she head butted a fifth and punched a sixth and seventh and after that it was impossible to work out what was happening as Rhiannon's fists and feet were swinging left and right sending the dwarf pirates flying.

Just as fast as they had charged past them, so now the pirates came scurrying back to join the others, only this time none of them had any weapons and all of them were crying.
"I don't think much of these pirates," said Aracuria in disgust.
"Whoever heard of pirates crying?" said Bill. Not even Klut had. Rhiannon came back to join them again just as the last of the pirates disappeared out of view.
"And next time I'll RIP YOUR HEADS OFF!" she roared after them, before turning to Aracuria, "Do you see what they did to my jacket?" Aracuria, however, didn't answer, as he had suddenly noticed that up ahead the tube was coming to a complete end. In front of them was what looked like a yellow wall and the next moment they crashed straight into it at an amazing speed. But no sooner had they hit it than Aracuria and the others found that they had bounced off and were now flying through the air again. Then, with a bump, they came crashing down on to the ground.

Aracuria was dazed; his head was still spinning. He stood up, fell over and then stood up again: this time he managed to stay upright. Looking around, he saw that they were in a large room. Behind them was the yellow wall which was, in fact, a big yellow rubber mattress that lay flat on the floor. Above the mattress, set into the ceiling, was a huge tube, out of which they had just fallen. In front of him there was a gigantic, curved window through which Aracuria could see all the stars and suns of space. In front of the curved window were rows of dials and instruments with flashing lights. In front of the instruments were dozens of swivel chairs, and seated in the chairs with their black leather boots resting on the dials and flashing instruments were some of the most evil looking people Aracuria had ever seen.

"Oh no!" he groaned to himself, as one by one the chairs began to swivel around to face him. "Klut: who are these people?"

Klut picked himself up from the floor, staggered up beside Aracuria and took a good look at what Aracuria was talking about. He took a good look at the black leather boots, he took a good look at the ripped denim jeans they were wearing. He took an even closer look at their pitch black leather jackets with the words DEATH and HATE and I'VE JUST EATEN MY GRANDMOTHER AND WHAT DID YOU HAVE FOR LUNCH? written across them in blood red paint. He also looked closely at the black hats some of them wore and the black patches that others had over their faces covering missing eyes, and the various knives, guns and razor blades that seemed to cover them like ornaments on a fireplace. Klut straightened himself up and cleared his throat.

"In my considered opinion, these people are the Zombie Space Pirates from the Dead Zone Solar System, owners of the 'Brain Damaged Virus Software Company', creators of "Head Banger," a virus laden computer program that laid waste the planet of Thlagtha and numerous other civilizations, destroyers of the Idol of Thlagtha and the ones who stole the Idol's gemstone eye that contained the second Ring of Ra. They are also the most evil, the most monstrous and probably the most stupid non-deified life form in the Universe."

But Aracuria hadn't heard a word that Klut had said, because he had noticed that around the feet of the Zombie Space Pirates clung several dozen dwarf pirates, all of whom were in floods of tears.

"I think we are in BIG trouble," said Aracuria.

Just then Rhiannon picked herself up from the floor. The instant she did so, all the dwarf pirates pointed straight at her and screamed out, "She's the ONE! " Immediately a dozen of the biggest, ugliest, most eyeless, patch covered Zombie Space Pirates stepped forward. "WHAT have you DONE to our little DARLINGS?" they bellowed at Rhiannon. Rhiannon turned to Aracuria in astonishment.

"I don't believe it: these are just the WOMEN!"

Aracuria couldn't believe it either, but these were in fact the mothers of the dwarfs and the dwarfs weren't dwarfs at all, but just about the ugliest group of toddlers that any of them had ever seen in their whole lives.

"We are going to SKIN YOU ALIVE for upsetting our LOVELIES!"

Rhiannon stepped swiftly behind Aracuria as the female pirates began pulling out razor blades and hatchets from their leather jacket pockets.

"Aracuria: PROTECT ME!" cried Rhiannon, which was rather odd as Rhiannon had shown herself time and time again to be tougher than the rest of them put together. Then an idea occurred to Aracuria.

"You've got nothing to worry about: tell them about ROGER!"

The moment she heard that name, Rhiannon stepped out from behind Aracuria again, placed her jacketless hands on her hips and smiled confidently. "I wouldn't try it if I were you: a friend of mine is going to be along in just a moment who will puree the lot of you." She pointed back at the giant tube just as Roger emerged from it at a fantastic speed. However, Roger was made of several hundred tons of high grade steel and when he hit the yellow rubber mat he didn't bounce off; instead he burst straight through it and hit the steel floor beneath. But the steel floor wasn't strong enough to stop him and Roger just crashed straight on through it. Then he hit the floor beneath that and burst through it, and so on, crashing through floor after floor of the spaceship until he disappeared in clouds of dusts and shattered metal fragments a thousand meters below.

"WHO is going to puree us?" asked one of the female pirates nastily. Rhiannon quickly jumped back behind Aracuria.

"DO SOMETHING!" she yelled into his ear. Aracuria had to do something fast: the female pirates were brandishing some of the most horrific knives that he had ever seen and they were coming to get Rhiannon. Aracuria raised his arm and was about to say, "Stay back," but he never did, because as he raised his right hand he caught sight of the glowing Ring of Ra that was on his index finger.

"We've got nothing to worry about!" he cried, "I forgot I had the Ring of Ra: the most powerful thing in the whole Universe! I can do anything I want!" He aimed the ring at the women and shouted, "Stay back or I'll..."

But Aracuria never finished his sentence, as just then one of the other pirates sitting in one of the swivel chairs picked up a huge lime green gun, aimed it at him and pulled the trigger. By the look of the gun, it seemed as if a ray of laser light was going to come out and blow

Aracuria away, but instead a long, green plume of phlegm came shooting out of the barrel, arched through the air and covered Aracuria's head. Instantly a lightning bolt burst out from the Ring of Ra, shot up above the heads of the women pirates and blasted a hole in the side of the wall. This was followed by another lightning bolt, and another, and then another, as Aracuria, who was now completely blinded by the green goo that covered his head, spun around, sending out lightning bolts everywhere.

Everyone dived to the ground; Rhiannon, Klut, Bill and all the pirates, male, female and toddling, as Aracuria whirled around like a top, zapping everything he couldn't see.

"Aracuria STOP IT!" screamed Rhiannon, "Stop it or you'll destroy the spaceship and us along with it!" Somehow, beneath all the goo that was now solidifying into a kind of rubbery head mask, Aracuria heard Rhiannon's voice. The pirates picked themselves off the floor and surrounded the four of them with a massive array of weapons, while Rhiannon nudged Klut, who was lying beside her. The same thought occurred to both of them.

How were they going to get out of this mess? Neither of them had an answer but at least one of them was going to have to think up something pretty quick or they would all be dead before they even reached Draco.

CHAPTER FOUR: SKULL EATER

The Zombie Space Pirates stood all around them in a great circle, dangling their knives and guns, flicking their switchblades in and out. Rhiannon, Klut and Bill waited for something awful to happen, but when nothing did the three of them stood up. All of the pirates were staring at Aracuria's ring as it glowed hauntingly on his outstretched arm, but none of them did anything, almost as if they were waiting for someone to tell them what to do.

Just then there was a deep, asthmatic cough. Immediately the circle of pirates opened up so that Rhiannon and the others could see through to the window, in front of which was a large, fur covered chair. Someone big and hairy was sitting in it. For a moment nothing happened, then out of the chair rose a huge man. He turned around to face them and came over to where Aracuria was standing. On his feet he too wore black leather boots, only the uppers of his were covered in white fur. His denims were ripped and dirty. Around his waist he wore a monstrous motorcycle chain as a belt. His black leather jacket was the dirtiest and scruffiest Rhiannon had ever seen. His face was half hidden by a huge, white beard while on his head he wore a black leather peaked hat with a death's head badge on the front. While all of this looked very impressive, what caught Rhiannon's attention more than anything else was the fact that across his face ran a huge, red scar. The scar cut straight through the center of one of his eyes and that natural eye had obviously been removed at some time, as it had been replaced by a glass eyeball made of bright red glass. It glowed in his head like an evil sun. He turned to face Rhiannon.

"Hoo u dink u r, man? U cum zap my spacezip; u cum boot my pikini; u cum bust my floor with u weird hevvy metal man. U kinda freeky meeky. Maybe we cut you AWAY."
Rhiannon turned to Klut. "What did he say? I didn't understand a word of it."
Klut shrugged his shoulders."Like I said, the Zombie Space Pirates are some of the most stupid people in the Universe."
"Hue u call zupid: flat head punk freak?" said the pirate, "U wan end up stuffed?"
Klut froze in terror. "Ah, no, no: not at all," he stuttered.
"Me 'ate alien punk freaks; me eat alien punk freak: you wanna end up in stew?"
Klut didn't answer, instead he jumped behind Rhiannon.
"You do the talking: I'll translate," he said hastily.

The pirate turned back to Rhiannon. "ANZER!" he bellowed.
Rhiannon was lost for words.

"We'll make her answer," said one of the ugliest women as she fingered her razor blade:

Rhiannon had to act fast.

"We were on our way to Draco!" she blurted out, "And we didn't want to come on board your spaceship but we couldn't help it..."

The pirate looked at her closely. "U 'erd of uzz? We Zombie Space Pirates from Dead Zone Solar System. Me, I called Evil Eye; what you called?"

"Rhiannon," she said timidly.

"Ok Rianton," said the Evil Eye, "we gonna kill you." The ugly woman stepped forward to do the dirty work.

"NO!" screamed Rhiannon, as she realized that this was for real.

Klut immediately jumped out from behind her. "You can't kill her!" he shouted.

"Y?" said Evil Eye.

"Because, because she's a princess."

The woman stopped dead, which encouraged Klut to continue. "And, and a princess is worth a lot of money. She can be ransomed for a lot of money and if you kill her she won't be worth anything at all..." All of the ugly women turned to look at Evil Eye, who stroked his beard thoughtfully.

"How much she worth?" he asked.

"Oh a lot," said Klut. "Her grandfather's a king, she must be worth a million Inter-Space Dollars at least."

"More!" said Rhiannon indignantly.

Evil Eye looked her up and down.

"How I know u not lie?"

"Because princesses never tell lies," said Rhiannon. Evil Eye grinned, revealing a mouthful of black and missing teeth.

"We see," he said. "Fetch Skull Eater!"

Rhiannon looked at Klut in horror as one of the women ran off to fetch something. A second later she returned with a blood red lizard with six legs. There were three claws on the end of each leg and a head at each end of its body. Each of the heads consisted of an enormous, fanged mouth but there were no eyes to be seen anywhere.

"Zis Skull Eater," said Evil Eye. "We put it on u head, and if u tell lie it eat u brains!"

"NO WAY!" shrieked Rhiannon. But it was too late. Some of the women rushed forward and grabbed her by the arms, while the other woman placed Skull Eater on Rhiannon's head. She felt the claws on its six legs grasp her head and almost fainted at the thought of it all.

"Zis dame say she a Princess: is zis true Skull Eater?" The lizard clamped a tight hold on Rhiannon's head and then raised its own heads high in the air. It held itself like that for a moment and then released her.

"U tell truth." said Evil Eye. Rhiannon breathed an enormous sigh of relief as the women took Skull Eater off her head.

Klut had become very excited.
"This is amazing!" he cried. "This creature is telepathic: that's why it has no eyes. Instead it reads people's thoughts. Someone must have trained it to eat the brains of people who tell lies!"
Rhiannon gave him a withering look. "Now you tell me! You could have let me know before it was put on my head!"
"I only worked it out just now," said Klut, rather timidly.

Just then Bill spoke up. "What's going to happen to Klut and myself?" he asked quietly,
"U two die horribly," said Evil Eye calmly.
Klut gulped in alarm. "No you can't! There are people willing to pay a ransom for us too!"
Evil Eye looked at Klut with his burning eyes.
"OK, let's zee if zis true: stick Skull Eater on Alien's head."
"NO!" screamed Klut, but it was too late. The women grabbed him roughly and placed the blood red lizard on his head.

"He say people pay ransom for both of dem: is zis true Skull Eater?" Skull Eater grasped Klut's head, which wasn't easy as the top of it was completely flat and the lizard didn't seem used to that sort of head. When it finally had a firm grip the two heads of the lizard arched upwards. Klut was shaking like a leaf.
"The Northern Corporations, the Northern Corporations will pay our ransom!" he repeated over and over again, with his eyes closed tight. Suddenly the lizard let go of Klut's head and the women pulled it off.
"U tell truth," said Evil Eye, as Klut collapsed to the floor in relief and exhaustion. "We just kill zis punk hoo zap my spacezip," he said turning to Aracuria, who was still hidden beneath a covering of solidified green goo.
"NO!" screamed Rhiannon, Klut and Bill.
"He's worth more than all of us put together," said Rhiannon, but it was clear that Evil Eye wasn't listening. Instead he was staring intently at the Ring of Ra which glowed eerily on Aracuria's finger and which he had only just seen.
"Wat zis?" he said in amazement at the ring. "I want zis, I want zis, zis ring is mine!" He gripped Aracuria's finger and tried to pull the ring off. But no matter how hard he pulled it wouldn't budge.
"Give me a knife!" bellowed Evil Eye.
"No!" cried Rhiannon, "You can't have the Ring! We need it! It belongs to Aracuria!" Still Evil Eye didn't listen. Half a dozen of the women offered him knives or razors. He snatched up one of them and went to cut off Aracuria's finger.
"EVIL EYE!"

A woman's voice suddenly broke out in the room. It was soft and gentle but seemed immensely strong. Everyone froze, including Evil Eye.

"Hoo zat?" said the pirate, looking around the room to see where the voice had come from.
"If you want to know who speaks to you, look out of the window."

Evil Eye turned and stared out of the window into empty space, and as he turned so did everyone else.
"Where r u?" said Evil Eye, "If zis is trick, I gonna..." Suddenly the whole of deep space burst apart in a blaze of blue light that blinded everyone.
"This is not trick, Evil Eye. Harm one hair on Aracuria's head and I will grind you and yours into dust." The blue glow had come to cover the whole window, obliterating all the stars, and at the center of the glow appeared a woman, clothed in the sun, standing with her bare feet on the moon, with a crown of twelve stars on her head.
"It's that woman!" cried Rhiannon, "The one we saw underground on Thlagtha!" Klut and Bill recognized her as well. Then, just as suddenly as they had appeared, the glow and the woman vanished, leaving everyone staring out into emptiness of space.

Evil Eye slowly turned around. His face was bleached white. His hands dropped to his side and he let the knife with which he had been about to cut off Aracuria's finger fall to the ground. Without saying a word, he went back to his chair and sat down. Without Evil Eye it was obvious that none of the other pirates knew what to do, so Klut decided to ask them some questions.

"This is the Morrigan Deep Space Transport we're traveling on, but I thought that this spaceship belonged to the Demi-Demons of Draco. So how come you lot are in charge of it?"
"We stole it," said one of the pirates. "We stole it after we gave the green gemstone of Thlagtha to the demons for safe keeping."
"Which you had also stolen," said Klut.
"Yeah," said another. "Nothing wrong with that."
"Some people might disagree you," said Klut, "However, what is of more interest to me is where you are currently traveling."
"Draco," said one of the women pirates.

Klut and Rhiannon exchanged looks, then Klut continued, "And why, might I ask, are you going to Draco?"
"We're taking DreamTime to the demons for safe keeping," said another of the women.
"DreamTime?" asked Klut.
"It's a prison," said one of the men. "We stole it from the Inter-Space Police. It's the only one in the Universe and it's supposed to be really valuable." This intrigued Klut. He was just about to ask a host of questions about DreamTime when suddenly Evil Eye rose out his chair.

"DreamTime," he said. "DreamTime," he repeated walking over to Aracuria and the others. "If I can't 'ave zis ring, zen no one will use it, ever. DreamTime."

"What's he talking about?" Rhiannon whispered to Klut, but before he could answer Evil Eye shouted out, "Throw zem in DREAMTIME!"

Immediately all of the pirates rushed forward and picked up Aracuria and the others. They charged towards a large double door in the wall, passing by the hole in the floor as they did so. Rhiannon shouted out to Roger, but Roger was nowhere to be seen. Once they had burst through the door, they ran down a long corridor and came to a halt in front of a small round tower painted with red and white diagonal stripes. In the side of the tower was a door with a handle on it. The pirates opened the door and placed Aracuria and the others in front of it. With the exception of Aracuria, who didn't have a clue what was going on, they all stared in amazement through the door, because beyond it, instead of there being a small round room, there was in fact a vast expanse of space filled with glowing, sparkling colors that continually changed shape and shimmered.

"What is this?" asked Rhiannon.

Klut groaned. "It's, it's a pan-dimensional prison, a man-made Black Hole: once we get thrown in there, I don't know how we'll ever get out."

"EXACTLY!" roared Evil Eye, as he picked up Aracuria and threw him through the door.

"ARACURIA!" cried Rhiannon, as she watched him drift off into multi-colored space. But before she had time to say anything else, one of the women pushed her forward, while Evil Eye booted Klut and Bill through the door.

"AARRAAGH!" they all screamed, as the next second all four of them found themselves floating through empty space into the Black Hole of DreamTime.

CHAPTER FIVE: DUCKSEA

Rhiannon was floating in a sea of light. Aracuria and the others were there, only they seemed so far away. At first, they all found themselves spinning in the light, but then they began to stay upright and before long they all came back together. It was almost as if they had landed somewhere. They were in a wide open place and in front of them was a large sign with the words WELCOME TO DREAMTIME: THE ETERNAL PRISON.

Rhiannon groaned. "This is awful!" she said despondently to Klut and Bill. "We can't stay in this weird place for ever. We've got things to do, a whole world to save..." But Klut and Bill were too upset to answer. Rhiannon looked at Aracuria, who was standing alone with his head still covered in a rubber mask. "Klut!" she said, "Give me a hand to get this thing off Aracuria's head: maybe if he uses his Ring of Ra it might get us out of here." Klut came immediately, pleased at the thought. He caught hold of the rubber head mask.

"I think we can pull it off," he said, "although it might hurt Aracuria a bit."

"Better that than he be stuck inside it forever," said Rhiannon, as she too grasped the rubber mask. "PULL!" she cried. Klut did as she said and with a heave they pulled Aracuria off his feet, but the rubber mask hadn't budged at all. "Bill!" ordered Rhiannon, "take hold of Aracuria's legs." Bill did as he was told while Rhiannon and Klut pulled on the head mask with all their might.

For perhaps ten minutes they staggered first one way and then the other trying to pull off the rubber mask while Aracuria kicked around furiously with his legs and waved his arms manically. Finally, after one gigantic tug the rubber mask peeled off Aracuria's head with an enormous PLOP, which was then followed by an enormous scream as Aracuria's head came into view.

"AARRAAGH!" For a few seconds he hopped around rubbing his hair and his face and then finally when the pain had subsided he sat down on the ground and looked around in wonder at all the shimmering colors.

"Where, where are we? Are we in Heaven?" he asked.

"More like Hell," said Klut grimly.

"What happened: how did we get here?"

"The pirates threw us in here," said Rhiannon, "after that woman stopped Evil Eye from cutting the Ring of Ra off your finger."

"Woman, Evil Eye, here? Where is 'here'?"

"This is DreamTime," said Klut, "It's a man-made Black Hole, designed as a prison for people like the Zombie Space Pirates. We were wondering whether you could use the Ring to get us out."

Whatever had happened, Aracuria felt very relieved that he still had the Ring of Ra. He looked down at his finger and suddenly his heart almost stopped.
"The Ring! The Ring has stopped glowing!" Everyone gathered around.
"Oh no!" said Rhiannon.
"See, see if it still works!" said Klut in alarm. Aracuria aimed the Ring at the signpost, closed his eyes and wished for something to happen: nothing did. He tried again and again, but each time the result was the same.
"It's broken!" he cried. "Those pirates might as well have cut it off my hand."
Klut stared wistfully at the Ring and then looked at Aracuria, "The Rings of Ra brought our Universe into being: they don't work outside of our Universe, which means that this DreamTime Black Hole must be outside of our Universe, and yet not in another.
"So where are we?" asked Rhiannon.
"Floating somewhere in the Cosmic Sea that fills all the spaces in between all the Universes." said Klut.
Bill looked up in terror.
"This is scary." he said, and he never spoke a truer word.

For a few moments the four of them just stood around, not knowing what to do. Then, when Aracuria had regained his senses, he walked off in the direction of the signpost.
"Where are you going?" asked Rhiannon.
"I don't know, but I'm not standing around here waiting for nothing to happen."
Hastily, Rhiannon and the others set off to follow him.

Aracuria passed under the signpost and continued in what he hoped was a straight line. After about a hundred meters, a cloud of mist began to appear on the ground and the shimmering colors around them started to disappear. The farther they walked the more the colors faded, until finally, after another hundred meters or so they appeared to be in normal surroundings. In front of them was a large, brightly lit building. At the bottom of the building was a revolving door with words THE CITY OF DUCKSEA written above it in neon lights.
"What is this place? How can it be a city when it's only a tower block?" wondered Rhiannon, but no one had an answer. Instead Aracuria led the way to the building and entered through the door. He found himself in a lobby with a counter in front of him at which a middle-aged woman stood, all alone. Aracuria approached her cautiously.
"Can you help us?" he asked.
"Of course," she said, smiling kindly.
"We want to get out of this place, out of DreamTime," said Aracuria.
"Of course you do," said the woman sympathetically.
"Is it possible to get out of it?" asked Rhiannon.

"Of course it is possible to get out. All you have to do is show that you're a responsible citizen and you will be released from DreamTime."
Rhiannon beamed broadly at this information.
"That's great!" she said. "You see, we are the most responsible people you could ever hope to meet because we're responsible for saving a whole planet from death, decay and destruction. At this very moment we're on our way to save it from being turned into a giant snowball."

The woman behind the counter suddenly looked very unimpressed. "THAT is no concern of MINE!" she said haughtily. She picked up a pen from the counter and prepared to fill in a form. "What crime did you commit?"
Rhiannon looked at the others in horror. "We haven't committed any crime!" she cried.
The woman gave her a withering look. "DreamTime is a correctional facility for justifying maladjusted citizens. No non-maladjusted citizen would be admitted into DreamTime, therefore you four are maladjusted citizens in need of justification."
Rhiannon turned to Aracuria. "What did she say?" Aracuria didn't understand either. Klut stepped forward.
"By 'justified' I assume you mean made a law abiding citizen," he said.
"What else COULD it mean?" snapped the woman.
"Well madam," said Klut, reasonably, "I can assure you that even though we are only kids, we are indeed all responsible citizens and therefore... you are wrong."
The woman's expression changed. "Did you say you were 'kids'?" She smiled as she spoke: the four of them nodded. "Well then you have committed a crime after all. To be a child is not to be a citizen in the full sense of the word. After all, you can't vote, you don't pay taxes; teachers and parents can beat you up if they want to and there is NOTHING you can do about it. Therefore you are maladjusted to society and maladjusted citizens are criminals." Rhiannon and Aracuria looked at each other: they didn't like her.

The woman picked up her pen and set about filling out the form. When she had finished, she handed it to Aracuria.
"Take this to the first room on the next floor up: they'll tell you what to do next."
Aracuria glanced at the form. "But there's nothing written on it." he said.
"Of course there isn't anything written on it: if I filled in all the forms for all the people who come in here my pen would soon run out of ink and then I wouldn't be able to fill in any forms at all."

Feeling rather bewildered, Aracuria walked off down the corridor with the others following behind. When they were out of earshot Rhiannon spoke.

"That woman is a head case," she declared. Aracuria had a funny feeling she wouldn't be the last one they would meet.

Aracuria led the way down a corridor and up a flight of steps; they found themselves in front of a door. Aracuria knocked, but when no one answered he opened it all the same. The four of them stepped into what looked like restaurant. On the left hand side of the room were row upon row of seats and tables and behind the tables there was a self-service cafeteria with some wonderful looking food on display. There were pasties and pies, plates of chips and heaps of sandwiches, cream cakes and éclairs and every imaginable kind of cola and pop. It had been so long since any of them had eaten anything decent that sight of all the food made them realize how hungry they were. However, none of them moved because on the right hand side of the room were some of the scruffiest, poorest and most ill fed people that any of them had ever seen in their lives. There were hundreds if not thousands of people, all standing one behind the other, staring at the food. But none of them was doing anything.

"This is weird," said Rhiannon. She walked up to one of the people standing nearby. "Why don't you lot get something to eat? You all look so hungry."

But the man just looked at her with his cold, empty eyes and said nothing. When Aracuria saw this, he went over to the service area of the cafeteria. A women in a bright red apron behind the counter beamed brightly when she saw him approaching.

"Can I help you, sir?" she asked politely.

'Yeah, we're, kind of hungry. Could you get us some food?"

"Of course," said the woman. "What do you want?"

This really confused Aracuria. He couldn't understand what was going on.

"Hmm, before we order, could you tell me why there are all these hungry people here?"

The woman frowned. "Oh, those, those people haven't any money and you can't buy food without money." she said. That seemed a bit harsh to Aracuria. He reached into his jacket pocket and pulled out a wad of Inter-Space Dollars.

"I've got loads of money: could you give the four of us something to eat and then give these people as much food as all this will buy. There must be about ten thousand dollars here."

The woman glanced down at the wad of notes in Aracuria's hand.

"Oh, that isn't REAL money," she said scornfully. "Those people have loads of that stuff. In fact, that's all they've had to eat since they came in here. No, if you want to buy something here then you'll have to have real DreamTime money."

By now, Rhiannon and the others had joined Aracuria and they all looked confused. "Where, where do we get that?" said Rhiannon.

"Oh, you have to work for it." said the woman.

"Where do we find a job? We're new around here," said Aracuria.
"Why, at the Jobcentre, of course," said the woman. "Just go down the corridor, up the stairs to the first room on the right and they'll tell you what to do."

Aracuria and the others walked away from the cafeteria and made for the door, but just as they were about to go through it, a thought struck Rhiannon.
"If it's that easy to get a job, then why don't those people work instead of going hungry?" No one had an answer for that, except Klut.
"Maybe they're lazy," he said. But as was often the case, Klut was completely wrong.

CHAPTER SIX: GET A JOB

They left the cafeteria and climbed the stairs to the first room on the right. Aracuria marched straight in this time, with the others close behind. This room was smaller than the first and it looked a bit shabby and dirty. It was empty, except for a counter set against one wall behind which stood a middle-aged man, reading a newspaper. Seeing Aracuria approaching, he hurriedly put away his paper and smiled.

"What can I do for you, young man?" he asked.

"I want a job," said Aracuria.

"And so do we," added the others.

"Good, good," said the man enthusiastically, "and what kind of jobs would you be interested in?"

Aracuria's face went blank. "I'm, I'm not sure," he said, "I've never worked before, none of us have."

The man nodded sympathetically, and pulled out a set of forms and four pencils from behind the counter.

"If you'd like to answer the questions, you might find out what kind of job you would be interested in," he said helpfully. Each of them took one of the forms and one of the pencils and began to answer the questions. They were mostly to do with the kind of things you liked doing. Klut filled his form in in about eight seconds, while Aracuria and Rhiannon took about ten minutes. It was only when she had finished that Rhiannon noticed that Bill was still trying to answer the first question, "Do you like biting the heads off chickens?" When Rhiannon saw this, she was astonished because all the others forms started with the question, "Do you like being with other people or do you prefer your own company." She pointed this out to the man behind the counter, who apologized profusely and handed Bill the correct form.

As Bill handed the wrong form back to the man, Rhiannon caught sight of the next question, which was "Have you ever drunk a bucket full of pigs entrails?" and she wondered just exactly what that form was for.

After Bill had finished filling out the correct form, the man read through them all. As he finished each one, he wrote down something in pencil on a separate sheet of paper. It took him about half an hour to read all the forms, by which time Aracuria and the others were feeling really famished, so they were all eager to start work to earn some money and get something to eat. At last the man finished the last form and looked up.

"Klut, which one of you is Klut?" Klut raised his hand: the man smiled at him warmly.

"It is obvious from this form that you would be most suited to become a nurse."

"What!" cried Klut. "That's rubbish! I've always wanted to be a nuclear-physicist."
The man shook his head, "I think not: you really have all the qualifications here to become a nurse, and I'm sure you'd make a lovely one."

Before Klut could open his mouth to protest, the man bad moved on to Rhiannon.
"Rhiannon, I think from the way you filled this form in you would make an excellent miner."
"What!" she screamed, "I could never become a miner: I hate dirt and filth. I've always wanted to become an Air Force fighter pilot."
The man shook his head slowly. "I think not: Mining would suit you down to the ground."

While Rhiannon fumed the man turned to Aracuria.
"Aracuria, this form tells me that you really want to be a dustman."
"What!" yelled Aracuria, "I hate rubbish, I come from a planet that's covered in rubbish. At one time I used to live inside a tip of rubbish. The last thing I would ever want to be is a dustman: I've always wanted to be a gardener."
The man looked straight at him. "The form says that your heart is in garbage, young man." Before Aracuria had time to answer, the man had turned to Bill.

"Bill, the way you filled this form in indicates that you would make a superb Managing Director of a multi-national corporation: you're really a high powered high flyer." Aracuria and the others looked at Bill in astonishment.
"Yes," he said quietly, "I've always wanted to do that." For a moment everyone was dumbfounded, but, thinking it over, Aracuria decided that as a Managing Director Bill would earn enough in an hour to feed them all and as he was the only one who wanted the job he alone was going to work.
Aracuria turned to man. "Well then, do you have any vacancies for Managing Directors of multi-national corporations?" The man reached under the counter and pulled out a portable computer. He pressed a few buttons and then stared at the screen.
"No, no sorry we don't have any at the moment: if you would like to come in later, we may have some vacancies." Bill's face fell, and the others felt awful too.

For a moment there was a gloomy silence and then Aracuria, who felt that he was going to have to sacrifice himself in order to fill his stomach, said, "OK then, I'm willing to work as a dustman to get something to eat: do you have any vacancies?" The man turned back to the screen, pressed a few more buttons and shook his head.
"No, I'm afraid we don't .Sorry to disappoint you: if you would like to come back later we may have some vacancies.' Aracuria didn't know whether to feel sad or glad.

It was now Rhiannon's turn, "Even though I hate the very thought of becoming a miner, if that's the only way we are going to get something to eat

then I'll just have to be one: do you have any vacancies?" The man turned back to the screen. He pressed yet more buttons and then shook his head.
"Sorry, there just aren't any jobs going for miners: if you would like to come again later we may have some vacancies." Aracuria and the others now turned to look at Klut.
"What are you lot looking at?" he said.
"You're going to have to become a nurse," said Aracuria.
"You must be kidding!" Klut exploded. Aracuria shook his head. "I'm a genius, any idiot can be a nurse: I'd rather be roasted alive than become one."
"That could be arranged," said Rhiannon in a cutting tone: Klut could see that she meant it.
"OK, OK. I'll sacrifice all my talents, all my genius, all my priceless intelligence to become a nurse so that you three can have something to eat, but I can assure you I have gone right off the thought of food." Rhiannon turned to the man. "Do you have any vacancies for nurses?" The man looked at his screen, pressed yet more buttons, and then shook his head.
"Sorry, no jobs for nurses at the moment: if you would like to come later we may have some vacancies."

Aracuria couldn't believe this.
"What on earth is the point in us filling in those forms if there are no jobs available as managing directors, dustmen, miners or nurses?" The man shrugged.
"Well, I didn't know that those were the jobs you were going to be suited to." Aracuria had to admit he had a point.
"OK then, have you got any other jobs available for us to do," said Rhiannon.
"We'll do anything," added Klut. The man looked back at his screen, pressed a few more buttons and then said, "Ah, no."
Aracuria looked at him in complete bewilderment. "What do you mean, 'no'?" he asked. The man shook his head apologetically.
"There are no jobs."
Rhiannon reached out and turned the computer screen around: it was displaying a computer chess game.
"What!" she bellowed, "there are no jobs displayed here."
"I never said there were," said the man reasonably. He might have spoken the truth, but all the same Rhiannon was about to club him. Aracuria hurriedly stopped her.
"Look, we're hungry," he said. "Stop playing games with us: if there are no jobs for us to do then where can we get some money to buy something to eat?"
"The Department of Social Insecurity," said the man. "Go up the stairs and it's the first door on the left.

Aracuria and the others went up the stairs to the next floor. They were all as angry as could be at having wasted their time looking for jobs that

didn't exist. They all marched straight into the next room. Here there was another counter with a middle-aged woman behind it, only this time the counter was topped with a thick glass screen.
"We want some money," said Rhiannon bluntly.
"Are you unemployed?" asked the woman.
"Well, we haven't got a job," said Aracuria.
The woman smiled a cruel smile. "That ISN'T what I asked you," she said.
"You mean there's a difference?" said Rhiannon.
"Of course," replied the woman.
Klut looked astonished. "It's a logical impossibility that being unemployed and not having a job are not the same," he said with authority.
"Logic has nothing to do with it," said the woman. "Are you unemployed, yes or no? We can't give you any money for being unemployed unless we know that you are unemployed and not just pretending."
"Yes," said Rhiannon angrily, "we ARE unemployed."
"Well, let's make sure you are," said the woman, pulling a mass of forms out from under the counter. She pushed a blue form under the glass.
"This is the Blue Form which you fill in to prove to us that you are unemployed: we require that a Blue Form be filled in every eight seconds."

Klut picked up the form and looked through it.

"But this form is twenty pages long and asks an average of seven questions on each page..."
The woman interrupted him as if he had said nothing.
"And then when you have filled in the Blue Form you have to fill in the Pink Form in which you tell us what you were doing for the seven seconds prior to filling in the Blue Form." The woman slid the Pink Form under the glass.
Klut picked it up and looked through it, "But this Pink form is fifteen pages long and it asks you to put your name and address on each page before you even answer any of the questions..."

The woman once again cut him short.

"Then, when you've filled in every tenth Pink form and Blue Form, you have to fill in a Red Form in which you tell us what you've been doing to find work since you started filling in the Pink and Blue forms."
"But that's crazy!" blurted out Rhiannon, "How can we look for work if we spend all our time filling in these forms?"
"If you haven't been looking for work, for whatever reason, then we can't give you any money as it would be wrong to help people who won't help themselves."
"But it's impossible!" said Klut. "No one could fill in all these forms in the time you give them, let alone look for work as well." The woman smiled in satisfaction.
"Well that's only because you weren't really unemployed in the first place."

Everyone was now very angry, except Bill who asked quietly,

"How many unemployed people are there in DreamTime?"

The woman pulled out a computer screen from beneath the desk, and tapped some of the keys.
"Ah, none." she said.
"None!" yelled Rhiannon, "Then who are all those unemployed, hungry looking people in the restaurant?"
"What people?" said the woman.
"The ones standing looking at all the food," said Aracuria, "Or have you never been in there?"
"I go in every lunchtime and I have never seen any unemployed people there: how could I? They don't exist."
By now Rhiannon was red with rage and it looked as if she might smash the glass and hit the woman over her head with the computer.
"We want to complain," said Aracuria.
"Yes, we want to complain," said Klut.
"All complaints have to be addressed to the Ducksea Councilors. They are in permanent session upstairs, first room on the right." The woman put her computer screen back under the counter and then put away her forms. Aracuria and Klut led Rhiannon outside before she did something violent.
"But it's so cruel," raged Rhiannon, "It would be better if they said there were no jobs or money to be had at all rather than deceive people like that." Rhiannon was right, but they were soon to find that complaining was a waste of time as well.

CHAPTER SEVEN: THE BUTLER

Aracuria led the way up the next flight of stairs to yet another room. He pushed open the door, expecting to see another counter, but what he actually saw made him freeze in amazement: in front of him was a beach which ran down to a large, wide bay. The bay arched around in a great circle and in the distance, which seemed many miles away, it ended at two little islands.

"This, this is incredible," gasped Rhiannon.

"Indeed," said Klut sagely.

"Weird," added Bill, but Aracuria said nothing, because he had suddenly spotted that the beach was littered with dead fish.

"Ugh!" said Rhiannon, catching a whiff of the rotting fish and holding her nose. Aracuria noticed that at the water's edge was a long table at which sat six middle-aged men.

"Who are they?"

"They, I believe, are the Ducksea Councilors," said Klut, because it was difficult to see who else they could be.

Aracuria led the way down the beach to where the Councilors were seated, just a few feet away from the sea. They all seemed to be in deep conversation. For a moment Aracuria stood in silence, but when no one took the faintest notice of him he coughed. One of the Councilors immediately looked up.

"Do you realize how many germs you have just spread over us with that cough?"

"You should be ashamed of yourself," said another.

"More than ashamed," said a third, who started to flick through the pages of a huge book that he had open in front of him, "Under the Local Government (Ducksea Special Edition) Act of 2055 AD it is a criminal offence, punishable by 300 years in prison, to wittingly, or unwittingly infect Local Government Officers or their Representatives with the known or unknown contents of a cough." Aracuria didn't know what to say, but Rhiannon did. However, before she had a chance to shout it at one of the Councilors, Klut spoke up.

"Excuse me, but you said that that act was framed in 2055 AD. AD means 'In the Year of our Lord' and it is an expression taken from the religious history of Earth. Now this is not Earth, so how can you make use of the expression 'AD'?"

The Councilors looked at one other in amazement. "AD means In the Year of Ducksea," said one of them, pulling a top hat from under the table and putting it on. "And when you talk to me in future you will call me The Honorable City Treasurer Butler."

"Are you a butler then," asked Rhiannon innocently. The man's face suddenly flushed bright red with rage.
"My name is BUTLER! I am not a BUTLER, I am the City Treasurer!" he bellowed.

Rhiannon waited patiently for him to finish, then she stepped forward and leaned on the table.
"Look here, you miserable little squirt, it doesn't matter to me one bit what job you've got in this non-existent little seaside town called Ducksea. On the planet where I come from I'm a Princess and if I wanted I could have you chopped into little pieces and fed to hamsters for shouting at me like that..." Before she had time to finish one of the other men started shouting.
"Out of order, out of order! You are all out of order! This is a private, closed session of Ducksea City Council and none of you is allowed to speak, EVER!"

Rhiannon was about to round on him when the man with the big book in front of him began reading from another page.
"Under the Ducksea Local Government Act of 755 AD it is a criminal offence, punishable by public beheading, to interrupt a Councilor while he is speaking." Rhiannon was about to put the big book where it would hurt the man most when Aracuria spoke.
"We are sorry that we interrupted your meeting, but we've come here to make a complaint."
All six Councilors looked at him in astonishment. "WHAT!" they screamed.
"We've come to complain about the way in which people are treated in your 'city'," continued Aracuria, " but to be honest it can't be much of a city if it's only housed in one tower block, even if you have got a beach on the roof."
Immediately one of the Councilors leapt to his feet and yelled at Aracuria. "How DARE you insult our lovely city! Ducksea is a BEAUTIFUL city!"
"Lovely!" said Rhiannon sarcastically, "What about all these dead fish then?"
"What dead fish?" demanded the Councilor, looking up in the sky, "I can't see any dead fish."
"That's because fish, dead or otherwise, don't fly," said Klut. He was just about to tell the Councilor to look on the beach for the fish when Rhiannon picked up one of the dead ones that was lying at her feet.
"Oh yes they do, Klut," she said, as she hurled a stinking cod into the Councilor's face.
"ASSAULT!" screamed the Councilor before the well-aimed cod forced him to shut up.

The man with the book at once began reading out another page.
"Insulting Ducksea is a criminal offence, as is assaulting a Councilor with a dead fish. The relevant acts specify 1000 years in prison and public hanging."

Aracuria had had enough. "You Ducksea Councilors are all crazy, just like your so-called city!" He picked up the book and threw it into the sea. Only it never reached the sea, because just as the book should have splashed into the water it hit something solid and then fell back on to the beach. But as it hit the beach so a door opened up where the book had hit the sea, because the sea wasn't a real sea at all. It was, in fact, painted on to a wall and the book had just opened up a secret door.

When Klut saw this he quickly scuffed the sand aside with his foot and found that there underneath was a carpet.

"This is all a con," he cried. "This isn't a real beach at all."

Aracuria walked around the table. "What's behind that door?" he demanded.

"You can't go in there!" shrieked Councilor Butler. "That's the secret room where Lord Ducksea lives: if you promise not to go in there we'll listen to your complaints."

"It's too late for that now," said Rhiannon, pushing the Councilor into his chair and knocking his top hat off in the process.

"I think we'll all go pay Lord Ducksea a visit," said Aracuria. "It's obvious you six idiots couldn't run a clockwork train set, let alone a city, so this Lord must be in charge of everything."

He pushed the door wide open, while the Councilors fell to their knees and started begging them not to go and see the Lord. Behind the door was a small corridor, which abruptly stopped at another door with the words 'Lord Ducksea' written on it in gold letters. Aracuria pushed on the door, but it wouldn't budge.

"Give me a hand here, it appears to be stuck."

Rhiannon came to help him push, then Klut and then finally Bill, but still it wouldn't budge no matter how hard they pushed. All this time the Councilors were crying and weeping, so to shut them out Rhiannon went back and closed the first door: the moment she did so the one against which Aracuria, Klut and Bill were pushing suddenly opened, sending the three of them flying into another room.

Klut was the first to pick himself up off the floor, only to find himself in a completely empty room.

"The doors are linked," he said, "presumably so that no one can look from one room to another."

"That means those Councilors could never have known that there's nothing in here," said Aracuria standing up. Rhiannon stepped into the room and looked around it. Even though it was empty she noticed that there was another door in the far wall. She walked across and opened it, and then stood back in horror as the door opened out on to empty space, that was filled only in glowing colors.

"Well, what do we do now?" she groaned. "It looks like we're back where we started."

Aracuria came over and stared out into the shimmering colors of DreamTime. "I don't know what to do," he said at last. "I really don't know how to get out of this place: nothing here is real, least of all the City of Ducksea and I bet the rest of DreamTime is just like this."
"This is dreadful," said Rhiannon sadly.
"If only that woman would help us again," said Bill.

Aracuria watched Rhiannon nod in agreement, but he didn't have a clue what Bill was talking about. "What woman? Rhiannon said something about a woman when you ripped that rubber mask off my head, but no one explained who she was then either."
"That woman, the one we saw on Thlagtha, the one with the stars on her head and the Moon under her..."
Aracuria's face lit up. "You mean SHE has appeared to you as well?"
"As well?" said Rhiannon, "Do you mean she's appeared to you? She seemed to like you. She told Evil Eye she'd smash him to dust if he hurt you in any way, though she didn't do anything to stop him from terrifying us."
"Yes, I know her," said Aracuria. "She appeared to me in the Fountain on Thlagtha."
"In the Fountain!" said Rhiannon in disbelief,
"Yes, in the Fountain of Theom."

As Aracuria spoke the last word, the glowing colors in the empty space beyond the door all changed to blue.
"Who calls my name?" said a voice.
Everyone was astonished, but Aracuria stood up, "I, I do. Aracuria, does." he said.
"Why have you waited so long to call me? The time is late. Already Lucifer knows that you are on board his stolen spaceship and the spaceship is just about to reach Draco."
"Oh no," gasped Klut, shivering at this news.
"Can you get us out of DreamTime?" asked Aracuria.
"DreamTime, DreamTime is an intrusion into the Cosmic Sea. First I will release you and then I will destroy it."
"But what about all the people in Ducksea?" asked Rhiannon.
"There are no people here except you: all the rest are images. Aracuria, step into the light, and your friends must follow you." Aracuria looked down into the bottomless blue emptiness of space.
"But I'll fall," he said uncertainly.
"Trust me," said the voice.

Aracuria closed his eyes and stepped out into empty space. For a moment he expected to fall like a stone, but when he didn't he opened his eyes.
"I, I can walk in mid air," he cried. "Do as she says: follow me!" Rhiannon closed her eyes and stepped out into empty space. When she to didn't fall she

walked over to Aracuria. “Come on you two,” she said to Klut and Bill, “it’s easy.”
Klut and especially Bill were dubious about following, but since Aracuria and Rhiannon were now clearly hovering in mid air, it was obvious it could be done. Both of them stepped out into thin air and, when they didn’t fall, Aracuria led the rest of them off through empty space. Up ahead there was a square, white light. Aracuria headed straight for it and hoped that it would lead them out of DreamTime. He was right; but it also led straight to Lucifer.

CHAPTER EIGHT: CAPTAIN OF THE SHIP

Aracuria approached the square of light. The next moment he passed straight through it and found himself stepping out into the cargo hold of the Morrigan Deep Space Cargo Transport, a cargo hold that was itself filled with light.

"We're out of DreamTime!" he cried. He turned around and saw that the door to the white and yellow tower was open and beyond it were all the shimmering colors that he hadn't seen when he was thrown into DreamTime. A few seconds later Rhiannon, Klut and Bill stepped out of the door as if appearing from nowhere. Once Bill had stepped through the colors in the tower suddenly vanished and, instead of looking through a door into empty space, all they could now see was the inside of a small, round room whose walls were covered in tin foil.

"I guess that's the end of DreamTime and Ducksea," said Aracuria, but no one else seemed to be listening.

"The light: where's this blinding light coming from?" asked Rhiannon, shading her eyes. Down the corridor that led to the cargo hold a brilliant white light was shining.

"Wasn't it like this when we were thrown into DreamTime?" asked Aracuria.

"No way," said Rhiannon. "This place was dark then."

"Well, we'd better find out where it's coming from," said Aracuria, as he shielded his eyes with his right hand and started off up the corridor.

At the end of the corridor was a set of doors that were propped open. Aracuria went through them and found himself back in the control room of the space ship. In front of him were the rows of instruments and dials and the seats filled with Zombie Space Pirates, but in the huge, curved window, instead of thousands of stars there was now only one. But that single star shone as brightly as any sun. Instead of hanging alone in the sky, it stood on top of a blood red planet whose flaming surface of molten lava glowed eerily.

"The Tree of Life!" cried Aracuria: they had made it to Draco. At the sound of Aracuria's voice, all of the pirates suddenly swung around.

"How u get out of DreamTime?" roared Evil Eye, who like the others was now wearing a pair of dark glasses. When Aracuria didn't answer, Evil Eye jumped out of his fur lined chair:

"Kill zem! Kill zem ALL!"

Rhiannon rushed to Aracuria's side. "You've got to use your ring! Remember you don't just have to send out lightning: you can wish for anything!"

Aracuria glanced at the Ring of Ra and saw that it was now glowing again. He pointed it at Evil Eye, who was just about to charge at him.

"You remind me of a bull," Aracuria said to himself: immediately Evil Eye turned into the most ferocious bull that Aracuria had ever seen.

All the other pirates stopped dead in their tracks when they saw what had happened, but Evil Eye didn't realize anything was wrong and he was still about to charge.

"I mean a pig!" cried Aracuria aloud. Instantly Evil Eye turned from a huge bull into the most ferocious boar that Aracuria had ever seen: it had huge tusks and evil-looking eyes that seemed to glow through the pair of sunglasses. The boar began its charge, heading straight for Aracuria's stomach with its pointed tusks.

"I mean a, a PIGLET!" shouted Aracuria. The next moment, the boar, who was now in full flight, turned into a little piglet, crashed straight into Aracuria's shin and knocked itself out.

"Change back to a man!" said Aracuria, pointing the ring at the unconscious piglet. In a flash, Evil Eye reappeared on the floor looking dazed. Some of the women ran forward and helped him to his feet.

"What, what U do to me?" he said, rubbing his head.

"If I want to, I can destroy you all!" said Aracuria, waving the ring in the air. Just then Evil Eye remembered how they had overcome Aracuria before with the phlegm gun.

"Smother him!" ordered Evil Eye.

At once, half a dozen pirates picked up the guns and prepared to fire at Aracuria. Aracuria pointed the ring at one of them and shouted out,

"Become, become a, a, kitchen!" He was almost lost for words, but as he said the word 'kitchen' so the six pirates turned into a set of fridges, cookers, washing machines and other kitchen appliances.

Evil Eye was speechless, and one by one all the other pirates stepped away from Aracuria.

"OK then," said Aracuria, "now you know what I can do. You with the big beard, you look as if you're in charge."

Rhiannon whispered in his ear, "He's called Evil Eye."

"OK Evil Eye, listen to me," said Aracuria, "You pirates are in great danger, more danger than we are, in fact, because down there is the planet of Draco and you dumb numbskulls have turned up here in a spaceship that belongs to the Demi-Demons of Draco. For that they are going to eviscerate you, after they have taken DreamTime off you. Well, DreamTime no longer exists, because a friend of mine, whom you saw in the window a little while ago, zapped it." The pirates now all looked rather upset. "But don't worry," continued Aracuria, "I want to make a deal with you..."

"You can't make a deal with these louts!" interrupted Rhiannon. Aracuria ignored her. "I want to make you this deal because it will be in all our interests. Down there, glowing like the sun, is the Tree of Life, which you might have heard of..." The pirates all looked at one another and then shook their heads.

“Oh, they really are dumb,” said Klut.
“Well, never mind, all you lot need know is that this is what we have come here for, and nothing else. However, the Tree of Life is held in a Treasure Chamber that is filled with all the most priceless treasures of the whole Universe. If you help us to get the Tree of Life then we will let you take as much treasure as the holds on this spaceship can carry.”

For a moment there was total silence, as Evil Eye thought over what Aracuria had said. At last, the pirate chief stepped forward, held out the palm of his hand and spat on it. For a moment Aracuria was perplexed at this strange action and was unsure what to do, then Rhiannon whispered, “You’ve got to slap it to cement the deal.”

Before Aracuria did so, he said, “And do you agree to take orders only from me?”
Evil Eye nodded, “Yeah!” he said.
As revolting as it was, Aracuria then slapped Evil Eye’s hand, sending a shower of spit over the lot of them.
“U got a deal, Boss,” said Evil Eye, as he pulled off his sunglasses and gave them to Aracuria to wear.
“Great!” said Aracuria, putting them on, as the women and other pirates stepped forward to perform the same spitting and slapping ritual with Klut, Bill and Rhiannon, all of whom found it disgusting but necessary.

When the spit had stopped flying around, Aracuria turned the various fridges, cookers and washing machines that littered the control room back into pirates. Evil Eye told them what had happened and then they in turn started another round of the spitting slapping ritual. When this second load of spit had finished splattering, Aracuria went to take his place in Evil Eye’s fur-lined seat. Just then there was an enormous groaning sound as Roger hauled himself up out of the hole in the floor.

“ROGER!” cried Rhiannon, running forward to hug his metallic knee. “It took you all this time to climb up all those floors! You’re wonderful.” Klut and Bill seated themselves on either side of Aracuria, while the pirates stood around.
“OK then,” said Aracuria, putting his feet up on the instrument console and staring out of the window at the burning planet, “The first thing we’ve got to do is work out how we are going to pick up the Tree of Life.
“Roger! Come here,” said Klut. “We are going to need your computing power.” Klut tapped a series of instructions into the console in front of him. Roger came alongside. “Right then Roger, Do you see this Video Terminal in front of me?” Roger looked down at the green, glowing screen in front of Klut.
“Well, I’ve just asked the on-board computer to display all the information it has on how the space ship originally picked up the Tree of Life from Eden. What I want you to do is to read all the information as it is displayed and then tell me how we do it.”

Roger stared at the screen, then Klut hit a button and the screen flooded with numbers, letters and diagrams, all of which flashed on and off at a fantastic speed. After about five seconds the screen went blank again.
"OK, how do we do it?" asked Klut.
"...Electro...nuclear - magnetic...fields...are...housed...in...the...Y..." said Roger. "...Position ...spaceship...above...Tree...and...press...this.. button..." He flicked up a little cover on the console to reveal a red button with the word LIFT written across it. Klut looked very pleased, but Aracuria and the others were baffled.
"Klut," said Aracuria, "could you explain to the Captain of this ship how we are going to lift the Tree of Life out of the Treasure Chamber?"
"It's simple," answered Klut. "The Tree of Life is as hot as any sun and for that reason it would burn through any normal container if anyone tried to carry it. So when the Demi Demons built this spaceship they put super-powerful magnets, powered by nuclear generators, in each of the ends of the 'Y' fork. All we have to do is position the space between the forked end of the spaceship above the Tree of Life, press the LIFT button and the Tree of Life will shoot up, burn its way through the top of the Treasure Chamber and come to rest in the middle of the fork. As long as we keep the magnets on, then the Tree of Life will stay there while we journey back to Earth. And when we get there we simply turn off the magnets and the Tree of Life will hang forever in space, keeping Earth warm."

Aracuria's face lit up: it was possible after all.

Rhiannon tapped him on the shoulder. "The trouble is, Lucifer isn't going to let us get away with it: how are we going to deal with him?" At that instant, the image of a handsome, suntanned man, dressed in a silver clothes appeared in the window. His hair was thick and black and his deep set eyes were filled with evil.
"IT'S LUCIFER!" screamed Bill. Everyone's jaw fell as they saw once again the man who a long time ago had tried to stop them from ever leaving Draco.
"My name is LUCIFER!" said the silver man, "Do I have the 'honor' of addressing the Zombie Space Pirates from the Dead Zone?"
Aracuria whispered to Evil Eye, "Say yes," Evil Eye nodded.
"Don't nod, you imbecile, answer him," hissed Klut. "He can't see you: it's only a computer projection on the window."
"Yeah!" said Evil Eye.

When Lucifer heard his voice he smiled. "Good, I know I can do business with someone as, 'intelligent' as yourself. I happen to know that you have a person called Aracuria on board 'your' spaceship, as well as some of his friends. His friends are of no interest to me, but I WANT Aracuria. Do you understand?" Aracuria nodded to Evil Eye.
"Yeah!" said Evil Eye.
"Good!" said Lucifer, "Well, if you hand Aracuria over to me in chains then I and my followers will overlook the fact that you stole our ageing spaceship.

We will not cut you and your wives into a billion pieces or throw your disgusting children to the twelve-eyed Child Gobbling Beastie of the Draco Schools' Inspectorate. In fact, if you give us Aracuria, we will let you keep our spaceship, for as long as it can fly."

Aracuria turned to Evil Eye and said quietly, "Tell him why you came here."

"We, ah, we came to deposit DreamTime," said Evil Eye.

"DreamTime!" exclaimed Lucifer. "So you bunch of uneducated gorillas stole THAT from the Inter-Space Police: I must congratulate you. Well, you can deposit DreamTime as well as Aracuria, but I want him NOW, or I'll blast 'your' spaceship into nothing, and no one will ever be able to put any of you back together again. You see, I don't trust Aracuria, not after what happened last time. So this time I'm not taking any chances. You have five seconds to do as I say or you will all die!"

Aracuria looked at Rhiannon, and Klut and then Bill: what on earth was he going to do now? One thing was sure: he had less than five seconds to find an answer...

CHAPTER NINE: ONTO DRACO

Rhiannon, Klut and Bill stared in horror as Lucifer started to count slowly down from five to one, all the while playing with the glowing gold chain that hung around his neck. When he got to three Rhiannon said desperately to Aracuria, "Do something!"

When he got to two Klut and Bill closed their eyes, but when he got to one Aracuria had an idea. He turned to Evil Eye. "Tell Lucifer that you threw me in DreamTime..."

Just then Lucifer shouted, "Your time is UP!"

"We threw Aracuria in DreamTime," said Evil Eye.

Lucifer said nothing.

Aracuria whispered to Evil Eye. "Tell him you'll bring me down to Draco as a prisoner in DreamTime."

"Aracuria is in DreamTime," said Evil Eye, "so we bring zem both down to u."

Suddenly Lucifer's evil face lit up in a smile. "How ingenious, my cerebral mollusk: I can't think of a better way to hold Aracuria than to keep him forever in the eternal prison of DreamTime. Very well, bring him down and then you and your brood can fly away to which ever Grotsville star system you come from."

Aracuria turned again to Evil Eye. "Tell him you want his word for it."

"We want your word, man," said Evil Eye.

Lucifer looked magnanimous. "As a god and a genius, you have my word." Then Lucifer's image disappeared from the window.

"A god and a genius!" scoffed Rhiannon. "How can you trust a man like that? I wouldn't trust him with the time of day."

Aracuria nodded. "Yeah, I know, but it might give us a little extra time when we try to get out of here."

He leaned back in his fur-lined chair and put his feet back on the computer terminal.

"How many people do you want to come with you when you go down to Draco?" asked Rhiannon.

Aracuria shook his head. "None."

"What!"

"You must be kidding," said Bill.

"If you go down there alone. you won't stand a chance against all those demons and monsters, let alone Lucifer," said Klut.

Aracuria scratched his chin. "I was thinking the exact opposite," he said. "I was thinking that the only chance we've got is to convince the demons that I can't possibly harm them. If I'm down there alone Lucifer won't be worried that I'm going to steal the Tree of Life. After all, he thinks Evil Eye and his pirates are holding the rest of you hostage. So the plan is simple; Evil Eye and his pirates take me down to Draco in DreamTime, where they leave me..."

Bill butted in. "What about Glenys?" he asked. Glenys was a Solar Duck that they had had to leave behind on their last trip to Draco.

"Glenys!" cried Rhiannon. "I'd forgotten all about her: oh, Evil Eye has to bring Glenys back up because I promised her we'd come and collect her one day."

Aracuria nodded. "OK, Evil Eye and his pirates will pick up Glenys while I fight my way to the heart of Draco. While I'm occupying the demons, I want you to place this spaceship above the Treasure Chamber and when you're in position, hit that LIFT button and pick up the Tree of Life." He turned to Klut. "What will happen to all the other treasure in the Treasure Chamber when the Tree of Life burns through the roof?"

"It will all be sucked out into space," said Klut.

"Do we have some way of picking it up?"

"Easy," said Klut, "We can pump it all on board and store the lot of it in the dozens of vast cargo holds that this space ship has."

Aracuria grinned. "Great, then that's the plan."

"Aracuria," said Bill quietly, "How do you get out of Draco once we've picked up the Tree of Life?" Aracuria didn't have an answer for that. Rhiannon looked anxious. "This is really dangerous Aracuria," she said, stating the obvious.

"I know," he said, "but that woman said it was my destiny to get back the Tree of Life and this seems like the only way of doing it. Lucifer's greatest weakness is his arrogance. He can't believe that a kid from a small planet on the other side of the Universe could take away from him what he managed to steal from God. Once you've picked up the Tree of Life, hit the Hyper-Space button and get the hell out of here back to Earth."

"OH NO!" shrieked Rhiannon.

"We can't leave you here to DIE!" cried Klut.

"Don't do it," pleaded Bill.

Aracuria shrugged his shoulders. "The fact is, I don't know how I'm going to get out of Draco," he admitted. "But if I don't go down there, Lucifer will blow you all out of space the second you lift the Tree of Life and if you hang around too long after you've picked it up he'll destroy you anyway, promise or no promise..."

A deep silence fell on everyone, broken only by the gentle crackle of the electronic instruments. Finally Aracuria took his feet off the console and stood up.

"Come on Evil Eye, get some of your men to take me down to Draco." Without another word he led the pirates out of the room and down the corridor towards DreamTime. Rhiannon, Klut and Bill watched him go with tears in their eyes, and even Roger looked upset.

When Aracuria reached the white and yellow tower, he opened the door and stepped inside the circular room.

"OK Evil Eye, you know what to do?"

The pirate nodded. "U very brave," he said, "braver than anyone I ever knew." All the other pirates nodded. Evil Eye took Aracuria by the shoulders and hugged him, which almost brought an end to his life there and then. "I wanna give u warrior's present," said the pirate chief. He took off his leather jacket and placed it on Aracuria. The jacket was about ten times too big and the leather arms hung down to Aracuria's knees.

"Thank you Evil Eye: it's the nicest thing anyone has ever given me."

Evil Eye closed the door to the tower. For a moment Aracuria was in complete darkness. "I wish this jacket would fit me," he sighed, and as he spoke so Evil Eye's jacket started to shrink, until it fitted him perfectly. As the arms shortened so the ring on his finger became visible and Aracuria found himself alone in a small round room lit only by the haunting glow of the Ring of Ra, as its light reflected off the silver foil walls.

A few moments later, Evil Eye and his men picked up DreamTime in a space shuttle and took off from the Morrigan Deep Space Cargo Transport. They flew under the shade of the giant belly of the spaceship and came out into the glaring glow of the Tree of Life. Inside DreamTime, Aracuria found himself floating in mid air, which could only mean that DreamTime was now out in space being transported to Draco. Evil Eye guided the space shuttle away from the spaceship, then swooped down to glide over the blood red surface of Draco. The whole planet was covered in burning molten metal and the space shuttle glowed a brilliant red as it passed over the fires. Up ahead was a huge mountain on top of which was the Treasure Chamber. Out of this glowed the Tree of Life like a captive sun. Evil Eye made straight for the mountain and, just as it seemed he might crash into the side of it so a huge, slit-like door in the rock opened up, allowing the space shuttle to fly in.

It took only a few moments for the shuttle to land. The pirates unloaded DreamTime and began to look around for Glenys. The hall that they were in was very large and seemed to be made of pure glass, but it also appeared completely empty. Then one of the pirates spotted something in one of the corners. Evil Eye and the others made their way across and saw that there, lying on the floor and absolutely covered in dust and cobwebs, was what looked like a dead Solar Duck, only without any legs. But then Evil Eye hit Glenys on the head, and when her eyes blinked wearily he knew that there was still life in her, in spite of the long years that she had obviously been waiting for Aracuria and the others to return. The pirates brought the space shuttle across, picked up Glenys and took off again to return to the mother spaceship, to re-unite her with her two sister ducks, who were still sitting together in the dark and vast cargo hold.

Aracuria was now all alone inside the white yellow tower on the dreadful planet of Draco. He was scared and, not for the first time in his life, he didn't have a clue what he was going to do next. Suddenly he heard something shuffling outside. For a moment there was silence, then the sound of heavy breathing, then a snort, like the sort of noise a horse might make. Then the most awful smell, like the stench of rotting maggots and festering wounds hit him full in the face.

"Ugh!" yelled Aracuria, putting his hand over his mouth. For a little while he tried to stay still, but in the end the smell became unbearable and he was forced to throw the door to DreamTime open.

From what happened next it was difficult to tell who was the most shocked, Aracuria or the thing that stood in front of him. He let the door close behind him and, with his hand still over his mouth, he kissed the Ring of Ra.

"I'm going to need you more than ever now."

In front of Aracuria was a huge dragon with outstretched wings and a long winding tail. Its mouth was closed, but on its back rode a creature with three heads. The first head was a ram's, the second a bull's and the third a man's .The creature carried a spear, which he pointed at Aracuria.

"You, you, are Aracuria?" said the man's head.

Aracuria nodded, "And I know who you are, you stinking monster. You're the demon Asmodee."

The dragon strutted towards him, and then stopped. When they had last been here, Klut had taken off his helmet, bowed to the demon and said, "Oh, Asmodee, I do this as a mark of respect." But that was a long time ago and this was war. When Asmodee saw that Aracuria had no intention of bowing, the man roared out, "Why do you insult me! Asmodee!"

Aracuria took his hand away from his mouth and grinned;

"Because you are the smelliest, ugliest, foulest looking thing that I've seen all morning and if I had been lucky enough to have had some breakfast, I sure as eggs would have brought it back up on seeing you."

For a moment there was complete silence as Asmodee took in the heap of insults that Aracuria had just hurled at him. Then the bull's head began to snort, the eyes in the ram's head went blood red, the man's head went bright green and the dragon lashed out its purple tongue and licked its white fangs.

"I WILL DESTROY YOU!" screamed Asmodee, and at that the creature pulled back its hand and hurled the spear straight at Aracuria's chest. Before it could hit its target, Aracuria held his left hand out in front of him and said, "A shield." Instantly a golden shield appeared in his hand and the spear harmlessly bounced off it. For a moment Asmodee was stunned, then the dragon raised its head high in the air with smoke pouring from its nostrils as it prepared to spew out a sheet of flame that would burn Aracuria to cinders.

"A fireman's hose!" cried Aracuria.

At the same instant as the dragon belched out a plume of flame Aracuria's shield changed into hose, from which a fountain of foam emerged. The sheet of flame and the fountain of foam hit each other in mid air. For a moment they seemed to battle it out together, then the fountain of white foam put out the burning fuel and carried on flowing straight into the dragon's mouth. A few seconds later a small fountain of foam emerged from each of the dragon's nostrils. It started to cough, splutter and sneeze and Aracuria had to make the hose disappear as the dragon was now spreading foam all over the place. The dragon collapsed to the floor exhausted.

Aracuria was still laughing at the dragon's plight when the man who sat on its back got off and came towards him. Each of the three heads was as wild and as angry as could be. As the man stopped in front of Aracuria, seven arms burst through the skin on each of his sides, and in each arm was a silver sword. The fourteen arms began a dazzling display of swordsmanship as all the swords spun around in the air like the flashing blades of a combine harvester. Then, with the swords still spinning, the man stepped forward to cut Aracuria to pieces. Getting out of this wasn't going to be easy...

CHAPTER TEN: INTO THE PLANET.. AGAIN

Asmodee's three heads were alternately snorting and grinning as he advanced within cutting distance of Aracuria.
"A sword!" cried Aracuria. Immediately a huge double-handed sword appeared in his hands. Aracuria raised it above his head and brought it swinging against Asmodee, hoping that the massive blade would cut him in half. However, the fourteen swords of Asmodee were spinning around so fast that it was like trying to cut through a wall of steel. The blade of Aracuria's sword hit Asmodee's swords and the next moment Aracuria lost his grip as all of the swords twisted around Aracuria's blade and flung it high in the air. He watched it arch away, noticing at the same time that the dragon had now recovered from its foam induced asthma attack: it was standing just a few meters behind Asmodee and was preparing to enter the fray once again.

"Pin the dragon's head to the ground!" shouted Aracuria to sword. The flying sword turned around in mid air and then came shooting down from the top of the glass hall like a javelin. It entered the top of the dragon's head, came out through its jaw and rammed itself hard into the marble floor.

While Aracuria had been watching all this, he had momentarily forgotten about Asmodee, who was still advancing on him. Just then one of Asmodee's swords hit Aracuria's leather jacket and cut straight through it, slicing through the skin on his left arm.
"AARRAGH!" he screamed, as the pain shot through him. The blow threw him off balance. He fell over and rolled across the floor. Asmodee was now in the ideal position to finish Aracuria off, but then from behind him, he heard the guttural groan of a dying dragon and the pumping glug of dragon's blood oozing out on to the marble floor. Asmodee turned to see what had happened and for a moment his fourteen arms stopped swinging their swords. This was the moment Aracuria had been waiting for: so as not to alert Asmodee, he whispered a request for another sword. As the second sword appeared in his hands, he rushed forward and buried its blade deeply into Asmodee's chest. Aracuria pulled out the sword and a green gel began to pump out of the monster. Asmodee fell to the floor, dead.

Aracuria collapsed exhausted beside his opponent. He was going to have to fight his way past seven more of these demons before he could reach Lucifer and if they were all as difficult as this one then he was in for a terrible time. For a moment he watched Asmodee's still twitching body, then he stood up and made both swords disappear. He turned and looked at the clear glass walls: somewhere in them were at least two doors; one led to the Treasure Chamber, where Aracuria didn't want to go, and the other led down into the center of the planet where he did. He looked back at mess he had made of Asmodee and his dragon and decided it would be best if he cleared it up. He waved his hand over them and said, “disappear,” and all the blood, gore and bodies vanished, as if they had never been there.

Just then a girl appeared. She seemed to walk straight out of the glass wall. She was young, beautiful and wearing a long silver dress with a white brooch shaped like the moon. She held out her hand.

“Would you step this way, please? The game show is about to begin.” Her voice was gentle.

“Game show?” said Aracuria, remembering that this was how they had got down into the planet last time. “Do you really want me to play games with you, Astarot.” Suddenly the beautiful calm features on the girl’s face changed to an expression of anger.

“You’re a fool, Aracuria, to ever return here,” she said. “We’ll play games with you until there’s nothing left to play with.” With that the girl turned and headed back towards the glass wall, only now there was a large white door in it. The door opened and she stepped through to the other side with Aracuria close behind. The next moment Aracuria found himself in a large TV studio: he had come in at the back of an entire audience of people. While Astarot walked down a long flight of steps towards the front of the audience another girl appeared and tagged a little label with his name written on it onto his leather jacket.

“Aracuria; come on down!” shouted Astarot at the front. Immediately the audience began to clap, shout and whistle their applause. Aracuria could not resist a grin at the stupidity of it all. All the same, he went down the steps and crossed the studio to stand beside the girl. “My name is Astarot,” she said. “I’m your hostess for this evening and I’m sure you’ll all wish to offer up a big hand for the return of our star contestant, Aracuria, who last appeared on this show 34 million years ago.”

“Was it that long ago?” said Aracuria, astonished that it had taken so long for them to return.

She looked at him in disdain. “Time has no meaning in this Universe, Aracuria, and if you don’t know that by now you must be a real WALLY!” The audience laughed cruelly. Aracuria looked into the girl’s deep blue eyes.

“You’ve got to understand, Astarot, that if there is a Wally around here then it isn’t me.” He faced the audience and said, “You’re really just a pack of seals!” Immediately the audience changed into hundreds of gray seals, each of whom was sitting on a chair, clapping its flippers and barking dementedly.

Aracuria turned back to the girl, who suddenly looked rather flustered.

“Right, ah, right then, the prize in tonight’s round of ‘Going for the Chop’ is a ticket down to the center of Draco, because for some stupid reason Aracuria wants to meet our Lord LUCIFER!” The seals began to clap frantically.

“OK then, Aracuria, this is your first and only question: and if you get it wrong then you’ll be ‘Going for the Chop!’ instead of ‘Going to see

Lucifer!"' The seals started to bounce up and down. Astarot pulled out a piece of paper from nowhere and read out the first and only question. "In all the Universe, Aracuria, there is only one thing more beautiful than the Twelve-Eyed Child-Gobbling Beastie of the Draco Schools' Inspectorate, whom you had the good fortune to encounter on your last visit to us. Is it Miss Dusty Matahari from the constellation of Amazonian Beauty-Parlors and thrice holder of the Gorgeous Girls of the Galaxy Competition, or Draco's own two-headed Rancid Rita, quadruple winner of the Obesely-Overweight Prize, better known as the Wobbly Award?"

Aracuria's face was completely blank. "To help you in this difficult task, I can tell you that while both of them are men-crazy, Dusty only ever eats yogurt and Rita has a taste mammoth oversize hot-dogs."

"Rita," said Aracuria, knowing what to expect next.

"You're RIGHT!" shouted Astarot, as the seals suddenly and unexpectedly produced two hundred red balls and began bouncing them around on their noses. "And here she is to give you the biggest cuddly hug you'll ever have the fatal misfortune to suffer!"

At that moment a huge curtain parted to reveal a monstrous woman sitting on a golden throne with a tiara on each of her heads. Behind her was a banner emblazoned with the words, MISS WOBBLY 1873. The woman was absolutely gross, with buckets of flesh oozing over the two-piece swimsuit that was trying, vainly, to cover her. The second she caught sight of Aracuria both her heads licked their lips with their long, forked green tongues and then she pulled herself out of her throne and began the long walk down a set of steps to where Aracuria and Astarot were standing. As she walked so her mammoth stomach began to swing from side to side like a massive pendulum, while the flesh on her bulging thighs began to ripple like the white sails of a ship. The more she saw of Aracuria, the more she wanted to cuddle him and the more she wanted to cuddle him, the faster she walked and the faster she walked, the more her stomach swung around until eventually it threatened to throw her of her feet altogether. With a great effort of will, she grappled with her stomach and managed to stop it heaving, thus preventing the inevitable from happening.

For a moment Aracuria felt like laughing, then he realized that if Rita really did give him a hug he would drown in her flesh and that would be the end of him. But at the same time, he didn't want to destroy her as she didn't really mean him any harm. He glanced at Astarot and saw that she was smiling an evil smile.

"Why are you smiling?" he asked.

"Because Rita is about to kill you and you're too good a person to harm someone like her." Astarot was right, but just then a better idea came into his head.

"The thing is, Astarot, will she want me once she sees what you've become?" Astarot swung round in terror, just as Aracuria waved his hand and said,

"Astarot: become a giant hot dog." Instantly Astarot changed from a girl into the biggest hot dog that had ever existed. By now Rita was only an arm's length away, but just as she was about to grab Aracuria the smell of hot dog and onions hit her full in the face. She stopped dead, turned to see where the smell was coming from and suddenly lost all interest in Aracuria. Instead she dived for the hot dog and began to munch away at it, until in a short while there was nothing left except some tomato ketchup that had squeezed out on to the floor.

Once she had eaten her meal, Rita lay flat on the floor and fell fast asleep. Her whole, massive body began to shake and rumble as she started to snore. The last time they had been here, after having outwitted Astarot, Aracuria and the others had fallen through a hole in the ground which had taken them towards the center of the planet, but as it was a concealed hole there was now no sign to be seen of it. Aracuria searched the floor for an entrance, but he was getting nowhere fast. He turned to the ring in desperation.

"Ring of Ra: give me X-Ray eyes," he said. Suddenly he noticed that Rita was no longer made out of bulging flesh, but consisted solely of big bones that were all joined together. He looked across at the seals and saw that they were all bones as well.

"This is great!" he said, enjoying the experience. Then he looked down at the floor and saw that right in the center of the studio was a circular hole. He went across and stood on top of it: he wasn't looking forward to what was going to happen next.

"OK Ring, you can take away my X-Ray eyes: I won't be needing them again," he said, raising his hands up and covering his head. "Now just blast away the cover to the hole that I'm standing on..." No sooner had the words left his mouth than the cover to the hole disintegrated and Aracuria found himself plunging down a seemingly bottomless shaft that would take him to the next sub-prince of Draco.

CHAPTER ELEVEN: PUS AND GORE

Aracuria fell down the shaft like a stone. The last time this had happened, thirty four million years ago, he and the others had been terrified, but now for some reason he wasn't scared. Perhaps it was because he knew what he had to face next, or maybe it was because this whole thing had been destined to happen for such a long time, perhaps before he was even born, so there was nothing to worry about.

The shaft turned left and right and then he hit something soft. The next moment Aracuria found himself bouncing up and down on a large trampoline. When he at last managed to steady himself, he climbed down off the trampoline and looked around. He had come out in the middle of a tunnel with a shaft running to left and right. The last time they were here, they had turned right and ended up face to face with another sub-prince demon of Draco, whom Aracuria had killed, but turning right was the wrong way to go. Aracuria turned left and started walking down the dark tunnel.

He had only walked for about two hundred meters when he came face to face with an old man in a white coat sitting at a large oak table. The old man had his head bandaged and he didn't look at all well.

"Dr Magot!" said Aracuria. "I thought I'd killed you."

The old man looked up. "You killed a MAGGOT, not me. Now please take a seat," he said curtly. A seat appeared on Aracuria's side of the table.

"My name is Doctor Magot. If you want to get past me you have to pass your medical, is that clear? The medical in this case is to see if you, Aracuria, are strong enough to survive what is to come."

Aracuria pushed the seat aside angrily. "You demons are so stupid," he said. "I'm not going to play your stupid games this time: I want to fight with Lucifer and I intend to get to him as soon as possible."

Dr Magot took his glasses off. "I think it is you who are the stupid one, Aracuria. Why do you think we set these tests for you, and indeed anyone who comes here to see Lucifer? We do it in order to find out your weaknesses and your strengths, so that if and when you finally meet our Lord Lucifer he will know all there is to know about you. And don't think that there is anything you can hide from us: we know what you did to Asmodee and how you tried to hide his body and we know what you did to Astarot. Now take a seat like a good little boy."

Aracuria had never thought that that was why they gave them the tests and he hadn't realized that they knew all about Asmodee and Astarot. Caught off guard, he sat down on the chair with his arms at his side. But the instant he sat on it, the chair suddenly sprung to life: its back became two wooden arms that rose up and over his shoulders and grabbed him around the neck, while the two front legs became giant hands that clasped his legs and the two back legs gripped his arms. The doctor stood up.

"Remember Aracuria, in order to fight with Lucifer all you've got to do is get past me: but I have a score to settle with you!" Suddenly, the buttons bounced off the doctor's jacket, and it ripped open as he began to grow in size. His skin became wet, white and slimy. While the chair began to strangle Aracuria and starve his legs and arms of blood, so before his eyes the doctor turned into a gigantic maggot that filled up the whole of the tunnel, crushing the table. Then it started to slither towards him.

Aracuria had to do something fast. He couldn't wield a sword and with his arms pinned to his side he couldn't aim the Ring of Ra, but he could do something else.

"Clothe me in a fire-proof suit!" he shouted. Suddenly his head and body were covered in a silver suit just as the maggot's slimy skin touched him. "And place me in a furnace!" At his words flames rose up around him. The maggot that had just been about to eat him hastily drew back as the flames grew hotter. The chair in which Aracuria was held fast began to burn and as it burned so it started to scream. A moment later the burning chair was no longer able to hold him and he broke free. He waved his arm and dispensed with the furnace and the fire suit. However, the chair was still burning and it was now running around in circles trying to put out the flames.

Aracuria pointed the ring at it and called for a wind to fan the flames. From behind him a strong wind began to blow and as it blew so the chair turned and ran down the tunnel in the direction of the maggot. The maggot was clearly terrified of fire, for it began to retreat down the tunnel as fast as its slimy skin could slither, with Aracuria following at a gentle trot.

The farther they traveled down the tunnel the warmer it became. Aracuria watched the walls of the tunnel begin to glow red and he realized that were coming close to the firefall. Whenever the flames on the chair threatened to go out Aracuria would fan them up with an even stronger wind in order to keep the maggot moving. At last, he saw that up ahead the maggot had come out of the tunnel into the firefall cavern just as the chair finally collapsed in a heap of cinders. Aracuria ran forward, dashed past two large statues that stood on either side of the tunnel exit and emerged on to a bridge made out of solid stone that stretched from one side of the cavern to the other, with the tunnel continuing on the other side. Beneath the bridge, the cavern dropped sheer through hundreds of meters to a red bubbling river of fire. Above him it rose into the giddy heights until it reached a vaulted roof. To his left a brilliant red torrent of fire was coming from the roof and falling thousands of meters to the river below. The firefall was bubbling, and screeching, and flames shot out in every direction. The cavern itself was glowing bright red from the flames. Aracuria conjured up a huge double handed sword out of the air, which in spite of its size was as light as a feather, and then he ran towards the maggot.

“It’s just like last time!” he shouted before bringing the sword crashing down on it. The maggot split open from end to end and, each side spilling gallons of pus, fell off the bridge into the burning sea of fire below.

Aracuria felt rather pleased with himself. He looked across at the firefall and stared in fascination as the millions of tons of molten rock and metal came pouring down from the surface of the planet. He was so engrossed in this that he forgot all about the two statues that he had passed on the way out of the tunnel, or about the other two statues that stood on the far side of the bridge. Suddenly he heard a loud creak, like the sound of moving stones. He turned around and saw that two of the stone statues were walking towards him. In their hands they held stone swords and each sword was stretched out as if they were about to fight. Aracuria was just taking this in when he heard another creak behind him. He wheeled around and saw that the other two statues had moved off their pedestals too and were advancing on him as well.

Aracuria knew he couldn’t fight the four of them at once, but he reckoned he could take them on two at a time so he ran towards the two statues that were closest, raised his sword above his head and brought it crashing down on the first statue. That, as it turned out, was a pretty stupid thing to do, as when the sword hit the stone, instead of cutting through it, it just vibrated massively. Aracuria was shaken to his knees; the sword quivered out of his hands and he watched as it fell off the end of the bridge, down into the lake of fire.

At that moment, the statue that Aracuria had hit raised its sword in the air and brought it crashing down on to Aracuria. He just had time to dodge away as the sword hit the surface of the bridge instead. But the blow was so powerful that the whole bridge shook and a large crack appeared in its surface. Before Aracuria had time to think about that, the next statue had brought its sword down to try and cut him in two. Once again he managed to roll out of the way and once again the sword hit the bridge, only this time an even bigger crack appeared and parts of the bridge actually began to fall away. He scrambled to his feet, looking around desperately for somewhere to run, but the other two statues were coming across the bridge to get him as well. Aracuria was trapped. The four statues advanced towards him from either side of the bridge. Hastily, he aimed his ring at one of them and fired a lightning bolt, but it had no effect. He aimed the ring at another and fired a laser blast but the stone was too strong to be harmed. No doubt if he had had the time he would eventually have found the right weapon to destroy them, but it was already too late: the four statues were now only a meter or two apart and Aracuria was stuck in the middle.

The four statues all raised their swords, aimed them at Aracuria and then brought them crashing down. Aracuria dived frantically out of the way just as the blows were about to hit him. Instead, the four swords hit the surface of the bridge. There was a massive wrenching sound and Aracuria watched in horror as hundreds of huge cracks appeared across the surface of the bridge. It clearly wasn't strong enough to take that sort of hammering and it began to fall apart. He scrambled up and, before the statues could raise their swords again, he dashed through their legs, just as the whole bridge gave way beneath him.

Suddenly Aracuria found himself flying through the air. He reached out wildly and just managed to grab the edge of the bridge as the whole central section fell away into the lake of fire below, taking the four statues with it. For a moment he hung there precariously, with the glow from the exploding fires below warming his body. Then, with an enormous effort, he managed to haul himself up on to what remained of the bridge.
"Wow, that was a close one!" he gasped to himself as he fell down exhausted on his back to get his breath back.

As Aracuria looked up at the glowing ceiling of the cavern, he began to hear the sound of buzzing. For a moment he thought that he had been deafened by the stone swords, but as the buzzing got louder he realized what was happening. He stood up and saw that from the other tunnel, the one that led to the heart of Draco and Lucifer, hundreds of gigantic flies were coming towards him, with their leader Beelzebub, the Lord of the Flies, in front. Aracuria realized that if he let the flies get out into the cavern he would be fighting them all day, and with only part of the bridge left to stand on he wouldn't have much room for maneuver. The tunnel itself was as straight as a die so Aracuria aimed his ring directly at it and waited for the first fly to emerge. After a few moments the fat, black head of Beelzebub appeared at the tunnel mouth. Aiming the ring at a spot between Beelzebub's two massive eyes, Aracuria shouted, "The most powerful laser beam EVER!"

Immediately a ray of golden light burst out from the glowing ring. It shot straight at Beelzebub and hit him square between the eyes. Aracuria watched in horror as the fly exploded into a thousand pieces, scattering bits of wing, body and pus everywhere. The laser beam, however, hadn't stopped. It carried straight on and hit the second fly, which had flown right into it. This second fly also exploded into a shower of bits. But the laser beam hadn't finished traveling; it carried on down the tunnel and hit the third fly, then the fourth and so on. One by one each of the flies exploded in front of Aracuria until eventually every one of them had been blown away.

Aracuria stepped forward. "Oh yuck!" he muttered to himself as he looked at the walls of the tunnel on to which the hundreds of enormous flies had been splattered. "And I've got to walk down that!" He turned up the collar of his leather jacket and conjured up a cap to cover his head. Without waiting any longer he ran down the tunnel whose walls were dripping in bits of dead fly, towards the last four sub-Princes of Draco, all that stood between himself and Lucifer.

CHAPTER TWELVE: EARTH, AIR, FIRE AND WATER

Aracuria had passed the last of the splattered flies and he could finally stop running. He pulled the mucus covered cap off his head and threw it to the ground.

"Ugh!" he groaned to himself, "the things I do to save planet Earth." He wiped off some of the fly stuff that was still clinging to his leather jacket and then carried on his way.

The tunnel now began to get bigger, the roof rose and the walls widened. A wind began to blow. The farther he walked, the stronger the wind blew, until eventually the tunnel, which had become a vast cavern, was filled with a storm. Aracuria remembered what had happened the last time they were here, how the wind had picked them up and carried them through the air and every second threatened to dash them against the walls of the cavern. He realized that if that were to happen again it might be a an easy opportunity for Lucifer to get rid of him, so he sat down on the ground and thought out what he should do next.

"That's it!" he cried out, pointing his ring at the ground. The next moment a sand yacht had appeared from nowhere. It had three old car tire wheels, one at the front and two at the back, all joined together by a piece of board. Out of the center of the board came a large, triangular sail. Aracuria had never driven one of these before, but he had always wanted to. He jumped on board, let out the sail so that it caught the wind and, just as it was about to tip over, he released the brake. A second later he found himself whizzing along the ground at an amazing speed. The wind became ever stronger and the stronger it blew, the faster the sand yacht went. The trouble was that the wind was now so strong and the sand yacht moving so fast that it did the one thing that Aracuria didn't want it to do: it took off.

Left to itself the sand yacht would have turned over and smashed itself to pieces, but now that he was airborne Aracuria quite liked it, so he shouted out, "Wings!" and the next moment an enormous pair of bird's wings appeared out of the sides of the sand yacht. Now Aracuria had actually been thinking in terms of airplane wings, but as the sand yacht began to fly well, he decided that the bird wings would do for the moment.

He flew the sand yacht up and down, turning to the left and right to work out how to control it, but just when he was starting to enjoy it, the wind began to die away, until eventually he was forced to land. The sand yacht carried on bowling along the ground for a short distance, and then it stopped completely, as there was now no wind at all.

Aracuria got down and looked around. He was in vast place with a roof of rock miles above his head. The walls were too far away even to see. In front of him stood four statues, each a mile high. They stood facing outwards from the edge of an immense circle, in the center of which was a pit which went right down to the center of the planet. Out of the pit leapt flames and lightning flashes. He had made it to the four Guardians of the Pit.

The first statue was about half a mile away and since Aracuria had no intention of walking that far, he climbed back on the sand yacht and called on the bird wings to take him there. He brought the yacht swooping in across the ground to come in to land in front of the first statue. He looked at the name of the statue that was written on the gigantic pedestal which its legs rested on.

"ORIENS!" he cried, craning his neck to look up at the statue. It was tall and white faced. In its right hand it held a sword and in its left, a smoking cauldron.

"Who spoke my name? Answer! Or I will burn you with fire!"

"Aracuria." he answered. "Remember me?"

The head of the statue peered down at him. "I am the Guardian of the East," it said. "What is it that you want of me, Aracuria?"

"I want to get past you, you overweight lump of stone: what do you think I want?"

"To get past me, you must answer a riddle of the Guardian of the East. If you fail to answer, accursed be you and all your kind and kindred. If you fail, I will burn you with fire, your tongue will molder in your mouth and your eyes will rot in their sockets. Will you turn away?"

Aracuria had been through all this before and then it had taken the four of them to answer the four riddles that the four Guardians had asked. He knew he didn't stand a chance of answering any of them, so he was going to have to trick his way past.

"No, after having pureed all the other demons that have come my way, I have no intention of turning back now. Ask your riddle."

The white face of Oriens stared down at Aracuria. "Very well, this is the riddle of the Guardian of the East: who is small, stupid, wears a leather jacket and is about to be burned to death in the fires of Hell?" Aracuria hadn't been expecting that sort of question. He looked up in amazement at Oriens and as he looked up so his expression turned to one of horror because the statue had just tipped over the huge cauldron that he held in his left hand and millions of gallons of burning fire were at this very moment cascading down towards Aracuria's head.

"That's cheating!" he shouted angrily, as he jumped on the sand yacht and yelled at it to fly. As the bird wings began to beat, so the flaming firefall plunged down through the air while Oriens laughed a sick, asthmatic laugh. The sand yacht took off and Aracuria aimed it out of harm's way just as the sheet of flames burned past him and exploded on to the ground, sending out a sea of fire that filled a good proportion of the cavern.

"What is the answer to the riddle?" said the statue.

Aracuria swung the sand yacht around and rose up in the air to meet Oriens face to face, "Aracuria! That's the answer, you evil monster!" Oriens laughed. "You have answered the Riddle of the Guardian of the East, now you must answer the riddles of the other three Guardians." Aracuria stared into Oriens massive eyes and then flew away to the next statue: at least this time he knew what to expect.

He swooped back down low over the ground so as to read the name of the next statue.

"Amaimon!" he shouted, "This is Aracuria and I want to get past you: what kind of stupid riddle do you have for me?" He looked up and saw that Amaimon was a statue of a man with a monstrous dragon's head. It had a blood red mouth lined with razor sharp fangs out of which spurted a flame of burning sulfur. In its right hand it held a sword and in its left a globe of the earth. Amaimon looked down at him. Its bloodshot eyes swiveled around in its eye sockets: there were no eyelids.

"I am the Guardian of the South," said the statue, in a much louder voice than the first. "To get past me you must answer this riddle: who has a smaller brain than an ant, hasn't a snowball in Hell's chance of outwitting our Lord Lucifer and is about to be buried in Earth?"

As it spoke, the statue crushed the globe of Earth that it held in its left hand into a million pieces. Suddenly, as the dust began to shower down from above so the whole ground underneath Aracuria opened up revealing a sea of fire underneath. The sand yacht tipped over and plummeted down into one of the huge cracks that had appeared in the ground. With the stench of burning sulfur filling his nostrils, Aracuria desperately clutched at the yacht's controls and shouted, "Fly us out of here!" The wings began to beat frantically, the sand yacht turned upside down, righted itself and then began to climb up though the air just as the ground, which was now over their heads, began to close up again: they were being buried alive. As the ground above him closed over, Aracuria ordered the yacht to fly straight at it, at the same time aiming his ring at the folding rock.

"Blast a hole through it!"

A beam of light burst out of the ring and punched a hole straight through the rock a split second before the yacht hit it. The sand yacht just managed to scrape through the hole before the ground sealed up yet again.

"You haven't answered the riddle," bellowed Amaimon angrily. Aracuria caught his breath while the sand yacht flew away to the next statue.

"The answer is Aracuria, again! I don't think much of your riddles!" he yelled back.

"And we think nothing of you!" roared the dragon's head.

The sand yacht stopped in front of the pedestal of the third statue so that Aracuria could read the name that was written there. Then he looked up at the massive figure that towered above him. In its right hand it held a sword that was hundreds of meters long. The point of the sword rested on the

pedestal next to its feet, each toe of which was bigger than the sand yacht. In its left hand it held a bowl, but Aracuria couldn't see if it was filled with anything. The statue had the head of a goat.
"Paimon! This is Aracuria speaking and you look really spooky," he said.
"I know nothing of this 'spooky'," bellowed the statue. "I am Paimon, Guardian of the West. I am the third Guardian of the Pit. What do you want of me?"
"I want to get past you to see Lucifer."
"To get past me you must answer this riddle: who will never see the Tree of Life again, will soon wish that he had never been born and is about to be drowned in water?" Paimon tipped up the bowl, out of which a huge waterfall came cascading down. This was far less terrifying that either being burned to death or buried alive, so all Aracuria did was to conjure up a giant umbrella. But while he waited for the waterfall to hit him something inside him said that he was in great danger. Without waiting for any explanation, he leapt off the sand yacht and ran as fast as his legs could carry him.

Glancing over his shoulder he was just in time to see the cascade of water hit the sand yacht: in an instant it began to burn and dissolve in front of his eyes. Aracuria watched in horror as the sand yacht melted away to nothing in a cloud of smoky mist. When it had finally vanished all that was left was a large circular burn mark on the ground where the 'water' had hit the earth.
"What kind of water is that, Paimon?" cried Aracuria.
"Ordinary Draco water," said the statue, "or as you call it on Earth, Sulfuric Acid." Aracuria had been lucky, but before he had time to think any more the statue shouted again, "What is the answer to the riddle?"
"Aracuria," he said forlornly, as he set off towards the next and last statue.

He walked for a few meters and then conjured up a set of roller skates to hurry him along. He finally stopped in front of the last statue and read out the name.
"Ariton!" his voice echoed out, "tell Aracuria your riddle, although I have a feeling I already know the answer." Ariton was less frightening than all the other statues. He had a man's head; in his left hand he held a sword and in his right a set of keys.
"I am Ariton, Guardian of the North, Keeper of the Keys of the Pit. What do you want of me? Answer or I will deprive you of air!"
"You know what I want! I want to get past you to see Lucifer," shouted Aracuria.
"Then you must answer this last riddle: if a Hydrogen Bomb is equivalent to 10 Joules of energy then what is the equivalent figure to describe the energy displaced by a Supernova?"
"WHAT?" cried Aracuria. He really hadn't a clue what Ariton was talking about.

"If you can't answer the riddle of the last Guardian of the Pit, then you can't have the keys to the Pit and if you can't have the keys to the Pit, then you can't see our Lord Lucifer and if you can't see our Lord Lucifer, then you can't overcome him and if you can't overcome him, then you can't get the Tree of Life and if you can't get the Tree of Life, then your whole, short, miserable life will have been wasted, Aracuria, because we all know that for that reason and that reason alone you were born."

Aracuria was speechless. He began to wish that he had been taught science in school: there was no other way he was going to answer Ariton's riddle, not in the time that was left to him, because at that very moment the Morrigan Deep Space Cargo Transport had positioned itself above the Treasure Chamber, ready to pick up the Tree of Life, and Lucifer had to be occupied when it happened, or else...

CHAPTER THIRTEEN: THE LIGHT BEARER

Aracuria had had enough: there was no way he was going to answer that riddle in a million years. He aimed his ring up at Ariton's left arm.
"A giant laser blast!" he shouted. Out of the ring came a brilliant green pulse of light. It shot up through the air and blew off Ariton's arm, "AARRAAGH!" it screamed as its stone arm shattered, sending out a fountain of green, boiling blood and releasing the keys in the process. Aracuria dived for cover as the giant fingers and bits of arm crashed to the ground along with the keys, then he ran forward and tried to pick them up before the fountain of boiling blood hit him. But the keys were too heavy to move. Aracuria conjured up a huge, yellow balloon which picked up the keys with ease.
"Take us to the Pit!" he shouted, as he grabbed the keys and was carried aloft. He drifted out over the massive circle which surrounded the pit, across which was painted a huge picture. The picture was of a red dragon, set within a golden pentagram, which was in turn surrounded by two golden circles between each of which was a series of strange letters. As Aracuria looked down at the painting so the four statues stooped to pick up their swords and moved off their pedestals.

Ariton was moving extremely slowly; the fountain of steaming green blood was beginning to cool and it was obvious that Ariton was dying. The statue picked up its sword and swung it around its head with its right arm. The huge blade shot through the air above the balloon, narrowly missing it, but Ariton no longer had the strength to do any more. It turned over on its side and then toppled off the pedestal. Ariton let out an enormous scream and, watching in amazement, Aracuria saw the huge statue come crashing down across the center of the circle. The instant it hit the ground so the arms, legs and head of Ariton broke away releasing billions of gallons of steaming green blood which flowed out over the red and gold painting and then began to pour over the edge of the pit.

While Aracuria watched all this, the three remaining statues stepped into the circle to destroy him. Oriens tried first. It stepped forward, raised its sword and swung it at the balloon. Aracuria conjured a wind to blow the balloon away just in time. Then Amaimon stepped on to the blood of Anton and raised its sword high above its head. Aracuria was now floating high enough to stare into Amaimon's monstrous dragon's head. He didn't think he was going to avoid this blow as they were so close to each other, so he aimed his ring at the statue's smoking blood red mouth lined with razor sharp fangs.
"A laser bolt!" he shouted. The next moment a golden beam burst out of the ring and disappeared into the dragon's mouth. Nothing happened. Amaimon looked down at it and laughed. Its bloodshot eyes without eyelids swiveled

around in its eye sockets while Amaimon prepared to deliver the fatal blow. Aracuria had to act quickly: he aimed the ring at one of the eyes.
"A laser bolt again, and this time it had better work!" Another golden beam burst out of the ring. It hit the eye right in the center and as Aracuria stared in horror the whole bloodshot eye exploded like stained glass shattering. A torrent of white liquid burst out over Amaimon's face as the monster screamed a terrible roar.
"AARRAAGH!" Aracuria aimed the ring at the other eye and fired another laser bolt. Once again the bloodshot eye exploded sending a river of white liquid down the dragon's face.

Amaimon was now blind. It began to lash out wildly with its sword, hacking and thrusting in all directions. Meanwhile Paimon had come up behind Aracuria and was about to strike him with its sword. At that moment one of Amaimon's blows swung aimlessly through the air, missing Aracuria by miles. But instead it came crashing against the goat's head neck of Paimon. The head of Paimon was hundreds of meters tall and as many wide, but the blow from Amairnon's sword was enough to shatter the neck and send the goat's head spinning to the ground. Immediately a huge fountain of green, steaming blood burst out of the severed neck as Paimon toppled over. As it fell, so it hit against Amaimon, which blindly lost its balance and toppled over as well. The two monstrous statues fell in the direction of the pit. They smashed into pieces against its edge and then in a sea of steaming green blood and broken limbs, they rolled over the edge and cascaded down into the bottomless depths of the pit over which Aracuria was now hovering.

Aracuria watched as the statues crashed down into the smoke filled pit with a torrent of steaming blood falling behind them. He was so absorbed in watching the spectacle that he had forgotten all about Oriens, which now raised its sword and brought it crashing against the balloon, bursting it like a bubble.
"AARRAGH!" screamed Aracuria, as he and the keys plummeted down into the depths of the pit.

He clung to the keys for dear life as he shot through sulfurous clouds and past great streaks of lightning that every now and then broke out through the pit. A stream of steaming green blood was still flowing down from above and was drenching Aracuria as he fell. After what seemed a dozen miles, Aracuria became scared of hitting the bottom, so he conjured up an oversize parachute which rapidly slowed him down. Gradually he drifted down the remaining miles of the shaft until he emerged into a vast cavern, coming in to land on an island of rock littered with broken bits of statue.

All around Aracuria was a vast sea of fire. The island of flat rock was only inches above the level of a bubbling lake of molten fire. From the island a narrow walkway led across the fiery lake to a hole in the rock in the far wall behind which was a circular shaft that went right up into the Treasure Chamber. In front of the walkway, not a hundred meters away, was a vast serpent. It had a massive skull-white head and a long coiled body covered in red and yellow scales. Out of the head came seven horns and along its back were two long, transparent wings. The head was as big as a house with huge, bloodshot eyes and a cavernous mouth filled with white teeth. In front of its mouth was a mass of broken green glass, which at the time meant nothing to Aracuria, while on the end of the serpent's nose were another three horns. The serpent was curled up around a solid gold throne that rose up out of the center of the earth. It coiled around a dozen times or more. On the throne sat a man dressed in silver.

"Congratulations Aracuria. After smashing your way through all the sub-princes of Draco, killing Asmodee, Astarot, Magot and Beelzebub, as well as littering my little domain with the broken remnants of three of the four Guardians, you finally arrive in person."

This was Lucifer. Aracuria was just about to say something when the huge parachute collapsed around his head, smothering him in white silk. Immediately he suspected a trick and began to fight with the parachute.

"Aracuria: for goodness sake use that ring of yours to sort yourself out. If you can't beat your own parachute, what chance do you have against me?"

Aracuria felt stupid: he wished away the parachute and was about to say something to Lucifer when he saw something which made his jaw fall wide open. Lucifer was sitting sideways in his throne with his legs crossed. He held his right hand up at his face and was polishing the massive blue diamond of a new ring that he wore on his long index finger. The blue diamond glowed hauntingly, lighting up Lucifer's evil but handsome lace.

"The, the other Ring of Ra!" gasped Aracuria in horror.

"Yes," said Lucifer calmly. "Thank goodness the Great Gods made two of them, otherwise I would have been in a right pickle with you zapping everything that moves with your own Ring of Ra. I suppose if you had kept it secret and got down here by answering the riddles properly then maybe you might have taken me by surprise. But once my fellow demons saw that you had this amazing ring, then we had to try and find out what had happened to the other one. What a fool I was not to realize that the only other Ring of Ra in the whole Universe had been locked away in our Treasure Chamber for goodness knows how long. It was rather hurriedly brought down to me and then dear Leviathan broke it out of the green gemstone: he has such strong jaws you know."

Just then Leviathan roared and Aracuria finally realized what all the broken glass in front of his mouth meant. Lucifer continued.

"So, Aracuria, when I tell you that I am glad you could 'drop' in on us, I really mean it from the bottom of my heartless heart. After all, one Ring of Ra confers enormous power, but after I have killed you and taken the other Ring of Ra off your little finger, I will become the most powerful creature in the whole Universe. That means I will no longer have to live locked inside this blasted planet. Instead I and my demons will be able to go forth and extend our rule wherever we will. Think of it, Aracuria, in ten thousand times ten thousand years people will still be cursing your name for putting the two Rings of Ra on my fair hands, because if it hadn't been for you, none of what is to come could ever have happened!"

Aracuria felt worse than awful. Even if Rhiannon and the others managed to take the Tree of Life away, once he was dead both the rings would belong to Lucifer. Then it would only be a matter of time before Lucifer would hunt them down, take back the Tree of Life and enslave Earth as well as every other planet in every other solar system. The worst nightmare imaginable began to unfold before Aracuria's eyes as he saw what kind of a place the Universe would become if he failed. And Lucifer was right: he would be to blame for it all if it were to come true, as he was the one who had objected to all the rubbish on Earth, who had stolen the Silurian Dripping Cheese from Draco to feed the people, who had then dumped all the rubbish on the Sun to get rid of it, which had then threatened to put the sun out, and who had then decided to steal the Tree of Life from Draco in order to stop Earth becoming a snowball. The trouble was, he had never expected to defeat Lucifer, only to occupy him while the others stole the Tree of Life, which was why he now felt so terrible.

Lucifer stepped off his throne and began to walk over the scales of the serpent, climbing down each of its coils as if he were descending a staircase.

"I only really have one question to ask you before I kill you, Aracuria, and that is, how did you get out of DreamTime? I do hope Evil Eye and his pirates didn't try and play a trick on me, because if they did I will have to blow them and their stolen spaceship out of space." "They, they didn't," said Aracuria.

"You're not lying, are you Aracuria?" said Lucifer. As he spoke, the Stone of Destiny burst out of the ground beneath his feet raising him up in the air. "You know the Stone of Destiny cracks when anyone tells a lie over it, Aracuria, so tell me the truth: who let you out of DreamTime? "

Aracuria began to think furiously. When he come out of the white and yellow tower on Draco, DreamTime no longer existed, so that meant that the first time he had come out of DreamTime was after they had had all that trouble in Ducksea.

"Theom let me out."

Lucifer's face suddenly became very frightened.

"WHO?"

"Theom, Tiamat, Ananta, Inanna: she has thousands of names," said Aracuria.

Lucifer waited for the Stone of Destiny to crack, but when it didn't he screamed out, "How did you come to know about HER!"

Aracuria realized to his amazement that Lucifer was scared. "Why do you want to know?" he asked, "You sound scared of her."

This sent Lucifer into a furious rage. "Me! Scared! Thanks to you I am on the verge of becoming the most powerful god in the Universe, and here you are asking if I am scared! What a fool you are!"

Aracuria smiled: for some reason he no longer felt scared of Lucifer, even though he still had every reason to be.

"I'm not a fool, Lucifer," he said quietly. "I know I'm not as bright as some or as brave as others, but I know my own weaknesses, which is something that can't be said about you."

Lucifer's face reddened with fury. "What weaknesses! Tell me Aracuria, what weaknesses do you discern in me, you impudent little wretch? I could crush you into atoms, grind you into dust, split you apart like meat on a butcher's table! Which weakness is it that you can point to first?"

"Pride," answered Aracuria. "You're so arrogant that you don't know that you're heading for a fall."

Lucifer burst out laughing. "And who is going to trip me up: YOU? You bag of nothing!"

"Maybe," said Aracuria. "Or maybe Theom."

Lucifer's face suddenly became very still and then he raised the Ring of Ra to his lips and kissed it. "Prepare to meet your God, Aracuria, and if she doesn't save you, I can assure you no one else will, least of all yourself." Lucifer aimed the ring straight at Aracuria and prepared to blow him away...

CHAPTER FOURTEEN: THE END OF THE UNIVERSE

Aracuria had no intention of waiting for the inevitable. He looked down at all the bits of statue that littered the ground and, on the spur of the moment, started hurling them at Lucifer. One by one the huge blocks of stone rose off the ground and flew at Lucifer, who hadn't been expecting this at all. The blast of lightning that he had aimed at Aracuria hit a huge rock instead, which exploded into fragments. But when this was followed by every other piece of stone available, Lucifer became strangely calm. As each stone came at him, he diverted it behind his back, where they all started to join together into something. At first Aracuria didn't notice what was happening, but then he realized in horror that a multi-headed stone monster was beginning to form behind Lucifer. Each stone that Aracuria threw at him became another part of the monster.

When the last of the bits of statue had been used up, Lucifer glanced behind at his creation. "Pretty, isn't she?" he said coolly, as he looked up at the twelve-headed, four-legged, long tailed statue, which seemed utterly lifeless.

"I didn't know you were into sculpture," said Aracuria.

"Oh, this isn't a sculpture," answered Lucifer. "This is the real thing." He raised himself up on his toes and blew into the nostrils of one of the heads. Suddenly the monster came to life: each of the heads began to flex on its long, winding, snake-like neck, while the huge scaled tail began to swish back and forth. "Not only is she alive Aracuria, she's hungry." Lucifer clicked his fingers and the huge beast stepped over him and came straight for Aracuria with each of its heads vying for the feast.

Aracuria looked up at the monster, aimed his ring at it and said, "I think you're full of hot air." Suddenly the sides of the monster began to bulge, the twelve necks began to inflate and the faces on each of the heads began to puff out.

"What are you doing?" asked Lucifer, who was now directly beneath the beast. But Aracuria didn't have to answer because the next moment the monster, who was now as puffed out as a balloon, suddenly took off and began to float away in the air. Lucifer gazed in amazement as the monster drifted off until it was high above his golden throne. Then Aracuria aimed his ring at it and fired a howitzer shell. There was a huge explosion as the beast burst like a balloon, sending out a shower of yellow, sticky liquid which drenched both the golden throne and Leviathan.

Lucifer wheeled around to face Aracuria: he looked really angry.

"I suppose you think that's funny, punk face?" he snapped, raising his ring at Aracuria and firing a shower of burning hail at him. Aracuria conjured up a steel umbrella which the burning hail bounced off. But once behind the

umbrella Aracuria couldn't see anything, which was why Lucifer had sent the hail in the first place.
"You're a danger to yourself," he laughed, as a laser bolt burst from his ring and burned through the steel umbrella, narrowly missing Aracuria's face. Hurriedly, Aracuria made the umbrella disappear, just as an enormous javelin came straight for him. He dived to one side, but it was too late. The javelin cut through the arm of his leather jacket, knocked him off balance and pinned him to the ground. He was at the mercy of Lucifer, who was just about to do something terrible to him when, across the walkway at the bottom of the circular shaft built into the wall, an enormous explosion took place. Lucifer turned around, in time to see the floor of the shaft tear itself up and a huge fountain burst out into the shaft, filling it completely.
"Did you do that?" he asked in astonishment.

Aracuria was about to deny it when he realized what had happened. The floor of the shaft held back a sea, and when the shaft was filled with water it would send anyone who was in it straight up into the Treasure Chamber with which it was linked. For the floor of the shaft to have given way like that could only mean one thing: that the roof of the Treasure Chamber had been broken open, spilling out all its contents into space, and sucking the water out of the ground. The only thing which could break open the Treasure Chamber's roof was the burning, glowing Tree of Life, which meant that Klut had pressed the LIFT button and the Tree of Life was theirs.
"Yes, I did it," he said, so as not to arouse Lucifer's suspicion. Just then a loud voice boomed out into the cavern.
"Our Lord Lucifer: there is something we must report." That had to be the demons coming to tell Lucifer what had happened and if he were to find out then their game would be up. Just as Lucifer was about to ask what it was, Aracuria told the spear to come out of the ground and fly at Lucifer. The spear did as it was told and flew straight at him.

Lucifer had been so distracted by the voice that he only saw the spear at the last moment. He dived aside, but the spear cut through his clothes, slicing open his arm.
"AARRAAGH!" he roared in pain and anger. "Don't bother me with your reports!" he screamed, "Wait until I kill this boy before I hear anything from you imbeciles again: you almost cost me my life with your blasted interruption!" The demons went silent and Aracuria smiled to himself.
"I'll wipe that smile off your face boy!" hissed Lucifer, catching sight of the blood staining his clothes red. "And I'll wipe your face off as well!" He raised his arm and sent a laser beam of light straight at Aracuria. Because it traveled as fast as light, Aracuria didn't have time to do anything. The beam burned through his leather jacket and cut into his upper arm.
"AARRAAGH!" Aracuria screamed as the pain shot through him. Then Lucifer sent another beam and then another and another, until Aracuria didn't know what to do as some of the beams burned into his flesh and others just

missed. He had to act or he was going to end up with more holes than a tea strainer.

"A mirror!" he cried. At once, a huge mirror appeared in front of him. He couldn't see what happened next, but he heard Lucifer's shriek. When he wished the mirror away, he saw Lucifer lying on the ground with a burn mark across the side of his face. The last laser beam must have hit the mirror and bounced off, striking its sender in the face.

Slowly, Lucifer picked himself up off the ground.

"You'll regret that, young man." he said quietly. Suddenly a sheet of flames rose up around Aracuria. With his hair singeing, he conjured up a fire-proof suit which momentarily protected him. Then Lucifer began to laugh and at the same time Aracuria felt itchy all over. The next moment he saw hundreds of ants crawling all over the surface of his visor: Lucifer had filled his fire-suit with ants. Aracuria conjured the suit away. The millions of ants that covered his body were burned away in the flames that still surrounded him and then, before Aracuria himself was burned, he brought a waterfall down on his head, which put out the flames and washed away the dead ants. Aracuria was soaking wet and he was angry. He pointed his ring at Lucifer and suddenly a mass of flames burst out around him. When Lucifer saw that he was surrounded by flames he started to laugh even louder.

"You idiot, Aracuria! Don't you know that I am the Devil and the Devil lives in the Hell of Draco which is filled with flames!" He rocked with uncontrollable laughter. "Flames can't hurt me at all, but they can hurt your kind a great deal!" Suddenly, in the midst of the flames Rhiannon, Klut and Bill appeared.

"Rhiannon!" cried Aracuria.

"Look what you've done now, Aracuria. You've sentenced your friends to be burnt to death: what kind of a person are you?" Lucifer's laughter echoed around the cavern as Rhiannon, Klut and Bill cried out for help.

"This isn't possible: this isn't happening!" shouted Aracuria. He tried to put out the flames, but they wouldn't go out. "Why won't the flames go out?".

"Because I will them to continue, Aracuria: don't you know that once a wish has been made by one Ring of Ra, it can't be undone by another. Only the sender can undo his own wishes: these flames are now mine and I will them to burn your friends to dust."

Aracuria shook his head in disbelief. He shouted to Rhiannon and the others, but all they would do was scream.

"How can you have taken them off the spaceship?" shouted Aracuria. "Simple," said Lucifer, "I just took them from Evil Eye, who was holding them hostage."

Aracuria suddenly realized what was happening: Lucifer was lying. This wasn't really Rhiannon, Klut and Bill because they weren't held as hostages on the spaceship, they were in charge of it. But Lucifer didn't know that. Aracuria raised his arm.

"Let me see things as they really are." Instantly Rhiannon, Klut and Bill turned into monstrous demons, each of which stood dancing in the flames. Suddenly the monsters and the flames disappeared and Lucifer picked himself up off the floor.
"That was rather intelligent of you, Aracuria," he said, "I'm quite surprised that someone like you might suspect I had tricked you." He let out a short laugh, "But now the games are coming to an end, I have only a few more tricks to play on you and then you'll go to meet your maker, if she'll have you." As Lucifer spoke, the ground beneath Aracuria's feet opened up, revealing a chasm below which disappeared into a black nothingness. As he fell, Aracuria managed to grasp the edge of the hole and haul himself out. He walked back from the hole until he was standing on the edge of the circular island with his back to the sea of fire.
"The fact is, Aracuria, you can never trust me not to trick you. I mean, who knows what might happen to you with your back turned."

Suddenly Aracuria felt a terrible burning sensation around his ankles. He looked down and saw that two fiery arms had come out of the sea of fire, grabbed his ankles and were about to pull him off his feet and into the sea. "Bye bye Aracuria," said Lucifer cruelly. But Aracuria wasn't beaten yet. He aimed his ring at the hands and blasted both of them off with a laser bolt.
"AARRAAGH!" A huge scream burst out in the sea of fire as a creature burst through the surface of the flames and then fell back beneath the fires.
"What, what was that?" said Aracuria.
"Oh, something or other," answered Lucifer, "That sea is filled with all sorts of things. I really haven't a clue what half of them are called, not that it interests me at all."

Aracuria rubbed his burning and blistered ankles and then stood up. "The games are over now Aracuria," said Lucifer. "You tire me, so it's time for you to die."

The Lord of Draco raised his Ring of Ra high in the air and cried, "Let the Cosmic String destroy you." At his words, from out of the glowing diamond, thousands of millions of tiny string-like specks of light began to flow slowly through the air in a great, winding arch.
"What, what's happening?" asked Aracuria.
"Everything in the whole Universe is made of this, Aracuria. This is the super string that flows through the atoms of space and matter and there is nothing that can resist it. I suppose you should take it as a compliment that we have reached this stage at all." Aracuria watched in amazement as the millions of glowing lines flowed out through the air, heading in his direction.
"What will happen when they touch me?" he asked.
"You will revert to what you are, you will become a part of it: you will dissolve into superstring like the air in front of you already has. That is why nothing can stop it, least of all you."

Aracuria stepped back, but the millions of glowing lines were making straight for him. Then he had an idea. He raised his own Ring of Ra and said, "Let the Cosmic string destroy you too." Sure enough, millions of glowing white lines appeared out of Aracuria's ring heading in the direction of Lucifer, whose face had suddenly bleached white.
"I didn't expect you to do that," said Lucifer.
"If I am going to die then so will you," said Aracuria.

Lucifer shook his head. "You really don't understand at all what you've done, do you?" he said. Aracuria said nothing. Instead he watched as the millions of strings of light from the two rings flowed up though the air in a great arch. Then suddenly they all met each other. Aracuria felt the ring shudder in his hand and at the same time he felt the whole planet of Draco rock gently.
"What's happening?" he shouted. But Lucifer just stared intently at the lines of light as they began to glow in various shimmering colors, from reds, to yellows, to brilliant purples and back again.
"You just don't know what you've done," said Lucifer again without explanation. Now the millions of glowing lines of light began to twist, first one way then the other. Finally they began to coil up like a rope, which started getting straight and taut. Suddenly instead of there being a wide arch of light between them, Lucifer and Aracuria were now joined by a glowing, taut rope of light that ran from each of their rings. Along the continually twisting rope huge pulses of white light began to flow back and forth. Then the ring in Aracuria's hand began to move uncontrollably, to and fro, up and down. He could feel in his hand immense powers rocking the ring first one way then the next but whatever was happening to it was completely beyond his control, as it was beyond Lucifer's, for his ring was moving in the same way too. Aracuria was scared. He looked up and saw that the whole cavern seemed to be draining of color; the walls, the floor, the sea, even he and Lucifer seemed to be becoming transparent.

"What's happening?" he cried again. Lucifer looked him in the eye.
"The Universe is being drained of power so we can fight our fight." All of a sudden, there was an enormous ripping, wrenching sound that made the whole planet shudder. In between Aracuria and Lucifer, right in the middle of the air, a crack of blue light had appeared. The crack ran through everything. It ran through the air, through the floor, through the sea of fire, up through the walls, right through the planet and then out into space, running through the stars like a jagged gash. On board the Morrigan spaceship, Rhiannon and the others stared in amazement at the huge crack that had appeared in space, as a glowing sea of blue light began to flood into the Universe, obliterating the stars. In the center of Draco, Aracuria stared in amazement at the flood of blue light as it flowed out of the crack and began to dissolve everything that it touched.

“What’s happening?” he cried in despair. Even Lucifer looked stunned.

“The Rings of Ra brought the Universe into being: we have wished them to destroy each other, which they cannot do, so instead they are destroying the Universe that they created: that crack is where the Universe is dividing into two and the blue light is the Cosmic Sea which is flooding in from outside to drown us all. I was wrong Aracuria, no one will curse you in a hundred million years for giving me control over the Universe, because in a few moments there will be no Universe at all and then no one will ever know that any of us, anywhere, ever even existed.”

“Is there nothing we can do?” cried Aracuria.

“Oh yes,” said Lucifer, “all it takes is for one of us to undo our wish, but you’ve got to understand that I have no intention of undoing mine. I would rather see the whole Universe die than let it be controlled by someone else. But if you undo your wish, then not only do you die, but you hand the whole Universe over to me. In other words Aracuria, either I control it all, or there is nothing to control. The choice is yours.”

CHAPTER FIFTEEN: IN THE BEGINNING

Aracuria watched as the Cosmic Sea dissolved the very air that he was breathing. What was he going to do? There was only one answer. He undid his wish and let his right hand fall away, breaking the cord of light. Immediately the millions of superstring strands unwound in a colossal burst of energy. A huge, glowing pulse of light burst out of Lucifer's ring and hit Aracuria in the chest, while the giant crack in the Universe suddenly slammed shut with a deafening roar that was heard everywhere. Aracuria was flung high in the air. His body was covered in a mass of electric charges that flowed over him like a thousand tiny snakes. He did a backward somersault and then crashed to the ground, dazed and battered. Seeing what had happened, Lucifer undid his wish and let his own ring drop to his side: he no longer needed the superstring to kill his opponent. Aracuria was already beaten.

It took a moment for Aracuria to regain his senses. His thick, dirty leather jacket had been blown off and now lay around him in shreds. It had absorbed most of the blast and probably saved his life. Slowly, he got to his feet and waited for the inevitable.

"Why did you do it?" asked Lucifer.

"Because it's better for people to live in hope than not to live at all," said Aracuria quietly.

"I think you have learned one simple lesson today, Aracuria," said Lucifer, "that whenever good and evil come into conflict, if they are both equally matched, then evil will always win. Because at the end of the day, evil men would rather see the whole Universe incinerated than lose their fight. That is something the good could never do, because it is really the Universe and its people that they are fighting for. You probably think that I am evil by nature, but in fact I am evil by choice because it makes me stronger than anyone else, and strength is what counts. Now it is time for you to die and for me to possess both rings." Aracuria said nothing; he just closed his eyes as Lucifer raised his ring for the last time.

"Spin the ring."

Aracuria opened his eyes wide.

"Who said that?" The voice had seemed to come from inside of him, but it was so clear and distinct he wasn't sure, although it was too soft to be Lucifer's voice. Then it came again.

"I, Theom. Spin the ring around you." Lucifer was just about to kill him. Without a second's hesitation, Aracuria began to spin the ring around and around until he was turning like a top.

Lucifer hesitated for a moment, convinced that Aracuria had finally gone mad.

"Dancing won't help you, my boy." But Aracuria kept turning, and as he turned so a blue thread-like substance began to come from the Ring of Ra. It formed a complete circle around Aracuria and then it began to grow up and down, curving around in a sphere like a sheet of blue glass. Aracuria was getting dizzy, but still he spun around while Lucifer stared in amazement. Finally he could spin no more and he collapsed, his head reeling. But he didn't fall to the ground. Instead he landed inside what looked like a large blue egg made of transparent glass.

Lucifer didn't know what to make of this. Then his face turned white, then red and he screamed out with all the venom in his soul, "The RING! What have you done with the RING!" Aracuria looked down at his hand and saw that the ring of Ra had disappeared. He looked up at the blue egg which surrounded him, and he realized that the ring had turned itself into it.

Lucifer went absolutely crazy. He aimed his ring at Aracuria and fired a laser pulse: it bounced harmlessly off the egg. He fired a lightning bolt, burning hail, a howitzer shell and finally a thermonuclear blast that nearly brought the cavern down around their ears, and yet still nothing happened: Aracuria was impregnable inside his egg.

"Make a wish," said the voice of Theom inside Aracuria.

"I want to go back to the spaceship." Immediately the blue egg began to lift off the ground.

"He's getting AWAY!" cried Lucifer in anger and despair, as the egg began to rise towards the shaft. At his master's voice, Leviathan uncoiled from around the throne, raised his huge head high in the air and brought his massive jaws crashing down on the egg. From inside Aracuria watched as the razor sharp fangs, weeping venom and spittle, clamped on to the surface of the egg and tried to crush it into nothing. Leviathan bit as hard as he could, but then, with a horrible crack, each and every one of his fangs suddenly snapped and Leviathan fell back to the ground roaring in pain, as the blue egg started to rise up the shaft.

Lucifer was jumping up and down with anger and frustration.

"Stop HIM! Everyone and everything: STOP HIM!" From out of the burning sea of fire, thousands of the most indescribable monsters and ghouls burst forth. They rose through the air and, with multiple fiery hands and claws, they grabbed hold of the egg. This really terrified Aracuria, as huge eyes and mouths, claws and multi-fingered hands suddenly surrounded him. He closed his eyes and clasped his hands to his ears as the monsters chattered and screamed: but there was nothing they could do. The egg continued rising through the shaft and as the fiery monsters stayed out of their sea of fire for too long, so they began to die and one by one they fell lifeless back into the burning sea.

With nothing to stop it, the blue egg rose up the shaft at an ever faster rate. However, Oriens had been alerted and he was waiting for

Aracuria above. As the blue egg rose out of the shaft, Oriens brought his sword crashing down on it. The egg shuddered, but the huge sword shattered into pieces, leaving Oriens helpless as he watched the blue egg shoot up through the cavern and burn its way through the stone vaulted roof.

Aracuria now found himself floating in space. High above him he could see the huge Morrigan spaceship, which had what looked like a glowing sun in tow between its Y fork. Looking down on to the planet, Aracuria could see a huge hole in the top of the Treasure Chamber, out of which the last of a long trail of gold statues and coins, diamonds and ingots was being sucked on board the Morrigan spaceship. The blue egg maneuvered itself into the end of the trail of gold and Aracuria sat silently in his egg as he was the last to be hauled on board the spaceship before the giant cargo doors closed.

He found himself sitting between a silver statue of an ancient god and a pile of gold ingots, "How do I get out of this egg?" he asked.

"Stand up," said the voice of Theom. Aracuria stood up and suddenly the egg cracked into a million pieces, which fell around him like blue dust. Now he had to act fast. Lucifer was bound to try and destroy the spaceship, so Rhiannon and the others had to hit the Hyperspace button as quickly as possible. But since they didn't know that Aracuria was on board they might hang around waiting for him. He picked up his heels and ran down the long cargo hold which was now filled with thousands of gold statues, vast piles of diamonds and millions of gold ingots. The whole place glowed wonderfully as he dodged between the piles of gold and silver, heading for the control room. At the end of the cargo hold he saw the solar Ducks, Margaret and Deborah, standing together. Between them was Glenys, propped up on a pile of gold ingots, and next to her was Roger, who was joining a new pair of legs to her.

"ROGER !We did it!" shouted Aracuria, as he rushed by and through the hole in the wall that led to the pirates' nursery.

A moment later he found himself floating through the air tubes and then he came crashing out on to the control room floor. No one seemed to notice him. Rhiannon, Klut, Bill and the pirates were all standing by the window, looking out at the stars as they suddenly turned into long streaks of light reminiscent of white spaghetti. That could only mean one thing: they had hit the Hyper-Space button and Lucifer could no longer touch them.

Aracuria walked silently up behind them. Everyone was crying, including Evil Eye.

"With all that gold, we'll build the most massive statue to him that anyone one has ever seen," said Rhiannon, through her tears.

"We'll name schools and universities after him." sobbed Klut.

"Everyone will be told what he did," added Bill sadly.

"Never mind the statues and the universities: a can of cola will do me fine," said Aracuria with a grin. Everyone spun around.

"ARACURIA!" they all screamed and suddenly Aracuria found himself buried as Rhiannon, Klut, Bill and two hundred pirates ran to hug him.

It took quite a while for Aracuria to free himself from his admirers and then everyone had wanted to know what had happened. Once he had finished explaining, he settled down in his fur-lined swivel chair, put his blistered feet up on the console and sipped his drink while Rhiannon and the others stood around him. The spaceship had now come out of Hyper-Space and the stars had returned to normal. Up ahead there was a strange little blue planet that really didn't look like anything else in the whole Universe. Next to it was a much smaller, silver planet and in the distance was a sun that didn't look as bright as it ought.

"How long have we been away from Earth?" asked Aracuria. Klut typed the request into the computer and out came the answer.

"Eighteen months and four days. Earth will be going through a bad winter now, even though it should really be summer."

"All that will soon change," said Rhiannon. "Once we float the Tree of Life in space next to the old sun things will soon warm up again." Everyone nodded.

"It's going to be really strange in the future," said Bill, "because every morning when people get up they'll see two suns in the sky instead of one."

"And when they do," said Rhiannon, "they'll think Aracuria."

"They'll think of all of us," said Aracuria, "and what we did."

"And in a thousand years' time the people of Earth will still be telling their children about us," said Klut.

"And in ten thousand years all the adults will say it was all a myth invented to account for the two suns that no other planet in the Universe has," said Aracuria, "and no one but the kids will believe it anymore."

Aracuria suddenly felt rather sad. When they got back to Earth everyone would love them and they would never have to want for anything ever again, but the adventure was over. Soon they wouldn't be children any more; they'd grow up, have children of their own and grow old, but no matter how long they lived they would never do anything like this again. And then one day, as the woman crowned in stars had said, another adventure would start that would never end. Only that one would be a dream.

"Klut," said Aracuria, "This Tree of Life: where did Lucifer and his demons steal it from?"

"In the beginning there was a place called the Garden of Eden in which the Tree of Life grew; it was an apple orchard I think: you know what these old stories are like," said Klut.

"That doesn't sound real, does it," said Rhiannon. "How could that huge, glowing Tree of Life have apples on it?

"Sounds like a myth to me," said Aracuria. "It probably isn't true at all. I guess we'll never know where Lucifer stole it from, but one thing's for sure: from now on it's going to shine on Earth."

And as they approached the gently turning blue-white planet, which was growing larger by the second in front of them, so the Tree of Life was finally going home; although only Gayomart, Theom and the Tree of Life knew it.

And, of course, Lucifer.